Curse of Prometheus: a tale of Medea

by

Morgan St. Knight

All events depicted in this book are entirely fictional. Any resemblance to real persons is purely coincidental.

Cover photo by Piotr Krzeslak/iStock/Thinkstock and Ivan Cholakov/ iStock/Thinkstock

Interior art by Asmakar/iStock/Thinkstock

ISBN: 978-0-9913960-9-2 (Paperback)
ISBN: 978-0-9913960-0-9 (Kindle edition)

For the Lady who never abandoned me, for my parents who never gave up on me and for David and Kristian who never doubted me

Chapter 1

In Atlanta, someone old is new again—and he's hungry. He's on the hunt, but also on the run. It's my job to catch him. My motive couldn't be better.

I'm the bait the gods have set out for him.

I'm taking a chance walking through the streets after dark. I used to love the city best on nights like this, when the heavy fog rolls in. Tonight, with all but the lowest levels of the skyscrapers veiled in heavy mist, it seems sinister even to me.

That's saying something. "Sinister" has been my middle name for centuries. But it's my first name people tend to remember most: Medea.

Medea Keres, now that having a surname is obligatory. I doubt any of my few human acquaintances would know that *keres* are the spirits that rip away the souls of those who die a violent death. Fitting, considering how many times I've been the instrument of such deaths.

Certainly, none of my neighbors would suspect I'm the original Medea. I live a quiet life in their eyes, a trust fund heiress who travels a lot as a consultant for various charities. It would be hard to reconcile that image with the witch of three thousand years ago who threw away almost everything for a pair of strong arms and soft lips that lied as smoothly as they kissed. A woman who didn't balk at murder, even fratricide, all to help the valiant Jason.

Well, he got his precious fleece, and I hope he chokes on it in Tartarus. I've got my own problems. I've worked hard to hunt demons that would gladly overrun the world and destroy humanity given half a chance.

Now the gods have decided the hunter needs to become the hunted.

"He will try to capture you," Zeus told me bluntly. "And when that happens, we will be waiting for him."

It sounded bad enough when those words echoed through the shining halls of Olympus. The memory is even more ominous playing through my head on a lonely, fog-shrouded street. If they're really watching, can't the gods give me a sign that I'm not alone? Of course they gave me their word, but that's not worth quite as much as it used to be. Not after what's happened.

One thing I *am* certain of is that he's waiting for me. I listen closely, trying to filter out the subtle hum of the city at night. My breath slows, catches in my throat.

Was that the sound of wings? I wait one heartbeat. Two, three. Finally I accept that it was another errant whisper. Perhaps it was just a car sliding carefully through the misty street a block or two away. Sound carries strangely in the fog. Minds play tricks in such conditions. Even mine.

If only I had just let things play out on their own without interfering. I learned a long time ago that no good comes of sticking my nose into bad business. But I'd done it anyway, even though the warning bells were loud and clear when they first started ringing just a few days ago.

Now there's hell to pay. Any way I look at it, I'm the one who gets stuck with the bill.

* * *

The satchel with my weapons of choice made a satisfying *thunk* as it hit the carpet in my bedroom. The faint clang of metal hitting metal inside the leather bag was like a little burst of joy at being back in familiar surroundings. "Joy" is a subjective thing, and probably not a term most would associate with silver stakes impregnated with the blood of the three-headed hellhound Cerberus. But they're handy for killing all manner of demons.

I'd spent the past two weeks being led on a merry chase by one of Lamia's brood across northern Ohio. She'd been one of the nicer ones, as the daughters of Lamia go. I'd come across several of her victims before the police did. All had died in her embrace, drained of their life energy in seedy hotel rooms during what had undoubtedly been the best sex of their lives.

That's how the succubi kill if they're being kind. Otherwise, they slip their barbed tongues right into the base of the victim's skull and just suck out the life force. Not a very pleasant way to go.

This one was posing as a low-price hooker, as many of Lamia's daughters did. She was no dummy, though. She managed to stay one step ahead of me for several days. Each time I thought I'd trapped her all I found was a lifeless, shriveled husk of a would-be john lying half-wrapped in stained, threadbare sheets.

Finally she left the outlying towns and headed for Cleveland. I found her lurking in a crypt in Lake View Cemetery. After nearly half an hour of fighting and chasing her among the tombstones, I got the upper hand and dispatched her.

I'd been up nearly a day-and-a-half, but I didn't bother finding a place for a quick nap before hitting the road. It was a ten-and-a-half hour drive back to Atlanta from Cleveland. At least the October foliage was uplifting as I drove through the mountains.

It would have been quicker to fly, but that was out. Like most demons Lamia's daughters can only be killed by specialized weapons like the silver stakes. Just try to get a bag of those through check-in at the airport. Never mind that any TSA agent who touched one would go up in flames from the poisonous blood of Cerberus. We witches don't need any more bad PR.

My orders are clear: hunt the baddie-bads and keep out of the spotlight. Don't give humans a reason to suspect who I am or what's really lurking in the shadows. Just find it, get rid of it and keep quiet about it.

Quiet, except when the mission is accomplished. In that respect, I was in the same boat as every cop around the world. Reports, reports, reports.

My stomach rumbled as I headed downstairs. It was tempting to make a side-trip to the kitchen, but I knew better than to try it. My boss is much more hard-assed when it comes to procedure than any police chief. Since my boss is Hecate herself, it would be foolishness of the worst sort to think I could delay giving her a report just to get a snack.

My stomach groaned again.

"All right", I said as I headed downstairs to do my duty. "You've earned a treat." Another rumble, with perhaps a hint of gratitude.

"Medea, you have to get out more. Conversations with your stomach aren't going to cut it," I muttered.

I could certainly treat myself to a night out or two, maybe a casual fling with one of the pretty-but-dumb boys who frequented the in-spots. A morale booster, something to enhance my on-the-job performance. All work and no play makes Medea a royal bitch.

Clubbing could wait until I had a good night's sleep. For a short-term fix I'd treat myself to a pint of Baskin Robbins ice cream. I had a stash in the chest freezer down in the basement.

But first, the sanctuary.

"Welcome home, mistress." Just once in awhile I would have liked to get a smile from the carved stone mask over the door, but that wasn't the Guardian's nature. Its hollow voice echoed a bit in the hall.

"You have a report." A statement, not a question.

I opened my mouth to respond then cut it short. The Guardian had sentience of a sort, but it wasn't a feeling being. More illusion than anything, though it would certainly live up to its name if anyone tried to enter the sanctuary without my presence. Its power was real enough, and that was all that mattered. Social niceties like conversation were irrelevant.

I spoke the charm that unsealed the sanctuary door. It swung open, and simultaneously candles in sconces around the walls flared to life.

But they weren't the only things that were glowing.

Next to the altar that held a statue of Hecate, a censer and vessels for libations, there was a small side-table. The single object on it was radiating an eerie light. It was a Sybil's mirror, my direct link to Hades. It was a convenient way to send in my reports.

It was convenient most of the time, anyway. Just not at that particular moment. It should *not* have been glowing before I spoke the incantation to activate it.

The smart thing to do would have been to run right out of that room, lock the door from the outside and chant an invocation to call up some of the entities I was on friendly terms with. But smart is never high on my list when I'm tired and hungry.

So I went closer to the mirror. Mistake number one. The surface rippled like water, and I knew that images would soon break through.

At first, all I could see was something ill-defined, like an object bobbing just below the surface of a cloudy pool of water. The image became more defined. I dimly saw a bejeweled hand caressing what appeared to be a crumpled mound of crimson velvet. The image sharpened even more: it was not velvet.

It was flesh. A gaping, bloody hole in a human torso. The hand was stroking it slightly, dabbling ringed fingers into the gash as someone might lazily trail their hand in a cool pond on a warm spring day. I could tell it was a man's body, but the image wasn't wide enough for me to see his face, or the woman who was stroking the wound.

Everything had a cloudy sheen to it and her jewelry had an off color, making the gems unidentifiable. They were an odd, bluish-green.

A soft voice filled the room, as if it was coming from every corner.

"Drink, drink…" it cajoled. A woman's voice, light and soothing with the hint of myriad promises.

The image receded a bit, enough for me to see more of the torso as well as the body's arms. I could see it was a man, but no more.

The vista slowly sank back into dimness. Another was surfacing. A mouth, surrounded by a lush beard. It was like black sable, sleek and oiled, arranged artfully into intricate curls and ringlets. A classic Greek style. The mouth and beard were all I could see, no other features to give me a clue about who it was.

The mouth was full and sensual, or at least it normally would be. I could tell that much even though it was twisted and pulled into a grimace. Pain? Ecstasy? A little of both, it seemed. It was not the expression which disturbed me the most.

The lush lips were streaked with blood. I could see, as the mouth opened in a silent groan, traces of blood on the teeth.

The image sharpened further, coming closer as if it was trying to come out of the mirror into my reality. My eyes widened as I realized it was no trick of light. The mouth *was* emerging from the mirror. Only a slight protrusion at first, then more, more…

The rim of the Sybil's mirror was changing, becoming the same color as the blood on the lips pushing through the mirror's surface.

As I backed away my ears started buzzing and I felt the floor wavering beneath me. I heard a sound that quickly grew louder, a throaty whisper that turned from a hoarse cry of need into distinct words.

"Join us. Join us. Join us… Medea…"

Hearing my name sent a shock through me, enough to make me want to bolt. But I couldn't.

The hideous mouth opened wider and scarlet clouds spilled from it like steam from a seething cauldron. They swept across the floor, flowing over my feet and up my calves. My legs were rooted to the spot even though my mind wanted nothing more than to run in terror—out of the room, out of the house, out of the city if I could run that much.

The room reeked of copper and ordure. Noxious fumes poured up my torso and over my chest and face, choking me.

Without warning or intent I fell backwards. It took me a moment to realize that I hadn't stumbled. I had been pulled.

I could see the arms reaching from under my own, curving up over my chest towards my shoulders. They ended in hands that were as white as alabaster. White, except for the black nails that curved like talons from the fingers. Talons that were coming dangerously close to my throat.

I barely noticed that the vile clouds were being sucked back into the mirror, as if some gigantic monster on the other side had drawn in a large breath. The light started to fade from the mirror.

I was spun around. As the mirror's glow dimmed I saw a face pale as moonlight, a mouth crimson as a ripe pomegranate, and eyes the color of amethysts just inches from my face.

The most pronounced feature was the hair. It seemed to be made of cobwebs and mist, floating in a silvery-grey cloud. Some of it was moving. Alive. As I looked at it, things looked back at me. Vipers.

The intruder's mouth opened, revealing long curving fangs.

"Medea…" The voice came from a distance, echoing as if I was in a deep cavern. The last thing I saw was the mouth opening wider, the fangs coming closer. Then the darkness took me.

Welcome to my world.

Chapter 2

A headache was firmly ensconced in my skull, blearing my thoughts. It took a few moments to realize I was lying on the couch in my den. How had I gotten there?

I tried to sit up and barely kept from retching.

"Don't move!" a raspy voice commanded. I turned abruptly, and just as quickly wished I hadn't. It made the headache even worse. But suddenly the pain seemed merely an inconvenience compared to seeing the owner of the voice. It was the creature who had grabbed me in my sanctuary room during the mirror's attack.

"Orphne!" I cried out, unable to restrain the happiness at seeing my oldest friend. Admittedly the fangs peeking through a lopsided leer-not to mention the talons and viper-hair-might not be the most welcome sight to mortals, but what can one expect from an underworld nymph?

Unlike their cousins who frolic through streams and dance in woodlands, the underworld nymphs are a rather somber lot. You would be too, if you spent your life in perpetual subterranean darkness dealing with souls of the dead.

That was what suddenly made me feel uneasy. To the best of my knowledge, Orphne had never left the Underworld to venture to Earth. What was she doing here now?

"I said, don't move," Orphne interrupted my hazy musings. "Give yourself some time to recover."

She came to the couch, her grey draperies floating around her like fog. She held out a glass of water in one taloned hand. Apparently she'd had no difficulty navigating my house, even though it was her first time on Earth. She'd found the faucets.

Or had she?

"Where did you get the water?" I tried to be offhand with the question. She just shrugged.

"From that small white cistern in the next room," she said matter-of-factly as she pointed to the hallway bathroom. "There wasn't much left in the bowl, so I dipped it out of the storage tank in back. Don't you have a proper well?"

I hoped my smile of gratitude was convincing as I put the glass down untouched.

"Why are you here?" I asked as I drew my legs up on the couch to make room for her. I realized too late that it was a very ungracious way to greet a friend.

Orphne took no notice. "I was sent. She tried to reach you through the mirror, but there was interference. At least I found out why. Bad business, that was."

My veins iced. There was no mistaking who "she" was. If Hecate was initiating contact....

"She had a warning for you," Orphne confirmed my dread. If Hecate thought she had to warn me, there was nothing but trouble on the horizon.

"A warning about what?"

Orphne shook her head. "She didn't say, and I didn't ask. I was just supposed to find out why we couldn't get through to you and make sure you were alright."

"I suppose that's a matter of opinion. I'm intact, at least, thanks to your fast thinking." I couldn't resist a slight groan as I pushed myself to my feet. The room spun a bit, but I got my bearings quickly enough.

"Let me get you wine and something to eat," I said as I eased a few steps forward.

"No, you should rest—" she protested.

"I'm okay, really. Besides, I could use a drink myself at this point. Make yourself comfortable. I'll be right back."

She hardly looked convinced, but at least made a gesture of acquiescence by leaning back a little into the cushions.

I didn't trust my equilibrium enough to risk a trip down the steps to the small wine cellar in the basement, but I had a respectable bottle or two in the kitchen.

I made a quick stop in the half-bath. The toilet tank lid was still lying neatly across the seat. I'd have to make sure Orphne knew what the thing was for before she went back to Hades. She'd appreciate the joke. I looked into the mirror to assess the damage.

There were no marks on my face, but the ache from the front of my collarbone told me there could be some bruises from Orphne's rescue efforts. As an elemental she was incredibly strong. Fortunately I knew plenty of spells to help speed the healing process along.

The lights caught the highlights in my golden blonde hair. It always amuses me that artists, having never met me, usually depict me with dark hair to match my dark reputation.

I was dismayed to see the eyes looking back at me from the mirror. They were a far more vivid shade of gold than my hair.

CURSE OF PROMETHEUS: A TALE OF MEDEA

The eyes, like the hair, are a legacy from my grandfather Helios, a trait I share with my aunts Circe and Pasiphae. But the eyes are also a distinct inconvenience when I'm trying to pass for human. The mirror's attack had been strong enough to knock out the minor charm I kept in place to make my eyes appear blue.

That was the least of my concerns. Standing all night in front of the mirror certainly wouldn't make the more pressing ones go away.

In the kitchen I poured two glasses of wine then gathered some light food on a serving platter: olives, a dish of olive oil, flat bread and some sheep's-milk cheese.

By the time I headed back to the study I was feeling worlds better, although the headache was not totally gone. I was able to make a passable appearance at being a good hostess as I set the tray down on the table in front of Orphne. With a slight bow of my head I handed her a wine glass with both hands.

She took the glass, then made a pointed look at the fireplace on the far side of the room. Catching her meaning I nodded and took up my own glass. We moved to the fireplace.

I raised my glass and poured out a small amount of the wine into the shallow dish I kept on the mantle. The fireplace was the modern day equivalent of an ancient home's hearth, where the gods were always honored.

"Hail to you, shining Olympians. May you bless this home forever," I murmured.

"Hail to you, shining Olympians. Grant your bounty to this home, and lay your protection on all within," Orphne responded as she poured some of her wine into the dish.

I quickly glanced at her, because that last part about protection was ad libbed, although she made it flow as gracefully into the short prayer as if it had always been part of the ritual homage.

Although the hearth was unlit I felt a little stirring of power, the gentle recognition of our simple but heartfelt prayers. But the good feeling swiftly departed when I glanced into the libation dish.

I saw a shallow pool of brilliant scarlet, brighter than the wine should have been. It started bubbling thickly, and as I watched in horror it began spilling over the dish onto the floor.

I gasped and involuntarily blinked. In that brief moment the image was gone. There was nothing on the mantle or the floor, and the wine inside the dish was its normal deep purple shade. Orphne frowned and looked at me.

"What is it?" she demanded as she put her free hand on my arm. I looked back into the dish. Ordinary wine.

"Nothing," I said quickly. "I'm still just a little shaken, that's all." I tried unsuccessfully to make myself believe that it had just been a trick of the light, that I really was still shaken from the incident with the mirror.

That the libation dish had *not* looked like it was overflowing with blood.

"Welcome to my home," I said, forcing a smile as I lifted my glass to Orphne. She smiled back—a rather gruesome look for an underworld nymph—and raised her glass in return.

As I expected, Orphne only took a few polite nibbles of the food. Normally that would have been considered an insult, implying that the guest didn't think the host had enough means to spare the food. As she had no need of physical nourishment it was pointless for her to pretend to have a hearty appetite. I had little enough stomach for the repast myself, simple and comforting as it was.

I finally gave up the effort to choke down any more food. "It's wonderful to see you again," I reached out and laid a hand on Orphne's knee, not at all put off by the chill of her flesh under the insubstantial robes. "I have to admit I'm still a little surprised to see you on Earth. It's so... unusual."

"As you just found out, this is hardly an ordinary night," she reminded me. "What happened in there?"

The million-dollar question, of course. But I needed to parse it out anyway to figure out what was happening. Might as well do it with someone who could give some feedback.

I took it slowly. "I went into my sanctuary to send in my latest report. I found and destroyed another succubus. But the mirror was already activated before I even got into the room."

She considered that a moment. "Strange. I didn't sense anyone but you in the house when I got here. That was just about the time those mists started coming out of the mirror."

I mulled that. "The Guardian didn't give me any warnings, either," I mused. "It would have alerted me to intruders."

"Unless the intruder had the power to block its presence from the Guardian." A disturbing possibility, which meant whoever or whatever was behind the mirror's attack could still be lurking around.

"Didn't you see anything else but the mists?" I asked. It was perplexing that she chose to mention the mists, rather than the enormous mouth protruding from the mirror.

"No," she said slowly. "But my view was partially blocked. You were in the way. My first concern was getting you out of that area. You seemed spellbound."

No argument there. I decided to go on with my story.

"I saw a body. Dead, very recently. Blood was still flowing from a huge gash in the torso."

"Male or female?"

"Male. Fairly young and in very good shape. But I didn't see his face."

"What else did you see?" Orphne pressed.

"A mouth. A man's mouth, but not the man whose body I saw. This mouth was moving. He was still alive. He had blood on his lips."

"Wounded?"

I paused, remembering the female voice. *Drink, drink.* "No. I think he drank the blood." She didn't comment so I pressed on. "The mouth was all I saw. The man had a thick beard. Old, old style too. Curled and oiled like they used to do in Greece."

Orphne cocked her head. "Any chance the style has come back among humans?"

"None. Too much work to maintain it. Besides, no one these days would want to kiss a man with a beard oiled like that."

"I'd think that kissing a man who drinks blood would be the bigger issue, but then again mortals are strange creatures. Sometimes they overlook the most obvious signs of trouble. Anything unusual about the vision?"

The whole thing wasn't unusual enough for her? "Someone called my name. And they said, 'Join us'."

"Are you sure?" She looked perplexed.

I took a deep sip of my wine and nodded.

"Was it the man with the bloody mouth?"

I tried to recall whether the mouth had moved in time with the words, but the memory was too blurry. "I just can't say," I admitted with frustration.

"Was there anything else unusual?" she prompted.

I shuddered because it was the part I least wanted to remember.

"That mouth. It started to come out of the mirror."

She sat upright. Not quickly, but enough movement to make me realize how alarmed she was at that.

"It's not possible," she said. "The mirror isn't a portal. Nothing can come through it."

"Something tried," I said a bit more sharply than I intended. I took another deep breath to steady myself. "No mistake about it. I was frightened, it's true, but I've lived long enough to keep my wits about me even when I'm scared. I wasn't hallucinating. That face was trying to break through into this reality."

She remained silent for several moments. Finally, she sighed.

"We have a problem then."

Chapter 3

Orphne's understatement would have been funny in other circumstances. A problem? Sure. And a rampaging Cyclops was a minor inconvenience.

The way I saw it, we had more than one problem. First, that the Sybil's mirror had shown me anything at all without my asking for it.

Sybil's mirrors are ancient devices. They were formed from the mists that gathered as Nyx, the goddess of night, bathed in a Stygian pool. Her devotees used a dark magic long since lost to coalesce the mists into solid objects. They are a direct link to the Underworld, and were used by sorcerers to contact the spirits of the dead as well as some of the beings who call Hades their home. That is their one and only power. The mirrors aren't scrying devices.

Even with such limited potential, they were deemed too dangerous for mere mortals to possess. The mirrors were all removed from the Earth, except for mine. In a sense, mine was a relic of a bygone age, the last of its kind on the planet, left behind for a very specific purpose.

Just like me. It had been more than fifteen hundred years since the Olympian gods, disgusted with man's continued inhumanity, withdrew Olympus from the Earthly plane altogether. All of the beings devoted to the Olympians had been withdrawn into other dimensions, as were the realms they sported in. Only the nymphs and daemons who were bound to the natural forces of the Earth… trees, fields, clouds and waters… were allowed to remain.

Gone were the lands of beauty, like the Garden of the Hesperides, and the lands of terror, like the dimly lit plane of the Gray Sisters and the cliffs of torment where Prometheus was bound. Even the enchanted islands like Aiaia, home to my aunts Circe and Pasiphae, were taken up onto another plane.

Everyone in those realms, with the exception of the Olympians themselves, was under a strict ban never to come to Earth. They could visit each other's respective abodes as much as they liked, as they always had, but under no circumstances could they come back to Earth. The penalty was annihilation.

But someone had to stay behind and clean up after the demons that would inevitably escape the nether regions, not to mention the monsters that were still wandering the Earth because no other realm would give them sanctuary before the withdrawal. Like my age-old nemesis Lamia and her cursed daughters.

I'd been chosen for cleanup duty. As Hecate's priestess, I was a logical candidate. I had the power and the knowledge to deal with such threats. Hecate made it sound almost like a promotion when she broke the news to me.

Funny. It didn't seem like such a compliment at times like this. I'd been granted immortality and eternal youth centuries before the Olympian withdrawal in recognition of my largely unnoticed efforts to keep humans safe from the dark forces, but sometimes that didn't seem to be enough. I'd have to ask her about hazard pay.

Speaking of which…

"Where are you going?" Orphne asked as I got up from the sofa.

"Back to the sanctuary. If Hecate has a warning for me, I need to find out what it is."

She rose abruptly and grabbed my arm, a little more forcefully than necessary. "You can't."

It took a second for my body to realize my arm wasn't going anywhere. The jolt of having my forward momentum curtailed brought me back to reality. It would have been nice if I hadn't almost dislocated my shoulder in the process, but it served me right for being so stupid.

I couldn't use the Sybil's mirror to communicate with Hecate. It had been compromised. If some other being had gained enough control of the mirror to show me images in it and worse still, to try to use it to manifest in my home, then that same being would be able to eavesdrop on my conversations with Hecate.

Having made her point, Orphne gave me my arm back. "So what are my options?" I asked, heading back to the sofa. I figured Hecate had devised some sort of plan. She must have, if she'd somehow finagled permission to send Orphne up to Earth despite the ban. Chthonic nymphs were supposed to stay in Hades where they belonged.

She sat primly next to me. "Hecate laid the choices out for me before she sent me here. You have three." She waited. Uh-oh. This wouldn't be good. I nodded for her to go on.

"If you feel you're in too much danger, you can come back to Hades with me."

I didn't wince, but I was certain my face wasn't entirely neutral. I'd spent my adolescence in Hades as part of my apprenticeship to Hecate. Souls of the dead, hideous monsters, chthonic nymphs like Orphne wandering around singing baleful hymns to Hades and Persephone, and from just over the horizon, the shrieks of the damned being tortured in Tartarus.

Ah, the memories…

One thing was for certain: they didn't have Baskin Robbins ice cream down there.

I restrained myself from giving an immediate "yes" or "no" to that offer. I'd learned the hard way over the years that you really do need to hear all your options before choosing.

"And behind door number two?"

She frowned at that, not understanding the reference. "Hecate says you can take refuge on Aiaia for the time being. She'll arrange for you to go there."

Well, Hecate certainly deserved her reputation as a miracle worker. She'd managed to conjure up an option that was just as unappealing as an extended stay in Hell.

It's not that I don't love my aunts. I do, really. They're both quite lovely. Statuesque, in fact, being the daughters of Titans. About seven feet tall. Circe has long, cascading red hair that curls and shifts like living fire, and Pasiphae's hair is like spun gold. Both are clearly the daughters of Helios, shining creatures of beauty.

But unfortunately, they're both a bit... off.

Circe's penchant for magical eugenics is more disturbing than interesting. True, she's created some of the most beautiful and exotic wildlife you'll ever see, not to mention herds of the more common sorts. Unfortunately, she doesn't create them from nothing. She uses humans for raw material.

When Aiaia was taken into another dimension during the withdrawal, it wasn't the end of her experiments. She'd thought ahead and created some workarounds. They included the faery mounds that dot Europe, where people disappear if they wander too close on dark moonless nights.

I'd always felt the Bermuda Triangle was her *piece de resistance* for getting a steady supply of humans. Truly a stroke of foresight. But then, for someone with her power, seeing far enough into the future to know that humans would one day sail and fly in the region hadn't been all that much of a trick.

Circe's sister Pasiphae had started out well enough, as the living goddess of the ancient Minoans. But her success drew envious stares from the Olympians, who coveted her worshippers. Worshippers equaled power in the old days. The more you had, the higher you were in the pecking order. The Olympians wanted hers, and wanted them badly.

They finally succeeded in getting her to abdicate, thanks to a fiendish plot by Dionysus and his lackey Theseus, who slew her son Megalitheros (or as commoners called him, the Minotaur) and kidnapped her daughter Ariadne to hand over to Dionysus as a plaything. Pasiphae gave up her throne but swore she'd exact a terrible revenge.

To prove her intent, she blew up the island of Thera, now known as Santorini, creating a tsunami that wiped out thousands of the worshippers the Olympians wanted to co-opt. If she couldn't have them, they certainly wouldn't.

You'd think that would have been the end of it, after she went to live with Circe on Aiaia. Wrong. Unless she'd changed since I last saw her, one of her favorite topics of conversation was how she would get revenge for the wrongs done to her.

She'd dreamed up several fantastic scenarios for getting back at the gods, most of which could have gotten her (and anyone caught listening to her ranting) thrown into Tartarus for plotting against the Olympians. Fortunately for her, and all of the creatures on Aiaia, the high gods hadn't chosen to take her seriously. Yet.

Altogether, a stay with the aunts would not be a vacation. But I took heart. There was still a third option open to me, and it couldn't be any worse than the first two.

"All right," I finally said. "What's my last choice?"

Orphne smiled, a little triumphantly. "You stay here, figure out what the menace is, and deal with it yourself. Without any direct help from Hecate."

I usually manage to keep my jaw from dropping completely open. It's so undignified. But sometimes, no other facial expression will do.

"She's turning her back on me?" I didn't quite gasp it, but I did squeak a little.

Orphne hastily waved her hands in a gesture of denial. "Not at all. She said she'll be watching, ready to help if needed. But you're not, under any circumstances, to call her of your own accord."

"But *why?*" None of this made sense. Hecate was not the sort to play games, especially if anything of hers—and like it or not, I qualified as a thing of hers—was being threatened.

Orphne allowed herself a disgruntled sigh. "She wouldn't tell me. She said the only way to proceed, if this is your choice, is to keep quiet about it. So of course, she didn't tell *me* what's going on. I can only guess that she's hoping silence will prevent us from betraying our hand about how much we know. Or don't know, in this case."

It might work. But one person who wouldn't be fooled, was me. I knew that if Hecate wasn't giving me more information, it was because she didn't have it. We were both flying in the dark.

"There's one other thing about the last option," Orphne said brightly.

I managed a feeble smile of encouragement.

"If you stay here on Earth, Hecate has ordered me to stay with you."

I gave myself an awful lot of points for not laughing in her face. That would have been cruel. But the truth was, her face as well as the rest of her were problematic. She was a chthonic nymph, after all. Vipers in the hair. Fangs. Ghastly pallor. Talons. Even if I lived in Little Five Points, the Bohemian's Bohemia in Atlanta, she wouldn't pass.

I lived in an upscale suburb where she *definitely* wouldn't pass. Uber-Goth was not in among the up-and-coming.

I grabbed the glass of wine I'd left on the table and took a thoughtful sip, trying to figure out a way to break it to her without being hurtful.

She seemed to have anticipated my objections. "You don't have to worry about my appearance," she chortled. "I've got just the thing." She slipped a hand beneath the neckline of her ghastly draperies.

I tensed a bit, ready to move just in case she pulled out something that jumped at me. You can never be certain what an underworld nymph will be nursing in her bosom.

I didn't jump when she pulled out her hand and showed me her prize. I couldn't move at all.

The wine glass slipped from my hand and shattered on the Italian tile floor.

Chapter 4

"Where did you get it?" I breathed. I could barely believe what I was seeing. It was small, as things of great power often are. The pendant was finely wrought silver with elaborate scrollwork, about the size of a fifty-cent piece.

It was the jewel in the center that was the real prize. Glimmering, opalescent like a rainbow moonstone, only more perfect. It was tear shaped, an odd choice for a cabochon in a round pendant. But then, that's what it was.

A Tear of Nereus. I remembered the legend well. Heracles had tracked down the Old Man of the Sea, Nereus, and fought a pitched battle to force him to reveal the secret location of the Garden of the Hesperides. Heracles grabbed the wily god and held fast, while Nereus used his primary power: shape-shifting. He became first one fantastic beast, then another.

During the battle Heracles clasped Nereus so hard that tears welled from the god's eyes, solidifying into jewels as they hit the beach. When it was over, and Heracles had won, Nereus sent his daughters the Nereids to collect the gems. They were hidden in a cave deep beneath the ocean, guarded by a sea dragon.

No wonder. They were more than just pretty baubles. Anyone who possessed a Tear of Nereus could use it to change into any shape they desired. The transformation would hold for as long as the Tear's possessor wanted.

"Where do you think I got it?" Orphne finally answered my question. She let the pendant drop, and I noticed it was suspended on a fine silver chain.

Where else would she get something like that? It seemed Hecate had some sort of plan after all.

"Do you know how to use it?" I'd never thought I'd see one of the Tears. It brought back an unexpected feeling of *déjà vu*. Heracles... I remembered him only to well. Remembered nights of holding him close as he'd held Nereus, only the fight I was in was to save his sanity. If only...

But I'd denied it back then. Had to, even though it was difficult.

Well, no use crying over spilled milk. He was beyond my reach now, happily married to Hebe, goddess of youth, who was now retired from her role as cupbearer of the gods. Not by choice, of course, but then, even a princess of Olympus is subject to the whims of Zeus.

"Do you know how to use it?" I asked again when Orphne remained silent. But then I realized she was already answering my question.

18

CURSE OF PROMETHEUS: A TALE OF MEDEA

The shift was so imperceptible at first that I thought it was simply a breeze that made her robe ripple gently. Then I noticed her skin was also rippling. Before I could blink her features blurred, and it seemed as if her head was becoming gigantic.

Within another second her form resolved itself and I saw her head *was* gigantic, because it was topped with a powdered wig that looked nearly a foot tall.

From the tip of that monstrous hairpiece to the now dainty feet in soft gold slippers, to the ostentatious artificial beauty mark on her cheek, she was the spitting image of Marie Antoinette. I never would have known the difference, and I remembered the original quite clearly.

Even the elaborate dress in soft shades of mauve and lavender looked precise in every detail. Her skin was still pale, but now a more believable human shade with pinkish undertones.

Gone were the talons, replaced by beautifully manicured and rouged fingernails—a nice touch which the real Marie Antoinette never sported. I wondered how Orphne even knew about Marie Antoinette, but perhaps the ill fated queen had ended up in Hades.

"C'est bon, oui?" The switch to French reminded me that like many of the older classes of beings, chthonic nymphs had the Gift of Tongues, enabling them to speak and understand any human language. Her unearthly rasp had been replaced by a light, girlish voice very close to the original Marie's simpering tones. Apparently the Tear allowed the bearer to sound like whatever creature they were trying to emulate visually.

As impressive as the illusion was, it wasn't especially helpful. Orphne could hardly go out to the supermarket dressed like that. She wouldn't be much use in helping me figure out whatever threat was looming if she had to be confined to the house. I doubted I'd be spending much time there.

Still, if her technique needed refining, there were ways to do it.

"All right," I said. "I'm staying here, and I'm going to fight."

"Are you sure? The aunts would love to see you." There was no smile on her face, but her voice had a touch of cynicism. She knew full well that Aiaia was an asylum tricked out as a paradise.

"I'm sure I'll make do. But if you're going to stay with me, you need to study up a bit. You have to pass for a modern day human if we're going to be seen together."

Within an instant she was back to her original shape. I made a mental note to pull down all the shades in the house until we could find a suitable form for her to use as her human persona. The yards in my neighborhood were fairly spacious, but the neighbors were also fairly nosy and not above staring boldly into my windows from the edge of my property line if they thought anything strange was going on.

"Let's start with men. I've never had a live one. They're all dead by the time they reach me, and I expect there's a difference." She was smiling eagerly now. In her original form, it made her look a bit like a cat that had sighted some easy prey.

Which a human man, dead or otherwise, would be to her. Underworld variety she might be, but Orphne was a nymph nonetheless. There's one thing all nymphs do well. Very well.

I ought to know. My mother Eidya is a nymph herself. Aside from inheriting her power, unique even among nymphs, to bespell any mortal with my eyes when I wanted, I had inherited some of her other abilities. They were diluted since my father had been mortal, but even a half-nymph's powers in the sexual arena can be formidable.

As a full-fledged nymph, Orphne would need careful watching. Atlanta is a progressive city, but even that has its limits.

"We'll talk about that later," I said firmly. "First, we need to get you up to speed on how modern humans behave."

I could tell she was disappointed that I'd deflected her from the subject of men, but she took it in stride. "All right. Do you have any scrolls that would be useful?"

Scrolls. Nowadays they would be books, but the malapropos phrase was the least of my worries. How could I possibly teach Orphne everything she needed to know about modern life?

I looked around the den, filled with shelves of books that I loved to collect on everything from science to cooking to history, hoping beyond hope that something would inspire me.

When my eyes hit the plasma TV, inspiration came. As they say, experience is the best teacher. Vicarious experience should count as well.

I switched it on. She jumped a bit as the image of a man driving a car filled the screen.

"What a magnificent scrying glass!" she cried.

"It's not a scrying glass, Orphne. It's going to be your teacher. Welcome to Earth in the twenty-first century."

I set about showing her how to operate the remote and scrounged up an old channel guide, circling channels that she should avoid so as not to waste time. She didn't need the latest mission briefings from NASA or the latest warnings from the right-wing fringe about how our country would be ruined by people who thought for themselves.

As I headed up the stairs to get a hot shower and a good night's sleep, she was quickly absorbing the finer points of teen angst from a show I'd never seen until then. I had a moment of guilt. Orphne needed no sleep, so she'd be channel surfing all night. If television was the only representation of humans she had, she'd think—

What? That humans were sophomoric, over-sexed, ruthless, violent, and appallingly stupid about the simplest facts of life?

Even if that was the only thing she came away with after an evening with the boob tube, she'd have a more sensible view of modern life than ninety percent of the humans.

Chapter 5

The great thing about my neighborhood is that there's plenty of activity early in the morning when I like to go running. Parents were bundling kids into cars for school, others were heading off early to work, and a few health conscious souls like me were getting in a quick jog before starting the day in earnest. Considering how much time I spend alone, it's nice to just be among people for a little while.

I had a moment of doubt before hitting the streets that day. Something was after me. Should I leave the safety of my house, which I'd warded strongly?

But the answer was clear. Whatever was stalking me had enough power to corrupt a Sybil's mirror, and the Guardian hadn't known something was afoot. There was every chance that if something was coming for me it wouldn't matter where I was. There was no point curtailing my life too much.

Anyway, if it was spying on me now and saw me boldly going out without any apparent care in the world, it might think I had something up my sleeve and hesitate to strike. Might, but not necessarily.

Still, I couldn't become a hermit.

The air was brisk, but there was that unmistakable moist scent that foretold a mild day. We'd been having a stellar autumn and I intended to enjoy the days as much as possible before the cold weather moved in.

I was halfway through my jog when I ran into Mr. McCaffrey, who lived alone in the house behind me. He smiled and reeled in Molly and Jasper on their leashes. The collies were highly playful, something I've never minded in dogs. I appreciated his gesture of courtesy just the same.

"Morning, Ms. Keres," he offered amiably as I reached down to scratch Jasper's head.

Not to be left out, Molly quickly nudged Jasper out of the way and took his place under my hand. "Haven't seen you in a few days," McCaffrey commented. It was a veiled question, but I didn't mind sharing.

"I just got back from Cleveland." I find it's easier to stay as close to the truth as possible when the neighbors enquire about my travels. He just didn't need to know I'd been there slaying an insatiable succubus.

"More charity work, eh? Well, that's very nice. Not too many young people are interested in helping others these days, especially if they can afford not to work."

I smiled up at him as I crouched and used my free hand to give Jasper some attention. Through bits and pieces dropped carefully at neighborhood get-togethers and casual encounters, I'd woven a plausible tale of having inherited a decent amount of money and using my free time as a "nonprofit consultant." My neighbors fancied me a well-heeled do-gooder who traveled a lot to advise various local charities.

Dispatching demons was charity of a sort. I'm sure their potential victims would agree.

"Well, it's good that you're back in time for the funeral," he sighed. My hands stopped in mid-scratch, prompting Jasper and Molly to nuzzle my palms to let me know *they* weren't finished.

"What funeral?" The neighborhood had a mixed age group, so the passing of an elderly resident wouldn't be out of the ordinary. But I could see from the look on his face that this was something different.

"Of course, you were traveling and wouldn't have heard. Shannon O'Neill was killed two days ago."

I've seen enough death, not to mention caused enough, that the news didn't throw me totally. I was surprised, though, and something tingled at the back of my mind. A killing in my neighborhood coming just before the menacing vision I'd had might not be coincidence.

I stood up, feigning a look of shock and sympathy. Neither is really in my nature, but one has to observe the niceties in such circumstances. "How did it happen?"

He waved a dismissive hand. "Don't know the details, really. Mrs. Kitson from the next street over phoned me when she heard. I watched the news that night, but I turned it off when they started doing the story. 'Butchered in Buckhead', it said on the screen. I can't stand that kind of sensationalism."

I couldn't blame him for turning off the news, but I wished he had more details for me.

There was one bright spot. She'd apparently been killed in Buckhead, a different section of town than our enclave in Vinings. Her death might be a coincidence after all.

"Do you known when the funeral is, and where?" I was resigned to attending, even though I couldn't really afford the time. I had to prepare for battle with an unknown enemy.

But McCaffrey had seen me, so I couldn't pretend I didn't know about it. If I didn't go, it would generate animosity and maybe a little suspicion among the neighbors. Such beginnings can quickly evolve into angry mobs with torches and pitchforks.

I'd had enough of those, thank you very much. Torches would probably be against the home owner association's covenant, but all you need is a Zippo to get the fire burning under the stake these days.

Several people in the neighborhood smoked.

"It's at the Catholic cathedral on Peachtree Street, at one o'clock," he said helpfully. "Sad thing, isn't it? I think she was only twenty-five."

"Twenty-seven," I corrected gently. "Killed, too. How awful. She was supposed to get married next spring."

"I know, I know. I was at the engagement party they threw back in August, remember?"

I didn't, but there had been at least a hundred people there. Shannon's parents and her fiancé's family were both well-off, and the party had been lavish. Ice sculptures on the buffet tables scattered across the ample back lawn at her parents' house, a subdued string quartet that didn't violate the HOA rules on noisy parties, and great food.

I'd especially enjoyed the wine. When I asked Shannon, she just smiled at Paul and said "It's a local label." He smiled back, and I guessed they were sharing a fond memory, or maybe a private joke. I'd let it pass without enquiring further.

Shannon and Paul made a handsome couple. She'd literally been glowing that night, surrounded by family and her closest friends, including five who were bridesmaids-to-be. They were all bubbling with excitement for her, not a trace of jealousy that she'd landed a good looking, successful man and was the first among them to walk down the aisle.

I took a deep breath to bring me back to the present. McCaffrey and I were just standing there in quiet commiseration over the tragedy of it all.

"I'd better be going," I finally said. "I have some errands to run before getting ready for the funeral. I wish I'd had time to send flowers to the wake."

McCaffrey cleared his throat meaningfully. "Didn't have a wake. I thought that was odd, them being Irish Catholic and all. They're usually big on viewings. But…"

He was clearly looking for permission to go on. I cocked my head in mock interest.

"Well, she *was* killed," he said, almost as if it explained everything. He stroked his wispy grey Van Dyke beard thoughtfully. "And the TV did say 'butchered.' I wonder if that has something to do with them not wanting a viewing. If… you know."

I did, but I was surprised that such a seemingly nice old man had thoughts that trailed into darkness like that. Apparently sensationalism was out of bounds for the media, but not for a good klatch.

"Maybe," I said uneasily. I turned, calling over my shoulder, "See you there." I gave a quick wave and headed back home. I'd suddenly lost the urge to keep up my normal routine.

Chapter 6

Seconds after I walked through the door I heard excited footsteps coming down the stairs.

"How do you like it?"

The question came from a six-foot-three naked Amazon who had just rounded the corner. And I do mean Amazon, right from the Brazilian rainforest.

Never mind the fact that the real inhabitants of that area weren't that tall. We had other issues to deal with. I wasn't sure whether I was more distracted by the giant plate that distended her lower lip so much I winced, or by the breasts hanging almost to her navel.

I quickly slammed the door behind me. This was the time of morning the couple across the street usually headed off to their respective jobs. Orphne was one house guest they didn't need to know about, especially in this form.

This was going to take more than a little polishing. "Do we have a second choice?"

The giantess shrugged and suddenly shrank before my eyes. In less than two seconds I was facing someone who could have been a queen from Ireland's heyday.

Her flowing red hair had just a touch of wildness in the curls. The mane was a skillful blend of reds and bronzes, making her porcelain skin seem that much paler.

Not so much as a dusting of freckles on the nose marred that milky softness. The eyes were a green so vivid it bordered on unnatural, but they were so stunning in that face that I doubted anyone would notice. She was only about five-foot-six, yet there was a voluptuousness to the curves of her body that made her seem larger.

"This was my original pick, but since I saw so much violence on television last night I thought I should try something a little more intimidating. It was too much?" She asked it with no hint of insecurity. She had a lot to learn about getting by in the mortal world, and knew it.

"Well, I suppose you would have deterred any muggers. But you would also have been a little out of place. Now *this* form... I like it. You look stunning."

"So I'm ready to go out?"

Aside from the fact that she was naked as a jaybird except for the Tear hanging around her neck, I was dubious about her readiness to deal with large quantities of still-living humans. Down in Hades she was higher in the food chain, but she couldn't pull any rank here on Earth if we wanted to keep our cover intact.

She cocked her head with a wry smile. "You don't think I could handle it? What's the worst that could happen?"

The possibilities were limitless, and most of them ended badly in my hasty assessment. "Just for giggles, what would you do if a man tried to assault you? Say you were alone in a dark street."

"I would kill him," Orphne replied as if it was the most natural thing in the world. For a chthonic nymph, it was. She was strong enough to rip a human apart with her bare hands. It was highly likely she would, if provoked, which was one reason I was going to keep a very sharp eye on her while she was on Earth.

"Wrong answer," I said as I moved past her. I motioned for her to join me upstairs.

She smiled as I strode over to my bedroom closet. "Don't tell me you haven't killed someone who assaulted you on the street."

She knew me too well. I deliberately paused while I studied the casual outfits hanging on the left side of the closet. I chose a few items before emerging and answering.

"You know I have. But not recently. When I did it, times were different. People were different. If thieves were caught in the act they were likely to be executed anyway, and they knew it. It didn't matter whether I did it or a professional did it."

She smiled knowingly, and I noticed she'd taken the time to add dimples to her new form. Fetching indeed.

I held up a grey cashmere cardigan against her shoulders. The sweater's tone was just a little too pale for my complexion but I'd never gotten around to returning it to Neiman's. Next to Orphne's transformed skin, it seemed to glow like a grey pearl. Perfect match.

"But things aren't like that anymore," Orphne said. It wasn't a question. I held a pink silk shell against her shoulders. The color would go wonderfully with the grey sweater, but it didn't do much for her hair. I replaced it with a black scoop-neck shirt.

"No," I ducked back into the closet to find some pants. "If you did anything to a human, even in self-defense, and especially if you changed back to your original form, you'd risk exposing us. There are surveillance cameras everywhere these days and you could easily be filmed. The authorities would never give up the hunt."

She shook her head in disbelief. "You're saying it's too risky to defend yourself against an attacker these days? Explain to me again why you like living on Earth so much."

I selected beige slacks to go with the rest of the outfit. I gathered the clothes and went over to the bed, sitting down and patting the space next to me. Orphne obligingly came over and eased onto the bed as I lay the clothes to the other side.

"I never said I did," I said patiently. "I suppose it's grown on me. At least here, things change. People change. Not always for the good, but it's still better than nothing. Nothing ever changes on Olympus, or the Elysian Fields, or Aiaia. Nothing much changes in Hades either, as you well know."

An odd look crossed her face, as if I'd hit a tender spot. But it was gone in a moment.

"You're trying to distract yourself, and me," she said with new vigor. "You've made a great show of choosing clothes for me, even though they clearly won't fit. I'm at least three inches shorter than you in this form, and our body types aren't even remotely similar. Never mind that the whole thing is unnecessary, since I can conjure outfits as part of my disguises."

She had me there. I was in avoidance mode and she wasn't willing to join me. She pressed forward.

"What are you really concerned about, Medea? I know I've got a lot to learn about living on Earth, and I probably should limit my contact with humans at first. I promise I won't use the Tear to change into the Hydra and eat anyone. But that's not the core issue."

She waited a few seconds for a reply. I didn't have one so she continued. "Have you thought about who might be behind the threat?"

I had. And I'd come up with one likely suspect.

"Lamia," I said. I took a breath, tried to calm down. Hard to do whenever Lamia came up in conversation. Fortunately it wasn't too often.

She frowned. "What makes you think that? Wasn't it a man you saw in the mirror? Wasn't it his mouth that tried to break through?"

I took another breath. "Yes. But there was something else, something I didn't tell you last night because I didn't remember it. At the beginning when I saw the dead body, there was someone else. A woman. I saw her hand caressing the death wound."

"But you didn't see her face."

I had to admit the truth. "No, but..."

"Then why focus on Lamia?"

My eyes hardened as I looked up at her. "How can you ask that? Who else would want to threaten me? I've been hunting her daughters for centuries, trying to wipe them out so she can finally be killed."

Orphne gripped my arm hard. "You have to *think*, Medea. Lamia doesn't have the power to affect a Sybil's mirror. And blood drinking... that's not what she does, or anyone involved with her. She and her daughters suck the life energy from humans, not their blood. You can't focus on her just because it satisfies a vendetta. You know what the blood drinking might mean, Medea. You *know*."

I did, and just because I hadn't mentioned it didn't mean I hadn't thought about it.

"The Curse of Prometheus," I said. A lot more quietly than I should have, if I was trying to convince Orphne that I hadn't lost my resolve.

But who was I kidding. If the Curse was involved, I would need more than an attitude.

"Just so," she said. "If that's what's happening, you could be in great danger."

Great danger indeed. The Curse of Prometheus had its origins in the founding of the Olympian gods themselves.

When they overthrew the Titans, the Olympians inherited a universe that was sheer chaos. The Titans had been content to let the forces of nature work at random, caring little for the havoc that happened away from their palaces. Stars wheeled madly through the heavens, rivers were as likely to flow with fire as with water. The Earth itself would have flowering fields one day, brutal winter the next, forcing every creature to take advantage of the rare moments of peace to eat, to mate, and to give birth.

Zeus ordered an end to it. Each of the new gods set about taming a specific force of nature, and then merging with it, becoming inseparable from that force. Demeter became one with the Earth, Poseidon with the sea, and Hades agreed to the grim task of ruling those dark realms where the worst nightmares were born. Ever proud, he named his dark domain after himself.

The plan was simple: if the powers of nature were linked directly to the gods, they would work together in harmony as the gods lived together in harmony.

As they say, the plan looked good on paper. But as with all changes in leadership, there were those who thought they could use the uncertainty of a fledgling regime for their own ends.

CURSE OF PROMETHEUS: A TALE OF MEDEA

The Titan Prometheus, who sided with Zeus during the war, had his eye on advancing his place. He didn't intend to wait for Zeus to reward his loyalty. His plan was simple: gain control of one of the elemental powers himself, and use it to force the Olympians to make him one of their own. What easier way to reach this goal than to steal an elemental force that had already been tamed?

Prometheus targeted the least warlike of the new gods—Hestia. Her calm and mild demeanor had ironically given her the firmest base for taming and merging with the wildest of the elements: fire.

Fire, as humans know it now, was far different then. It's true, untamed power made the fury of a supernova look like a shot from a squirt gun. Of all the natural forces, Hestia's conquest was the greatest, and Zeus knew well that had she been anything less than a dutiful sister, she would have been the biggest threat to him because her power alone could challenge his.

Capturing her in an unguarded moment alone, Prometheus attacked Hestia and stole her power. He fled to Earth, intending to find a way to incorporate the power of fire into his own being. But he was nearly destroyed while trying to absorb it directly. He was a Titan, but not one of the strongest. It would never be his destiny to wield such a force and sit in the highest places of Olympus.

Still, he had some power as well as great cunning. Knowing the gods were hot on his trail, he used his power to isolate the spiritual component of fire, the essence that made it more than mere flames, and planted it into the odd, squealing creatures that had gathered in awe around him. Humans. He fused it with their blood, and laid a binding that would allow the power to propagate with each successive generation of humans.

Just as the gods arrived, Prometheus shrieked a curse. Any god could regain total control over the true, near-limitless power of fire by absorbing it step by step from the blood of humans. But there was a terrible price: for each drop of blood they drained, they would slide further and further into insanity.

Not being gods, humans could not benefit fully from the new power that literally flowed through them, although it enabled them to understand fire enough to make it useful for cooking and forging metal. Modern scientists exploring the complexities of nuclear energy and plasma physics had no idea that the power to control a far more formidable force lay within their very veins.

As for the gods, there was little they could do. There was no way to try to regain true control over fire without taking the greatest of risks.

The possibility of a mad god roaming the universe wielding such power was unthinkable. A ban on human sacrifices went into effect. None seemed inclined to break it, owing to the huge risks. If any dared they would become anathema to the rest of the Olympians, as well as losing their minds.

But maybe that price was becoming more acceptable to someone. There had been more than one attempt among the gods to revolt against Zeus. They had failed, but what if one of the gods had decided to try again by reclaiming control over the most powerful element? If that god killed enough humans, and drank enough blood, it could happen. Having that kind of power would make such a god the equal of Zeus himself. And if that rogue persuaded others to join him, the battle might be short indeed.

The thought was chilling. If someone from Olympus was going that route, it meant they had already lost their head. If I tried to stop them, I would be in way, way over mine.

Chapter 7

There was no outward sign of extravagance at Shannon O'Neill's funeral. Everything was subdued, but I had an experienced eye. The casket and flower arrangements were all of the finest quality. There was a profusion of star-gazer lilies on the coffin.

I caught the occasional whiff of their heady fragrance even though I was sitting towards the back of the church. Other neighbors were scattered here and there. McCaffrey had decided to sit one pew ahead of me. I didn't know why he bothered keeping even that much distance, since he kept turning around every few minutes to offer some observation to me.

A small group walked in, two women and a man.

"There they are," McCaffrey stage-whispered. "They" were the surviving O'Neills, Shannon's parents and sister.

I couldn't believe that Evelyn O'Neill had actually gone so far as to wear a large black hat and oversized black sunglasses. That seemed to be taking the melodrama a little too far.

I caught the uncharitable thought before it progressed to a catty observation about the length of her skirt (far too short for a woman her age, especially one who was supposed to be in mourning for her daughter). Her husband Michael was appropriately dressed in a black suit, and her daughter Lyn was wearing a dress that came to mid-calf. But then, she always seemed to wear such dresses. Not my taste, but her mother could have taken a few pointers from Lyn on this occasion.

A few minutes went by before another group joined them. I instantly recognized Shannon's fiancé Paul Kirkpatrick. The reddish-blond hair would have been enough of a giveaway, but even without it he stood out. He was well over six feet tall, and took very good care of himself.

Very good.

Now *I* was the one being inappropriate. I decided two could play at the gossip game.

"There's Paul," I whispered to McCaffrey. "But who's that with him?" I was referring to an older woman and a young man dressed entirely in black.

McCaffrey squinted a bit. "Oh, that's his mother and brother. I met them both at the party. Very nice woman, though she seemed a bit dotty." As if he should talk. "She's been widowed for several years, from what I gathered. And Peter, that's the younger one, he's very nice too. But then, he would have to be, considering."

Considering what? I wondered.

I got the answer a second later when he turned around abruptly and looked straight in my direction. It was no small distance from the front pew to the rear of the cathedral, but I had the uncanny feeling that he was looking directly into my eyes. The momentary shock took my breath away.

The other thing I noticed was the catch of white at his throat, barely visible because the rest of his outfit was pitch black.

He was a priest. Now I remembered him more clearly. He stayed mostly in the background at the engagement party. I'd assumed he was a family friend, maybe the one who was going to perform the wedding. He didn't look a thing like Paul.

Music started, and he looked down and turned his back to me again.

What the hell was that about? I wondered as the mourners rose for the beginning of the service. The fact that he'd zeroed in on me sitting alone in the back of the church was unsettling enough, but that look— even from far away, there was something in it. Some connection.

I decided the atmosphere was playing tricks with my mind and tried to pay attention to the service. I went through the general motions of the ceremony with the rest of the mourners. Sitting and standing, though I didn't kneel when the others did. This was not my faith, after all. I had plenty of gods to kneel to already without adding another to the list just to keep up appearances.

As the eulogy began I paid closer attention to Shannon's parents. During my one-on-one encounters with her, mercifully few, Evelyn O'Neill had been strident, almost abrasive. She didn't seem any worse for the wear despite her daughter's death.

By contrast, Mr. O'Neill's shoulders were bunched with pain. I understood, perhaps better than anyone else there, the abyss that opens up inside of you when your child dies. Murder makes it even harder.

Finally the service was over. McCaffrey made his apologies and rushed off. He had to give the dogs their mid-afternoon walk or they'd start chewing up the rugs again.

The O'Neills were gathered outside. Already the condolence line was sizable. I decided to wait off to the side until it thinned a little.

I was admiring the lovely gold of the autumn trees just down the street when I felt a hand on my arm. I spun a little more abruptly than I intended. For some inexplicable reason, I had the thought that Peter Kirkpatrick had found me.

But it wasn't him. It was Paul.

"It was good of you to come, Ms. Keres," he said in his soft, rich baritone. I could see why he was a successful stock broker, with such a reassuring voice. I was ready to invest myself, even though I hardly needed it after three millennia of savings.

To be honest, I was a little flattered that he'd remembered my name. We'd only met briefly at the engagement party. I'd spent most of the time talking to Shannon and the other neighbors.

I decided I could risk a quick touch on his arm. "I'm so sorry, Paul. I only got back into town last night and found out today."

He gave a quick, tight smile. More of a grimace, really. "We still don't understand why they did it," he said, a little choke in his voice.

It clued me in that it wasn't just some random crime, but there was no tactful way to ask him more with his dead fiancée lying in a hearse a few yards away.

He looked over to the O'Neills. "They've just gone to pieces. I'm not much better, to tell you the truth. But considering what they've been through, I guess I'll have to take care of canceling..."

He trailed off, but there was no mistaking what he was talking about. The wedding. I had no doubt Shannon's mother had been handling things up to that point. She was that sort of woman. Like they say, a girl's wedding day is usually for her mother, not her.

Based on the mother in question, not to mention the splashy preamble of an engagement party, I figured Evelyn was planning the wedding of the century. No doubt with a cast of thousands, or at least several hundred. There'd be elaborate catering, huge floral arrangements, probably personalized party favors for the guests.

That was a lot of canceling for one man to handle. Or so I told myself afterwards, to justify what came out of my mouth next.

"I could help you," I said, just then realizing my hand was still on his arm. Well, he hadn't done anything to remove it, not even taking a half-step backwards. And if he was opening up to me like that, he probably needed someone who wasn't involved with the immediate situation to talk to.

He seemed a little confused. "Help?" he asked, looking more than ever like he needed it.

"I could make some calls. It would be no trouble, really, to take care of canceling some of the arrangements."

Understanding crept into his eyes. "That would be fantastic." He kept his voice at a modest pitch, but I could see the relief in his eyes. "Lyn and I were going to take care of notifying the out-of-town guests. We were supposed to get together Friday to divvy up the list. Could you...?"

I knew exactly what he meant. He was going to stick me with Shannon's mousy sister Lyn. I couldn't blame him there. The girl, while quite attractive, had been so thoroughly cowed by Evelyn that she hardly had enough spine to walk upright. It was more of a slouching amble, at that. She was hardly someone you'd spend much time with, given a choice.

It served me right for making such a shameless invitation to a man in mourning. Of course, I'd done it mostly because I intended to find out more about Shannon's death, just to reassure myself it had nothing to do with the threat from the Sybil's mirror. I couldn't shake the feeling that somehow they were connected.

But there was no reason I couldn't just dig a bit on the local television websites and the Atlanta Journal-Constitution's online edition. I absolutely did not need to spend time with Paul to find out more about it.

Funny how "needs" and "wants" so rarely overlap. Well, it didn't matter. Maybe I could get some answers from Lyn, though I doubted she'd have the stomach for discussing something so violent as murder, let alone her own sister's.

"Of course, Paul," I smiled reassuringly, finally taking my hand off his arm so I could reach into my bag for a calling card. I wondered if the notion of a calling card seemed antiquated to him.

"Why don't you give her this? She can call me to set up a time. I don't know her very well, and I'm sure it would be easier for you to smooth the way with her."

And you can copy that phone number down for your own records, I thought hopefully. I nearly gave him a second calling card for himself, but that would have been too obvious. An outsider might consider my interest in him distasteful given his loss, but really, it had been awhile since I'd met a decent man. And the nights in between demon hunting can get quite lonely.

I'm half nymph, after all.

He put the card in his wallet.

"Thank you again," he said with a slight nod before moving off to take his place a bit apart from Shannon's family in the condolence line.

Several neighbors were still there, along with other people I recognized from the engagement party. But as I gazed around, I had an uneasy feeling. It seemed I should know more of the people there.

I shrugged it off. No one is ever really themselves at a funeral. It was probably just the awkward silence that made it seem as if there were too many strangers, young and old alike. More older people than young ones, though. Something was odd about that.

I decided it was time to make a discrete exit. I turned to where the hearse was parked to say a final goodbye to Shannon.

He was staring directly at me.

How long had Peter Kirkpatrick been standing by the hearse looking at me? There was no doubt this time that it was more than just a chance meeting of eyes. We were close enough that I could see those eyes this time, a surprising shade of blue. Quite unexpected considering his skin was almost dusky. Maybe Peter liked to hit the tanning bed. He was motionless, but his mouth opened slightly as if he wanted to say something.

He didn't. His lips compressed and he simply gave me a nod. A nod of recognition, even though we hadn't formally met.

Keeping my gaze level, I gave him the same nod before turning and heading towards the parking garage across the street. I had no intention of looking over my shoulder to see if his gaze was still on me. He was just a human, nothing more.

I had bigger things to worry about. Peter Kirkpatrick didn't have an elaborately curled and oiled beard, or any trace of blood on his lips. He wasn't the threat.

No threat at all.

Chapter 8

Practicing witchcraft and being more than three thousand years old wouldn't make me a likely candidate for techie of the year in most people's eyes. That would be their mistake.

I pride myself on my computer skills. It's much easier to track down aberrant reports that could indicate demonic activities these days, what with the huge number of local media websites.

Of course I backed them up with traditional scrying methods. I'll trust a pendulum over an investigative reporter any day. Still, thanks to the media I'd sharply reduced the time lapse between detecting a possible problem and zeroing in on it.

I had the best computer system money could buy in my den, and that's where I curled up after changing out of my funeral attire. I tuned out the sounds of the daytime talk show on the television and the sporadic giggles from Orphne, who seemed to find the segment on women who killed abusive husbands highly amusing.

It took almost no time at all to track down information about Shannon's death. When I found it, I was grateful that I hadn't openly invited Paul over for a one-on-one chat with a side order of mild interrogation.

"Holy shit," I muttered, the spoon of Baskin Robbins mint chocolate chip halfway to my mouth. I was attacking the pint I'd forgotten about the night before.

"Something good?" Orphne enquired.

"Not good by a long shot," I returned as I scraped the ice cream from the spoon back into the container. The craving had just disappeared. "Take a look at this."

She obliged, and after a few seconds of reading drew in a sharp breath.

"She was killed by her friends?"

"Not just her friends," I corrected. "Her *bridesmaids.*"

This was stuff worthy of Euripedes.

I quickly scanned a few sites with Orphne leaning over my shoulder. It had even made CNN's web page. No wonder, with such horrific details. Those details varied slightly between media outlets, depending on which "confidential source close to the investigation" was supplying the information.

Shannon had apparently gone to a party at the Buckhead condo of one of her bridesmaids-to-be a few nights ago. When she didn't come home that night the family thought little of it, since she sometimes slept at friends' houses. But when she didn't show up for work the next day, her coworkers got worried. One of them called Paul.

He went over to the condo, found the door unlocked, and found a horrible scene inside. Shannon was dead, and the other five girls were in some kind of stupor or passed out entirely.

Two of the accounts indicated the place was covered with blood. One, quoting an anonymous police source, said the girls were as well.

All of the stories confirmed police were releasing few details, but said they had "firm evidence" that each of the girls had a hand in her death.

I finally understood why something seemed odd about the crowd at Shannon's funeral. None of the bridesmaids I'd met at the engagement party were there. None of them had even been granted bail. Three of them were on suicide watch.

By that time Orphne had pulled over a chair to get more comfortable. "That is fucked out," she observed as I called up a video report on the murder from a local station.

"Up."

"What?"

"The story is fucked *up*, not out."

She shrugged. "I'll try to pay more attention when they're swearing on television. With something this strange, does the direction even matter?"

Probably not, especially for a chthonic nymph who'd likely done it in every direction imaginable. With dead guys, no less.

Of course, that meant she might have some unique insights into something like this. "Have you heard of anything like this recently? Maybe someone has come your way who was involved in something similar?"

I wasn't just thinking of victims. Perpetrators of this caliber would have breezed through Hades on their way to Tartarus for a few hundred years of torment. Shannon wouldn't have been the first good Catholic girl to get mixed up in some weird cult, but if there was any kind of activity like that in my area there'd been no reports of it. The Underworld might be the first place where signs of something abnormal showed up.

"No, nothing like this," she said thoughtfully. "The closest was a lovely Asian gentleman who drifted down a few years ago. He was being hustled off to the torture pits, of course. Something about genocide and a military junta."

I bet Orphne was the only one who'd thought he was lovely. Clearly the judges of Hades hadn't, since he'd been heading to Tartarus. I wondered briefly why he didn't end up in one of the Buddhist hells, but figured he'd probably been an atheist. It's always a toss-up where they'll land.

"You're thinking this has something to do with what happened last night, aren't you?"

CURSE OF PROMETHEUS: A TALE OF MEDEA

Orphne was right on the money. Unfortunately it's a long way between thinking there might be a connection and establishing one.

"Her death is definitely strange, and so is what happened with the Sybil's mirror. Not to mention, Hecate sending you here to warn me to keep my guard up for something. Something she couldn't identify."

I got up and stretched. My neck had a slight crick in it from working at the computer. I went over to the sofa to get more comfortable.

"That's all I've got, though," I admitted as I settled in. "Some odd stuff going on, but no clear connection between events. The dead body I saw in the mirror was definitely a man's, so I couldn't have been witnessing Shannon's murder."

"Could it just be coincidence?" She didn't sound convinced herself.

"I doubt it," I chuckled. "Maybe, though, one or the other incident is a diversion. Something to draw me away from the real truth."

She smiled. "Just what I was thinking. So, obviously—"

"We'll have to check into both of them," I finished.

A snatch of a rich scent drifted in from the direction of the kitchen. The lamb shanks I'd put in the crock pot before the funeral were almost ready. My appetite perked up again.

"Come on," I got up and headed that way, motioning Orphne to join me. "I'll show you how we set a proper table."

"Shouldn't we be getting some weapons ready, just in case?"

"Plenty of time for that after dinner. And we might even have time for a pay-per-view movie before bed." With popcorn, of course. Orphne should learn the magic of the microwave while she was adjusting to life on Earth.

I almost felt guilty for being hungry after just wolfing down half a pint of ice cream. But with my line of work, you have to eat when you can and enjoy the few home cooked meals you've got the leisure to make. You never know when you'll have to turn around and use the cauldron to cook up something else.

"So, what movie did you have in mind?" Orphne asked as she grabbed a couple of plates from the cupboard.

"I here there's a remake of 'Rosemary's Baby,' " I offered.

"What's that?"

I opened my mouth to explain, then remembered who I was talking to and what her perspective was.

"It's a light comedy."

Chapter 9

Something is wrong.

I have to get back. They're in danger. I can sense they've left the safety of the temple of Hera, where I'd hidden them before fleeing.

I command the dragons to turn back. The chariot swoops and dips in the air as we wheel around back to Corinth.

I have to make sure they're safe, no matter the risk to me. At Hera's altar, none would dare touch my children until Jason comes. If he comes, if he's not too wrapped up mourning his precious princess. If he doesn't claim them the priests will take them in. They'll be safe.

No. This is just a dream. Wake up. WAKE UP!

With the strange flow of time that dreams take, I was suddenly in Corinth, the half-hour frantic journey back there elided out.

The chariot lands on the roof of the temple. I spring out, hear a commotion to the side. It's night, but there is a faint flickering light from below. Torches.

I run over, look down.

No. Don't look!

He's there. Jason. Charred rags cling to him, all that's left of his wedding finery after the cursed robe I sent to his bride burned her alive. His body is going slightly soft but is still fine at forty years of age. He's holding...

NO!

He's holding their bodies. My boys. My sons. In a city where I was scorned, thrown aside even by my own husband, they still loved me.

A low moan escapes my lips, rising in pitch to pain, fear and terror. What happened to them? They look—

"Medea!"

Jason's eyes are on me now, grief and rage twisting his face to a hideous mask. "Why? Why did you leave them? Wasn't it enough that you killed Creusa and destroyed my hope of marrying into a kingship? You left them alone! And look what happened! It's because of you they're dead. You killed them! You killed them!"

I'm powerless to form words to protest, to tell him I had to leave them, that they would have died in my fiery chariot because they didn't inherit my magic. All I can do is keen, venting the agony in wordless wails. And then it hits me. Where, where is my daughter? I left her with the boys in the temple.

The serpentine dragons hitched to the chariot start to hiss a warning.

Shouts come up from below as the accusation moves through the gathering crowd.

"Did you hear? She killed them! The witch killed her own children!"

"Ah, the curse of the gods is upon us!" moans another. "The king and princess are dead, the palace burned to the ground, and now the evil foreign witch slays her own children!"

NO! It wasn't me!

I look across the sky, hoping some god will show mercy, descend and make things right. But there is nothing. My gaze drifts downward.

On a rooftop below I spy her. I know now what happened, why my sons look like that.

Cold eyes, unnaturally blue with serpent-slit pupils stare back at me. Lamia. She did it. She killed my boys, sucked their very life from them as she did with countless children, jealous of any mother's happiness after losing her own children to Hera's wrath.

But she is not alone. Another set of eyes look up at me. Amber-brown. She got those eyes from Jason. But now, they've changed.

The pupils are serpent slits! I realize why her eyes are standing out so much in the dark.

They're glowing. Just like Lamia's. Glowing enough to highlight a humorless smile. A ghoul's smile on a three-year-old girl's face.

"See now, Medea!" Lamia hisses. "I have taken in the daughter you forsook to save your own life. She will be the first of many daughters for me. I have learned how to transfer my power to others. Only females, but they shall be enough. With them, I shall have my revenge!"

A cry bursts through my lips. "Clymene! Not my baby! Not my little girl! Give her back to me!"

Fireballs spring to my hands, but it is too late. In a swirl of greenish light they're suddenly gone.

I hear a clamor from below. Someone is bringing ladders, ropes. They're going to try to come up to the roof.

Desperate, not for me but for Clymene, I spring back to the chariot. We're airborne a second later, swooping low over the roofs of Corinth as I search the shadows for any sign of them. Any sign of my daughter.

"I'm coming! I'm coming!" I scream, uncaring that the terrified people fleeing for cover below must think I'm cursing them. How horrible it must be, to see me in the flaming chariot drawn by dragons. But their fears mean nothing to me.

"I'll find you! I'll find you!"

"I'll find you!" I bolted upright from the sofa where I'd fallen asleep.

Arms grabbed my own. I struggled, cursed, got a hand free. A fireball appeared almost by instinct in the cupped palm. I tore free, turned to the fool who had grabbed me from behind and flung the fireball with all my strength.

Orphne ducked just in time. The fireball slammed into the plasma TV, shattering the screen. A million sparks fell to the ground as the wrecked shell burst into flames.

"Medea! It's just a dream!" Orphne screamed.

Awareness flooded back into me. I spoke a charm in a ragged voice and the fire died down, revealing a large scorch mark on the wall. I sealed the magic with another spell, this one to cancel any possible danger from smoldering plastic or damaged wires.

I sank back down into the sofa cushions.

"Sorry," I muttered weakly. Orphne was already over at the bar pouring me a stiff brace of brandy. She must have seen that in an old movie.

I gulped the brandy in one draught, glad that she'd thought to bring the decanter with her when she handed me the glass. I resisted the urge to pour another one immediately.

She sat down next to me. "The same dream?"

She knew the answer, but I nodded anyway. "It comes back when I'm under stress."

We sat in silence a few moments.

"There'll be time, Medea. Time when the immediate threat is over to go back to your hunt. You'll find her."

"Them," I said flatly. I'd long ago stopped denying the reality. Stopped denying what I'd have to do to put an end to Lamia's curse. She wasn't the only one I'd have to kill.

Lamia had been beautiful. A queen, a woman with everything. And she'd gotten more when Zeus' eye fell on her. For awhile, it must have been a dream come true. Not only did she have the best of what the mortal world had to offer, she was paramour to the king of the gods himself.

But as they say, all good things come to an end. Zeus's wife Hera found out, as she always did. She couldn't do anything to Zeus, of course, so she turned all of her anger against the hapless Lamia. She killed the queen's children.

Zeus could have brought them back, but it would only have made Hera exact an even higher price against Lamia. Instead, he swore an oath that no one, not even death, would harm Lamia again so long as she had a child of her own. To guard her he set his own sigil on her, as gods did with every mortal under their special protection. To harm a human with such a mark was sacrilege, even for another god.

The queen knew she had a rare chance with such protection and quickly adopted a dozen children. Her grief still heavy on her, she turned to studying dark arts from foreign lands until she learned the secret of staying forever young by sucking the life force from humans.

By continuing to adopt new children, she usurped Zeus' gift and cheated death, becoming essentially immortal. By preying on humans, she remained eternally youthful and seductive.

Her evil grew with the years. She tormented other parents by killing their children, sucking out their energy until they were dry husks.

Eventually she learned to spread her evil, imbuing other women and girls with the same energy-sucking power. The infected girls grew to adulthood, but aged no further, although unlike Lamia they could be killed. The gods were appalled, but Zeus could do nothing. He had given his word to protect Lamia and couldn't take it back.

The only way Lamia could ever be killed was to kill all of the females she "adopted" as daughters, the women she turned into deadly succubi. If she had no more children, the terms of Zeus' protection would be voided.

I'd been charged with killing any demons that escaped from Hades, but it was understood that Lamia would be my top priority. She'd killed my sons. Worse, she'd taken my baby Clymene under her dark wings and made her a monster.

For centuries, people bought into the myth that I'd slain my own children to punish Jason for leaving me. They were wrong, but it didn't matter. One day, I would have to live up to that myth.

Hunting and killing all of Lamia's "children" meant I had to find Clymene, the first girl who'd come under Lamia's dark tutelage.

It meant I would have to kill my own daughter.

Chapter 10

The next two days passed without any incident. I decided to move the Sybil's mirror to the storeroom off the kitchen. I knew, of course, that out of sight was definitely not out of mind. Anything strong enough to break through the mirror wouldn't be deterred by a locked door. But not seeing it made me feel better.

I used the time to get together some weapons. Most of them were already primed for fighting demons. I had several silver stakes impregnated with the blood of Cerberus, one of the few things that can kill a demon.

Getting his blood had been a fun little chore, part of my apprenticeship in Hades all those centuries ago. Fortunately the power of my eyes to bespell a human worked on some otherworldly creatures as well, even if they have three heads. I was able to put him in a stupor long enough to get enough blood for my needs.

The stakes were dangerous, though. A mere touch would incinerate a human, so I had to keep them well wrapped when I went on the road hunting demons. I couldn't risk having one poke through a duffle bag and jab an unsuspecting bellhop.

Another problem was their size. Effective as they were, they were too large to stick in even my most generous purse.

I had other options, though, including a knife that was infused with the Hydra's venom when it was forged. It was strong enough to incapacitate even an immortal with a mere scratch. For anything else, it would bring an agonizing death in a matter of seconds. I closely examined the sheath to make sure there were no gaps that could allow the blade to scratch me accidentally. Raging agony is not one of my favorite things, unless I'm the one causing it.

The knife fit nicely into my purse, along with a couple of amulets that kept most low-level nasties at bay. I knew I was up against something much stronger than a mere bugaboo, but it might have little henchlings. No reason to waste time and energy fighting them if I could banish them by flashing the right talisman.

Orphne watched my preparations with interest one afternoon. She had permanently adopted the red-headed human form, complete with a different outfit every day. She was getting some of the subtleties of human behavior down fairly easily.

"Nothing bigger than a knife and few talismans?"

"I'm just packing a few things to take along. The rest of the stuff is too bulky for a trip to the store. Not to mention, I wouldn't get very far toting the bigger items around town before the police stopped me. I need something easily concealed, and easily disposed of, if need be." Truth be told, I hadn't even scratched the surface of my arsenal. But swords, spears and shields would have to stay at home unless I planned on a formal assault. Which, having absolutely no information to go on, I didn't.

I stashed a few of the larger weapons in each room of the house. If the thing in question decided to hit me on my home turf I could get to them quickly enough.

I was debating whether to put together a couple of emergency potions to carry with me when the doorbell rang.

"Who the hell could that be?" I get a little snippy when my concentration is broken.

"It's Friday, remember? Maybe Lyn is here."

Damn, I'd forgotten all about that. "Wait in the guest bathroom until I get her into the den."

"Still afraid to take me out in public?" I could tell she was teasing, but it wasn't the right time.

"No, but Lyn is awkward around strangers. Even in your human form you might spook her, and I need to see if she has any information I can use."

She obliged, giving me a thumbs up sign before closing the bathroom door. She'd picked up a bit more than I expected from watching television.

The gods had a pleasant surprise in store for me. Paul was standing there when I opened the door.

He returned my smile a little hesitantly. "Sorry, I hope I'm not interrupting anything."

"No, not at all. Just doing a little housekeeping." I moved to the side so he could come in.

I led him to the den, which was big enough to double as a receiving room. It was cozier than the living room. "Come on in. Can I get you a drink?"

"I don't want to be any trouble." He was standing a little self-consciously just inside the den's door. "Wow," he said as he took in the wreck of my television and the large scorch mark on the wall. "What happened there?"

"Oh, I was playing tennis with my Wii," I began. He picked up on the implication.

"Control slipped out of your hand and hit the television, huh?"

"Yeah. Guess I'd better invest in a wrist strap along with a new television." I hoped he wouldn't look too carefully, because I didn't want to explain where the nonexistent Wii had gone off to.

I gestured to the couch while I went over to the bar. "Please, make yourself comfortable. I'm having a *mavrodaphne* if you'd like to join me." I uncorked the bottle and poured slightly less than I usually take.

"A what?"

"It's a Greek wine. Kind of like sherry."

He didn't look too keen on it. "A water will be fine, thanks."

I had to laugh at his expression. "The *mavrodaphne* does take some getting used to. Perrier work for you?"

"That'll be fine." He seated himself, still looking uncomfortable. I wasn't sure what to make of his unexpected appearance, but I figured I still had a few inches of safe territory before things got really awkward.

Orphne poked her head around the door. The couch faced the other direction, so Paul didn't see her. I made a subtle gesture with my head and she ducked back. Knowing her she was probably listening just outside the door, but that was fine. This might be a chance for me to get some more information about Shannon's death, and I wanted her to hear it.

"I thought it might be Lyn when the doorbell rang, though she hasn't called me yet. Do you know if she's still planning to tackle the guest notification today?"

He took the glass from my hands without looking me in the eyes. "That would be my fault. I forgot to give her your card. She mentioned today that she didn't have your number."

Hmmm. Forgot to give her my card? Maybe he subconsciously wanted to hang onto it himself. I tried to remind myself he was still in mourning as I took a thoughtful sip of the wine, but it didn't help. Vulnerable men turn me on.

"You saw her today?" I was trying to keep the conversation going. He seemed to have something on his mind.

"Yeah, I gave her a ride home from the university. It's not close to the office, but… well, you know. After what happened I didn't want to be too standoffish with her. She's shy, and sometimes she takes things too personally, if you know what I mean."

I did. It made me even less happy about having to deal with her.

"Nice of you to go out of your way like that," I commented. Subtle flattery is a good way to get most men to warm up.

He waved it off. "Her mom's car died, so she borrowed Lyn's today. On the way over I mentioned I was stopping by your place, and Lyn asked me to see if it would be OK for her to come over around seven-thirty tonight. If you don't have plans?"

That last sounded a bit hopeful, as if he'd like it if my Friday night was free. A sign I wasn't seeing anybody. I'd been planning to do a little work with the pendulum to see if I could pin down any hotspots for trouble in Atlanta, but that could wait.

"Sure, that would be fine. I could call her now and confirm."

He cut short a sip of his water, as if I'd just suggested something peculiar. "No, don't worry about it. She said if she didn't hear from me or you she'd assume she could come over."

He was definitely acting a little off. Nervous. True, I'd only met him a couple of times, and the longest conversation we'd had before now had been at Shannon's funeral. Not exactly a mood-setter unless you're Bela Lugosi. Or me.

I figured it was time to stop dancing around things. "So what brought you over? Not that I mind a casual social call."

He drained his water, still looking pretty uncomfortable.

"Are you sure you don't want anything else?"

He sighed. "Maybe a scotch. A small one, please. I'm driving."

I was halfway back to the bar when he finally dropped it on me. "Medea, what do you know about Shannon's death?"

I waited until I was pouring the scotch to answer. "Only what the TV stations are reporting. It was horrible. I can't tell you how sorry I am."

I stopped myself from asking him if he had any idea what had possessed her friends to kill her. He wanted to know what I knew. Maybe he was planning on giving me information that would be even more useful than the murderers' motive.

He paused. It was still painful for him to talk about it. I bent down to get some ice from the mimi-fridge. The moment I disappeared from view he opened up again.

"Did you know Shannon well?"

"No," I said from under the bar. I took a second to compose my face. He was taking his time getting to any point.

"Oh. I was just wondering…"

He let it hang as I came back over and handed him the drink.

"Please, don't worry about it. You can ask me whatever you like. I'll try to help if I can," I assured him.

He took a sip, then another. "I was just wondering if you'd noticed anything… *different* about her."

That was easy enough to answer. "I only saw her casually. Occasionally I'd catch her while I was out for a morning run and she was heading off to work, but we just said 'Good morning'. That was about it. I didn't notice anything unusual the last time I saw her a couple of weeks ago. Was she behaving strangely?"

I knew I'd have to get the ball rolling with some questions of my own. Here he was in a strange woman's house, looking for answers to a deeply personal tragedy. Of course his search was understandable. When you lose someone close to you, you always want answers.

I didn't have any to give him, but I was certain he had some to give me.

"She seemed… I don't know." He took a deeper sip of his drink. "Preoccupied, I guess. Like something was on her mind."

No mystery there. "Well, she had the wedding to think about. That's a lot for someone to handle."

He laughed a little. It was a nice laugh. When his face relaxed, he was quite handsome. I remembered how he'd looked at the party.

"That was no problem. Her mother was handling everything."

"Well, if Shannon was letting her mother take care of things—"

He laughed outright at that. A nice laugh, deep and rich. "*Letting?* You must not know Evelyn well. She wouldn't have it any other way. Try stopping her when she sets her mind to something."

That sounded like the woman I knew. But we were getting off the subject. "Paul, I know you two were happy together. But getting married is a big life change. Remember, she's been living at home since she was a girl. Shannon went to school locally, didn't she?"

He nodded. "Yeah. She spent a year in a sorority house. Hated it and moved back in with her parents."

"There you go. She was very close to her family. It would be a big change, living at home your whole life and then moving in with someone else. Maybe she was just thinking about the adjustment. But I'm sure she didn't have any doubts at all about marrying you."

I'd wanted to reassure him but the sadness that crept into his smile made me think I'd gone too far. "Thank you. I guess I was just a little paranoid, trying to figure out a reason for it all. Surely if she'd thought anything was going to happen she wouldn't have gone over to Laurie's."

We sat in awkward silence for a few moments. I knew if I didn't act I might lose a good chance. He looked like he was ready to go.

I pulled out the secret weapon, dropping the spell that camouflaged my eyes and allowing them to go back to their natural golden color.

It took a second for him to notice. He tensed a bit when I caught his gaze. They always do, like an animal that's just stepped into a snare.

Then he was mine.

47

Chapter 11

I moved closer to Paul, holding him with my eyes. His jaw went slack. I managed to rescue the glass in his hand before he dropped it and set it on the coffee table.

"Tell me what happened. You went to the condo when Shannon didn't show up for work, right?"

"Yes," he said, a little thickly. He wasn't aware of his surroundings or what was happening to him. I might have to drag it out bit by bit.

"Tell me slowly then," I prodded. "What did you do when you got there?"

"I went inside. The door was open."

"What did you see?"

He tried to speak but his voice caught in his throat. I concentrated a little harder. There were some self-defensive barriers there, which was understandable, but I needed to get the information. No time for taking the easy route. It would pain him now, but I could make him forget we'd ever had the conversation.

"What did you see?" I pushed.

His mouth worked a bit before he finally answered. "They were all there. Shannon... she was... there was blood everywhere. Everywhere! And the rest of them... they were covered in it."

"Were they awake or asleep?"

"They weren't asleep. They just stared into space. I yelled, tried to get them to tell me what happened but they all just sat there. Laurie was the only one walking around. She wouldn't tell me anything.

"I tried. I grabbed her, shook her until I could hear her teeth rattling. She wouldn't say anything. She didn't even know I was there. She was in another world."

The scene he painted was horrific, yet not alien. There was something oddly familiar about the description.

"Why?"

The unprovoked outburst from Paul took me off guard.

"What?"

"Why did they do it?" His voice broke. A tear formed in his eye.

I saw it slide down, felt a similar wetness on my own cheek. That's one of the dangers of connecting too closely when putting mortals under my spell. Sometimes their emotions can affect me.

I forced myself to regain control for both of us. Needless sentiment wouldn't serve any purpose. Impatiently I brushed my tear away. Then, a little more tenderly, I wiped Paul's cheek.

"They were her friends," he whispered, his voice catching again. "Why would they do it?"

"You don't know why?" It seemed obvious, given what he'd just said, but I had to be sure.

His eyes closed. It didn't matter if he could see mine anymore. He was in my control. He wouldn't come out of it until I willed it.

"No. They won't say. The police say they're hysterical, babbling, not making any sense."

There wasn't anything else I could get from him. It was pointless to keep him spellbound any longer. I reached over and put my hands on either side of his face, tilting it so he could see my eyes clearly. His opened at my touch.

"Listen to me Paul. You will forget you told me these things about how she died. Do you understand?"

His eyelids fluttered briefly, then settled into a half-opened state.

"Understand," he slurred.

I withdrew my hands, stepped back several paces, restored the spell that masked my eyes, and deliberately shifted my gaze away from his for a few seconds.

When I glanced back Paul looked like he might slide to the floor. Then he jerked a bit and came out of it. While he was blinking and shaking his head I composed my face into an expression of perfect congeniality. "I'm glad you came by, Paul."

He shook his head again. When he looked at me he still seemed slightly dazed. It would take a minute or two for him to fully reorient himself.

"Thank you, Medea. And thank you for working with Lyn to notify the wedding guests."

He got up and headed to the hallway. I hurried after him, but when I got there Orphne was nowhere to be seen. Maybe she hadn't eavesdropped after all.

Paul smiled down at me as I opened the front door, but a second later his smile faltered. "Take care of yourself, Medea," he said.

It wasn't the usual carefree tone people used when saying that. He touched my arm briefly, then walked out into the fading afternoon.

I took a deep breath before turning around. Orphne was standing right there.

"Where were you?"

"Outside the door, listening of course. Sounds like he doesn't know much more than we've learned from the news reports."

I frowned. "Did you learn how to become invisible somewhere along the way? I didn't see you when we walked out of the den."

She touched the Tear hanging around her neck. "Didn't have to. I just changed into a fly when I heard him getting up. I didn't think I could duck out of sight otherwise. I got the idea from a show I saw the other night. Someone mentioned something about being a fly on a wall."

Smart move on her part. She really was getting the hang of things. I went back to the den and grabbed the glasses from the coffee table. I dashed the remains of Paul's scotch into the bar sink before finishing off my *mavrodaphne.*

Orphne flopped onto the couch and stretched out. "This is getting fairly interesting, isn't it?"

I leaned on the bar, thoughtful. "More details, but not particularly useful. We still don't have a motive for the attack on Shannon. I don't suppose you've seen anything else on the news that would shed some light on this?"

"Can't help you," she shot back. "But you're going to have another visitor this evening. Maybe she can shed some light on things."

I could only hope. I needed to have more to go on to formulate some sort of plan before the nasty thing threatening me decided it was time to make another move.

Chapter 12

"This is going to be a treat," I muttered irritably.

"You've already had dinner, so don't eat her." Orphne knew my tolerance for simpering women was beneath the zero-mark.

Creusa had been simpering. I think that's what Jason found attractive about her, in addition to the throne that came with her hand.

The bell rang just as the clock in my den chimed the half-hour. At least she was punctual.

I turned to Orphne, but she was already gone. Her place on the couch was occupied by a small white statue. It was Michelangelo's David, with one very obvious enhancement.

"For the love of Hades! It looks like you have a third leg!" I laughed as I picked it up and placed it on the bookshelf.

"Do you think she'll notice?" the statue said in a small voice.

"I doubt she'll look too closely at anything that's less than fully clothed. She's that kind of girl."

The statue winced but didn't comment. The disguise was Orphne's idea. Lyn spoke softly, so lurking by the door wouldn't work as it had with Paul if I wanted Orphne to hear everything she had to say. This was an unobtrusive way to have Orphne in the room for Lyn's visit.

A bundle of brown was waiting for me at the door. The strong lights on either side of the door didn't do anything to improve the look.

Another warm front had moved through Atlanta, and there was talk of an Indian summer by the time Halloween rolled around. Despite the lovely evening, Lyn was wrapped in a drab brown overcoat, a matching beret on her ash-brown head. The coat was so long I couldn't tell what was underneath.

I supposed someone like her wanted to fade into the background as much as possible. Mission accomplished.

I didn't let my expression reflect that assessment. I smiled and stepped to the side. "Come on in. I'm glad you could make it, Lyn."

She stepped in hesitantly. Two steps, no more.

I cleared my throat a bit. "Excuse me," I whispered as I started to close the door, hinting that I needed more room to get it shut. She bumped forward two quick steps.

"Sorry."

It's never a good sign when the first word from someone's mouth is an apology. I had a feeling it was the first of many for the evening. Yes, it would be a treat indeed.

I pointed towards the coat closet. "You can leave your wrap in there, Lyn. We'll go back to my den." She did as I asked without a word, revealing (surprise) two more shades of brown; a blouse and a long skirt.

I didn't bother looking at her shoes. I put a reassuring arm around her shoulder and led the way.

"How are your parents doing?" I asked as we got comfortable on the sofa. I'd used a glamour to hide the damaged television and wall for the moment, although on second thought it seemed a wasted effort. She didn't seem interested at all in her surroundings.

Lyn looked like she was about to cry. Good thing I'd put a handy box of tissues on the coffee table. I anticipated it might happen, knowing her temperament, but I hadn't imagined it would come so quickly.

"It's been horrible, Ms. Keres." Lyn said weakly as she stared just over the top of my head. I knew she was willing herself not to blink. If you blink, the tears come.

"Mother and Father don't even look like themselves. They hardly say a word to anyone, even to each other. Every morning at breakfast, they just look like they're going through the motions of eating, but they hardly touch the food. It's like watching a pair of robots."

She looked down.

"Mother doesn't say a word. It's like she's not even there anymore. I can't stand it. I never imagined this would happen."

"Of course not," I said quickly. "How could anyone have expected your sister would be killed?"

I was on dangerous territory, and knew it, not least of all because I was still in the dark as to *why* it happened.

I didn't want to remove the glamour over my eyes and use my true gaze to compel her to talk. Paul had been strong enough for it, but with someone like Lyn it might cause irreversible damage to her psyche even if I erased the memory of our conversation.

Lyn looked down. "They haven't said anything, but sometimes I wonder if they blame me. Maybe they're thinking that if I'd just stayed with her, it wouldn't have happened. That if I hadn't left early, she would still be OK."

Left *early?* Paul hadn't said anything about her being at the condo where Shannon was killed. Neither had the news reports. Did he— or the police—know about this?

I only felt a little guilt at taking advantage of Lyn's distress. Obviously she wanted to talk, and it sounded as if she didn't have anyone else to listen. If she had, wouldn't she have already gone to them?

"Lyn," I began quietly, "I only know a little about your sister's death. What makes you think your being there would have changed things?"

"Maybe they would have listened to me. Maybe I could have gotten them to stop. Maybe if there had just been someone else there... I don't know."

She shook her head, and I could see the tears creeping down her cheeks. I pushed the tissue box towards her. She grabbed a couple and dabbed at her eyes.

"I shouldn't have left early. I should have been there with her. Maybe the two of us together could have fought them off."

I didn't think Lyn would be much help to anyone in a fight, but I certainly wasn't about to say that.

Lyn suddenly looked up. She surprised me with direct eye contact. I hadn't thought she had that much temerity, even on a good day.

"They were her friends. How could they have done it to her?" she demanded, almost as if she thought I owed her an answer. She was far more strident than Paul had been when he asked the same question.

"What happened, Lyn? What happened that night?" I asked it quietly, encouragingly, like a therapist trying to coax a patient to face a buried memory.

She swallowed hard, looked past me again. "We all got together for dinner at Laurie's place," she said, so softly I strained to make out the words.

Lyn smiled faintly. "It was supposed to be a surprise bachelorette party, just for us. We were going to have another one later with her coworkers and other friends, but she knew about that one. We wanted to *really* surprise her with an early party."

I remembered then that Lyn was supposed to be one of the bridesmaids as well. I nodded for her to go on.

"Shannon was stunned. She thought she was just meeting Laurie for drinks and a movie. She even cried a little. Shannon never cried at things like this, but I guess it really got to her.

"Dinner was great. Laurie had it catered. We must have spent an hour-and-a-half just talking and joking during the main course and dessert. Everything was really fun up to that point. But one of the girls brought over some movies. I knew what kind they were, and... well, I didn't really want to watch them. I didn't think Shannon would either, but it turned out she'd already seen one of them! Can you imagine her watching porn?"

I had to admit that I could, but then I'm a bit jaded about these things. I'd seen the real thing back in Caligula's day.

I wasn't going to lie to Lyn and pretend I shared her idealized version of her sister, but I saw no reason to deliberately shatter her memories. When in doubt, demure.

"Well, maybe she'd watched it in college. You know how things can get in those sorority houses," I suggested.

Lyn smiled again, and this time there was something real there, something that indicated I was on the right track in trying to relate to her, rather than just listening to her.

"Yeah, I know all about that. Sometimes the girls in mine..." She trailed off with something that was a cross between a grin and a grimace. I was surprised that Lyn had even ventured to join a sorority, much less been accepted. She seemed far too shy.

"So you left then, before they showed the movies?" I asked.

"It was already getting pretty late, so at least I had an excuse. I had a ten o'clock class the next morning. So I went home and went to bed.

"I was just about to leave for school when the police came. Father had already left for work and Mother was still in the shower. I had to get her out and downstairs." I didn't envy Lyn that task. Her mother wasn't the sort who would be patient with interruptions.

"I didn't know what had happened," Lyn said. The strain in her voice was becoming more pronounced. "The police officers didn't want to tell me until Mother was there. I thought Father had been in an accident. I didn't know..."

She choked a bit and I put a steadying hand on her arm. I was about to tell her everything was all right—even though it plainly *wasn't*—but she surprised me by going on without any prompting.

"I heard Paul telling Father about it later that day. They thought I was in my room, but I was on the landing and I heard them talking. He was the one who found them."

I knew that, but instinct told me there was something more. "What did he say?"

She hesitated, but the words wouldn't be denied now. "He said blood was everywhere. All over the place. All over them. It was on their hands, their faces. Their mouths."

I didn't bother hiding my "holy shit" expression. It was genuine enough, and certainly appropriate. "Their *mouths?*"

After a second Lyn went on, still staring into space as if she could see the whole scene somewhere on the horizon. "They didn't just kill her," Lyn said softly. Like a child afraid of speaking about the bogeyman, lest he hear his name and come after her. "They tore her apart. They ripped her arms out of the sockets, yanked off so much hair she looked like she'd been going though chemo, bit off—"

"Bit?" I interrupted before I could stop myself. Suddenly, the room seemed very, very small. Very cold. Very dark. Lyn looked at me again, but calmly this time. It was chilling to see that much calm in her while the rest of her story unfolded.

"They ate her, Ms. Keres. Her friends ripped her to pieces with their bare hands and they ate parts of her. Pieces of flesh from her arms and legs..." Lyn trailed off, looking down again.

I felt a change come over her. Maybe saying the words, making the horrible images real, was enough to break down the last part of the wall that had obviously kept so much pain inside of her. Too much pain for any one person. The tears came freely.

As I rushed to the bar I felt a trace of darkness following me, a wisp of miasma that played at the edges of vision but vanished the minute I tried to look at it directly. Something was here. Not in my house, but here in Atlanta. Something that should not be here. Something that should have died out centuries ago.

Tissues weren't enough at this point. She needed a good stiff shot of brandy. Another glance at her convinced me to make it a double.

"I'm sorry," she said with a wan smile as she took it. "I shouldn't be doing this. You offered to help me and here I am taking up your time with sniveling."

Hmm. At least she was self-aware. We pretty much sat in silence after that. Lyn's tears came and went, but the intervals grew longer as the brandy snifter grew emptier.

"I'm sorry," she said again. "I just don't think I can do much work tonight. I brought a list with me..." She fumbled in her skirt pocket a bit, finally locating a folded sheet of paper. "Mother wrote it out for me. She said these were the people we haven't called yet. Most of them are on Paul's side."

Lyn handed the paper to me. I took it and unfolded it, giving it a cursory glance. I quickly calculated about forty names. Not bad. I could rip out two or three reasonable letters on the computer in half an hour, just for variety among the former guests. It wouldn't take long to enter these names in the form letters and make up mailing labels with the addresses Evelyn had thoughtfully provided.

I decided I could just handle it myself. It would cut my time with Lyn in half. Although she wasn't quite the wimp I'd imagined, she was starting to grate on me.

I figured that I no longer needed to find a motive for the bizarre attack on Shannon. Something was afoot, and clearly those girls had just gotten caught up in it. Why Lyn had been spared a role was still a question, but maybe the evil involved had less tolerance for weakness than I did. "Don't worry about a thing, Lyn," I said with a careful pat on her shoulder. "I can handle this. I'll put together a brief notice and you can come by to look at it when you like, just to make sure it's OK. Maybe next Friday?"

"That would be great." She smiled as she finished her brandy. The smile was a bit broader than normal.

I hoped she wasn't so plastered her parents would notice. I didn't need it getting around the neighborhood that I corrupted young women with hard liquor. Not that it would be anywhere close to the top of the list of my crimes, but I try to keep the list from growing longer unless absolutely necessary.

"Do you need me to walk you home?" I asked at the door.

She shook her head. "I think I'm fine." For a moment I thought the tears would come again, but they didn't. She blinked a couple of times, and her expression shifted to a lighter stage of uncertainty.

"Thank you, Ms. Keres. For everything."

I gave her what I hoped was a reassuring smile and closed the door, leaning back against it as I exhaled in relief.

Chapter 13

Orphne was already back in human form when I returned to the den.

"Looks like it was a good idea to keep your date with her tonight," she commented.

"Please don't characterize it like that!" I begged with a laugh. Sure, I'd experimented. Three millennia is a long time, after all. I'd just never experimented with an invertebrate.

"But we did learn something," she added as she grabbed a notepad and pen from my desk and met me at the couch. I suddenly remembered I had part of that pint of Baskin Robbins left, but I was on a roll now. It could wait.

"We're dealing with some kind of blood lust," she started off, writing quickly. I noticed she was using hieroglyphs. Middle Kingdom, it looked like. Gotta love the Gift of Tongues. I didn't have it but I'd learned to read them, and they were much more concise than English.

"It's something that affects both men and women," I added. "The face I saw in the mirror was a man's, but unless there's something we don't know about, everyone involved in Shannon's death is a woman."

"It's still possible one or the other is a decoy, though," she said thoughtfully. "I'd vote for the girls at Shannon's party. Maybe the man in the mirror killed her, and set them up. Drugged them or bespelled them so they didn't know what they were doing, then got them soaked in her blood to make it look like they were the killers. It would explain why they were dazed when Paul found them."

I considered that, but there were points against it. "Maybe, but Lyn seemed very specific. She said they ate parts of Shannon. It would take a whole lot of magic to get a person to do that to someone else, especially someone they knew. There are too many barricades to that sort of behavior in the human mind. I couldn't compel someone to go that far, let alone five people. And people who are drugged or enchanted to the point of compliance are usually passive. This was a violent attack."

"But how could Lyn be certain they actually did those things?"

"Easy. If the authorities suspected it they would get warrants." She didn't seem to understand that.

"A way to compel people to turn over evidence," I explained. "They could force the girls to get their stomachs pumped so the police could examine the contents."

"Impressive," she said with a smile. "Humans are more clever than I imagined."

"But probably not as clever as whatever we're up against. It's up to us to figure this out."

"Right. So what fits this scenario?"

I glanced over at the bookshelf that had my reference works but didn't bother getting up. I had that material pretty well memorized. A few of the more exotic tomes were stored in the basement, and I might have to look at those later. Well, maybe I'd need an extra pint of Baskin Robbins by that time, and the chest freezer was down there as well...

"Between the two of us we should be able to come up with a reasonable list," I pushed on, forcing myself to the task at hand.

An hour and a half later we'd finished it, and I was starting to finish that leftover mint chocolate chip ice cream as a reward. I gave the list a final look.

Our working supposition was that this was something that could be spread from human to human, given the number of people involved in Shannon's death. That ruled out natural-born predatory monsters, which don't infect those victims who manage to survive an attack. It helped narrow the list, but it still left a lot of possibilities.

We had no idea how far it had spread or whether there was some sort of period of dormancy before the infection kicked in. Were Shannon's friends the only ones affected and, now that they were isolated, was that the end of it? Or were there more out there? Could a full-scale epidemic erupt any moment?

The usual suspects were on the list. At the top, the *nosferatu* and other not-quite-dead things that fed on blood and could potentially infect humans.

Orphne was particularly intrigued when I added *penanggalan* to the list. They aren't vampires specifically, but a variety of witch native to Malaysia. Their heads detach at night and fly around trailing their intestines behind them as they search for humans to attack.

"Now *that* would have been a party!" she giggled.

I had to admit the image of Shannon's friends detaching their heads and flying around with their intestines splotching up the hardwoods was weird to the point of absurdity, but we didn't want to rule anything out just yet.

We also added lycanthropes to the list, including the *loup-garou* of Haiti and New Orleans. Contrary to popular belief they didn't need a full moon to change, plus their bites were infectious and their victims were often people they knew. And cannibalism, rather than just blood drinking, was one of their distinct characteristics.

I figured we'd done all we could do for the night and decided to turn in.

"Any of these books good?" Orphne asked with a glance to the well-lined shelves when I told her goodnight. Since she didn't need sleep, it would be a boring night for her. She was trying to hide it, but I could tell she was jonesing for television.

Who could blame her? For thousands of years the only things she'd known were what she'd seen in Hades, and what she gleaned from the souls who ended up down there. Even though most of it was mind-numbing to me, the stuff on television (nearly 200 channels worth, with digital) must have seemed a treasure trove to her.

I had an idea.

"Come up to my room. You can have my television. We'll just take it over to the upstairs guest bedroom." There was no way I was going to try to hook anything to the disabled cable outlet in the den before an electrician looked at it. Although it was wired for cable I'd never bought a television for the main guest room. When I was in the mood for an overnight guest or two they stayed in my bed, and television was definitely not on the menu for those occasions.

She seemed pleased with the suggestion. It took us only a few moments to hook up my television and converter box in the other room.

"You're pretty good at this technical stuff," she said.

I shrugged. "I figured out how to fly a dragon-drawn chariot when I was just nineteen. This is a piece of cake compared to that."

I switched on the TV and flipped over to a local channel. The ten o'clock news was a few minutes away, but it wouldn't hurt her to see that. She could find something else if they didn't have anything interesting.

"Where are the little beasties, by the way?" she asked as she settled down on the bed.

"Hibernating a little further north. Chariot and all, just in case I need it." Which would have to be a pretty special case.

It had been a great getaway vehicle in the old days, but it wasn't such a hot idea in the days of NORAD. The military gets very touchy about odd aircraft flying around. Those dragons would be just fine under the Etowah mounds, where I'd safely ensconced them in an enchanted slumber.

Speaking of subterranean environments, I'd have to hit Orphne's room with a vacuum and duster. It was much more cheerful than Hades, but if she was going to spend time there I could at least clean it up for her.

That could wait until the next day. I had to think of my next steps. I bid her goodnight and went back to my room for a little light plotting before bedtime.

Our list of potential suspects was a start, but it was only a group of theories. I'd have to make more progress. That meant one of two things. I could track down friends and family of the now-jailed bridesmaids and start making my own enquiries. It would be little trouble if I used the same technique I'd used on Paul.

Or, I could wait around in case there was another attack and see if new details emerged. The first seemed more practical, since I wouldn't have to wait for another victim to turn up.

As it happened, I didn't have to wait anyway.

Chapter 14

The shrill ringing was jarring enough, but when Orphne burst through the door it gave me just the adrenaline rush I needed to send me straight out of bed.

Straight up, that is. I'd drifted off into a light sleep, and in my clouded thinking I forgot that I had a guest in my house. I thought I was under attack and unconsciously engaged my ability to levitate, shooting nine feet up to the vaulted ceiling, out of harm's way.

Seconds later I woke up enough to realize two things. The phone was ringing, and Orphne looked irritated.

"Medea, get down here. You have to come see this!"

I drifted down quickly, but the first thing I did was reach for the phone. I figured a call that time of night was probably a real emergency. And it was cordless, so I could take it wherever Orphne needed me to go.

I motioned for her to lead the way, hoping she wasn't interpreting something on the Syfy channel as a real event.

"Hello?" My voice was a little creaky with sleep.

"What do you mean hello? I know you're here!" I waved impatiently at Orphne to be quiet, realizing she had yet to see me use a phone.

"Medea! Have you seen the news?"

It took me a second to recognize Paul's voice. He was clearly upset. No, more than that. He sounded almost panic stricken.

"No, I was asleep," I said as Orphne and I got to her bedroom. She pointed at the television. What I saw there almost made me drop the phone.

Orphne was still watching the local news. The banner on the screen read: *Just In! Second Gruesome Murder*. A picture of Shannon O'Neill was on the screen next to another woman's picture. She looked about ten years younger than Shannon. The picture's caption identified her as Monica de Silvo.

"I'm looking at the news right now, Paul. What happened?"

"A girl was killed at Elliswood today!" That was a small, upscale university in Atlanta. "The police say it was similar to Shannon's death. They've got several girls in custody now. How could that be? How could this happen again?"

He sounded nearly hysterical.

"I don't know Paul. Let me see what they're saying." I found the remote and turned up the volume.

But the report was already over, the reporter on the scene babbling some inanity to the studio anchor about police continuing to investigate.

"I saw another report just before I switched the channel," Orphne chimed in. She held up the notepad she'd brought up from the study. "I have more information."

"Who's there with you?" Paul was in high stress mode. I was awake enough to resist the urge to tell him it was none of his damn business.

"It's a friend visiting me from Greece." Technically Orphne was from *under* Greece, but he didn't need those details.

His voice was a bit more controlled when he spoke again. "I thought it might be Lyn."

"No. She came over earlier, but she left hours ago. Why?"

"No reason," he said a little too quickly.

Something that was nagging the back of my mind decided to make a front-and-center appearance. "Doesn't Lyn go to Elliswood?"

There was a significant pause. Then, "Yeah. She does. I brought her home from classes today, remember?"

"She didn't say anything tonight. I guess she didn't know about the killing. Looks like the news is just getting out now."

"I guess so. Look, Medea, I know this is going to sound crazy but… don't go out tonight, OK?"

"I hadn't planned on going out at this hour," I said. It was the truth, because up to that point I *hadn't* planned on going out. It was just short enough of a promise to ease my conscience in case the plan changed, which it very well might if something was on the prowl.

"Good. I'd really like to see you, if I could. There's something I need to talk about."

"It's a little late…" Now where was the Medea I knew in that statement? I'd never been shy about having a guy sneak over to my house in the dead of night. But something about his demeanor didn't seem right.

"Not tonight," he said hastily. "I was thinking tomorrow night. At the zoo."

"The zoo isn't open at night," I said hesitantly. I didn't want to put him off entirely, but I at least wanted to put him in the general vicinity of realistic expectations.

"It will be tomorrow. They're having a fundraiser. My family is a big donor, so we get comp tickets. Could you make it, say around seven-thirty?"

I considered pulling that old excuse about having to check my date book, but I knew what was penciled onto every day for the foreseeable future. Find out why young women were being slaughtered in some bizarre—and in Shannon's case, almost ritualistic—fashion.

This might be another step in that direction. He clearly wasn't just worked up about the new murder. He was hiding something.

"Sure, that sounds fine."

"Great. Meet me at the front gate. If I'm tied up for some reason, ask at the ticket office. I'll make sure your name is on the guest list. Just wait for me by the flamingo pond just inside the entrance."

Ugh. I'd been near flamingo ponds before. Nothing like the enchanting smell of ammoniated bird shit to put a girl in the mood. He'd better have something good.

"Sure. I'll see you then, Paul."

"See you then." The phone went dead.

I sat down on the bed, hoping the news would do an update on the murder, but they'd moved on to the weather.

Crap. It was going down to forty the next night. So much for Indian summer.

"What was that about?" Orphne indicated the phone.

"It was about the weirdest call I've gotten in awhile. Paul wants to talk to me. I don't know if it's anything useful, but the way his thoughts were running I'm betting it's connected to the latest murder. He seemed really upset about it."

"Isn't that understandable? I wouldn't think most humans would be too calm about it, especially if someone they knew had just died in a similar way."

"Not just knew. Someone he loved enough to marry," I corrected. "I guess it would be jarring." I reached for the notepad. "So what did you find out?"

"That woman, Monica de Silvo, was killed at that school today. They said her sisters did it at their house. At first I thought it was some family thing, but then they said it was something called a sorority.

"They said the police took several girls into custody, but they never said how many. But what they *did* say, was that something called an inside source revealed there were a lot of similarities to the way Shannon O'Neill died."

It was all on the notepad in neat hieroglyphs, except for three letters. I pointed to them.

"This is Greek."

"They showed the house where the girl was murdered. Those letters were on it."

I looked more closely at them. Delta, kappa, iota. Demented Killers Inc.?

Probably not. Nothing is ever that simple. But now I had a new place to look for answers.

Orphne had opened the window and a breeze carried in the beguiling scent of autumn leaves. I decided I could fudge my not-quite promise to Paul.

"Come on," I said. "Let's go for a walk. You have to get out of the house some time."

"Sounds nice."

She came back with me to my bedroom, where I quickly changed into a jogging suit. We wouldn't be out long. She used the Tear to give the illusion she was wearing a similar outfit.

The weather front that would push the temperatures down hadn't arrived yet. The night was cool but still comfortable. Once or twice around the neighborhood would be nice.

Occasional clouds drifted by, not quite heavy enough to mask the moon entirely. Orphne seemed enchanted by it.

"I never knew how beautiful it was," she said.

"We'll have to see if we can get further away from the city one night," I sighed. "There's too much light here. You can't really see the stars."

But the moon and stars were not what she was interested in the next moment. She'd looked back down and suddenly came to a dead stop. She stared straight ahead.

We were at the O'Neill house. She pointed to one of the cars. I recognized it as Lyn's. I'd seen her getting into it a few mornings while I was out running.

"I don't believe it," she said.

Didn't believe what? It was fairly inconspicuous as cars went. but it was hardly a heap.

"What's wrong with it?" I asked.

"There. On the end of the car."

As a chthonic nymph her night vision was 20/20. I needed to get a little closer. No lights were on in the front of the house, so I could risk walking up the driveway a little bit.

When I saw what Orphne must have been pointing at, I didn't believe it either. It was a small bumper sticker. So small that only three things were on it.

The Greek letters delta, kappa, and iota.

Chapter 15

      I like to think I have a vocabulary broad enough to include words like "coincidence" but with two gruesome murders and one blood-soaked visionary experience on my plate I couldn't afford to be broad-minded. The fact that Lyn O'Neill was closely tied to two of the dead people in my path was my best starting point.

      The next day found me wandering the campus of Elliswood, a venerable school that dated back to the early 1900s. It was still a small tight-knit school, with more than its share of upper-crust students from old Southern money.

      So I dressed to impress. I wore a comfortable but well-tailored trench coat. The day was sunny and mild so I left the coat unbelted and open, exposing the subdued business suit underneath.

      Sunglasses completed the outfit. I usually don't wear them, but they added a little flair. I could easily be mistaken for an official investigator. Not that I intended to openly deceive anyone, but if they made that assumption based on my appearance it could only make my task easier. And if that didn't work, the sunglasses could come off and the golden eyes could come out. I was playing to win. Too much was at stake.

      Even though it was Saturday the campus was buzzing with activity. I stopped to watch five boys playing Frisbee in a courtyard surrounded by several neoclassical buildings.

      I approached the group and seconds later I had general directions to the sorority house.

      It was slightly more out-of-the-way than I'd imagined. It was set further back from the curb than other buildings on campus, and surrounded by several large trees. Just as I anticipated, three police cars were in the street. The cars parked in the driveway probably belonged to the plainclothes contingent.

      I hadn't expected to get into the place, but it wasn't necessary for what I was planning.

      Bright yellow police tape was strung up on the other side of the trees. Checking both directions first, I slipped under it and darted to a tall evergreen right next to the house. The foliage would shield me from a casual glance.

      I slid behind it, reached out and touched the wall, dropping the psychic shields I kept up under normal circumstances. You'd be surprised how much negative energy swirls around a city the size of Atlanta.

      That energy paled in comparison to what I suddenly felt. For an instant it seemed like a bolt of electricity was surging up my arms, paralyzing me. Then I saw her.

She was terrified, screaming, trying to break free. Two girls were holding her arms in vise-like grips, one on each side of her. Another was tearing at her clothes, and a fourth grabbed her lower legs to prevent Monica de Silvo from kicking.

The girl ripping off Monica's clothes made short work of it. Within seconds Monica was naked. Then the real screaming began.

I saw one girl sink her teeth into Monica's arm, while another attacked her side. Within seconds the other two were upon her, and Monica was on the ground, struggling and shrieking. Occasionally a hand or leg slipped free... maybe because by that point, they were slippery with blood and harder to hold.

More girls joined the attack. One had a knife, others carried bowls. They looked like ordinary bowls, probably the ones the girls who lived there used for soups and salads. Neither was on the menu for this event.

I saw the girl with the knife go in but the others blocked my view of what she did. A second later I saw Monica's legs tense, thrash wildly—and suddenly go limp.

The bowl carriers pushed into the group and the original attackers made room for them. Within a few seconds the bowls were filled to the brim and the girls staggered to their feet.

They carried the bowls a few steps closer to where I was, blood sloshing over the rims with their halting gaits. Their eyes were blank, staring, lopsided grins on their mouths. Their breath was rapid, as if they'd just run a marathon. This close, they blocked my view of Monica's now-dead body.

It wasn't just their breath I was hearing. Another sound came from beside me, an exhalation of anticipation that sighed warm and sweet into my ear. I was powerless to move my head to see who it was.

A hand and forearm swam into my view. No garments covered the arm, but a heavy gold bracelet adorned the wrist. It was a man's, no doubt about it. The hand reached for a bowl and a girl pushed forward, almost spilling the contents as she fell heavily to her knees.

The hand took the bowl, withdrew. I heard deep, eager swallows. A voice beside me whispered. "Join us, Medea. Join us." It was a man's voice.

I couldn't speak, couldn't refuse.

"We're here, Medea. Join us. Join us, ma'am."

"Ma'am". But that wasn't right. That voice was coming from the distance, and it was—

"MA'AM!"

Without warning the vision shattered and I was staring at an imposing man. He was in normal clothing, but his demeanor had "cop" written all over it.

"What the hell are you doing here? This is a crime scene! Didn't you see the tape?"

His voice was raised enough that others might hear. I had to get the situation under control. The sunglasses came off, along with the spell that made my eyes look human.

His mouth opened, but nothing came out. A moment later his shoulders relaxed. He was under.

I spoke low and fast. "If anyone asks, I'm with the forensics lab, out here doing a spot check to make sure the team is covering all the bases. Do you understand?"

"Yessss…" The slow acknowledgement was good enough.

"What haven't you told the media about this case?"

He took a few moments to think. Probably hard to keep the public and non-public facts straight when he was under enchantment. But he finally came up with what I needed.

"Cannibals. They tried to eat her." I'd seen that much for myself.

"What else?"

Another pause, then, "Coroner says there's not enough blood. Not enough at the scene, not enough left in her body. At least half of it is missing."

"Is that the same as Shannon O'Neill's death?" I hoped that if this guy wasn't working Shannon's case, there was enough communication in the department that he had those details.

"Yesss… blood missing from her too."

And I would bet my immortality whoever had been drinking the blood in the vision I'd just had was the same one who made off with Shannon's. I'd also bet that he had an elaborately curled dark beard, just like the one in the Sybil's mirror.

"Is there any connection to Lyn O'Neill in either of these deaths?"

"Sister… Shannon's sister…" he muttered before his brows furrowed a little. "Belongs to the sorority. But she wasn't here when they killed de Silvo… witnesses saw her in class." So they knew about Lyn's connection to the sorority.

"Forget I even mentioned her. And now, Detective… what's your name?"

"Martinez. Alan Martinez."

"Now, Detective Alan Martinez, you're going to close your eyes and count slowly to thirty. When you reach that, open your eyes and go about your business. You remember what to say if anyone mentions seeing me?"

"You're with forensics, doing a spot check."

I scanned the area. No one was around. "Very good, Alan. Close your eyes, and start counting."

I quickly ducked back under the police tape and through the trees, hiding a bit while a couple of kids passed by. Then I got out of there and headed back to the car. *Little good a car will do,* I thought. Even with the fastest car in the city I wouldn't be able to shake the dread growing within me.

Whatever was out there knew me. Knew my name. Knew I had just been at the scene of the latest crime because it—no, *he*—had reached back into time and space to interact with my vision of Monica's death.

Worst of all, he wanted me to join him. Somehow, I had a feeling it would be an invitation I couldn't refuse.

Chapter 16

"Are you absolutely sure?" It was the tenth time she'd asked me. Orphne knew me well enough to know my answer hadn't changed since the first time. I concentrated on finishing my up-do.

"You saw a man in the vision," she pressed. "In both visions, the one in the mirror and the one at the sorority house."

After a few more seconds, she added, "Paul is a man."

"Not this man. Paul doesn't have a beard. And even though he's tall and well built, he wasn't the one in today's vision. The arm was different. Bigger, like it belonged to someone taller and stronger than normal. The skin was darker. And the voice was completely different."

"You know very well visions can distort things like that," she shot back. She was right. The whole vision in the Sybil's mirror looked odd, like some sort of cataract was over the mirror clouding things slightly. I hadn't even been able to tell what sort of gems the faceless woman was wearing as she stroked the dead body.

Instinct told me I was on the right track. I'd made real progress that day, and I wasn't about to start second-guessing myself. I'd only be moving backwards.

Based on my latest vision Orphne and I scratched several characters off our list of possible suspects. The girls I'd seen hadn't changed into some sort of beasts, so lycanthropes were out. They were humans so demons were out, except for the ones that could shape-shift. Those usually worked alone, but I couldn't rule out some sort of cooperative effort.

Certainly, the room in my vision hadn't been filled with flying detached heads trailing intestines. She hid it well, but I suspected Orphne was extremely disappointed about that.

Knowing her attempts to dissuade me from going to the zoo were futile, Orphne finally gave her approval to my outfit for the night. "I'm sure Paul will be mostly impressed."

"Mostly?" I think I kept the edge out of my voice, but as we stared at my reflection in the full-length mirror I couldn't see anything wrong.

"Correct me if I'm wrong, but wouldn't people giving money to a zoo be the type to like animals?"

"Yes...oh." I realized that the fur coat slung over my shoulder probably wouldn't go over too well at the fundraiser. Score one for the chthonic nymph.

"No problem. You've got your mind on other things," she said gamely as she produced an alpaca ruana from behind her back. I didn't push her to clarify which "other things" she was talking about. But yes, I was putting out a lot more effort than I usually did for get-togethers with men I hardly knew.

I spent the whole drive to the zoo convincing myself there was nothing more I wanted from Paul Kirkpatrick than answers.

The closest lot was full so I circled to a farther lot. After I got out of the car I immediately clutched the ruana around me. The air was nippy, perfect early fall weather unless you were traipsing around in my outfit.

I decided I wanted more than answers from Paul. I wanted him to give me a heated room of some sort for sure, preferably with an equally heated cup of coffee no matter how watery and bitter.

It was my first time to the Atlanta zoo, and I was betting it would be my last unless it was a stellar evening. I normally don't mind walking, but a downhill trek in high heels isn't exactly paradise. The chill didn't improve my mood. I wished I'd chosen a heavier dress than the sleeveless black number I was wearing. It looked great, but there are times when a girl needs to go for practical.

My internal temperature rose several notches when I got to the gate. No sign of Paul. All right, I was late, but he should still have been there. He was the one who asked me, not the other way around. I paced a few minutes before going up to the only ticket window with any sign of life.

True to his word, Paul had put my name on the list for comp tickets.

"Keep that ticket with you, it's good for one free drink," the elderly man in the booth said with a smile. Oh goody, one whole free drink. Well, it was a fundraiser. They had to make the bucks somehow.

"This is for you too," the man said as he slid me a folded paper through the window with my ticket. Maybe Paul had left me a note of apology for not being there. Several people were coming up to the ticket booth so I walked inside and stepped over to the flamingo pond. The handwritten message was short.

Meet me at the panda exhibit.

OK, great. I had no idea where the pandas were, just that they'd made a lot of news when China loaned them to Atlanta a few years ago, and more news still when cubs were born. Couldn't Paul at least have written the note on the back of a zoo map?

I crumpled the paper up and almost tossed it into the flamingo pond. My conscience got the better of me and I jammed it into my purse, quickly shutting it so no one could see the venom-infused dagger. It was great for slaying demons, but not for making good first impressions at public events.

A nice young couple trailed by two exited children not only gave me directions but walked me partway to the panda exhibit. The crowd was denser than it had been on the walkways. I craned my neck trying to find Paul, but it quickly became apparent he wasn't there. He would have stood out in any public gathering with his height and reddish-blond hair.

I spent another couple minutes jostling with the rest of the people for a look at the pandas. I could see why the exhibit was so crowded. They really were cute. But the enchantment faded as the wind picked up.

My cell phone rang and I whipped it out of my purse.

"Where are you?" Paul asked. The edge from last night was still in his voice. Obviously he still had my card with him—it had my cell phone number on it. The thought that he'd hung onto it helped me keep my irritation in check.

"I'm looking for you at the panda exhibit."

"Panda exhibit? What are you doing there?"

"Your note, remember?" Patience isn't exactly my strong suit but I wasn't out of it just yet.

There was a pause. "I didn't leave a note for you, Medea. There must have been some mix-up at the ticket office. I've been checking for you at the flamingo pond every few minutes. I thought maybe you'd changed your mind." His voice was slowing down a bit.

"Where are you now?"

"Up by the new gorilla exhibit. I got cornered by one of Mom's old friends. I just now managed to get away from her."

"Why don't you come here? We can take a walk." I stopped myself from adding that we could probably find someplace private. I didn't know how he'd take it.

"No problem. I'll swing around and come up the back way. Thank you, Medea. Thank you so much for coming." He heaved a heavy sigh.

"I know the news about that girl's death upset you last night," I finally put in when it was clear he'd run out of things to say. I hate long pauses on the phone.

"You don't understand, Medea," he blurted. "It's not just her. It's not even that they're saying she was killed like…" he trailed off. Message understood.

"It's Lyn," he said so quickly that I half-turned to make sure no one had overheard. My phone's receiver suddenly seemed extraordinarily loud.

I didn't intend to jump to conclusions. We'd already had one mix-up that night. I wanted everything to be clear from that moment on. "What about Lyn?" I asked. I knew I should wait to talk to him face to face but my appetite was whetted.

"She was there," he said with another exhalation. He started talking rapidly again. "She was there, in that sorority house yesterday afternoon."

I didn't bother protesting that it would probably be natural for her to stop by her sorority house on any given day, that it could just be coincidence. "When was she there?"

"It was about three, three-fifteen. That's when she called to ask me for a ride. It took me about half an hour to get there. She told me to meet her outside the house. The murders took place between the time she called and the time I got there. There was a timeline in the paper this morning. They figured it out based on when the other girls in the house got back from classes and found the body."

I hadn't seen Lyn in my vision, but I couldn't read too much into that. I hadn't seen anything of the mysterious man except his arm, after all. She could have been lurking next to him or somewhere else I couldn't see her.

But the cop had said witnesses saw her in class when the murder happened. Just because she met Paul outside the house didn't mean she'd ever gone inside it.

Paul cut off my thoughts. "What the hell…"

"What is it?"

"I'm at the new leopard exhibit. There's something down there."

Well, it was an exhibit, wasn't it? "What's wrong with that?" Wouldn't they want to showcase new exhibits at a fundraiser?

"The leopards are kept in the indoor portion of the display when the temperature gets down this low," he said. "But there's something in there now, moving around." He paused a moment. "Yeah, it's them. They're out there when they shouldn't be."

I started to think the leopards were luckier than me if they could beg off an appearance when the temperature dipped to forty. The thought was cut off abruptly.

"Oh my God," Paul said loudly on the other end. "Oh GOD!"

I was too stunned by the outburst to say anything. Just as I gathered my wits, he shouted again.

"It's her!"

That frantic exclamation jarred my adrenal glands into overdrive. I started walking quickly, even though I had no idea where I should be headed.

"Who's there? Who's there, Paul?" I repeated the question urgently as I brushed past people flowing up to see the pandas. There was nothing from the other end.

A loud crack erupted through the phone, as if he'd thrown it against something.

Or dropped it.

I ran to the closest person, a man who seemed absorbed in staring up at the sky even though the city lights blotted out the stars.

"Where's the leopard exhibit?" I demanded hurriedly. He was taken aback, but a second later pointed off to the left.

"Up there. You wind past where the gorilla enclosure used to be and hang a sharp left. There are signs—"

I was already hurrying up the path. It was nice and hilly, just the thing for someone in heels.

Inanely, I started thinking about the leopard exhibit. They'd moved the original gorilla exhibit to new territory to accommodate the leopard enclosure. The big cats were a gift from a prominent businessman from India who'd made his home, and his fortune, in Atlanta. Everyone was waiting for the leopards to mate and produce offspring.

As I ran I kept putting the phone to my ear, but there was nothing from it now. I was passing fewer and fewer people. I finally saw the signs for the leopard display and started up that walkway. No one was on that path. It was darker than the others, only a few lights turned on. Why was it so deserted? It was almost as if something was causing people to just stay away from what should have been a highly popular exhibit.

I'd gone about ten yards when the first scream stopped me in mid-stride. It was definitely not an errant animal call. The second scream was more high-pitched. A scream of pain.

A man's scream.

I tore off the high heels, clutching them in the same hand as my phone while awkwardly trying to keep my wrap from flying off with the other. My purse banged against my hip repeatedly as I raced up the path.

Annoying as it was, I remembered the dagger in there and was slightly reassured.

The chilly pavement froze my feet. I shoved the discomfort to the back of my mind. I could hear more noise. Animal snarls rose and fell ominously. Big cats. What made it more ominous was that I could tell the sounds were not anger.

Those cats were terrified.

If there were any lights around the enclosure they were off now, but the ambient glow from elsewhere in the zoo let me see dimly inside as I ran up to the fence.

As my eyes adjusted I could easily make out the leopards. They were crouched in a corner of the display. It was a decent-sized enclosure, with several large rocks and trees. There was a safety moat between the fence I was leaning over and the area where the leopards prowled.

"Paul!" I screamed. Was he around here somewhere? And who the hell was with him? A woman, if I could believe his last exclamation, but what woman?

Could it be Lyn?

I stepped on something hard and winced. I looked down and saw a faint glow.

A cell phone. I picked it up. The display showed my name and number. It was Paul's.

Other footsteps were clattering along the path. I saw a large flashlight bobbing wildly. I quickly jammed the cell phone into my purse. I didn't want anyone knowing I'd been talking with him until I found out what was going on.

"Who's up here?" A rough voice demanded.

"Hurry! There's something wrong here!" I screamed. A second later two men, both in security uniforms, were at my side.

"What is it, ma'am?" the older of the two men asked. He seemed to be pretty winded from his sprint so I turned to the younger man.

"Something's wrong. I was on the phone with a friend of mine who came past here and saw the leopards. They're not supposed to be out in cold weather."

"Someone heard screaming up here," the younger man said severely.

"I heard it too," I confirmed. "I ran up here but I didn't see anyone on the way up. I'm sure it was a man screaming. I think it might have been my friend. Please help me find him!"

I'd already decided that acting the part of the defenseless, needy woman would probably get me more points with these two. Never mind that I'd been about to conjure half a dozen fireballs to light the area for my own search. Let the guards search it for me.

The older man turned his flashlight into the leopard enclosure, and a second later the other one did too. They made quick, methodical sweeps of the display.

A lot of good that will do, I thought crossly as I slipped my shoes back on. *We already know the damn leopards are in there when they're not supposed to be.*

It turned out they had the right idea. The cats were still crouched in the corner, hissing and growling. But they were not alone.

A body was lying on the other side of the display. I'd mistaken it for a shadow cast by one of the larger rocks. The body was face down, but it was definitely a man. A large man with reddish-blond hair. I didn't even bother getting my hopes up.

The dark pool that was rapidly spreading out from under him was the last answer I would get from Paul Kirkpatrick.

Chapter 17

Paul's funeral was at the same cathedral and just as understated as Shannon's. Not that the Kirkpatricks were hurting for money. The coffin was of finest oak, the flower arrangements subdued but nonetheless top-of-the-line. Perhaps his mother and brother felt a man's funeral should be more conservative. That was certainly the way to describe the turnout as well. Only the first few pews were filled.

There was no question of an open casket or viewing in this circumstance. I was grateful I'd been spared the sight of Paul's ravaged body. The security guards hustled me away as soon as we spotted it. I ended up in a corner of that heated room I'd been longing for, drinking horrendous coffee with a bored cop nearing retirement age.

I answered his questions (most of them truthfully) for several minutes so the other cops who were milling around wouldn't think anything was amiss. Then I shifted my eyes to their natural state and gently suggested to the slack-jawed detective that he'd have much less paperwork if he "lost" his notes from my interview after he got back to the station.

As soon as I got home I performed a rite to ensure Paul's cell phone records would vanish from his carrier's computer system. It's surprising how easy it is to interfere with even the most sophisticated technology if you know a little magic. The police would never find them, never know he'd called me just before he died.

Over the next couple of days the media began to hint that Paul was so shattered over Shannon's death that he decided to end his own life by flinging himself to wild beasts. There was also a huge dust-up at the zoo, with a couple of people being fired over the leopards being in the display instead of their indoor enclosure. Everyone denied having a hand in that, but what else would they say?

I cast the thoughts about that night out of my head as the funeral service started. The least I could do was pay attention. But just as the opening chords of the first hymn began, something distracted me. A late arrival.

Lyn. Her parents were nowhere in sight.

I was fairly confident she didn't see me sitting alone in the back pew. None of the neighbors were in sight, which was a blessing. I'd just gotten an idea, and I didn't need any witnesses to what I was about to do.

As the clerics began filing in something else gave me a little start. Or rather, someone.

Paul's brother was the celebrating priest.

The sight of him up there drove home just how Catholic the family must be. Their two sons were named Peter and Paul. Just like the original, Paul had been martyred, though not because of his religion.

I was beginning to suspect it was because of what he knew.

What *I* knew for certain was that Paul didn't throw himself into the leopard display out of desperation after Shannon's death.

Someone put him there.

Peter proved to be movingly eloquent when he gave the eulogy. He didn't dwell too long on memories of a lifetime lived together but briefly encapsulated the essence of his brother with vivid examples of Paul's kindness, loyalty, and willingness to protect those who were weaker than him.

That hit home. No one had been there to protect *him*. But he hadn't been alone if I could believe his cryptic last remark. *It's her.*

I was determined to find out who she was, and there was an opportunity at hand that I didn't want to miss.

Lyn was sitting too close to the front to leave the church before the funeral was over. I, on the other hand, could slip out unnoticed.

It was a shame to do it before the eulogy was over, but I needed as much time as possible. I quietly made my way out of the cathedral's rear door.

A quick scan of the small parking lot directly outside the church proved futile. Those spaces were supposed to be reserved for the handicapped or elderly. I guessed they'd been filled by the time Lyn arrived. There were a few cars parked on the street, none of them hers.

Perfect. The parking garage across the small side street was exactly where I wanted to be. It would provide cover for my movements. I ducked inside and found pay dirt right on the first level. I wove a small glamour around Lyn's car and myself. Unless Lyn herself came right up to the spot, no one would pay any attention to my foray even if they knew it was her car and that I had absolutely no right to be in it. Right or not, I had a need.

I partially closed my eyes and focused my thoughts, holding my hands in front of me and allowing my power to flow out into the car. I was rewarded a few seconds later when the headlights gave two quick flashes as a small muffled *thump* sounded from the car doors. I'd gotten it open and disabled the alarm.

There were a couple of notebooks and textbooks in a tote bag in the trunk, plus a small gym bag that yielded nothing more than shorts, a T-shirt, socks and tennis shoes, all clean from the smell of things. I crawled inside the car, not really surprised to find the interior was immaculate. The front and back seats were totally empty.

I didn't really have any idea what I was looking for, but to my way of thinking that's usually for the best. Don't focus on finding a specific thing, and you can find something far more important.

Unfortunately what I found was a big fat nothing. But what was I expecting… a large jug labeled *Potion to Induce Homicidal Psychosis*?

I was just about to shut the door and make my way back to the church when I noticed a slip of green between the driver's seat and the door frame. I reached down and picked it up, expecting it to be nothing more than a stray twig of holly or some other evergreen plant. What I pulled out made me do a double-take.

I tucked the new clue into my purse and left the garage. As the service ended I stood up and moved towards the vestry. The door was open.

Peter nodded in my direction when he saw me.

"Ms. Keres," he acknowledged without further embellishment. So he knew who I was even though we'd never met, and he wasn't afraid to reveal his knowledge. I decided he'd be comfortable with a direct track.

"May I speak with you privately, Peter?" I asked, forgoing the usual platitudes and sympathies, as well as the usual courtesies. I was *not* about to call a man who was three thousand years younger than me "Father."

He didn't directly answer my question. "You left in the middle of the service," he observed.

"Yes." I didn't waste time with excuses or explanations. I wasn't entirely surprised he had seen me leave from his vantage point at the altar, although I would have expected him to be more distracted by the ritual and the fact that his brother was dead.

"There was something so important that you had to leave a funeral?" He began removing his vestments. He sounded curious rather than accusatory.

"Yes," I repeated. No elaboration. He seemed about to speak, but in the end gave yet another short nod.

Up close I could see no strong resemblance to Paul. Paul had been broad shouldered and tall, but Peter was about my height, running to lean. It was hard to tell with the priest's garb, but he certainly didn't look as well-built as his brother. Still, there was enough substance to his shoulders to indicate he kept himself fit. His dark hair and skin were puzzles. Both Paul and their mother were fair. Perhaps his father had given it to him.

I decided it was my turn to take the lead in the conversation. "Do you know any more about your brother's death than what's being put out in the press?"

He regarded me carefully for a minute. "You're trying to figure out who did it, aren't you?" he finally asked. He took a few steps towards me. I didn't feel threatened, although I kept my guard up.

"By the way you phrase it, I assume we're discussing murder," I noted.

He looked me straight in the eyes, and I briefly thought about letting mine go back to their normal golden hue. Now that we were inches apart I could see just how vividly blue *his* eyes were. Nothing you'd expect from his dark hair and slightly olive-toned skin.

I told myself it would be a perfect time to use my power to find out what he knew, just as I had when Paul visited my home. But he seemed willing to talk, so I quickly brushed it aside. No need to use magic when ordinary means would do.

"The police say there's no evidence anyone else was involved," he said with more than a little heat. "They're chalking it up to a freak accident, a man getting careless and for whatever reason ending up in a zoo display with leopards. They have no explanation, but they say there's no crime. What do you say? You were there."

Now how the hell did he know that?

Peter correctly interpreted my hesitation. "Paul stopped by my church that day. He asked me if I was coming to the fundraiser. He said you were, and he wanted to talk to both of us. Any idea why?"

"He seemed extremely stressed when I spoke with him the previous evening," I said carefully. "I knew he was going through a lot. He didn't tell me why he wanted to see me when he called, but he seemed so agitated I couldn't say no."

That, at least, was truthful. Then I remembered Catholics have an odd concept: sins of omission. What you *don't* do or say can be just as malignant as your actual deeds and words.

Well, guilty as charged then. I wasn't about to tell Peter his brother had revealed his reasons for calling the bizarre meeting before he died. I needed to find out what Peter knew before showing my hand.

He let out a slow breath. "I told him I couldn't make the fundraiser. Truth is I just didn't want to go to another one of those things. Our family is always giving money to some cause or another, and I've been to enough functions to last a lifetime.

"After we spoke Paul went over to the church itself. I was still in the office. Not that I minded, you understand, but I was a little surprised. Paul was not exactly religious. But with Shannon's death..." He paused, rubbed his hands together as if he was cold. "Well, I didn't think too much of it. But when I went out for a breath of air about two hours later, I saw his car was just pulling out of the parking lot. He must have spent that whole time in the church."

Not surprising, I thought. He was already worked up, frightened, clearly convinced that Lyn was somehow involved in Monica de Silvo's death, if not Shannon's as well. Fear can convert a man more quickly than the most inspired religious text.

"I'm assuming you don't know exactly why your brother wanted to see us either." He acknowledged it with a slight sigh. "Is there anyone who would want Paul dead? Anyone willing to go to the lengths necessary for such an elaborate death?"

"So you don't believe what they're saying on the news? That he killed himself?"

"Not any more than I believe those leopards were in that display by sheer accident," I said with certainty. "Someone had access to those cats. Someone willing to go to a great deal of risk and trouble."

"What I don't understand," he said, ignoring my query about suspects, "is how the killer knew it would work. How did he know Paul would even be walking by there? Let alone that the leopards would..." He didn't need to finish the sentence. "How could he be sure Paul wouldn't just be injured, maybe not even be attacked by the leopards at all? Those zoo animals are at least somewhat used to humans."

"You said 'he'," I observed. "How do you know the killer is a man?"

The corner of his mouth twitched slightly but didn't move into even a half-smile.

"I have nothing against women, Ms. Keres. But please, let's be realistic. My brother was a big man. When someone his size is struggling, how do you force them into a display that's designed to keep leopards safely penned up? There's no way in from the front, unless you force the man over the fence, and even then you'd have to get him across a huge retaining moat."

He started pacing. "The killer somehow had to get Paul up to the rocks in the back of the display and then push him down to where the leopards could get him. Access to those rocks is extremely tricky, and Paul weighed about two hundred pounds. Whoever did it had to be incredibly strong. A woman doesn't have that kind of strength."

But several women might, I thought, mulling the circumstances of the other deaths. Peter was very observant. From what I'd seen in the sketchy light of the security guards' flashlights the back of the leopard display was a good imitation of a steep cliff, clearly meant as another retaining device. The leopards had room to run and jump, but only so far.

"How do you know he was struggling?" I asked, focusing on one of his more pertinent comments. He shrugged.

"The coroner said there was no indication he was unconscious when he died. No drugs in his system, no alcohol, no signs of a blow to the head. So he wasn't just knocked out and dumped there. If he'd been unconscious and motionless, the cats would have had no reason to feel threatened, no reason to attack."

"But you're certain someone else had that motive." He didn't take the observation amiss.

"I can assure you, Ms. Keres, Paul was a fighter. He would never have given in to depression and jumped into that display willingly, and he would never have let someone force him there without fighting like a madman. Someone overpowered him and threw him in there."

There was a soft knock on the vestry door. "I have to go," Peter said as he looked away. The movement revealed a definite tinge of frustration. I pulled a card out of my purse and walked over to him. I held it out, but he didn't take it. We stood just inches apart, so close I could feel the heat from his body. I felt my temperature start to rise in response.

Great gods, what was I doing? I was in a church, looking at a priest like he was—

There was another knock. Peter gently removed the card from my hand. Then he surprised me by reaching into his pocket and pulling out a small gold card case. He withdrew one of his own, and I saw it had a church's name as well as his. Saint Helen's. There was an address and a phone number.

"Can you stop by tomorrow?" He was holding my eyes carefully with his own.

"Does one o'clock work?" I tried to keep myself as neutral as he was being.

"I'll clear my calendar for the afternoon. See you then."

It was not just a pleasantry. I knew we'd just agreed to an alliance.

Having another ally was small comfort, if what I now suspected was true. I headed straight home after leaving the church, making it near-record time. I needed to be on safe ground, even though I knew no ground would really be safe if I was right.

"How was the funeral?" Orphne asked brightly as I walked in. She said it in the same tone as someone else might ask "How was the movie?" But she was a nymph from Hades and had her own concept of entertainment.

She didn't find my response any more entertaining than I did.

"The maenads are back."

Chapter 18

I really hoped Orphne would jump up and say: "Oh, it can't be true," and then list a dozen reasons why. She didn't. Instead she walked with me in silence back to the den. I started to pour a *mavrodaphne*, then changed my mind and reached for the scotch. I made it a double. Orphne waved off my offer when I held up a second glass. I didn't insist. I might need the rest of the decanter myself.

"It does make sense," she said thoughtfully after we sat for a few moments. I'd pulled out the item I retrieved from Lyn's car. It was a grapevine, in full leaf and flower. Not the sort of thing you'd find in October in Atlanta under normal circumstances.

"Actually, I've been thinking about the maenads since you found out details about the sorority house murder. The method certainly fits."

It did indeed. In spades. And it confirmed what I'd feared all along. Someone was trying to take advantage of the Curse of Prometheus by drinking human blood to gain more power.

The "someone" in question had to be Dionysus, god of wine and the chief deity of the maenads. It fit with both my visions, even though I hadn't seen him fully in either. The lush full beard, the strong, powerful arm girded with a thick gold wristlet like they used to wear back in the day. And let's not forget, the crowd of eager women offering him bowls of Monica de Silvo's blood.

"This is going to be a tough one, isn't it?" Orphne asked quietly.

Tough was no mere understatement. For one thing Dionysus was a survivor, and had been since before his birth. His mother Semele had been tricked to her death by her jealous sister Agave, who knew Semele was having an affair with Zeus. Zeus managed to rescue his child and sewed him into his thigh until he could find a safe place to hide him from Hera. She never was particularly kind to the children of her husband's affairs.

Dionysus grew rapidly, and when he wasn't officially acknowledged by Olympus he went about claiming godhood the only way he could.

He instituted a cult that promised its followers—women, mostly —divine ecstasy. And it delivered. Caught up in the throes of rapture, the women quickly lost all sense of reason. They became murderous in their frenzies, often turning on wild animals and sometimes other humans and ripping them apart. When humans were the targets, the blood was offered to Dionysus.

One of the first victims was his own cousin Pentheus, son of his aunt Agave. Despite betraying her sister, Agave felt nothing but love for her divine nephew and quickly became his most fanatical follower. It was rumored that when she died he captured her spirit and hid it in a jeweled box, so that she wouldn't face punishment in Hades for all the crimes she'd committed in his name.

Since the Olympians didn't accept him as one of their own at first, Dionysus technically wasn't barred from conducting human sacrifices. Olympian or not, the Curse held true, and Dionysus became more and more insane as he drank more and more human blood. He also grew stronger. Much stronger.

Finally the Olympians couldn't tolerate it any longer. Dionysus was now in a position to challenge and possibly overthrow them. They welcomed him into their ranks, but as a condition they made him outlaw the human sacrifices among his followers, the maenads.

He accepted the terms. How he came to be cured of the madness that warped him after drinking so much blood, no one knew for certain.

Now I had to wonder whether the cure had really taken hold or just been temporary. Surely he would have to be at least a *little* insane to even think he could reestablish his blood cult on Earth without being found out.

But that's the thing about the Olympians. They turn blind eyes to the misdeeds of their own. That left me in a real jam. If Dionysus was really behind the murders, how would I be able to alert anyone in a position to stop him?

The gods valued my ability to deal with demons and other nasty things, but those same abilities pretty much tainted me in their eyes. I was the supernatural equivalent of a sanitation engineer as far as they were concerned. Necessary, but hardly someone to rub elbows with.

"You're thinking about contacting her, aren't you?" There was no mistaking who Orphne was talking about. And yes, I had been thinking about it. Or maybe it was the scotch doing the thinking.

Whichever was the case, I decided the issue needed more thought and finished off the glass.

"It isn't a good idea, though," I said, realizing I was already slurring my words a little. "Hecate told me not to contact her. For all I know, I wouldn't be able to anyway. He might block me somehow."

"And there's always the question, what happens if you're wrong and falsely accuse him?"

That really hit home. Orphne was right. If I falsely accused one of the twelve Olympians of something as heinous as taking blood sacrifices—which was both sacrilege and treason since it defied Zeus, king of the gods—I would be on Cerberus' dinner plate faster than you could say "Orestes".

I needed proof. Hard proof, not just visions that no one else had seen. I would just be accused of lying. The Olympians wouldn't be interested in the circumstances surrounding the deaths of Shannon or

Monica, or even Paul. All of them could be chalked up to bad fortune, choosing the wrong companions. The only possible clue I had to link the deaths to Dionysus was a grape vine flowering out of season, found in the car of a woman with ties to all three of the victims.

That would hardly be proof in the eyes of the gods. While it was fall where I lived, it was spring elswhere. Maybe grape vines were blooming in Chile now? Between planes and my flying chariot, I could get them.

No, I needed something so concrete that even the Olympians couldn't deny the implications.

But how the hell do you get the goods on a god?

Chapter 19

I had only one lead to follow up on, and it involved a trip to St. Helen's church in Dunwoody. Orphne came along for the ride. It was her first time in a car, but she was all business. No gawking out the window. We'd agreed that once we got to the church, she'd disguise herself as something small again. I wanted Peter to be as open with me as possible, and that meant no visible company.

Peter was kneeling in regular clothing, digging into a patch of ground around the side of the church. The day was warm, and he'd worked up a bit of a sweat.

Looked good on him. But it was something else that caught Orphne's eye as we parked.

"Nice ass," she murmured.

"Hide!" I hissed urgently. A second later there was a faint buzzing in my ear. I glanced down and noticed a fly on my shoulder. I was wearing a black top; she blended in perfectly.

"Stay there. You'll be able to hear everything."

By that time Peter had straightened up (damn) and turned to face the car. I got out, moving slowly to avoid jarring Orphne.

"Thanks for coming, Ms. Keres," he said, extending a hand. He caught himself, glanced at it and wiped it a bit on his jeans before trying again. "Sorry. I was just putting in some new tulip bulbs."

"Call me Medea," I insisted as I took his hand. It was warm. Strong.

Nice.

Enough of that, I admonished myself. *You're on duty, and he's off limits.*

"Would you like to see the church? We've just finished renovating it."

It was my third trip inside a church that month, more than I'd had in any single year since the late '40s when I posed as a nun to track down a trio of Lamia's whelps in Brooklyn. I didn't have great memories. Those early morning offices were killers, and the nuns' Latin was abysmal.

But that was more than half a century ago. Peter probably didn't know a word of Latin.

"Sounds nice," I smiled up at him.

I had to admit, it wasn't disappointing. The church didn't look that big from the outside, but from inside the vaulted ceiling seemed to soar at least three stories. Probably careful tricks of lighting and perspective, but the effect was impressive. I felt like I was in a much larger space.

The stained glass windows let in abundant light, and the brilliant colors seemed to glow on their own. He led me around the side walls where I admired the full-color plaques of the Stations of the Cross.

I was surprised to see Veronica portrayed as a striking black woman with elegant braids, wiping Jesus' face with what looked like Kente cloth. As we walked in silence I looked at some of the other stations and picked out Latinos, Asians and traditionally-dressed Native Americans among the crowds watching each scene.

The Roman soldiers leading Jesus were a monochromatic grey, almost leaden in color, as if they were mere shadows who had no real meaning in the tableaux. A fitting interpretation, I thought.

We reached the front of the church, where an alcove branched off. I frowned a bit at the statue there. It was definitely *not* traditional.

It was an older woman, clad in a simple, nearly shapeless robe and a headwrap that looked almost like a modest turban. Her eyes were closed, hands clasped in front of a small oil lamp. The flame flickered slightly as I approached, as did a few small votives at her feet.

I realized this was a very unusual representation of Mary. What was more unusual was how close to the real woman the artist had come, right down to the gentle, peaceful smile. Not the eternally young virgin most envisioned her as, but a woman who had lived and aged as other humans did. I remembered her much like this.

"This is quite lovely," I said, meaning it. I spied a small slot underneath the row of votives. On impulse I reached into my pocket and pulled out a clip of singles.

I felt Peter's hand on my arm. "Please, you don't have to donate. Not after you came here to meet with me. Feel free to light one, on the house."

It was a nice offer, and I took him up on it. I stood for a moment in silence, not praying but remembering a woman who taught me to come to terms with losing my children, as she had lost her son. It was a good memory.

I finally looked away towards the altar. We made our way towards the center of the church.

"This is very impressive. It's all new, but it still has the feel of an old cathedral."

"Took three years," he said. "I came in for the last of it, so I can't take any credit for the planning and design. I was just ordained last year."

A newbie, to be sure. But then, they all are compared to someone who's been a priestess for millennia.

"A stroke of luck that you got assigned to a parish so close to home," I offered. He looked a little chagrined.

"I don't really believe in luck. I was assured it was just the way things fell. My fellow seminarians got transferred hither and yon though, so I have my doubts. My family's been pretty tight with this parish for three generations, and I can't help being suspicious."

"Politics doesn't change much, I suppose, even in churches. Still, it's a good fit for you. It suits you."

In his worn jeans and T-shirt, slightly damp around the neck, he looked more at home with these modern interpretations of his religion than any traditional priest. Probably for the good, if he wanted to keep things relevant for his parishioners.

We'd made it to the front of the church by that point and sat down in the first pew.

"I never did tell you how sorry I was about Paul's death," I apologized. We were only half-looking at each other; the rest of our attention was on the altar. It was splendid in gold and marble, the cross depicting Christ rising in glory rather than suffering in agony. A nice blend of modern and traditional imagery, I thought.

"You don't have to," he said. "You're here, now, and that's more meaningful than a platitude. You're the only person who agrees with me about this being murder."

He turned fully to the altar, but his eyes were closed. I had to stop myself from putting my hand on his arm. Sympathetically, of course, although it did seem to be a very nice arm based on how tightly the shirt cuff hugged his bicep.

He collected himself a moment later and faced me again. "I've been putting some things together, based on what I know about Paul and Shannon's deaths. I've got some stuff back in the office, but if you don't mind I'd like to just brainstorm out here a bit. One thing I'm sure of is that their deaths *are* related."

"Yes," I said. "There's something too odd about the whole thing." I wondered if he knew about Monica de Silvo's death. Possibly not, I thought. He'd have a lot of duties even in a well-heeled parish, and he might not keep up with the news. I decided to keep Monica's death on hold, to see if he'd offer any new insights first.

"I've been trying to piece together what happened a few nights ago," I began. "The fundraiser was a risky time to try an assault like this,"

I checked his body language to make sure I was couching things enough. I didn't want to be too clinical in discussing the death of his brother. He seemed steady enough so I went on.

"There were a lot of people there, most of them wandering around. That meant the risk of witnesses. So however it happened it had to have been done quickly. I'm wondering if it wasn't just opportunity rather than preplanning which made the killer strike. Perhaps the leopards really were left in their exhibit by accident. If he spotted Paul alone, the killer might have decided to attack on the spur of the moment."

"Which means the killer was probably tracking Paul the whole time," Peter jumped in. "A chance encounter would be too coincidental. Seems more likely the murderer was just waiting for the right moment."

I glanced surreptitiously at my shoulder. Orphne was still in place. Perfect. This might be where the good stuff came in.

I had no idea just how good it was going to get.

"Medea," he turned fully to me, leaning forward and clasping his hands in front of him. He looked so nervous I had a quick, hysterical image of him dropping to one knee and proposing.

I almost wished he had, rather than what he said next.

"Have you ever heard of maenads?"

My jaw dropped in surprise at the reference just a split-second before the rose window above the altar shattered.

Chapter 20

I was on my feet in a shot, fireballs in my hands. Out of the corner of my eye I saw Peter half rising, dividing horrified looks between me and the things that had just burst into the church.

In the next moment I felt a solid presence beside me and turned to find an eight-foot ogre, the Tear of Nereus glinting around its neck.

"Keep him safe!" I screamed as I ran forward to meet the new menaces. More than keeping him safe, I needed Orphne to keep Peter from leaving. He'd seen the flames leap into my open hands, and I couldn't let him get away without using my power to make him forget that. I didn't need the added headache of a mortal who knew I wasn't human.

I sized up the threat as I sprang onto the wide marble dais where the altar rested. There were two of them. I didn't need to be right on top of them to know their eyes would have serpent slits. Succubi.

I focused my attention to my left, eyeing the larger of the two. I launched the fireballs at her. She ducked and rolled with amazing agility, escaping them both, but landed hard enough on the cold marble floor to daze herself.

One fireball splashed on the floor, leaving an ugly scorch mark on the pristine marble. The other slammed into the chair where priests sat during parts of the Mass. In a second it was reduced to ashes.

I didn't wait before hurling another fireball at the other one. More nimble than her sister, she did a quick back-flip out of the way. She landed with her back against the wall, but that was no problem for someone like her.

She kicked off her shoes. Hooking her fingers and toes behind her she quickly scrabbled at least ten feet up the smoothly polished marble wall, more easily than a human could scrabble forward on flat ground. The effect would have been truly horrifying if I hadn't seen it countless times over the centuries. A cat-like hiss erupted from her mouth, and she swiped one hand in a menacing claw-like gesture.

"Medea!" The guttural shout from behind me had urgency in it. I turned and saw Orphne easily keeping a struggling Peter restrained with a single hand around his wrist. She'd dug into my handbag with the free hand and quickly tossed me the knife infused with Hydra's venom.

A quick burst of magic from me guided it to my waiting hand where I quickly unsheathed it.

The first monster had regained her composure. She was only a half step away when I wheeled and drove the knife into her. She tried to change course at the last minute, but I still got her deeply in the side. I pulled the knife out with a slight twist. A terrifying shriek burst from her lips a second before sickly green flames burst out of the gaping wound. Within moments they covered her entire body like a thick, blistering gel.

She staggered only a few steps before the flames flared and died, taking all traces of her with them.

I ran and took a hard leap, engaging my powers of levitation. The momentum from my jump propelled my weightless body straight up to the second one. She tried to claw her way to the side but I swung the knife wide, catching her on the arm.

Her death was almost as quick as the first one's, and just as gruesome.

I cut off the levitation spell more abruptly than I should have. I cursed my foolishness. If I'd landed a bit harder I could have broken my ankle. My healing spells worked quickly, but if there were more of Lamia's brats around…

But it was better than that.

"Well met, Medea."

I hadn't heard that voice in more than a century. The last time had been in Paris. She'd been a red-head then, and the only word exchanged came when she called my name across the dimly lit street. We stared at each other, knowing there was no point in going any further. A carriage crossed between us, and like the wind she was gone.

Like the wind she'd come again, probably through the shattered window. She was floating above the altar, a long wine colored dress edged with lace swirling about her. As I walked around to face her squarely I could see she'd chosen her position to perfectly block the view of the risen Christ from a head-on vantage point. A sick joke no doubt, alluding to her own triumph over death.

Her hair was ebony now, with slightly reddish undertones. Of course she'd mastered enough sorcery to change her hair to any shade of the rainbow and any texture imaginable. No shade or texture of hair would have masked her aura of something alien, something that was glittering and beautiful on the outside yet corrupt and decayed on the inside.

But then, I'm a bit prejudiced.

"Lamia," I said coldly. "So you're the one responsible for what's happening after all!"

Her serpentine eyes held no humor even though she smiled.

"Hardly. Word reached me only the other day, and I came to see what was happening for myself. I knew you'd be up to your pretty golden eyes in it, and you didn't disappoint me. Here you are with the dead man's brother. And it seems he's solved the puzzle. Had you figured it out yet, or do you need humans to do your thinking for you now?"

Pointless baiting was one of her favorite pastimes. It was no surprise that she knew where I lived. I knew she was living in Greenwich Village for the moment. We had ways of finding each other, but there really was no need. I was too busy hunting her daughters, and until that deed was finished there was no reason for me to look for her.

But there was certainly no reason for her to tempt fate by seeking me out, either.

"Clymene is doing well now," she purred, her lips edging up slightly at the corner. "She's almost rivaled me in her knowledge of the dark arts. The arts she failed to inherit from you, after you diluted your bloodline with a mortal lover."

Centuries ago she could have tempted me to forget my control by reminding me that my daughter was born human, and didn't inherit the magic that was passed through the female side of my family. I wouldn't give her the satisfaction now.

"So why bother showing up if you're not involved? Having those clumsy puppets of yours attack me like that was stupid." I pointed to Peter. "Now he knows all about you. Why wouldn't he believe you had a role in his brother's death, and the others? And for that matter, why shouldn't I?"

"Why wouldn't he think it was you instead?" she countered. "You hardly kept your orders to pass for human just now. Your friend knows what you are, as well as what I am. Someone with your abilities could easily be responsible for the deaths. Or have humans learned to fly and wield blades imbued with deadly magic?"

I clenched my teeth. I had blown it, at least a little, by showing my powers in front of Peter. But I could correct that mistake once I'd dealt with the bigger issue hovering in front of me.

"And if you're not involved, Lamia, then what difference does any of this make to you? Why come here? Have you suddenly grown so concerned for mortals that you want to intervene?"

Her smile turned into a sneer. "I have as little love for them as you do, I suspect. I'm here because what's happening interferes with my own plans."

I hadn't thought about that. Like Lamia's daughters, the maenads were women. If we were correct about Dionysus' involvement, he could seriously cut down on her pool of potential recruits. Once he'd gotten hold of a woman she might become a raving murderer, but at least she would be *his* raving murderer. She'd be immune to becoming one of Lamia's killers.

"Then you're more foolish than I gave you credit for, coming here," I said with a cold laugh. "Do you think you can match wits with one of the Twelve?"

Her look was pure contempt. "He cannot touch me, any more than you can, Medea," she said, brushing her hand lightly across her brow, where the sigil of Zeus' protection glowed for those with sight to see it.

A thought came to me. "Are you proposing some sort of truce, Lamia?"

"I am proposing more than that, Medea. I know you are in a better position to end this little... problem... than I am." She drifted down slowly until her feet barely hovered above the floor. Rather than walk, she chose to float towards me. Her hand went to a pocket in her dress.

I raised the dagger reflexively.

"Do you think I have taken leave of my senses, Medea? I can do no harm to you." It was true. Because I was a high priestess, she had no more power over me than I did over her. If she attacked it would be sacrilege, and she would forfeit Zeus' protection, just as I would forfeit my immortality if I violated the sanctuary Zeus had granted her. We were in a perpetual stalemate unless I could eliminate all of her cursed daughters, and so remove the most important condition for Zeus' continued protection.

I lowered the dagger when she pulled nothing more sinister than a slip of paper from her pocket. She held it out. Still suspecting a trick, I took it gingerly.

"I have learned one thing about these murders, Medea. One thing I believe you do not know. And I am giving you that information. Consider it a gift."

Only a few words were written on the paper, but if it wasn't a trick they might be more valuable to me than all the treasures of Midas.

Find the old woman who was at all of the murders.

I was still staring at the paper when I felt a gentle breeze. I looked up and saw Lamia was gone, leaving nothing more behind her than a faint odor of decaying roses.

Chapter 21

"Let go of me!"

The shout reminded me I still had work to do in the church. I turned to Orphne and Peter. He was pulling against her grip so hard I was afraid he'd yank his arm out of the socket.

"It's all right, Orphne," I said as I dropped the masking glamour, letting my eyes go back to their natural golden color. "You can let him go. You won't be any problem at all, will you, Peter?" By that time I'd made it halfway from the altar.

He relaxed, his eyes firmly fixed on mine. After a moment Orphne eased her hold on his wrist and changed back to her human guise.

I took a few more steps. I had to make him forget he'd ever seen me flying around and throwing fireballs. That, at least, would be easy enough.

Or not.

Peter suddenly lunged to the side, twisting free of Orphne. He managed to get a few steps before she jumped after him and grabbed both his shoulders, throwing him down hard on the ground. For a minute I thought she was going to straddle him, but she confined herself to putting a foot neatly on his throat. She'd conjured up a nice black mini-dress, but it was the spike heeled shoes that really made the outfit. The one lodged lightly in the hollow of Peter's throat also made a convenient deterrent.

He tensed, thought better of it, and lowered his arms. I hurried over. Something was wrong.

I knelt down and grabbed his face in both my hands, forcing him to meet my gaze.

"I want you to look me right in the eyes, Peter."

"Why? So you can see fear in mine before you kill me? It's not going to happen. If you're going to do it, get it over with."

Definitely, something was wrong. They never talk back when they look me in the eyes.

He twisted his head out of my grip but didn't break contact with my eyes.

"I don't know what you are, or what that woman was, but she's right. I think you're the one responsible for Paul's death! Your friend here has enough strength to force a grown man into the leopard's cage at the zoo, and you can't tell me you and those *things* that broke in here are the good guys!"

"They're not. I am, though. At least in this case. I killed them, remember?"

He looked like he wanted to spit at me, something which would be very inadvisable in his current position. He must have realized that and opted to spew his frustration in another way.

"Bullshit!"

Orphne put a hand on my shoulder. I didn't look up at her. I was totally floored at finding a mortal who wouldn't give in to my gaze.

"I think he's immune, Medea," she offered.

I sighed. "So I gathered. I'm sorry, Peter."

He closed his eyes and clenched his jaw. "Just do it."

So I did. As the poisoned knife clattered to the ground I pulled back and gave him my best roundhouse punch. He grunted and went limp.

"Forgive me, Father," I muttered as I got to my feet. I stowed the knife back in my purse. The next moment the air around Peter was shimmering as I laid on a sleeping charm that would keep him under until I decided to wake him. At least, it worked with the dragons that drew my chariot. I wasn't so sure about Peter. He had some sort of natural resistance to my hypnotic gaze and might not be affected by other magic.

"So what do we do next?" Orphne asked. I took a couple of deep breaths while I considered my options. Of course if I just killed Peter outright, it would solve my problems. But I didn't have the heart. He didn't deserve it.

More importantly, if he knew about the maenads he might have information I could really use. I couldn't afford to lose him just yet. He might not be compliant under my gaze, but I had several other ways to get answers out of a man. Some were pretty fun. At least for me.

We loaded him into the back seat of the car. I laid a warding charm around it to keep intruders out, and another to mask his presence in case anyone happened along and peeked inside.

"What are you doing?" Orphne asked as I headed towards the rectory. "Shouldn't we get out of here?" Orphne looked a little nervous, and I couldn't blame her.

"We can't. He said he had some information in his office. Maybe it'll help us narrow things down."

Fortunately there was only one other building in sight. It seemed to be a good candidate for an office.

We carefully opened the door. There was a reception counter, but no one at the desk behind it. I motioned with my head for Orphne to peak around a nearby door. I went behind the counter, keeping as quiet as possible.

There. A slight sound of movement. I quickly went to a door at the back of the area.

I had no idea how a woman of her size had squeezed herself into the narrow coat closet, but I had no trouble hauling her out.

"Please! Don't hurt me!" She was nearly seventy if she was a day. I remembered Lamia's note, but one glance at her threw her out of the running. She was *too* old to be of much use to Dionysus in any practical capacity, even as a house mother for the maenads. I doubted he needed secretarial help.

My eyes were still unmasked. I grabbed her chin, forcing her to look at me. She relaxed almost instantly, all tension easing from her body. Unless she was a world-class actor, she, at least, was in my power.

"You know what happened. How?"

She pointed weakly to the counter. I saw a few small screens flickering just underneath. Of course, a well-to-do church would have security cameras. Two of the monitors showed different shots of the church interior, including the main altar where everything had happened. A third had a shot of the parking lot. My car was clearly visible. A fourth had split-screens of the other monitors and the office. I spied the camera in the corner by the main door.

"Did you call the police?"

"Yeessss," she drawled heavily. Damn and double damn. We had little or no time left.

"Are those cameras hooked up to recorders?"

She nodded slowly. "Show me." I demanded. She went over to the counter and opened a small cabinet. It was a simple digital recorder.

"Is this the only record of what happened?"

"Yessss."

A muttered charm and the input cables and power cord sparked and fell away from the back of the recorder. I popped it out and handed it to Orphne, who had just emerged from the other room. She had a folder in her hands. "I think this is what Peter was talking about. It has your name on it. It was sitting right on the desk."

I'd have to hope it was all the information he had in the office. We had to get out of there fast. I made the secretary look me in the eyes again.

"When the police get here, you're going to tell them three men broke into the church and attacked Father Kirkpatrick. Do you understand?"

She nodded again. "And they're the ones who did the damage. You hid in the closet, and you don't know what happened after that. There were no women, no women at all. You understand what I'm saying?"

"Yesss…" It was getting a bit monotonous, but her compliance was reassuring.

"You will forget you saw us. Get in the closet now. And stay there until the police arrive."

She turned, hustling a bit and breathing heavily as she forced herself back into the small space.

Orphne and I dashed out of the office and into the car. I saw a second driveway in the back of the parking lot. It let out onto a side street, and seemed a safer exit route than the driveway leading to the main road.

I'd made at least one good decision that day. Seconds after we pulled out onto the side road and headed away from the main street, I spied flashing blue lights in my rearview mirror. Two police cars roared down the main road in front of the church and wheeled in through that driveway.

I was reassured when the lights stayed in the church parking lot and made no move to follow me.

We rode in silence for a few moments. Finally Orphne sighed. "Well, it could have been worse."

I was in no mood for pointless reassurances. "I don't see how," I muttered. "I've been keeping score. Lamia, of all the possible scourges, showed up. Not only showed up, but forced me to use my powers in front of Peter. And forced you to reveal yourself, and your shape-shifting abilities. Let's not forget, Peter is now unconscious in my back seat. And as a *final* joy, he doesn't respond to my hypnotic power, which means I can't make him forget what he saw."

"But at least now you know Lamia isn't responsible."

Leave it to Orphne to find some way to make me laugh after a total fiasco. "Are you insane, Orphne? Do you think for one minute I believe that bitch when she denies involvement? If anything her being here, of all places, makes her even *more* of a suspect in my book."

"But the deaths don't fit her methods. And she wouldn't be stupid enough to try to frame Dionysus, would she? Especially by trying to make it look like he was reviving a forbidden blood cult."

She had a point, although I grudged admitting it. If Lamia wanted subterfuge and misdirection to cover some plot of hers, there were ways that were a lot safer than trying to implicate one of the Twelve in something so serious.

"What was on that paper she handed you?"

I'd stuffed it into my pants pocket. I pulled it out and handed it to her.

"Well, that may be something," she said, although she didn't sound convinced. "But you didn't see an old woman at the sorority house when you had that vision, did you?"

"Only young ones."

"What about the vision in the mirror? There was a woman by the dead body, stroking the wound, right?"

I nodded. "I couldn't see her face to tell whether she was old or young, although the hands didn't look old at all."

She mulled that a second. "And you're sure you couldn't tell what kind of stones were in her jewelry? It might be an important clue. Especially if they were amethysts."

Indeed, that would be a giveaway. The stones were sacred to Dionysus, although paradoxically they were supposed to prevent drunkenness.

"The color was off. I couldn't tell. There was something wrong, like the vision was clouded or obscured by something, remember? But they didn't look purple. More bluish-green."

The frustration in my voice was enough to make her let that train of thought go.

"Well, at least you have this," she said as she patted the folder from Peter's office meaningfully.

Sure, I had that, and the man himself lying unconscious in my back seat. What could possibly make me happier?

Chapter 22

Back in the seventies I'd heard a children's song—something about happiness being two kinds of ice cream. I had three flavors of Baskin Robbins melting away in the bowl next to me, but I was a long way from happiness.

Peter was safely asleep in my basement. I'd made him as comfortable as I could on a couch down there. He showed no signs of shaking off the sleeping spell but it didn't pay to take chances.

With Orphne's help I bound him to the couch with several lengths of chain. The chains were thin and light, but unbreakable. The smith god Hephaestus gave them to me when I was first assigned to hunt down demons.

The possibility that Peter might be a demon or a demon-human hybrid didn't escape me. I had plenty of ways to deal with either. What I needed to do first was focus on the murders, and figure out what was going on.

Unfortunately Peter's research about the maenads didn't help much. Most of the stuff in the folder was from the internet, and while it was fairly accurate it didn't shed any new light on what was going on. I was impressed to see one printout that mentioned leopards were sacred to Dionysus. A note in red ink above merely said "Paul", and it was underlined heavily. It had already occurred to me that Paul's death in the leopards' exhibit was another clue pointing to Dionysus as the culprit.

The cops might be delighted to get a lead like this but I didn't intend to give them the information. They'd only get in the way, and most likely get themselves killed in the process. There were enough bodies piling up in Atlanta without that. I had a horrible suspicion more were piling up by the hour.

I was pretty irritated with my lack of progress by the time I reached the end of the folder. What I saw there brought me out of the doldrums so fast, I felt like racing down to the basement and kissing my unconscious guest.

It was just a small note clipped to the back of the folder. My second small note of the day, but even more helpful than the one Lamia gave me.

Dionysus = wine = vineyard. Our vineyard?

The last two words were underlined heavily. So, Peter's family had a vineyard? This was too good.

Unfortunately my elation quickly ended when I hit the internet to find out where it was. I did every search imaginable to link the Kirkpatricks to a vineyard. I suspected it would be local, but none of the searches linked the family to any of the places that made or sold wine in Georgia.

Out of the blue the insane vision of Peter and Paul stomping grapes in a huge vat crept into my mind. It quickly turned into a remake of that famous "I Love Lucy" episode, where Lucy and another woman got into a catfight in the grape vat.

The image of Peter and Paul wrestling each other was much more entertaining. I didn't have time to indulge so I quickly filed it away. Maybe I'd get some down time to enjoy it later that night.

In the meantime I wasn't about to admit defeat. The internet might not have the answers, but I had another source of information available. I glanced at my watch. That source would be out walking his dogs right about now.

I cornered McCaffrey as he turned onto my street. We exchanged the usual pleasantries about the weather before I turned the conversation a different way.

"I just can't believe what happened to Paul Kirkpatrick," I said with a sigh as I walked slowly with him. The collies frolicked at our feet, oblivious to the dreary tones we adopted.

"Yes, it was horrible. Don't know what to make of it at all. He didn't seem the type to give in to depression, but then you never know. Losing Shannon like that—I can see where it might push him over the brink."

I waited a couple of seconds before tossing out the lure. "I imagine his mother is having a terrible time, especially since he was probably taking care of the family businesses. I don't suppose his brother will be able to help out much, being a priest."

"No, I don't suppose so," McCaffrey agreed. "But they didn't have much by way of businesses that I know of. They made their money through investing. I think the father made sure there was plenty of cash to hand before he died, so the missus won't have to do much."

"Mmm," I murmured. "Although didn't they have a vineyard or winery? I wonder if Peter will have to sell it, if he can't take time away from his duties to have a hand in it."

McCaffrey's eyes lit up. Pay dirt.

"Now, that's going to be interesting. I wonder who really will get it. Didn't you know, Paul signed it over to Shannon as a present? Did it right before the engagement party. That was the wine they were serving— came right from Hawk's Haven, up just past Dawsonville. That's the place."

I stopped in my tracks. "Some present," I breathed. And some clue. The first known victim of the newly-revived maenads had gotten a vineyard just a few months ago. Coincidence didn't even wave goodbye as it flew out the window.

"A couple of us were talking about it the other day. We wondered if Paul had asked for it back. Of course, the O'Neills should have given it back out of decency, but I don't know that they were thinking about that with Shannon so recently dead. And with Paul dying so soon after Shannon... well, it muddies things more, doesn't it?"

No. No, indeed. It just might make things a little more clear.

"So Shannon's family is in charge of it now?"

He chuckled. "Not exactly. Shannon knew her parents were set for everything. Word is—and mind you, this is just gossip, no way to confirm —but word is, Shannon had a will made out, right enough. And she left everything, trust fund, investments, and of course the winery, to her sister."

Bingo. The winery Shannon had gotten as a present was now in Lyn's hands? I had to wonder how much of Lyn's mousy, self-effacing demeanor was an act. I was willing to bet most of it.

Lyn had links to all three of the victims: her sister, her sorority friend Monica, and Paul. She'd been at the scene of at least two of the deaths, and could easily have been at the zoo the night Paul was killed. She certainly had ample opportunity to move through the crowds unseen.

She had something else, too: a clear motive for being rid of her sister and Paul.

Time to pay a visit to Hawk's Haven.

Chapter 23

The drive north up state route 400 is amazingly smooth once you get past exit 12. Unfortunately we started at exit 4. By the time traffic and construction eased up I was in a bad enough mood to be a candidate for Maenad of the Year myself. Ripping someone apart with my bare hands didn't seem so appalling after more than an hour of delays.

Eventually 400 ended and I started taking the back roads. At least the directions to the winery were straightforward. It hadn't taken more than a few seconds to pin down an address once I entered the name "Hawk's Haven."

There wasn't much information on the winery's homepage. There were a few pictures, a schedule of hours for a small shop on the premises and a link for email enquiries for wholesale orders. Of course I didn't expect the webpage to have a flashing marquis proclaiming, "Now Appearing: Dionysus and the Maenads!", but a little more information about nearby landmarks would have been useful.

It wasn't an area I was especially familiar with. But we had a full tank of gas, a gorgeous sunny day, and a lovely view of the autumn foliage painting the rolling hills in golds, ambers and scarlets. Even if I got lost I figured I'd come out ahead, because the scenery was taking my mind off the more lurid reasons for the trip.

"So what do we do when we get there?" Orphne queried. Her outfit of the day included a red sundress and a silk scarf closely wrapped around her head (she steadfastly denied the need for a coat because "this is paradise compared to Hades"). I'd lent her my sunglasses just for fun. She looked like a movie star from the fifties.

"We'll just scout around, see if anyone working there has seen anything unusual," I said, unwilling to formulate anything more detailed than that.

"Anything unusual. You mean like groups of women running around frothing at the mouth?" Orphne asked with a slight laugh.

I didn't bother responding. It was a distinct possibility. At least it would be unquestionable proof that Dionysus really was behind this, and that it wasn't some plot of Lamia's after all.

"What if we find more?" My silence wasn't enough for Orphne. "What if we find the body of the man you saw in the vision? Or the woman with the jewels?" She paused a second before finishing the thought. "What if we find *him*?" There was no mistaking who 'he' was.

"You have the Tear of Nereus. Use it to become a bird or a small animal, anything that can hide easily and get away. Find shelter with other nymphs. If you go to a spring or river, the water nymphs will help you get in touch with my mother. She'll be able to help."

"What about you?"

I took a steadying breath. "He can't kill me," I reminded her. "Besides, I'm a priestess. I'm protected by the rules of sanctuary."

Orphne waited a moment before replying. "He may not care about those rules any more. And he can damage you enough to make you wish you could die before anyone comes to avenge a violation of sanctuary," she said quietly.

"Damage can be healed, especially with Hecate's help. She can take away pain and the memory of pain if she chooses."

"Then why haven't you asked for her help in this, instead of running to meet a potentially dangerous situation like a long-lost lover?" she demanded. "I know you aren't supposed to call her unnecessarily, but when you decided to stay here on Earth rather than going to Hades or Aiaia, you had no idea what we were facing. I think she'd understand if you ask her for help to fight a god."

"But what if I'm wrong?" I countered. "I have to be sure. If I call her now and blame you-know-who for the carnage, and it turns out to be something else, do you have any idea what she'll do to me? Serving a goddess like Hecate isn't easy. She won't easily forget, or forgive me if I call her for something I can handle on my own. And her punishments…"

I shuddered involuntarily. "I just have to be sure," I finished weakly. I knew it was no argument.

"By the time you're sure, it could be too late."

I didn't have a response for that. She was absolutely right.

"You're too intent on finding definite answers," she said as I pulled up to a stop sign. No one was behind us so I used the chance to double-check the directions. We had a couple more easy turns before we hit the winery.

"Why shouldn't I want answers?" I shot back.

"Wanting them is one thing, but taking risks like racing right up to the potential lair of the maenads without any sort of backup is beyond insanity. Have you really thought things through?"

"What's there to think about? I've got a lot of signs pointing to one specific area, and I'm checking them out. What else do I have to go on?"

"You have the information that Lamia gave you."

"Which could be a lie. And it's not much help, is it, even if it's true. An old woman at the scene of all the murders. Do you have any idea how many old women there are in Atlanta alone?"

"But it may not be just any woman. Think, Medea. Don't you remember an old woman who would have good reason to want to help Dionysus?"

It took a few seconds, but when the realization hit I couldn't believe I'd been so blind.

"Agave," I breathed. The stories that Dionysus captured her soul to keep her from facing punishment in Hades could be true. She would have been an old woman by the time she died. In life, she'd been fanatical enough to kill her own son to help Dionysus establish his cult in Thebes. If he needed an accomplice, she'd be at the top of the list of candidates.

For someone with his power, it would be little problem to resurrect her.

"So it might not be Lyn at all," I muttered. "I hadn't thought of that. Everything tied together so neatly."

"Too neatly, if you ask me," Orphne said. "But you're right about our choices. I don't think we can afford to ignore this one. I just wish we'd brought more weapons than what you have in your purse. This could be an ambush."

And there I was, driving blithely into it.

"I notice we haven't turned around," Orphne said as she leaned back into her seat and stretched. "Just make sure you're going into this with your eyes fully open, Medea. If this vineyard is at the heart of things, don't be surprised at anything you see there. Or anyone."

The silence that followed was uncomfortable so I switched on the radio and tuned it to the classical station. Vivaldi kept us company as we drove in silence.

I was so engrossed in the music I almost shot past the driveway. It was fairly small, but it was the only one in the area. The odometer told me the mileage was right, based on the MapQuest directions.

I carefully eased up the driveway. It was closed in on either side by trees close to the road, but a few yards up it widened to a respectable size. We ended in a small parking lot, with enough room for maybe ten cars if everyone parked straight. Only one other car was there.

A large building with huge panoramic windows and cedar shingle siding was on the right side of the lot.

Directly behind the building I could see trellises. The building must be the shop, and probably the administrative offices.

"Looks like the best access to the vineyards is up that gravel path," I said as I pointed to the spot just beyond the far edge of the parking lot. "Wonder if it goes to the end of the fields?"

I sized things up. My car stood out too much in the empty parking lot. Hopefully no one inside the building had noticed our arrival.

I murmured a charm and the air around the car shimmered with a slightly prismatic effect.

"We're invisible now, at least to human eyes. Let's take the car as far up that path as we can. If we have to go part of the way on foot, I want it as close as possible so we can make a quick getaway."

I knew we were both thinking the same thing. If things went badly, we'd be extraordinarily lucky if we even had the chance to attempt an escape.

Chapter 24

The gravel path was barely wide enough to accommodate the car. I kept a close eye on it to ensure no deep ruts caught me unaware, but it was well maintained.

The trellises still had leaves, though the vines were starting to die back. Nothing here to indicate the presence of Dionysus, at least not yet. I could see a small rise just ahead. It blocked my view of whatever lay beyond.

The fields had to go further. There was barely an acre and a half of trellises ahead of the hill. Not nearly enough to sustain a winery.

As I pulled up to the base of the hill Orphne was already opening her door. "Maybe we can see how much territory we have to cover once we climb up." My thoughts exactly.

But when we got to the top I suddenly wished I'd walked more slowly.

"By all the gods of hell," I said faintly as we hit the top.

As far as our eyes could see, the trellises on the other side of the hill were heavily laden with vines as lush and green as if it was harvest time. Grapes were hanging in profusion, and the same vines bore blossoms as well.

Fruit and flower at the same time—proof positive that something far more significant than Indian summer was at work here.

But it wasn't firm proof Dionysus was involved. Given the right spells and ingredients, I could pull off something like this. I suspected Lamia could as well, with all her studies of arcane arts. I needed more than this if I was going to prove Dionysus was responsible.

I took a resigned breath. "Let's go." A hand on my arm stopped me after the first step.

"We need to talk about something first," Orphne said quietly. The look on her face told me it was a chat I wasn't going to like. Before I could protest she started back down to the car. After a second's hesitation I followed her.

"I haven't exactly been truthful with you," she said without looking at me, a second after I closed my door.

I waited. It was her story, and she'd tell it in her time.

She took a deep breath, let it out slowly. "I lied to you when I told you Hecate sent me here. She didn't. I came on my own."

I was too stunned to say anything for several seconds. Then I exploded. "You're a *fugitive?* By Hecate's hounds, don't I have enough problems without that added to the mix?"

Problem was a mild way to describe it. Like most elemental spirits, Orphne was assigned to a specific realm—in her case, the

Underworld. She couldn't leave that realm to wander around without express permission from Hades, Lord of the Underworld, or his queen Persephone. For Orphne to leave on her own was tantamount to insubordination. The consequences would be dire in the extreme if she was caught.

If he was feeling kind, when Hades found out about her little escapade he would simply snuff her out. Orphne was immortal by nature, but that was easy enough to cancel out for a deity like Hades. But more than likely, he'd take advantage of the fact that she couldn't die to make her suffer exquisitely in the torture pits.

If I was caught harboring her, there'd be consequences for me too. Probably only a few years in the torture pits, but by the end of the first day I'd be begging the gods to rescind my immortality. I doubted they would.

Until that moment, I'd had an out. I'd believed she'd been sent to Earth officially. I had no reason to doubt her. Now that I knew the truth I'd have some decisions to make.

Like whether to turn over my oldest friend, knowing her punishment would be excruciating.

Another thought came to me. "And the Tear of Nereus?"

"I stole it. I knew where Hecate kept it, a box in one of the rooms in her estate which is rarely used. I snuck in, took it and left. I long ago learned the routes that would let me leave Hades by stealth and arrive anywhere I wanted on Earth, though I never thought I'd use them."

Wonderful. Thieving from the queen of witches herself. A brilliant move. "And that whole story you told me, about Hecate sending you up because she suspected something was about to happen…"

"That was partially true. You have to believe that." She turned to face me for the first time, but turned away again when she saw the anger in my eyes. Whether she felt remorse or not, I couldn't tell. She was hiding all emotion.

"I overheard her discussing it with her counselors. There had been signs, omens, that something significant was coming. The river Styx started flowing backwards at one point. That was the first sign, but others followed.

"The Gardens of the Dead, where the pomegranates that Persephone ate grow, started having fruits and flowers on the trees at the same time, just like those vines down there. That's never happened. And Cerberus has been anxious, baying for hours at a time. He never gives more than a few barks and growls. Hades summoned Hecate and told her to figure out what was happening.

"I don't know what she found, but what she told her counselors was that the omens presaged things happening on other planes as well. 'First the dead,' she said, 'then the living shall feel this darkness. Finally it shall reach Olympus itself.' A reversal, you know. Backwards, from the way things are supposed to be."

A reversal indeed from the natural order in which decisions would be made, destinies woven on Olympus. Then those decisions would be enacted on the Earthly plane and, if necessary, carried through to the planes of death where extreme virtue or sin would be rewarded or punished appropriately.

If what she said was true, the omens had appeared in the land of the dead first. Now, we were dealing with consequences here on Earth. Which meant the next stop—

"They talked about alerting you, knowing you'd be in a prime position to spot anything unusual on Earth. Early signs, something they could take to Olympus. Something to merit intervention. But Hecate didn't make a decision. She said she needed more time, more information."

She sighed again. "I thought...."

She broke off, but I could guess the rest. She thought if she could find enough information to bring back to Hades, enough to give Hecate reason to go to the Olympians themselves, that she might be forgiven. It was a long shot, but it was the only one she had at the moment.

It wasn't just her subterfuge that numbed me. It was the fact that Hecate had some sign, some indication that something bad was going to happen—something that might very well involve me—yet she hadn't been inclined to warn me about it. She wanted more information, never mind whether I might be in danger in the meantime.

Hecate hadn't changed, and likely never would. Well, I knew who and what she was when I signed on for my gig as her high priestess. I couldn't be disappointed now.

For some reason, I couldn't feel disappointed with Orphne either, even though she'd put me in a hell of a position. Emphasis on hell. I didn't know whether it was friendship that motivated her, or whether she'd just thought about it after the fact, but one thing was for certain: Orphne *had* warned me that something was up. I owed her something, at least for that.

"I don't know what to say, Orphne. Except that I'm not going to turn you over, even though I should. Especially since I'm a priestess. I, of all people, should be following the rules. But done is done, and there might be a chance to win some mercy for both of us if you can help me uncover something useful."

"It's not too late, you know," she said. "You can still call on Hecate and ask for refuge in Hades or Aiaia. You don't have to stay here to face this."

"If I call her now, she'll know you're with me, if she doesn't already. It's gone too far. There's only one thing left to do. We have to hope that Dionysus really is responsible for this, and then get the goods on him."

"We could be in even worse trouble if it's true."

I didn't bother responding. The odds, already against us, had just gotten worse. I was now an accomplice to Orphne's crime. Unless we found something really, really good to distract the powers of Heaven and Hell, we'd both be paying a high price.

Chapter 25

We picked our way gently down the hill. The gravel path didn't continue on this side, but there was a low-mowed path of grass. It divided the fields neatly. They stretched to either side as far as I could see.

The trellises were slightly taller than me and so densely packed with leaves you couldn't see through to the next row unless you wanted to crawl on your hands and knees and peak beneath. The temperature was several degrees warmer in the fields, and there was a hint of moisture and the subtle scent of fresh foliage in the air.

"All right then," I said with a surety I didn't feel, "We'll take one side of the field at a time. You go down one row, I'll go down the next one over. We'll keep doing them by twos then tackle the other side of the field."

We set about dealing with the rows on the left side of the field first. I dearly hoped we'd have enough daylight to do the entire field. I could always conjure fireballs and set them afloat like lanterns, but I didn't relish the idea of being in that place after dark.

It quickly grew monotonous. There wasn't much to look at except solid walls of green on either side of me. I kept telling myself I could get lucky, and *not* find anything else. The state of the vineyard was pretty strong evidence.

But not conclusive, I reminded myself.

We walked in silence for about ten minutes. By that time the shock from Orphne's revelation had worn off. "What made you do it? You know the risks." I had to know. Had to understand why she'd been so careless with my fate as well as hers, or if she'd even bothered thinking about my fate.

She waited a few seconds before answering. "I thought it was worth it. But I wasn't thinking straight, because I didn't consider at the time that you could get into trouble for sheltering me. I'm truly sorry, Medea."

So she had thought about me, at least after the impulsive decision to flee Hades. That was some comfort. I couldn't fault her for not thinking everything through before her mad escapade—not I, who'd really messed things up by helping Jason get that stupid fleece. Killing my own brother in the process, no less. Not that the little shit would have lived much longer anyway, with his clumsy attempts at manipulating palace politics.

She wasn't offering any more insights though. "I know you wouldn't have willfully put me in danger. You had other things on your mind. But what were they? You never expressed unhappiness with your place in Hades before."

Another pause. "I suppose I hadn't really thought about it until recently. You know, we've been getting an uptick in the number of souls wandering our way."

No surprise there. Human souls end up in whatever afterlife they believe in most strongly. It's one of the great mysteries of the universe, how much control humans actually have over their fate, and not just in this world. With renewed interest in fantasy literature, television shows about the supernatural, and sci-fi conventions I could easily believe more people were ending up in the ancient Greek Underworld again. There'd been an increase during the Renaissance too, when artists started churning out works inspired by ancient Greece.

"But what about it?" I pressed. "It just means things are swinging back to the old ways here on Earth. But they've got quite a ways to swing yet before we'll be building another Parthenon."

"Maybe, but what struck me was how much people have changed since the ancient times. You know I can recognize souls. They may look different each time they incarnate, but once they're dead you can pick them out again easily enough. But even though they looked the same, they changed. After they'd been reincarnated a few times, they seemed much nicer. Complained a lot less. Some even were friendly, asked me questions as I led them to the river Lethe."

One of her jobs as a chthonic nymph was to help escort the dead to Lethe to drink the waters of forgetfulness, so their souls could be reborn. Over the ages it would be a true exercise in people-watching. Or shade-watching, if you prefer.

"It occurred to me that people were lucky. They could change. I haven't changed since the day I came into existence, as the Underworld was coalescing from the primal darkness. And I realized, I never would change, because it isn't part of my existence. It isn't something I'm destined for."

I suddenly understood it all. It made me a little sad to know she'd come to such a realization. Most elementals like nymphs are perfectly happy with their lot and never question it. But what if you suddenly saw there was something different out there and realized you'd never be able to enjoy it?

It was a question of opportunity. Humans had plenty of them. Elementals had almost none. Immortal they may be, incredibly strong most of the time, and some even have their own sorts of magic. But there is one magic they can never accomplish, and that is evolving past what they are.

We started down the next rows.

"It's all right if this is it for me, Medea," she said. "Because I've gotten the opportunity to do something different. It beats going on another hundred thousand years in Hades, doing what I've been doing for countless millennia. At least I've enjoyed being on Earth, doing things like riding in a car and eating human food. Though I have to say, I still don't see what you like about ice cream. Nothing but frozen fluff, if you ask me."

I couldn't help smiling. I supposed it wouldn't be up an underworld nymph's alley. "Maybe after we get done here today, we can go for sushi. You should like that. They kill it and serve it to you raw."

When she spoke again it was in a tone of voice that immediately banished all thoughts wasabi.

"It must look an awful lot like what I'm seeing right now."

Chapter 26

Orphne had been keeping pace with me until then, but that last comment came from about two yards behind me. She'd stopped to look at something, and it was clearly something important.

I immediately levitated over the top of the vine row. I didn't bother to mute the sharp inhalation of breath at what I saw.

There were five, all men. They looked like they might have clustered together in some sort of effort to defend themselves. It hadn't worked. From the look of their clothes and the scattered tools lying around, I surmised they were working in the vineyard when they were attacked.

"Looks like it might be the maenads all right," Orphne said matter-of-factly. "What do you say, Medea?"

I eased down on the other side of the vines and hurried over to the bodies.

The men were in various positions, their livid faces open-eyed, but the expressions were not at all terrible. They looked more like life-sized, badly damaged ventriloquist dummies which had been carelessly discarded, their mouths frozen open. The corpses seemed inane rather than menacing. That's real death for you. Nothing like the movies.

I knelt to get a closer look at a man who was face-down. There were several deep gashes that could have been made either by claws or human nails in his back. The wounds were bruised and jagged.

The next man, lying on his back with his legs bent painfully under him, had probably been decent-looking in life. Not so much now. One ear was torn off, his jaw was severely dislocated, and part of his nose was gone. He was in a T-shirt and zippered sweatshirt, jeans smeared with dirt as well as the soil a body releases after death.

He was missing an obvious death wound. Unlike the others his shirt had only a few splatters of blood on the front, as if he'd been near one of his companions when they were cut down. I sighed, knowing the examination was only half done. Putting one hand on his shoulder and the other on his hip, I rolled him over onto his stomach.

Well, so much for the death wound. It was staring at me quite blatantly from the remains of his sweatshirt, which had been ripped apart below the shoulders. The gaping wound was slightly to the left of center, about two thirds of the way down his back, and big enough to put a hand into.

I took another deep breath and did.

It took only a short probe to confirm his heart had been ripped out by someone strong enough to shove a bare hand through several layers of skin and muscle, and up under the rib cage. Considering how thick the back muscles are, it was no small feat.

But it might be possible for a maenad in full ecstatic trance. Certainly an Olympian god had the strength do it.

Orphne seemed puzzled by my actions. "What are you doing?"

I withdrew my hand and wiped it on the ground, to little effect. I got better results wiping it on the man's pants. "Trying to find out how he died, which I did. Heart's gone. And judging by the warmth of his entrails, it didn't happen all that long ago."

I gauged about three hours had passed, putting their deaths at about an hour after sunrise.

I only needed to give a cursory glance to the next two. One was lying on his stomach, but his neck had been broken and twisted so badly he almost looked like he was laying face-up.

The next man was missing the lower half of his T-shirt, along with the skin, muscle and kidneys that had been underneath it. He was also missing his left arm.

The last man was face down, his hair so caked with mud I couldn't tell its color. He was oddly different, and I couldn't put a finger on why. But since I'd just put an entire hand inside another man, I damn well didn't intend to leave without answering the question. I bent down to examine him more closely. As I did, a strange chemical scent hit my nose. Maybe some sort of pesticide?

His shirt was pale blue, and as I knelt down to get a closer look I realized it wasn't denim. It was a high-quality material. The pants, which at first glance looked like work khakis, were linen. He was wearing expensive loafers and dark socks. None of the clothes looked damaged or disarranged.

Whoever he was, with clothes like those he was not a field hand. I grabbed his shoulder and hip and gently turned him onto his back.

Paul Kirkpatrick's vacant eyes stared back at me.

Chapter 27

I stiffened but didn't scream, even though I really, really wanted to. Not out of fear, but out of frustration combined with anger.

Paul's once-handsome face was heavily caked with makeup. Even though the morticians had done a decent job filling them in, the deep claw marks were still visible from just above his nose down the left side of the face. The edges of more marks were visible above the collar of his shirt.

I was getting a good look at the handiwork of the murderer. It made me more determined than ever to get my own hands on whoever it was.

I started to jump up with a half-muttered imprecation. I only made it halfway when a sudden shove sent me sprawling directly on top of Paul's body.

"DOWN!"

Orphne's shout rang through the vineyard, but at that point I wasn't worried about drawing attention. We already had company.

I turned just in time to catch her transform into something I'd never seen before. It was hairy, it was stout, and it had arms as big around as a good-sized tree limb. One of them was drawn back, and before I could catch my breath it shot out with lightning speed. There was a soft thud as it connected with its target.

"OW!" The sharp exclamation was a mixture of annoyance, pain and surprise. It was followed by a grunt, then a hissing inhalation through clenched teeth.

"Ow!" again, but softer. "Dammit, that hurt! What the hell are you doing?"

My brain went into overdrive. Orphne's blow should have crushed the skull of whoever was on the receiving end. And even if they survived, I knew the querulous voice should not have been speaking ancient Greek in the twenty-first century.

I was able to make it to my feet and throw a restraining arm around Orphne's, which was drawn back for another blow. The hair on the arm turned out to be coarse fur which scratched my hands. I ignored the discomfort and tightened my grip.

"Orphne, no!"

She turned an extremely hideous face towards me. The features were blunt enough to look like they'd been smashed nearly flat on purpose, though I thought the third eye, red and angry, was a nice touch. I had no idea where she'd come up with this creature, and was pretty sure I didn't want to ever find out. All I was interested in at that point was stopping her from launching an all-out attack, because I recognized the voice of our new companion.

"He snuck up behind us without warning," she said thickly. The tusks protruding from her lower jaw evidently made talking difficult.

"And I suppose you'd have no issue at all if I'd descended from Olympus in a gold chariot, with a band of nymphs and satyrs blowing horns and banging gongs ahead of me!" the voice behind her snapped. "That would be a truly subtle way to arrive on the scene."

The owner of the voice stepped into my line of sight, which had been mostly blocked by Orphne's new and enormous body.

"Nice to see you again, Medea," he said with a rueful grimace, his hand gingerly cupped over his nose. Apparently that had been ground zero for Orphne's punch. Even with his face partially hidden, he was still as ruggedly handsome as I'd remembered him.

I let go of Orphne's arm and practically skipped into his. The hug was long and heartfelt, and, as always, there was more than a little heat to it. I quickly put those feelings to the side. He was a friend, nothing more.

"Heracles," I sighed as I stepped back, my hands still on his biceps in a clasp of grateful welcome. Well, most of the feeling was grateful. I was a nymph's daughter after all, and they really were exceptional biceps.

I couldn't resist giving him an affectionate kiss—on the cheek, of course—before releasing my hold, and ruffling his shoulder length golden brown hair. The matching beard was neatly trimmed, and, I was thankful to see, not artfully curled and oiled like the one I'd seen in the Sybil's mirror.

He managed a half-smile, but the look in his clear blue eyes made it obvious the movement caused him pain. "Good arm on your friend there. I don't believe I've had the pleasure?" He held out a conciliatory hand, which she took after a moment's hesitation. She shifted back to her human guise as she did.

Heracles raised his eyebrows as he gave her an appraising look. I remembered he'd had more than his fair share of lovers while he was human, not all of them women. His stamina in that department was as legendary as his strength.

"Pleasure indeed to meet you—uh!" He winced at her grip. Even in human form she retained the natural strength of an elemental. It sufficed to cool the ardor in his gaze, allowing a little respect to fill the void.

"Orphne," she finished with a slight nod as she withdrew her hand.

"Ah, yes. Heard of you, of course, but I never thought I'd meet you. I don't get down your way too often," Heracles said amiably.

115

I was surprised when Orphne turned her gaze back to the dead men. She hadn't even given Heracles the once over, even though he was in the garb he'd preferred since his time as a mortal. It was a classical off-the-shoulder tunic that bared the right side of his amply developed chest, as well as giving us a good look at his finely sculpted shoulders and massive arms. The garment fell to the knees, but one had only to look at the perfectly rounded calves to know that the hidden thighs above them would be impressively strong.

Even someone without a nymph's proclivities would have stopped dead in their tracks. Heracles was a real eye-candy buffet, but for once Orphne wasn't indulging.

"What on Earth are you doing here?" I finally controlled my excitement enough to ask the obvious question.

"This might not be the place to discuss it," he said, his grin now fully restored. I would have used a healing spell, but as a god his body healed on its own quite nicely. His face was fully restored from the damage Orphne had done with her punch.

"Let's just say, someone in a very high position sent me to check out a potential problem. And it looks like I didn't have to search far."

A high position? I had a feeling I knew what that meant. Apparently I wasn't the only one suspicious of Dionysus. Only the Twelve could come to Earth without permission. If a minor god like Heracles was here, it meant one of the high gods had given him leave. That was a good sign.

"I see you haven't lost your propensity for getting into quagmires of epic proportions. Wouldn't one dead body have been enough?"

His attempted levity only darkened my mood.

"That all depends on which dead body we're talking about," I swept my hand towards the victims. "Would it be one of the four who may or may not have been killed by maenads, or would it be the fifth one, who was attacked by leopards and mauled to death several days ago? And buried miles from here, by the way, not left lying around in this vineyard. We've got both sorts of bodies. Take your pick."

He took a deep breath and let it out with a low whistle. "I was only joking when I mentioned epic quagmires." He slowly walked around the bodies, giving each one a few seconds of scrutiny. "You really think there are maenads running around again? You know the implications."

"Don't forget the implications of finding Paul's body here," Orphne added. I nodded again.

"Someone is sending me another message," I said flatly. Someone was watching me and knew I was onto something.

"Why don't we go somewhere a little more private so you can brief me on what's happened," Heracles said after a moment.

"Any suggestions?" It would have to be a good one, since Dionysus had the power to listen in on us anywhere on Earth.

But Heracles offered a perfect solution to that. When he told me, I made an impulsive decision.

"All right. But I need you to help me bring something along."

"A gift for the hostesses?" he asked with a smile.

"Indeed," I answered with my own smile. His faltered when he saw it. Ah, he knew me too well.

Chapter 28

It had been centuries since I'd visited my aunts Circe and Pasiphae. After a particularly grueling decade of demon hunting back in the Middle Ages I'd gotten a special dispensation for some rest time on Aiaia. The island, once a jewel in the Mediterranean, had been swept into an alternate dimension along with everything else the Olympians claimed as their territory when they withdrew from Earth.

He might only be a minor god, but Heracles had the power to bring us there in the twinkling of an eye. Me, Orphne, and a couple of new acquaintances.

We were on a marbled portico overlooking a beautiful valley where the sun was just setting. Time runs differently in the Otherworlds, and I wasn't too surprised to see the day was ending here when it was barely noon back on Earth.

Slightly to the right, on the far side of the valley, a waterfall flowed into a serene pool. The water was tinged with gold from the rays of the setting sun. As I admired it three fantastic birds soared over the cascading falls. With trailing plumage tinted beautiful shades of cerulean and lavender, they looked like a cross between peacocks and quetzal birds. Strange and eerily beguiling calls resounded over the valley, but I couldn't tell whether the cries came from those stunning birds or some other creatures on the island.

There was activity in the pool at the base of the falls. I looked more closely and saw several satyrs playing in the shallows, while beautiful—and naked—women waded deeper into the pool. No humans, I knew, but some of the nymphs who served as caretakers to the varied wildlife on the island.

Some of that wildlife was not so wild. As I turned away from the bucolic scene before me with a contented sigh, I noticed two lions lounging beside the columns that framed the main entrance to Circe's palace. They gazed at us with jaded eyes, not at all uneasy at seeing creatures that looked as they once had. Although I recognized each one by its distinctive markings, I realized that I had forgotten their names.

I suspected the lions had forgotten their own names as well. They were once men. So were many of the other animals on Aiaia.

How long had it been since she changed these two into lions? A thousand years or more, I thought. Nothing on Circe's island ever ages or dies. Sounds nice, unless you've been de-evolved into an animal at her whim. Dying might not be so bad if the alternative is spending eternity licking your rear end.

As we moved past the columns one of the lions pushed himself up a bit on his front paws, then gravely bowed his head. The courtesy shown by some of the animals on Aiaia is enchanting at first, but eventually you see it for what it is: proof that the creatures haven't forgotten they once were human.

The main hall of Circe's palace was empty when we arrived, but a serving nymph instantly appeared. She obligingly went to alert the aunts, and moments later they swept into the room.

Their exclamations of delighted surprise were welcome and comforting. They embraced me quickly, covering my cheeks with kisses, before finally breaking away.

"It's so good to see you again," Circe said as she held me at arms length to give me an appraising look. I realized I must look a mess, in jeans and a T-shirt with a casual sweater tied around my waist.

But if Circe disapproved it didn't show in her smile. Her flaming red mane, shot through with fiery deep gold and softer copper, floated gently around her shoulders and down her back. She had combed it straight for the evening. Left to its own devices it would circle her head in thick curls that seemed to constantly flow and change like flame itself. No human could imagine such hair without seeing it in person. But after all, she was the daughter of the sun god Helios.

His other daughter turned and ordered a serving nymph to bring refreshments. Pasiphae's hair fell in a beautiful mass of pure gold, again reflecting her parentage. That particular evening it was in gentle waves rather than the elaborate combination of braids and upsweep that she often preferred.

She'd also forgone the diadem she habitually wore, with the double-bladed axe prominent on the brow. It was the royal crown of Minoa, which she'd worn when she ruled the empire. It might be absent that evening, but I knew full well she hadn't forgotten the time when she'd worn it daily, or how she'd lost that empire.

Both sisters were dressed in loose chitons light enough to float like a mist around them, and yet not at all transparent. The robes glowed with a subtle fire. No human hands could ever have made such cloth. It was woven from opals that had been softened through magic so they could be coaxed into fibers using a distaff, much as one could spin a clump of flax. Of course, the fact that both the aunts were more than seven feet tall added to their imposing beauty.

Pasiphae turned to Heracles and Orphne. "And you've brought guests. Heracles, back so soon?" She narrowed her eyes a bit. "And this is... Orphne!"

The aunts were expert enchantresses, but I was still surprised that she could see through the disguise conjured by the Tear of Nereus.

She turned back to Heracles, her nose wrinkling instinctively at the sight of the two corpses he was carrying, one slung over each shoulder.

"And these would be?"

"Someone I need help with," I offered tentatively.

Circe raised an eyebrow. "I know you understand the healing arts better than that, Medea. These two are a long way past help and... Heracles, what *are you DOING?*"

Her voice became progressively shriller as Heracles approached one of the hall's spotless divans. It was upholstered in beautiful pastel pinks and mauves.

"Just putting these chaps down, my dear," Heracles said cheerfully. I'd chosen the least mutilated corpses among the field hands, but they were still quite a mess.

"You most certainly are not!" Circe's golden eyes were already flashing. Heracles froze in mid-stoop, quickly re-adjusting his balance to stop the bodies from falling onto the sofa. I couldn't help giggling a bit at the comic pose, but I don't suppose he saw anything funny about it.

"For pity's sake, it took me nearly a hundred years to perfect the magic to weave dawn's light into fabric. I will NOT have you putting those—*things*—on the furniture," Circe fumed.

She turned to me.

"It's always delightful to see you Medea, and your friends," she condescended to give a slight nod towards Orphne. "And I realize you're living a more Bohemian lifestyle these days. But really! You can't tell me your human friends would appreciate you bringing two dead bodies when you come to call. Couldn't you just bring chocolates?"

"I'm not going to leave them here, Aunt Circe," I reassured her. "And I promise I'll bring some chocolates next time I come. But first, I need you to help me find out something about them."

She snorted impatiently.

"They're dead and they've started to rot. There, that's two things about them. Will you kindly remove them now?"

I smiled and shook my head.

"I mean something specific. And you and Pasiphae are the only ones I know who have the skill to do it." I was buttering them up shamelessly, and they knew it.

Heracles cleared his throat diplomatically.

"Not that they're really any sort of burden to me, but do you mind if I put these fellows down now? I think one of them is seeping."

Pasiphae rolled her eyes. "Certainly, just toss them anywhere. We don't mind oozing corpses on the floor at all. Why not invite the Harpies over for a potluck while you're about it?" Now that was overstating the case a bit. The evil half-bird, half-woman monsters were voracious eaters. If they left anything uneaten, they fouled it with their shit out of sheer spite.

Circe held up her hands in a gesture of defeat. "Just let me handle it," she said, facing Heracles and lifting her arms. The two bodies floated off his shoulders and remained suspended in mid-air. He stood up, making a relieved sound in his throat. Sure enough, there was a large smudge on his skimpy outfit.

"Here, let me," I said. I went over and put my hand on the stain. Of course I could have done it without touching, but what the hell, why not cop a feel if the opportunity arose? The muscles of a god are nothing to miss if you get the chance.

I removed my hand after a few seconds, and the tunic was immaculate.

"Could we please get back to the issues at hand?" Pasiphae interrupted as she gestured towards the floating bodies. "What do you need us to do with those?"

"I need you to bring them back to life, so they can tell me about their deaths," I said.

Circe and Pasiphae looked at one another. Whether or not they were communicating telepathically, I was certain they were thinking the same thing.

"Well, that settles it. You've become completely unhinged." Pasiphae said with resignation. "Why would you bring two dead humans here for something that you could just as easily ask Hecate to do? In the privacy of your own home, if needed. You're her priestess, after all. And if I'm not mistaken, she is an underworld goddess, no? This should be a specialty of hers."

"Yes," I admitted. "But I can't get her involved just yet. I've got… a slight problem to deal with."

The refreshments had arrived. Wine was being poured at a table surrounded by more divans, and another nymph had brought in a tray of pastries soaked in honey.

Circe gestured to the seating area, extending the move a bit to wave the bodies away to a corner of the room. They hung like sulking children denied a place at the grownups' table.

"Tell us all about it. And make sure to include all of the juicy details."

I wondered if she'd regret her invitation once she heard what I had to say.

Chapter 29

Fortunately the aunts have never been squeamish. They let me tell my tale without interruption. Heracles' interest peaked at certain points, especially when I relayed my encounter with Lamia and Peter's apparent resistance to my hypnotic gaze. He didn't interrupt me either.

After I finished we all sat in silence for a few moments, pretending to be engrossed in the wine and the pastries. It was very good wine, but considering what I was up against I didn't feel like indulging. Wine, being the province of Dionysus, had lost its appeal for the moment.

I turned to Heracles. "So now it's time for your story. You said you'd been sent to Earth. By who, and why? Is it the same thing I'm facing?"

As much as I dreaded confirmation that Dionysus was on the rampage, I certainly didn't want to have to deal with him *and* another problem.

He avoided my gaze. "I can't say who sent me, but I can tell you it wasn't Father." So, Zeus was out of the loop on something? Another bad omen. Or, he might be using one of the other Olympians to do his work for him. Perhaps understandable, since Dionysus was his son. It might be too hard to handle it in person, although he hadn't balked at making uncomfortable decisions before.

"But can you at least tell us why you were sent?" Circe persisted. She, of all of us, was least likely to just let a thing go.

He sighed, shook his head, and drank deeply. A nymph rushed over to refill his cup as he set it down with a clang.

"I'm under orders not to. What I can tell you, though, is that someone has noticed something isn't right. Someone high enough to send me to Earth, and you know what that means." We did. Only one of the Twelve could do it. If it wasn't Zeus—and certainly it wasn't Dionysus—that left ten gods and goddesses to choose from.

"I can also tell you that someone is missing who shouldn't be," he went on after another draught. "You can draw your own conclusions."

Was he saying I was on the right track? Damn the high gods and their secrecy, anyway. But certainly, that was a thought I would keep to myself.

Orphne seemed content to let us parse it out. She nibbled at a honey pastry and sipped her wine, sitting slightly apart from the rest of us.

Pasiphae was a little more diplomatic than her sister. "Let's leave that be, for the moment. Hypothetically, if someone did something very severe—something which clearly went against the edicts of Zeus—

wouldn't they automatically be banished? Without any decisions or trial, I mean. Their actions alone would make them anathema. So they wouldn't be able to return to Olympus without absolution, correct?"

I'd thought about that the moment Heracles suggested retreating to Aiaia. "Which means, the person in question wouldn't have any sway here either, since this is part of the Olympian domains."

"I've always considered my island safe anyway," Circe said smoothly, though there was certainly enough emphasis on the words "my island" to indicate she didn't appreciate being considered someone else's fife.

Heracles smiled, though there was little humor in it. "Precisely why I chose Aiaia, Medea. I needed to hear what you had to say without the risk of eavesdroppers. And of course, if the aunts agree to your request, anything we learn from the dead men here on Aiaia will remain a secret as well. It could give us an advantage."

"Mmmm," Pasiphae said thoughtfully. "I, for one, would be happy to help. Especially if your suspicion is right, Medea. There's no love lost between Dionysus and me, after what he did to my beautiful Ariadne and my poor Megalitheros. Having his underling cut my son down in my own sacred labyrinth like an animal..."

Circe held up a restraining hand. "Just because a traitor couldn't hear you here, doesn't mean others can't overhear you. Keep your temper, sister."

Pasiphae's eyes had become molten gold during her tirade. They flashed briefly at Circe's chastisement, but quickly cooled to their normal amber gold. "It makes little difference. It's clear whatever is happening around Medea is dangerous, and we're bound by family duty as well as duty to Zeus to help her stop it. Senseless slaughter is an outrage against the gods."

This, from the goddess who'd caused an enormous tsunami in the Mediterranean to wipe out thousands of worshipers rather than having them shift allegiance to the Olympians?

Well, maybe things *could* change on Aiaia. But I wasn't a believer yet.

Circe glanced over to the corner. "Those bodies aren't getting any fresher. Come, we'll go to my workroom."

She rose, making an imperious gesture towards the corner where the dead men still hung suspended by magic. They slowly drifted towards us as we turned to follow Circe. They didn't know it yet, but their day was about to get even worse.

Chapter 30

Circe's work chamber was deep inside the palace. There were no windows, though the domed ceiling was pure crystal and let in plenty of light from the moon that was now sailing overhead on Aiaia. But that wasn't the effect we needed, and Circe knew it.

She glanced up, narrowing her eyes slightly. The crystal darkened to obsidian, blotting out the light. Odd how the daughters of the sun have such a propensity for conjuring darkness. The place became pitch black in an instant.

Pasiphae snapped her fingers and torches that were placed along the walls flared to life.

Circe pointed towards a low, wide marble table in the center of the room, and the corpses gravitated towards it, tipping sideways gracefully and settling down on their backs.

Circe clapped her hands twice and a nymph appeared. She was of the plainer sort, the kind who hang around in deserted caverns. My aunt whispered in her ear and she vanished, reappearing a few seconds later with a black ram, a thin golden chain around its neck. I didn't know who he'd been as a man, but I had no doubts that he'd been born human and transformed by Circe's magic. She can't bring herself to sacrifice real animals.

Pasiphae laid a hand on the ram's head and guided him towards the far end of the table, where the dead men's heads were laying. Circe moved to join her. She held out her hand, palm up, and a knife appeared in it. It was long, the blade sturdy but honed to a razor-sharp edge.

Pasiphae took firm hold of the ram's head. He must have known what was coming, but he was under enchantment and couldn't even try to make a break for it. Circe held out the knife and Pasiphae closed her fingers around the onyx handle.

"Wait," Circe broke the silence that had descended on the room like a pall.

Pasiphae looked at her with curiosity, then smiled in understanding. She released the knife. "Medea, come here," she commanded coolly, I was puzzled but did as she asked.

"This is your inquiry, dear," Circe eyed me cannily as the silken words slid from her mouth. "I think you should perform the rite."

I couldn't believe what I was hearing. "You know I don't have that kind of power," I muttered. Reanimating the dead was worlds beyond my abilities. It had been a long-standing family joke that I, who had chosen to become a priestess of Hecate, lacked that particular ability. Why were the aunts doing this?

"Why not just call up their ghosts? Surely you could do that," Heracles put in, trying to be helpful. He could sense my discomfort, I had no doubt.

Circe's irritation flickered briefly across her face before she decided to be more diplomatic. "In the old days, when we knew their shades would end up in Hades, it would have been sufficient. But we have no idea which afterlife they've gone to. It might be a realm where our kind have no power. Using their bodies gives us a firm link, but we can have to call their shades back into those bodies." She glanced meaningfully at the altar. "They'll come, no matter where they are now."

I looked down at the dead men, calculating my chances of succeeding at what Circe and Pasiphae were asking of me.

Circe knew what I was thinking. "No matter dear, if it doesn't work out and things get messy. You said there are three more corpses back where you found these—we can make another go at it."

She was assuming I would be at least partially successful, which meant that the bodies in front of us wouldn't be in passable shape for long. Such magic as we were planning has a price, and it's much more than the blood of one black ram.

"Two bodies," I said finally. "The third is mine. I owe him a reburial, and the proper rites to ensure he stays buried and can't be desecrated again." I felt rather than saw her shrug of indifference.

"If you don't succeed, then you may bring those two here and Pasiphae and I will take over. But do this for me," Circe's mouth drew closer to my ear. "I know you have this within you. You are the granddaughter of Titans!"

"Have faith, Medea," Orphne broke her silence, her eyes hard and glittering. Heracles stood impassively by her, but after a moment he gave a short nod of agreement.

I gave up. The sooner I got through this little experiment, which I felt sure would end badly, the sooner we could get the real work done.

"All right then," I accepted the knife Circe offered.

I took a deep breath. "Hold him steady," I said to Pasiphae.

Moving forward, I struck true and clean with the dagger. The ram gave a strangled bleat and staggered. Pasiphae grabbed its horns, holding its entire weight as the beast's legs collapsed.

Circe was there immediately. She held a large brass bowl that had appeared out of nowhere. It was wrought with magic glyphs and letters in a primitive alphabet. Linear A, they call it now, though humans have yet to decipher much of it.

Around the curve of the rim I saw a word that translated roughly as "breath of life." It was all I could read before Circe thrust the bowl under the huge, welling gash in the ram's throat. It quickly filled with the hot sticky liquid.

CURSE OF PROMETHEUS: A TALE OF MEDEA

Pasiphae moved one hand to grasp the ram's hind legs. Holding it by horn and hoof, she lifted it as easily as a child might lift a stuffed animal. She strode to the side of the table, uncaring of the blood that stained her beautiful gown. She laid the brute down across the two bodies. Its lingering life-force would serve to strengthen the spell.

I exchanged the sacrificial dagger for the bowl Circe held, moving towards the head of the table. The coppery stench of the blood inside the vessel made my head swim.

I felt my eyes glittering hot and golden as they do when I summon my deepest sorceries, the ones bound to my own life force. They burned hot enough to disintegrate the glamour that masked my eyes in the human world.

I lifted the bowl higher, then tipped its contents down straight onto the faces of the dead men. It dribbled thickly on their foreheads.

I used my power to force their mouths open. Focusing the power, I guided the streams of blood into their throats and forced it down into their gullets so that most of it ended up inside of them rather than around their heads.

"Let this blood rouse your own to life once more! I compel your souls to appear and give true answer to all that I ask! Delay not, but answer now my call!" My voice rang through the chamber, echoing in its hidden recesses.

Was it my imagination, or were there whispers drifting just at the edge of hearing?

I could feel the power coursing through my arms. I let go of the bowl, but it remained suspended over the table. I placed either hand on the blood-streaked brows of the corpses.

"Awaken, and speak! Live again, and heed my commands!"

I no longer saw or sensed the room around me. All that existed was my mind, the men's bodies, and the flow of power crackling around my own body and the table in front of me.

It felt as if I'd had a star encased in iron in my gut, and now the iron was splintering, falling away. The star's energy was bursting forth in jagged, uneven beams.

Before I could stop it a scream escaped my lips. All the pent-up anger and frustration of the past few days came to a head in that wordless cry. It broke through a little more of the stifling iron shell, but most of the power was still imprisoned, inaccessible.

As the cry sprang from me, there was a shuddering from the table. First one, then the second body, drew ragged, gurgling gasps. It was hard to be sure with the flaring power that was surrounding us, but I thought the eyelids of the one on the right fluttered a bit.

I tried to focus my energy, willing it to wake their dead blood and wrest their souls from whatever afterworld they'd gone to.

Then I was reminded of an odd paradox: dying can be easy, but death never is.

Especially not that day.

Chapter 31

A form rose up between the two men on the table, as if it had been lying there all along. Dark and still amid the flashing power pouring out of me, it was perfectly black, the outline roughly human. There was no firm definition to the edges of the body. It flowed and rippled like onyx-colored water.

Billowing clouds rose behind its back, shot through with thick reddish-black strands that throbbed unevenly like huge, ulcerated veins. The clouds resolved into vague wing-like shapes. Icy winds whipped through the room, snuffing most of the torches along the walls.

{Forbidden}

The voice was hissing, the single word almost breathless, as if it was uttered on an inhalation rather than exhalation. Pounding blows of dark energy assailed me, a relentless tide from an ocean of decay. The power flaring within me shuddered under the punishing attack.

{Release}

The word rang within my skull as much as it echoed from the walls, the sibilance giving it a hint of something vaguely serpentine. It seemed my summons was not going to go unchallenged. It was the worst possible circumstance, and yet I felt oddly reassured. I knew this adversary wouldn't have bothered appearing if there hadn't been a strong chance my efforts would be successful.

"Yield, Thanatos!" I said through bared teeth, calling death by its ancient, though by no means its oldest name. I willed more energy from my center to push back its assault. I could show no fear, for it would be the one chink in my armor that Thanatos would find and exploit.

{Mine}

Fetid winds pummeled me, trying to force me to release my grasp on the two dead men. I knew if I broke contact with them for even an instant, Thanatos would be able to seal them off from me forever.

I wasn't willing to give up now. Too much was at stake. I was going to get the answer I needed, once and for all.

I balled my hands into fists, clutching the hair of the men beneath me. I forced first one, then the other of my legs to lift up so I could struggle onto the table. Without being able to use my hands for balance it wasn't easy, but I wasn't interested in impressing Thanatos with a show of nimbleness and grace. There was just enough space between the dead men's heads and the edge of the table for me to kneel precariously.

"You want them back?" I yelled. "See what they bring with them!"

With a cry, I jerked their heads up so that they faced the hovering monstrosity in front of me. I changed the flow of my power, drawing it up rather than pushing it into the bodies, using it to suck the ram's blood out of their stomachs. I concentrated with all my might, forcing the blood into jets that shot with blinding speed towards the living darkness.

The still-hot fluid hit home, and horrible screams pierced the air. They sounded like multiple sets of iron claws dragging on a blackboard in rapid succession. I'd guessed correctly. The one thing death cannot abide is life, and fresh blood is the essence of life itself.

There were huge rents in the darkness where the blood had eaten through the material form Thanatos had temporarily adopted. But the demon-like terror was not gone by a long shot. It wasn't about to give up so easily. It closed the distance between us almost instantly, the head coming within inches of my own.

I struggled not to retch at the stench of rot that poured from the area where a mouth would be on a human. On this creature, it merely seemed to be an inky black aperture, darkness within darkness.

It rippled slightly as another single word oozed from deep within it.

{Release}

Numbness spread through my arms, and in a panic I looked down. I was still grasping the men, but I couldn't feel my hands. It was a psychic assault. Nothing was actually wrong with my nerves or muscles. But if I didn't maintain perfect control my hands could easily slip and let go of the prizes I was trying to win. Thanatos hadn't been able to scare me into submission, so it was going to try another tactic.

Too bad we'd sacrificed a ram instead of a bull. If I had more blood to work with I might have been able to disintegrate the form of Thanatos entirely. But there wasn't another easily accessible source of life-force.

Suddenly I remembered. Maybe I *did* have another weapon. I looked up. The bowl which had held the sacrificial blood was still floating above my head, right where I'd released it. It was caught up in the same nexus of power that surround me and the dead men. I recalled the word meaning "breath of life" engraved around the bowl, and understanding came to me. The words weren't just decoration.

They were an incantation. The bowl itself was a magical object, and it was still coated in blood.

It was my only chance. I reached out with my mind, felt the shape of the bowl as clearly as if I held it within my own hands.

"Now!" I screamed, using my mind to thrust the bowl down. It struck the jet-black form of Thanatos directly in the middle. Cries of pain and anger that would have frightened devils erupted from the dark specter, so loud that I thought my head would shatter.

I felt the table jar as if we were in an earthquake, and it took all of my focus to maintain my hold on the dead men that lay on it. Their eyes were wide open now, their mouths working as if they were trying to say something. Hard to tell, but it could easily have been a look of terror on their faces. Well, no blame there. They'd died horrible deaths, and were now faced with new horrors when they should have been enjoying peace.

I thought the form of Thanatos might simply disappear, but I should have known better. Nothing is simple in battles like that. Instead, it shattered into myriad shards that shot in all direction, like thousands of tiny arrows. The ones flying towards me vanished as soon as they hit the wall of power around me.

Light flooded the room. It was streaming from Pasiphae and Circe. Heracles and Orphne were behind them, shielded by the bodies of my aunts. The twins were glowing brilliantly, their own forms barely discernible as outlines within the radiance.

The daughters of the sun were living up to their heritage. The dazzling light sparkled blindingly as it hit the rest of the darts that were the parting shot of Thanatos. The projectiles seemed to absorb the light, swelled, then burst into glittering showers of diamond dust.

Unbidden, my power refocused on the task at hand, no longer divided between fighting Thanatos and trying to keep the dead men's souls linked to their body. Surges raced through me, hot and flashing, liquid fire that flowed down my arms into the men. I looked down and saw the two men glowing, their eyes fully open, chests moving up and down evenly.

Alive.

I couldn't break the contact. It was like an electric current was flowing through me; my muscles were locked, my hands immobile on their heads. All I could do was move my lips.

"SPEAK!" I commanded in a voice that echoed through the room. "TELL!" I knew I sounded almost as monotonous as Thanatos, but I could only force one word out of my mouth at a time. It would be enough, for my very will was being carried into their bodies.

Unintelligible gurgles bubbled up from their throats. Their eyes were wide and staring, but not comprehending. From somewhere beyond my field of vision I heard a voice. Orphne. She seemed to be shouting, but the words barely penetrated the sparking shell of power that was dancing around me.

"Too late! They drank from Lethe! They've forgotten all..."

No! I was being thwarted at every turn, taken down every useless meander on a path that could only lead, in the end, to the heart of evil.

I thought of Shannon, Monica, the men in front of me. I thought of Paul, killed to keep him from talking to me, then dragged out of his grave to be flung on the cold ground in a vineyard as a warning to me. His face swam in front of my own, marred by the claws of leopards so that even in death there could be no peace on his countenance, only a tale of violence and tragedy.

I was through. These corpses in front of me could not talk, but by Hecate, I was going to have answers once and for all.

"Then SHOW!" I don't know how it was possible, but the power seemed to triple in an instant. The dead men had already started to smoke, as they often do when fully reanimated by an outside power. They burst into flames that burned white-hot, leaping to the ceiling.

I flung my arms over my head, the power shooting from my hands in red and gold waves that merged with the glowing tongues of fire.

"SHOW!" I commanded again.

And the images appeared in the seething mass of fire and magic.

Smooth flesh, cool, seductive. A woman's laugh. A petal-soft kiss, gentle at first, then more insistent. A caress on the cheek, the feeling of silken skin trailing along the slight stubble of the unshaven man's face.

A hand running sensuously through hair. The fingers suddenly flexing, tightening in a sharp grasp that brings needle-hot points of fire across his scalp.

A tongue, warm and probing on his throat. Teeth slicing into exposed flesh, pressure enough to crush the Adam's apple. Sudden pain, thick and penetrating, deep within the gut, tearing though skin and muscle. Legs and arms held by countless hands more adamant than stone. More slashes against the back, each a stroke of lightning.

Hot floods of pain as the warmth of life bursts from the wounds. Cold metal pressing close to the searing gashes; silver cups flashing into view, filled with blood. A woman's face swimming into focus, mouth opened in expectancy and demand. Her brow crowned with ivy and vine leaves. Eyes unfathomable, demented, no longer human but an animal's cold orbs.

The sounds of voices screaming in triumph.

"IO! IO EVOE! IO! IO!"

A large hand covering the smaller pale-fleshed one holding a cup, taking the vessel from the pliant woman, who reaches up in ecstasy. The hand holding the cup lifts it up.

Darkness tunnels the scene, closing in rapidly from the edges as life finally gives up its struggle to stay.

A face turns, smiling lovingly as the silver cup comes to lips that part in sensuous abandon. Lips surrounded by a lush, elaborately curled beard. The eyes above the mouth burn green as the leaves of vines in bloom, the same vines that spring living and full from a brow framed by sable locks.

The face of a god. Dionysus. He holds the cup out to me.

"It's not too late. Join us. Join us, Medea."
The cup coming closer... closer...
Then the darkness took me.

Chapter 32

"Well, obviously you succeeded in getting the answers you wanted," Circe said happily. We were sitting around a table on the portico, refreshments flowing all around. The moon sailed in a cloudless sky as crickets and other night creatures sang to each other.

After waking up from my dead faint in Circe's chamber, I'd had a bath while the serving nymphs cleaned and repaired what was left of my clothes. By the time I was dry they were as good as new.

"Not to mention, you gave Thanatos a good thrashing for trying to interfere," Pasiphae added. She had a huge grin on her face. I could tell they were both proud of my accomplishment.

"That was a marvelous improvisation, Medea," Circe jumped back in. "You knew the dead men couldn't talk because their memories had been erased, but you figured out that their bodies would retain a rudimentary memory of what happened. I couldn't have done better myself!"

"Yes, calling up a vision was most inspired!" Pasiphae was practically trilling. "I actually felt what was going on as well as seeing it. Did you, Circe?"

"I did, sister," she affirmed. "That takes real power to accomplish."

I knew my own smile was only half-hearted. Something didn't seem right. "But where did that power come from? I've never been strong enough to reanimate the dead. Much less, beat back Thanatos. Even a priestess of Hecate has limits."

"Perhaps that's the problem," Orphne added. She was sitting a little apart from the rest of us again, occasionally sipping from the cup of nectar. "You've been a priestess since you were a girl. Had specific duties as a priestess. Have you pushed yourself beyond them, to see what you can really do?"

"You mean by tracking down a rogue god? No, it hasn't come up. Until now."

She ignored the sharpness in my voice. "Well, we all saw what happened to those men." She turned to Heracles. "You have enough to bring before the Olympians now."

He averted his gaze from me. "I wish I could say that. But there's a complication."

"Oh?"

He took a deep drink from his cup, filled with more of that choice wine the aunts always had on hand. "I saw what all of you saw, right enough. But that won't be enough to convince the Olympians."

I slammed my hand down on the table. "And what do they need? For Dionysus to rip off a human's head in front of them and gulp down the blood? Or would they prefer waiting until he's strong enough to take them all on? Because it could happen. You know it could."

He sighed. "Yes. The Curse of Prometheus. I haven't forgotten that blood makes him stronger. Or *would* make him stronger, if he's revived the maenads and started ordering human sacrifices again."

"Can you doubt it, after what you saw in my chamber?"

Circe was more shocked than angry, but the winds that blew her world could easily shift to anger without any warning. I wanted to defuse the situation before she said something she'd regret. I'd already trod the line between cynicism and sacrilege with my outburst, and Heracles had politely ignored it. He might not ignore another remark like that.

"It's because I'm a witch, isn't it?" I said, quietly but firmly.

He looked down again. "I'm sorry Medea, but that's the sum of it. I saw a vision, but because you have a... history... there might be suspicion that you conjured the whole thing up from your imagination, rather than working a true summoning. The Twelve would know magic from miracle, but I'm not one of them. My word won't be enough."

Pasiphae finally hit the furious level on her temper meter. "Her history didn't stop the gods from leaving her on Earth when the rest of us withdrew. They trusted her enough to work on her own to hunt demons!"

Circe, at least, was being reasonable for once. "Demons, sister. Not gods. This matter is so serious, the accusation so scandalous, that it will take far more than a vision to convince them."

"So I need more evidence," I said glumly as I took some of the pomegranate juice offered by a nymph.

"Perhaps you just need a repeat performance," Heracles said thoughtfully.

"Do I get to choose which exploit I repeat? I've had some fine ones."

"We'll leave that for another day," he said, his laugh grating on me rather than cheering me as it usually did. "By the way, I don't think anyone bought your excuse for that incident with Pompeii. After what Pasiphae did in the Mediterranean, it looks suspiciously like a family pastime."

"It was an accident!" I insisted hotly.

He was serious again. "But we can't afford another accident. When I said repeat performance, I meant you should get the other two dead men you're willing to work with, and bring them back as well. Call up another vision."

Pasiphae was beside herself. "You just said it wouldn't be enough!"

He held up a hand. "But I was talking about the vision being called up in front of *me*, rather than someone who would know whether it was mere sorcery or a true vision. Aside from the Olympians, Hecate would be an expert in that area. No?"

"You're asking me to call her, and try to bring the other men back in font of her?"

He nodded. "Hecate's word would be good enough for the high gods. It would be the best way. Assuming the other bodies retain the same sort of memories as those poor fellows you brought back."

"And if they don't? If they fell so that they never saw Dionysus drinking the blood?"

"We'll have a little bit of a problem, then. So perhaps we can dig up some more evidence when we return to the vineyard."

The reference to digging things up reminded me I had to at least go back and retrieve Paul's body. I owed him that much.

"All right. Let's get going."

Everyone started to rise, but I stopped Orphne with a glance. "You're staying here. You've helped me enough already. Heracles and I can get the bodies safely back to my home. Besides, we'll need the room in the backseat for all of the dead. I don't think you need to be there for the summoning."

No, indeed. Hecate would no more be fooled by the shape-shifting illusion from the Tear of Nereus than Pasiphae had been. As long as the aunts didn't know she was a fugitive, they wouldn't be blamed for offering her hospitality.

Orphne's expression told me she wasn't at all thrilled with the prospect of staying behind, but she said nothing. Instead, she rose and headed silently towards the palace.

"We'd be delighted to have your friend as a guest," Circe assured me. "I'm sure she has some delightful gossip."

No doubt. Too bad klatches had never been my thing. It would have been far preferable to stick around on Aiaia for awhile, eccentric aunts and all. It beat what was waiting for me back on Earth.

Chapter 33

I suppose I shouldn't have been surprised at all to find the bodies of Paul and the two remaining field hands were missing when Heracles and I stepped back into the vineyard.

"This is the same spot, isn't it?" he asked needlessly. I didn't bother answering.

"What now?" Heracles asked. I could have sworn he was pouting. It was probably a trick of the hazy light from the cloud-wrapped moon that sailed overhead. I resisted the urge to give him a comforting stroke on the cheek. I was about to suggest we head back to the car when I heard it.

Footfalls. Unmistakable, though faint.

Someone was coming. The occasional dry leaf crackled as it was crushed by otherwise muted footsteps. There was a whispering sound, as if something was dragging slightly in the grass. Heracles heard the sounds too, put a hand on my shoulder and moved to stand between me and the source of the noise. I peeked around his massive bulk.

The first one appeared at the end of the row of vines we were in, walking casually as if out for an evening stroll. Nothing out of the ordinary at all about the figure, except for the tall, slender staff it carried. The staff was about as thick as a broomstick, topped with a vaguely conical shape that seemed more menacing simply because it was indefinite. The figure turned slowly towards us, knowing we were there and not at all afraid of us.

Another one came up the same path and stood next to the first. I could hear more faint sounds behind us, and I didn't have to turn to know that route of escape would be blocked by more of them.

The maenads had come back to the scene of the crime. Or at least the scene of *one* crime.

Heracles turned to me. He was probably going to give me some sort of order. Stay down, keep close to me, don't panic—something along those lines.

I opted for none of the above.

I ran forward, letting loose a battle-cry I learned from my travels among the Celts. I held up both arms, and fireballs sprang into my cupped hands. With another cry I flung one of the blazing orbs towards the two figures in front of me.

I ignored the muttered curses from Heracles and flung the other fireball off to one side. I intended to set the vines on fire to help illuminate the battle. But the fireball sailed through the vines instead, barely burning the leaves.

It hit another target. It turned out a third maenad was standing just on the other side. I could tell from the sudden flare of light—and the screams—that she'd burst into flames as the fireball exploded on contact.

The two directly ahead of me were thrown off guard when my fireball hit the ground in front of them. They'd been quick enough to dodge the sparks and avoid their sister's fate.

One was shorter than me, barely five-six, and sported what was probably a stylish pageboy in better circumstances. She was naked, and her dark brown skin was glistening despite the chill of the night. There was absolutely no glimmer at all from her eyes. They were cold and dead, the same sort of eyes I had seen in the visions in Circe's palace and at the sorority house.

Her companion had red hair that swept past her shoulders. She had an athlete's build despite the fact that she was well into her forties. But there was nothing active and lively about her eyes. Like the other maenad's, they were a shark's eyes, soulless and cold.

The fires let me see what they were both carrying. I should have known what they were from the shape, not to mention all of the paintings and frescoes I'd seen of maenads. The staffs were lightweight, the color of pale bamboo. They were topped with gilded pinecones surrounded by small tendrils of ivy and vines.

The thyrsus. Legends said the maenads could cause milk or wine to well up from the ground by hitting it with the thyrsus. Most often, they were used as weapons.

Clearly the modern maenads had enough training to know that. The shorter woman in front of me shot a glance towards her smoldering compatriot one row over, bared her teeth, and launched herself at me full force.

I was prepared for the savage down-sweep of the thyrsus. I easily dodged the blow, grabbing the staff with both of my hands.

Searing pain lanced through my palms, but I put aside the surprise and focused on my defense. The maenad was in no mood to let go of her weapon so I changed tactics. I abruptly rolled down onto my back, bringing my feet up slightly and using the thyrsus to pull her with me. The sudden shift caused her to tumble forward.

Working with the momentum I thrust my feet into her midsection. A strong upward thrust of my legs sent her flying over and past me. She crashed into the vines behind us and lay motionless.

I quickly let go of the staff. Looking at my hands, I saw ugly lines of blisters on each palm. The damn thing had been coated with some sort of poison. I had no doubt the maenads were immune to it through their link to Dionysus. It couldn't kill me, but the pain from contact with the staff would be debilitating if I took too many blows.

I murmured a charm of healing and was relieved to see the blisters fill out and become unscathed flesh. But I couldn't keep pausing to mend myself during a full-out fight.

I glanced behind me and saw that Heracles had his own problems. Three maenads had rushed at him from behind. Two were attacking him with their staffs; the third was circling like a wolf ready for the kill.

I could tell there was something odd about the third maenad's hands, but the light wasn't good enough to see just what. They were bigger than they should have been. Maybe it was some sort of armored hand-cover?

I couldn't spare much time to think about it. The red-haired maenad was brandishing her thyrsus, approaching me warily but with plenty of determination. I doubted I'd be lucky enough to surprise her the same way I'd taken out her sister.

Turned out I was the one who got the surprise. From out of nowhere a huge dog sprang into her path, snarling and snapping.

I didn't know where the thing had come from, but it sure wasn't this world. I saw its red-gleaming eyes just before it turned to face my opponent. Its tail had spikes and was more serpentine than stiff; it whipped freely from side to side, discouraging assaults from the rear.

The next surprise came when it turned its head to me.

"Behind you!" The gruff voice was half-human, half-animal. But the thing seemed to be on my side, so I glanced over my shoulder.

The maenad I'd thrown off was back on her feet, trying to sneak up on me. Her thyrsus was closer to me. I lunged for it, snagged it and swung low.

The blow caught her just above the ankle, and I had a brief hope that I might have bruised her Achilles tendon. Her leg buckled. I dropped the staff, quickly murmuring the healing spell to deal with the poison wounds that had developed within just those few seconds.

She was struggling to her feet. I shifted all my weight to one leg, leaned back and lifted the other with the knee partially bent. I snapped my leg twice in quick succession, delivering two hard side-kicks to her midsection. I was rewarded with the sound of cracking ribs on the second blow.

The maenad gave a sharp grunt of pain and doubled over. Before she could recover I seized the advantage. I leaned back into the same stance and repeated the double kick, only this time my target was her throat.

There was a crack. Her eyes widened and rolled back. They didn't close even after she hit the ground. She lay there, motionless except for her left arm, which jerked violently. It seemed to spasm for an eternity before finally falling still.

I turned back to my canine ally, only to find Orphne staring back at me. There was blood on her hands. A glance past her told me why. The other maenad wouldn't be getting up again.

"What the hell are you doing here? And how—"

"I turned myself into a fly, got into your purse and changed into a stone so I wouldn't get crushed. You really should clean that thing out."

So she'd snuck back with me when I thought she was sulking in Circe's palace.

"I'm willing to face up to my mistakes, Medea. I'm not willing to leave a friend in trouble while I seek shelter on Aiaia."

It would have been a real choke-up moment if we hadn't been in the middle of a battle. But when I turned to see how Heracles was faring, it was clear the battle was over. I counted seven bodies lying around him.

Heracles stepped over the body directly in front of him and came towards me. The watery glow of the moon wasn't enough for my comfort. I conjured up two more fireballs and gave them a gentle toss into the air. They hovered about three feet above my head. At that point, I didn't care how visible they were.

Dionysus already knew I was there. The gauntlet was thrown.

As he stepped into the light from the floating fire I saw Heracles had taken several blows from the venomous staffs of his opponents. The poison had eaten through his tunic, but the raw wounds underneath were healing as I watched. I knew they probably hurt him, but the pain didn't show on his face. There was only grim determination there.

He was holding something up, obviously so I could see it, so I thought it best to turn my attention from his exposed torso to his hand. Better, anyway.

"Didn't think you'd stay behind, Orphne. Nice to see you again." Well yes, in her current form I imagined it *was* nice. He hadn't seen her a few moments ago.

"What do you make of this?" He thrust the object he was holding towards me. It was absolutely grotesque. Anyone else would have recoiled, but I couldn't resist grabbing it.

It was almost a human hand, but not quite. The thumb was about an inch up the wrist and was more towards the center of the forearm, rather than to the side. The palm itself was distorted with what appeared to be huge calluses. I touched them and realized they were actually soft, like the pads on a cat's foot.

The four fingers ended in sharp claws. They were not merely long curved human nails, but actual claws, thick and round, tapering to a deadly point. The pseudo-thumb had a similar claw, but it was much smaller.

The whole hand was covered in soft velvet-like down which seemed slightly tawny. That might have been a trick of the firelight, but I suspected not. It would fit in with the large spots scattered across the back of the hand.

The thing I was holding was some sort of hybrid between a human hand and a leopard's paw. "You got this from one of the maenads?" I asked Heracles, my eyes still riveted on the hand in front of me.

"Yes. Her other hand matches it. I hated to tear the thing off, but she was dead already. I didn't want to drag her over here with me. Thought you'd still be fighting the others, and I didn't want any encumbrances. But I see you've kept up your skills."

"I bet we had more fun than you, fighting a woman with hands like that."

"Well, she wasn't as challenging as the rest if that's what you mean. She didn't seem to have any heart for it, just kept taking weak swipes at me. No force behind them. It was almost as if she was sleepwalking."

Now that didn't sound right. The maenads Orphne and I had tackled fought wholeheartedly, if not skillfully. I decided I'd better get a close look at the others, because I had a suspicion I'd recognize one face there. And if the woman with the leopard hands was fighting poorly, I felt certain I knew whose face it would be.

"The hands weren't the only thing," Heracles said as we moved towards the cluster of bodies. "She looked—odd. In other ways."

Heracles pointed her out to me, but I examined the others first. All of them were strangers. I estimated their ages ranged from early twenties to mid-thirties. None would qualify as an old woman, like the one Lamia's note warned me about.

By the looks of things, Heracles had tried to make their deaths as quick and painless as possible. Most had broken necks, one a caved in skull. All of them were naked, most wearing circlets of ivy and vine leaves, and none of them had the heavy jewelry that I had seen in the Sybil's mirror.

I couldn't put off looking at the mutant maenad any longer.

As it turned out I did indeed recognize her, but I was still surprised. I had expected to be looking at Lyn O'Neill's face.

Instead, I was looking at her dead sister Shannon.

Chapter 34

"May Hecate damn the one who did this," I said through clenched teeth. But my voice sounded flat. I'd dealt with too much that day, and sometimes even a witch has her fill of horror.

Heracles put a hand on my shoulder.

"Have no doubt Medea. The one responsible for this will spend eternity in Tartarus." He knelt beside me and regarded Shannon. "You knew her?" I nodded.

"She's the one I told you about, the one whose death dragged me into this bloodbath. She was a beautiful woman. Look at what they did to her."

The morticians had done what they could, but even they couldn't replace the large chunks of flesh that had been torn out of her neck and arms. By her bridesmaids, I reminded myself. There were similar wounds along her legs. Huge tufts of hair were missing from her formerly silken mane.

Her torso had been sewn shut, and I could tell by the way it was done that it had been ripped open before the autopsy. Like Paul, Shannon had scratch marks across her face, but they seemed shallow. Probably caused by human nails.

"Do you want to take her?" Heracles asked quietly, though he already knew my answer.

"Yes," I said as I heaved myself up to a standing position. Heracles bent down to lift her.

"I suggest we get back to your vehicle with all haste," he said softly.

I willed the fireballs to move ahead of us to light the way. Thankfully I was in good enough shape to maintain a swift run, though Heracles could easily have outpaced me if he wanted. Orphne kept pace as well. We made to my car sooner than I expected.

I let the fireballs burn out while Heracles laid Shannon in the back seat. I glanced at Orphne. She waved off the unspoken question.

"I've dealt with the dead my entire life. I'm fine sitting next to her back there."

Well, better than changing into a pebble and riding back in my purse. I knew she was right; I really should clean the thing out. It seemed odd to strap a corpse in with a seat belt, but it seemed more improper to just dump her in there like a sack of potatoes. I gently laid her torn-off hand on her lap.

I dissolved the glamour that kept the car from ordinary view but put a smaller spell in place to keep Shannon's body from human sight.

Even a casual glance from someone in another car would be enough to give her away as a dead woman.

The headlights had a good wide beam and the path was fairly straight, so I gunned the car. We shot forward at a perilous speed. Heracles started turning to say something when his head snapped forward again. Something was ahead of us.

My mind barely had time to register his face.

It was Paul. He was directly ahead of us. His mouth was open, and he was pointing at us as if accusing us of something.

I slammed on the brakes, but we were going too fast. The car skidded and slid down the path. I drew in a horrified breath as we slammed into him.

Almost.

At the instant of impact, Paul's form disintegrated into a mass of dark-winged shapes. I heard the hoarse screams of ravens flying past the windows as the car finally came to a halt. It sounded like there were dozens of them.

For the first time that night my breath came in ragged gasps. The shock of seeing Paul alive—or somewhat alive, anyway—coupled with seeing him transform into a flock of ravens, was the lowlight of the evening.

"What the devil—" Heracles began.

"Closer than you think," I said. I took a deep breath and gunned the motor again. The car spun sharply to the right before we straightened out and shot past the wine shop. I turned the car too quickly to get on the road and we nearly spun out again.

Finally, we were out of the damnable vineyard. But I knew we were a far cry from getting out of the woods. Even if I made it to 400, at this time of night it would be miles before we hit any real traffic. I doubted it would deter Dionysus anyway. He'd launch an attack no matter how many humans witnessed it. Of that, I was more than certain.

"It seems the dead are coming back to life at a fast clip today," Orphne said after a few moments of tense silence.

"Well, at least it explains why Paul wasn't lying where we left him," Heracles observed.

"You don't really think that was him, do you?" I couldn't believe he'd be that gullible.

"He didn't resemble anyone else I've seen."

Message understood. Unless he saw Dionysus with his own eyes, he couldn't swear the wine god was involved in any of this. For all he knew, Paul was some sort of magician himself.

Or, it could be a trick from the witch, I reminded myself. Good enough to stay on Earth to clean up the garbage, but not good enough to be believed in anything else.

Time for licking my wounded pride later. "Just on the off chance that I'm not the only one reanimating corpses, could you tell me how you stopped Shannon?"

He thought a moment. "I actually didn't. She just sort of toppled over, like a puppet with its strings cut. I assumed she'd gotten hit by one of the other maenads by accident. It wasn't until you told me who she was that I realized she was dead to begin with."

I pondered that for a moment while I stepped on the gas a little harder.

"Do you think she's going to come back?" He sounded uneasy.

For a heart-jarring moment I had a flash of a horrific possibility: me glancing in the rearview mirror and seeing Shannon's corpse sitting up, eyes open, smiling at me. Proof that I've seen too many horror movies over the years.

"Doubt it," I said, with what I hoped was confidence. Just to be sure, I snuck a peek in the mirror. No grinning corpse. "But if she does, I'm glad you're with us. Glad to see you again."

It was more than just a friendly comment, and he knew it. "Well, I might have asked Zeus for leave to come back before now," he sighed. "But when I brought the subject up to Hebe, she said she'd rather stay on Olympus. Without my wife there'd be fewer complications, of course. But I knew that if I came to visit you without her to keep me in check, I might not want to go back."

So there it was, hanging between us. No way to ignore it now. But how long could I expect the two of us to tiptoe around a longing that had lingered for three thousand years?

It had been there ever since I sought refuge with Heracles after killing Jason's whore. Ironically we'd met because of Jason. Heracles was among those who came on his quest for the fleece. But when I fled to him for help, he was hardly the man I'd first met.

I found him in the midst of a blood-madness that caused him to kill his own sons. It took three days and nights, using the strongest medicines and magics I knew, to remove that madness. During much of that time he lay in my arms, alternating between crying like a heartbroken child and raving like the lunatic he'd become.

I joined him in both his crying and his raving, for the deaths of my sons were still fresh in my mind and haunted my dreams. Waking or sleeping I couldn't get the images of their bodies, drained and lifeless, out of my head. Or the dead look in Clymene's eyes that told me she was lost to me forever.

Perhaps, in riding the waves of terror and sadness along with Heracles and refusing to leave him, I found some healing myself.

Of course such intimate ceremonies are bound to have repercussions. When Heracles was himself again, he remembered that I'd been a port of safety during his vulnerability. After a few days he wanted to become vulnerable again, though this time willingly and with a clear head.

I knew the bonds formed during times of stress often fail the test of time. I declined Heracles' propositions and went my way. We didn't meet again until after he'd become a god, and by that time it was too late for there to be anything between us. Just as there couldn't be now.

"I would have welcomed the company," I finally said in answer to his unspoken proposal. "But you know I have one rule about love. And I won't break it."

He sighed again, turning to face the windshield and look out into the night.

"You won't have an affair with a married man," he said lamentably, as if I had sworn off sex altogether. Furthest thing from the truth. But that one stipulation was ironclad. Jason's love for Creusa had destroyed our marriage and, ultimately, our children. How could I be hypocritical enough to become another man's mistress?

Another deep sigh sounded through the car. I would have started to feel sorry for Heracles, except he wasn't the one who sighed. Neither was Orphne. I certainly hadn't.

I could sense Heracles tensing next to me. I really didn't want to look in the mirror, but there was no avoiding it.

At least it wasn't *exactly* like the horrible thought I'd had moments before. Shannon wasn't leering at me. Instead she was staring out of the side window. She reached towards it, oblivious of the damage Heracles had inflicted on one of her arms. The remaining warped hand made spastic grabbing gestures. It was almost as if she was reaching for something. She made unintelligible grunts as she strained upward, adding to the ghastly tableau.

Orphne had backed as far away from her as possible.

"Why are you still driving? Pull over so we can get rid of her!" she said urgently.

But I wasn't about to pull over, or even slow down so we could toss her out of the car. I knew exactly why she was reaching towards the window. She was trying to get to the one who had reanimated her, which meant Dionysus was closing in fast.

He wanted her back.

At first, I didn't really notice the sound. But then I realized I heard something aside from Shannon's desperate, wordless pleas filling the car. It was a jarring, erratic sound, and for a minute I thought something was wrong with the engine.

Then I recognized it. It was the sound of ravens screaming. Lots of them. They were getting closer.

Heracles heard them too. "He's right behind us," he said. I stepped on the gas pedal and the hoarse cries faded into the distance. But the borrowed time wouldn't last long. Those ravens weren't bound by the ordinary laws of physics. They'd catch up soon enough.

At first I thought the grunts from the back seat were getting shorter, until I realized Shannon was trying to say something."

"Aaaa-gaaa... AAA... GAAA," was what it sounded like. Merciful Hecate, was she trying to talk? And was it to us, or Dionysus? I knew beyond a shadow of a doubt she was beyond any help *I* could give her.

I was more worried about the rest of us. How was I supposed to outrun a god?

A thought came to me. "Heracles! Get us back to Aiaia!"

It was our only hope. He'd gotten us there before. Of course it was a lot different trying to transport a car driving at a hundred miles an hour, but we had no other options. For his crimes, which now included despoiling the dead, Dionysus would be powerless in any of the realms tied to Olympus.

That was his problem. Apparently we had one of our own.

"Now would be a good time," I said, trying to keep my voice steady.

"I'm trying!" Heracles snapped. "It's not working."

Shannon's moves were becoming more frantic. She was kicking the back of my seat but she hadn't thought to unfasten her seatbelt, thank Hecate. If she was even capable of thinking.

"How can it not work? You're a god, aren't you?" Orphne sounded as panicked as I was.

"He must be blocking me. He's one of the Twelve still, even if he's exiled himself." Great time for Heracles to join the believer's club.

I could hear the raucous clamor growing louder outside. We were sunk. I was out of options.

At least I thought so, but apparently I was in the minority.

"You try it, Medea," Heracles said with authority.

"What?"

"It's our only chance," Orphne practically screamed. "Dionysus may just be focusing on keeping Heracles from opening a portal. Maybe you can—"

Her last comment was cut off. I glanced in the mirror and saw Shannon spinning towards her, pummeling her with her hand and arms.

"Leeettt meeee gooo tooo heeerrrrr!" Shannon's rasping slur was horrifying, even to me.

I turned around again, concentrated on the road in front of us, and wished, with all my heart, that a portal to Aiaia would open.

Nothing.

I closed my eyes again, trying to remember how it felt to move through a portal, how it had felt when Heracles took us to Aiaia that afternoon. A slight shift, as if we were stepping just a little to the side of reality, then back in again. I tried to project that feeling out ahead of us on the road. But nothing happened.

Like waves of seawater breaking over the car, the birds started overtaking us. Their rough shrieks filled my ears.

Out of nowhere an icy vise gripped my throat, and it wasn't fear. Shannon had stopped her attack on Orphne. Her good arm— the less damaged one, anyway—had snaked around the side of my seat. Her forearm was pressed tightly against me in what would have been a total headlock if the seat hadn't been between us.

I was choking, clawing at her arm to break free. Orphne was trying to pull her off, to no effect.

"Leettt... meeee... gooo tooo... heerrrr," Shannon gasped. The words were as hoarse as the raven's cries, carried on a breath that stank of chemicals and rot. Adrenaline shot through me, but it wasn't the only thing increasing my metabolism. Something else was reaching out from inside me, roused by my sudden fear and desperation to be out of there.

"By the balls of Zeus, open!!" I screamed as I flung my arms straight out.

The glow started subtly in front of us, but in less than a second it blossomed fully until it looked like we were racing straight into the sun.

The ravens surrounding our car shrieked and did improbable flips, flowing backwards over the car as if they were being repelled by an unseen barrier. A horrible scream burst from Shannon as her arm suddenly whipped back from my throat.

I struggled with the wheel, but it was too late. The orb of light in front of us was huge, and there was no time to react.

We were going into it no matter what.

Chapter 35

Aiaia was the first place on my mind, but the furthest place from where we landed. We sailed at top speed into the glowing aperture before me. The light intensified for a second then abruptly faded.

The car's engine roared momentarily as the wheels spun on something not-quite-there during the transit. But as soon as the glow died they squealed as they hit pavement again.

I had only a moment to react when I noticed other lights around us. Houses. Wherever we were, it was not Aiaia. I slammed on the brakes, praying there was nothing too close in front of us. We screeched to a stop.

I waited for an enormous cloud of birds to descend on us, but it didn't. There was only the pounding of my heart in my ears, a sharp intake of breath from Heracles, and a horrible burning smell.

I ignored the stench and took several deep breaths. Silence. I glanced hesitantly out the window.

We were on my street. We'd skidded to a halt less than one house from mine. Good brakes, thank Hecate.

Instinct told me the immediate danger was over. I eased down to my driveway and turned in. I waited until I was in the garage to glance at the back seat.

There was nothing left of Shannon but a few pieces of smoking flesh clinging to some charred bones. From what I could tell the rest of us were fine.

I quickly shut the garage door. Hopefully none of the neighbors had seen my car materializing out of nowhere in a flash of light.

"Welcome to Atlanta," I said weakly to Heracles.

He opened the door with a relieved grunt. "A good escape. But couldn't you have managed an incantation that didn't mention my father's balls? He tends to get sensitive about things like that."

Fine words from a fellow whose own balls had been on the line a few seconds ago. "I'll try to think of something better, assuming I can figure out how I pulled it off to begin with."

Orphne was easing out the car. "It did the trick, all right. Did you see how those birds were flung back by the light?"

I leaned down and peered through her still-open door. "Not to mention what it did to Shannon. And I'm guessing the reason it destroyed her body and left us unscathed was because she was in thrall to Dionysus."

Which meant I might have a potent weapon against another assault by maenads. But it could have been dumb luck, or even outside intervention from another source.

147

Perhaps Hecate herself had decided to get involved?

Speculation was pointless at the moment. "Orphne, take Heracles inside. You can both wash yourselves upstairs. Just show Heracles where my bathroom is. And Heracles, could you take Shannon's remains upstairs? There's a small storage room just off mine. I've got an old settee in there, and some spare sheets as well. You can wrap her—it— up and leave the bundle on the settee."

He smiled. "I can do better than that." With a snap of his fingers Shannon's body was gone, and my charred backseat was restored. The smell of burned flesh was gone as well. "I may not have been able to get us away from Dionysus, but I've still got some power."

"We're going to need all we can get," I said, not bothering to match the levity in his tone.

While they headed upstairs I slipped down to the basement. Peter was still asleep, and from the looks of the chains and his clothes he hadn't moved even a fraction of an inch.

I couldn't keep him down there forever, though. But another hour or two wouldn't hurt. I raided the chest freezer, snagging a pint of praline ice cream. My supply was getting low, but I had other priorities. Maybe Heracles could snap his fingers again and replenish my stores.

Orphne caught me at the desk in my study, eating straight out of the container. "More fluff and sugar," she sighed. "Good thing you're an immortal. Otherwise you'd be in the grave, judging by how much of that you pack away."

"It's stress eating," I said around a mouthful of ice cream.

"Did it myself back in the day. I once ate an entire boar after a particularly tough battle." Heracles said jovially as he walked into the room. His hair looked great even when it was still wet, but what really caught my attention were the jeans and T-shirt he had on. I knew he couldn't possibly have squeezed into anything I owned. And were those Sketchers?

He caught my glance. "I figured I might as well blend in with the locals. I assume we're going out again once we regroup. And I also assume you've got some weapons at hand?"

I feigned an insulted look. "Sorry I asked," he laughed.

Orphne poured herself a brandy before heading to the couch. "An extremely busy night it's been. Wonder if we'll have any further trouble."

"I'm thinking not," I said slowly as I leaned back in my chair. "I bet Dionysus was as surprised as anyone at what happened. I have no doubt that flock of birds was just one of his manifestations, and they looked like they got a pretty good jolt from that light."

"Speaking of which—" Heracles began, but I cut him off.

"I have no idea where it came from."

"Maybe it has something to do with your ancestry," Orphne put in. "Helios is your grandfather, after all. And remember what the aunts did on Aiaia, when Thanatos disintegrated into thousands of little missiles."

A good point. They'd called up a brilliant flashing light to combat his deadly darkness.

"Maybe it was the stress that gave you the boost you needed to open a portal yourself," Heracles said thoughtfully. He poured a scotch and tilted the decanter in my direction. I shook my head. He shrugged and took his glass over to the couch, sitting next to Orphne.

I brought my ice cream over, along with the small cloth bundle that no one had noticed on my desk. "I'll think about that later. Maybe I can practice, but it seems a bit dangerous to try in close quarters. All we can do is hope he doesn't try to attack us here. I've warded the place, but..."

I didn't need to finish the thought. "Well, he's probably trying to figure out what you did as much as we are. Maybe we can get some rest tonight," Heracles seemed to be more at ease already.

I unwrapped the bundle. It was Shannon's mutilated hand, the one Heracles had torn off. It had rolled under the car seat during her struggles and somehow had missed being destroyed by the light.

After a moment's study Heracles spoke. "Now that I see it in the light, it looks like some kind of animal paw."

"A leopard," I said firmly, indicating the spots on the back. He nodded agreement.

"But why would Dionysus do that to her?" Orphne asked as she leaned forward to examine it.

"I don't think he did. I think someone else did." They both looked up. "Do you remember what she was saying in the car?"

It took a second, but Orphne finally sat back with a look of understanding. "She said 'Let me go to her.' Not '*him.*' That's what she would have said if she meant Dionysus."

Heracles frowned. "I don't understand. Who was she talking about then?"

"Agave," Orphne and I said together. He sat back and exhaled deeply.

"More bad news, if she's involved. The woman was insane on her best days, worse still on most others."

"Shannon did make those sounds at first. 'Aaaa-Gaaa'. Remember?"

He shivered a bit and nodded. "You're right," he said. "She could very well have been calling for Agave."

"It would bear out what Lamia said in her note to you," Orphne added. "The old woman who was at all of the murders."

"But perhaps she's no longer an old woman," I mused as I took another spoon of ice cream. "Her soul may have taken over Lyn's body. It would be much more convenient, especially since Lyn now owns the vineyard."

"Whatever form she's taking, it's likely Dionysus has made her his high priestess," Heracles said flatly. "He'd want to reward her for the devotion she showed him."

"But why would she do this to Shannon?"

I'd been wondering that myself, but a cold realization was creeping through me. It was true, leopards were sacred to Dionysus, but that wasn't their only link to these atrocities.

Unbidden, Paul's last words rang through my mind.

It's her!

I exhaled heavily as I realized the extent of the horror. Paul had been lured into the leopard's cage, not thrown there by frenzied maenads or even Dionysus himself.

Lured by seeing his beloved Shannon in the cage with the deadly cats. And unlike mortals in the old days, who had sense enough to stay away from anyone who was supposed to be dead and clearly shouldn't be walking around, he'd rushed into danger, heedless of the risk to himself, not knowing what she'd become.

He'd died horribly, all because of his love for her. And the murder weapon was lying right there on my coffee table.

Chapter 36

"This is a lot to consider," Heracles sighed as he sank back into the couch. He took a healthy swig of his drink.

"All the more because Agave may be just down the street," Orphne added. That perked up Heracles' attention.

"Then all we have to do—"

"Is forget about it," I said. "I have no intention of trying to take her on face-to-face tonight. She's probably up at the vineyard with Dionysus. Even if she's at home we'll likely just walk right into another trap. We need to have a plan first."

Heracles threw his hands up in frustration. "So we just sit here and wait? For what?"

I shook my head. "We try to go back to the vineyard tomorrow. Try to catch Dionysus on his home turf, so to speak."

"And then? He prevented me from bringing us to Aiaia, and now he's preventing me from going back to Olympus to report his misdeeds. I know. I tried several times since we arrived at your home. He's strong enough to keep me bound to Earth until the end of time."

"I would hope that before then, whoever sent you down here would send out a rescue party," Orphne observed dryly. "He can keep you here, but could he restrain one of the high gods?"

He considered that a moment. "Maybe sitting here doing nothing isn't a bad idea, then."

"But in the meantime, who knows how strong Dionysus could grow? How many he might kill to satisfy his blood-lust?" I countered. "We can't sit around for days on end, even if it seems like the most likely way to get your patron down here."

"So we go back to the vineyard and he attacks us again? How does that help?" He drained his glass impatiently.

"If we walk back into his territory willingly, he may hold off the attack," I responded quietly. "We seem to have something he wants. Me."

The two of them just stared. "He said it twice: in the vision at the sorority house, and the vision I called up on Aiaia. 'Join us, Medea'. It was the same message I heard when I saw the vision in the Sybil's mirror. If I go up there willingly, he may assume I'm ready to talk terms."

Heracles almost broke his glass when he slammed it down on my coffee table. "You can't be serious! If he gets his hands on you—"

"He can't do anything. He can't do any violence, or try to coerce me with his power. I'm Hecate's priestess, remember? I'm under her sanctuary. If he does anything to me, he'll be in even more trouble. Instant trouble. You know how quickly *they* respond in cases where sanctuary is violated."

The room was silent for a moment. Heracles and Orphne knew who I was talking about. *They* were the Erinyes, the hideous avenging spirits who sought out and brutally punished the worst sins against the gods, including violence against sworn priests and priestesses. Zeus had given them leave to hunt down anyone—even a god—who violated the rules of sanctuary.

"The madness from the Curse of Prometheus surely is taking hold by now," Heracles said. "He may not remember—or care—about the rules."

"All the better," I said. "If he does violence to someone under sanctuary, the Erinyes themselves will come and he'll be caught red-handed, with no defense."

"We were just attacked, if you remember," he countered. "They didn't come to our rescue."

"The ambush in the vineyard might just have been an attempt to bring me to him. He didn't attack me himself. And it's a sure bet the maenads didn't know who I was, because they probably don't even remember their own names. The rules of sanctuary deal with intentional sacrilege. Mindless pawns don't merit attention from the Erinyes."

"And if he's coherent enough to remember that, and keeps using his pawns to attack you?" Orphne said after a moment.

"There's a very good chance he'll tip his hand some other way, probably in front of Heracles." I turned to him. "They may not take the word of a witch, but they Olympians wouldn't ignore *your* word. He may be able to prevent you from returning to Olympus to rat him out, but Orphne was right. Eventually, whoever sent you will get curious and send down reinforcements. We may just have to be patient after all. But at least this way, we'll be in a better position to get firm evidence.

"Otherwise, when the rescue party arrives, what do we tell them? That women we *think* were maenads attacked us? That's no proof at all, any more than the vision you saw with me on Aiaia. As you pointed out, I could have made the whole thing up. I could just as easily drug a dozen or so women and make them think we were some sort of threat to them."

"But why would you do that?" Orphne seemed truly puzzled. "What possible motive could you have?"

I looked at Heracles, but he avoided my gaze. I'd figured out why he brought up those doubts about the vision, and more importantly, why he'd voiced them in front of the aunts.

"Revenge," I finally answered. "It could be claimed that I was trying to exact revenge on Dionysus for what happened to Pasiphae. She's my kin, after all, and it's because of what he ordered his servant Theseus to do that she abdicated her queendom. Theseus slew Megalitheros, remember? And kidnapped his sister Ariadne. Both were my cousins, so I would be avenging them as well as my aunt if I could get Dionysus in trouble."

She nodded slowly. "So if he plays his cards right, we might just end up in a stalemate. No proof either way of his guilt or innocence. And as I've learned from television, humans nowadays assume people are innocent until *proven* guilty. I doubt the Olympians will have lower standards."

Heracles frowned. "Television?"

Orphne leaned forward eagerly. "You absolutely *must* see it. It's fascinating! And since it looks like we have a little time tonight…" She shrugged, trying to make it casual. I knew it was anything but. The only working television in the house was in her bedroom.

Well, why not? No reason to deny her a little fun. I'd play along with it.

"You might as well, Heracles. We're going to have a long day tomorrow one way or another. Get some rest tonight while you can." Or not, if Orphne had her way.

Orphne rose, but Heracles stayed put. "Upstairs, is it? You go on. I'll be up in a few moments. I have to talk with Medea about something private."

She smiled gamely, not at all put off at being shooed away. "I'll find something interesting to put on." I had no idea whether she was referring to television programming or clothes, but it was probably both.

"What's up?" I asked as I dug into the remaining ice cream. Heracles looked more serious than I'd ever seen him. I put a hand on his arm. "I know it's a dangerous plan, going up to the vineyard. But we don't have any choice."

"You seem to think he wants you. Why?"

I was too tired to even feign being insulted. "I don't know. But he has more of a reason to win me to his side now, if I have some way of hurting him. Which apparently happened when I jetted us back here. But wouldn't it be enough to have someone with my power—and my knowledge of modern Earth—as an ally? He's moving into uncharted territory by coming here. Agave might learn things from possessing Lyn's body but like they say, two heads are better than one."

"I agree," he sighed. "But I want you to know, I truly believed the vision showed me the truth on Aiaia. I hate playing devil's advocate, but I have no choice in these matters. I know you'd never deceive me."

I squeezed his arm, then pretended to busy myself with the ice cream. The touch had reminded me of what I couldn't have, even if I wanted it.

He kept his eyes on me. "I wonder, though, if you aren't deceiving yourself."

I stopped with the spoon halfway to my mouth. A blob of ice cream hit the coffee table, but I didn't put the spoon down. "What are you talking about?"

He put a gentle hand on my arm, guiding it down until the spoon was back in the container. "I know Dionysus wronged your family, but you have to believe me in one thing. I've lived with him for nearly two thousand years. Medea, he has absolutely no reason—*none*—to revive his cult or leave Olympus. No reason at all to risk being expelled, cast into Tartarus. So you have to ask, what made him do these horrible things? What made him bring back his blood-cult and start accepting human sacrifices again?"

I hadn't really considered motive. Power seemed enough motive to me, but when you were already nearly omnipotent, how much more power did you really need?

"Well," I began hesitantly, trying to parse it out as I went along, "you said it yourself. Accepting human sacrifices *again*. He did it before, and went partially mad before the Olympians accepted him and he was healed. Maybe the healing didn't take, and he's slipped back into his old ways. Like a drunkard willingly falling off the wagon."

He frowned again. He might have the Gift of Tongues like the other gods, but it didn't always confer the ability to understand idioms. "That sounds like a very dangerous thing for a drunken man to do."

The sidetrack, humorous as it was, had given me time to think. "Drunks don't always fall off the wagon. Sometimes they're pushed."

He understood that, right enough. "Exactly where I was going. What if he was tricked into doing this? I don't think, once a god has tasted blood, that the desire ever leaves them again. He may be able to stop himself from willingly taking blood, but what if it wasn't willing?"

I felt a little dizzy and sat back. "What if someone gave it to him without his knowledge? Put it in his wine, maybe? And once he tasted it..."

I didn't need to finish the sentence.

"The woman in the mirror," I said weakly. "The woman with the dead body. Maybe that's why the mirror showed her to me. Maybe she killed the man and took his blood, and gave it to Dionysus without his knowledge. Bringing the madness on him again."

Heracles nodded. "Just so, Medea. Dionysus has no reason to do it on his own, but I can think of at least one who has a reason for *luring* him into doing it. Someone who has access to Olympus as well as her own realm, and therefore has the opportunity to surreptitiously taint his wine or food with blood."

There was no reason to go any further with the conversation. It was clear he was talking about Pasiphae.

Was I being blind, and ignoring the possibility that she might have plotted Dionysus' downfall? Heracles was right. She had everything:

motive, opportunity, and means. Circe was able to capture humans and bring them to Aiaia to change them into beasts. Pasiphae was as powerful as Circe. She could do it as well, and use the humans for other things.

"I don't want to speak ill of your kin, Medea, but you know what Pasiphae did when she still held Minoa in her thrall. You know she sent humans down to the labyrinth for her son the Minotaur to eat, forced vassal kingdoms to send their finest youth to sate his hunger. She certainly has no compunction about killing."

"Megalitheros," I corrected him. I hated it when people referred to him as simply the Minotaur. He had a name. And terrible as he was, it was mostly due to the circumstances of his birth rather than innate evil.

Heracles didn't respond to that, but he let go of my arm. I restrained myself from grabbing his hand again. I needed the contact. Needed something to take me away from what I'd seen and heard that day, something to prove that I didn't always have to be strong alone.

Maybe he was waiting for it too. When I didn't move, he stretched easily and got up.

"I'll be interested to see what Orphne has to show me."

Well, no doubt it would be a show all right, although he might find himself part of the main act. But maybe they'd just settle for watching an old movie.

I sat quietly for awhile after he left, trying calm and focus myself. It wasn't working.

I told myself a little more ice cream might help. Later, I'd try to tell myself that was the initial reason I went down to the basement. Of all people, a priestess of Hecate should know best about the innocent intentions that pave the road to Hades.

Chapter 37

Peter looked so peaceful lying on the basement couch I forgot about the ice cream. It was pleasant just to watch him sleep, breathing evenly as if he didn't have any cares.

I remembered how my great-aunt Selene, goddess of the moon, had fallen in love with the beautiful shepherd Endymion. She'd put him into a magical slumber so that he would never age or die. She bore him many beautiful children too, lying with him while he slept. Although he didn't wake, she assured me he dreamt of holding her in his arms, so that he could have pleasure in it too.

I cursed under my breath as I realized why my thoughts had turned that way. The close contact with Heracles had awakened the old longing. Now it throbbed dully in my muscles, and deeper still in more intimate parts. That's the downside of being half-nymph. Once I'm turned on, turning off is hard.

There were two ways to go. I could sit around and wait for it to abate by itself. It would take hours, and I'd be miserable, but it would happen.

Or, I could take steps to satisfy my needs.

The irony was, the man who'd churned up those needs to begin with was now upstairs, happily sporting with Orphne. My iron-clad rule about married men kept me from going to him.

I swore again, frustrated with my own inflexibility as well as the image of him with Orphne. Well, he wasn't the only man in the house.

I knew it was reckless beyond belief. I had no idea who Peter really was or why he was immune to my hypnotic gaze. But I had other ways of bespelling a man, and they were much more satisfying than just looking him in the eyes.

Before I knew it I was kneeling down next to the couch, slipping off the chains which kept him bound. I looked at him a few more moments, savoring the angle of his jaw, the slight stubble on his face that made him seem more rugged.

I gently stroked his cheek. He turned slightly, nuzzling into the touch. The response pushed the heat within me up a few notches.

My other hand slid down his torso, and I relished the firmness of him. I slid my hand up under his shirt. The contact with his warm flesh increased the need I felt. I leaned closer to him, mingling my breath with his. His head tossed slightly when I began stroking his chest.

The need was too strong now, and unlike Selene I had no intention of satisfying myself with an inert partner.

My lips found his. My tongue slipped gently inside his mouth, parting his lips a bit. Slowly sinking into the new contact I half-whispered, half-sighed the incantation to wake him.

I could feel his eyelashes fluttering against my face as his lids eased open. He was still in a partial stupor, but that wasn't the reason he was so still. Even though I was only half-nymph, that first kiss was enough to have him completely in my spell.

The kisses continued for a long time, each of us giving and taking, moaning slightly. A small voice, what was left of my conscience (I don't give it much exercise), chastised me for seducing a priest sworn to celibacy. That voice was quickly drowned out by other sounds that were much more compelling.

His hands slid up my arms and across my back as I climbed onto the couch. My hands slowly worked his shirt up until it was just at his shoulders.

He stopped a moment, looked at me. His eyes were confused, but there was no resistance there.

"Where—"

"A safe place," I murmured as I coaxed him to lift his arms over his head so I could finish slipping off his shirt. I allowed myself a moment to savor his form, which was much nicer than I'd imagined it would be. He wasn't overly-developed, but fine muscles stood out clearly along his stomach and sides.

His hands found my arms again, but I pulled back slightly so I could take off my shirt as well. Knowing exactly where this was going, and having no compunction about it, I quickly slipped out of my jeans.

He tentatively raised a hand to touch my stomach, giving me petal-soft caresses. Odd how such a light touch could make me feel even more urgent...

"Shouldn't do this," he murmured, very unconvincingly. The argument really fell flat when he reached around my back and drew me down again.

We explored each other, touching, tasting, each move more certain, more insistent. Within a few moments I was completely naked, thanks to some surprisingly skillful moves on his part. Well, just because he was supposed to be celibate *now* didn't mean he hadn't practiced earlier in life.

A low vibration shook through me, and it took a moment to realize it wasn't just my response to him. A brief flash of light came from the darkened laundry area next to the finished portion of the basement, followed by another low thrum. There were windows in there; it must be a late-season thunderstorm.

Peter's attentions quickly drew my focus back where it belonged. My breathing was getting more labored, and his was absolutely ragged. The hunger quickly grew, and it was as delicious as the method of satisfying it promised to be.

The thunder was coming closer and more quickly as the storm intensified. It seemed to mirror the waves of our passion. Peter was clinging to me as if he had no other hold on the world. Maybe, at that moment, he didn't.

It was too much. I had to do something—now.

I moved over him, feeling him ready. He slipped into me easily, so smoothly that I briefly marveled at it. For a priest, he was really good at this.

But that idle musing quickly flew out the window as rational thought gave way to pure sensation. We were moving together now, a tandem race to reach a goal we both wanted badly. We weren't separate any longer, but one.

The lights in the basement flickered just as the first spasms of release began from deep inside me. Such delightful little tickles, but they quickly intensified until they were clutching me. We were half-sitting at that point, and suddenly I felt my insides giving way as I fell back, my legs and arms wrapped around Peter, bringing him down on top of me.

I moaned, a staccato tattoo that made my throat feel raw. The thunder crashed outside, a counterpoint to my screams. Peter was groaning too, deeply, as if he was experiencing pain as well as pleasure.

He started jerking against my grasp. "No—"

"*YES!*" I screamed as my legs pulled him closer. He gave a wordless gasp, then a short cry. Another, and another. His grip around me tightened, making it nearly impossible for me to draw in a breath. I felt myself getting lightheaded.

Wave after wave of release surged through me, concentric circles of pure pleasure. The thunder outside was so loud now my ears rang.

Peter stiffened, and I felt his own release as a scream broke from him. Thunder crashed again and again as the lights flickered, faded, came back.

Peter's grip was crushing me, but I didn't care. I could feel huge spasms across his back, as he bucked and sank into me. But it wasn't just a normal response. No, not by a long shot. We were locked in such a tight embrace that I could see clearly over his shoulder. Slowly, something filled my vision as my body shuddered from seemingly endless spasms.

Just before another flash of lightning sent the lights in the room out for good, I saw an enormous pair of white wings emerging from Peter's back.

Chapter 38

My cries were as much from shock as from the final throes of pleasure. My mind desperately wanted to run away, but my body had its own thoughts.

It was several seconds before I could even think about making my arms follow my commands. In that interval I felt soft brushes against my outer legs, and I knew those huge wings that had erupted from Peter's back were gently fluttering.

"I'm sorry... I'm so sorry," he gasped. "Oh God, I'm so sorry..."

Was he apologizing to me or to his god? In the corner of my mind, the cynical thought arose that he'd be better off asking forgiveness from his god, because there was at least a small chance of getting it. None whatsoever with me.

My arms finally were ready to listen to my brain. I yanked them away from his back, feeling the slowly fanning wings slide across them. The touch raised goose pimples.

Just as Peter started to roll to one side I jerked my body in the opposite direction. I had to shove my hands into his chest to get him to move off my body enough. He drew in a sharp breath but gave me the room I needed.

I heaved myself free and tumbled off the couch, scrabbling away on my hands and knees until I was almost to the steps. The flashes of lightning were more intermittent, but they were enough to let me see where I was going.

A sudden pounding on the steps told me help was on the way.

"Medea!" Heracles bellowed.

There was more than one set of feet on the steps. Orphne was with him, unless Heracles had become a centaur. Considering how things were going that evening, it was a possibility.

"There's a problem!" she yelled just as Heracles cleared the last step. A second before she hit the floor the lights came back on.

Suddenly they only had eyes for Peter, never mind that I was sprawled on my hands and knees on the floor. Naked, to boot. Both of them were still fully clothed, I noticed.

"I stand corrected," Orphne murmured as she took him in. "We have two problems, and it's hard to say which is more interesting." Peter was frantically trying to pull up and refasten his pants.

"By my father's beard," Heracles said softly. "What have we here?"

"Hello!" My sharp tone brought their attention back to me. "We have me, on the floor, crawling frantically away from... from..." I gestured halfheartedly towards Peter.

"From whatever he is," I grumbled as I held out my hand. Heracles took the cue and helped me to my feet. "And I'm fine, thanks for asking."

"I thought he was in some kind of enchanted sleep?" I could see the corner of his mouth twitching as he raised an eyebrow, trying, I supposed, to look authoritative. I wasn't having it. All of my pent-up desire had been worked out, and if any was left it would have been scared straight out of me by what was now huddled in the corner of my couch.

Peter reached out a tentative hand to touch one of the wings. "God," he whispered. "God, God, God, I'm sorry. What have you done to me?"

"Get off it!" I snapped. "Don't even pretend that this is some kind of surprise. Who or what are you? And don't bother telling me you're some kind of angel. No angel has moves like the ones you just made with me!"

"I don't want to interrupt, but we have something else to deal with," Heracles said, putting a hand on my arm. "I'm sure this can wait. He won't be going anywhere." He gently tugged me towards the steps.

"Stay with him," I told Orphne, hoping she knew the harshness in my tone wasn't directed at her. "Don't take your eyes off of him."

She half-smiled at that. "That'll be an easy promise to keep."

Heracles bounded up the steps but I took them one at a time, a little reluctantly at that. I'd had enough aggravation for the night. I didn't need something else on my plate.

"You'll want to put something on, unless the neighbors are very liberal." He was heading for the front door.

"Not by a long shot," I muttered. I pulled my London Fog out of the closet and belted it around me. We stepped outside into a steady fall of rain. There were still muted flashes and thunder rolls overhead, but nothing like there'd been a short time ago.

I threw my hands up. "This is what you wanted to show me? I know they don't have anything but wonderful weather on Olympus, but surely you haven't forgotten what rain is."

He walked towards the street. "It's not quite the way I remember it. Come along. You'll see what I mean."

I quashed the sound of annoyance rising in my throat and trotted to catch up with him. The rain seemed to be easing.

He strode across the street. "Over here. You'll get the picture."

The invective I'd chosen stopped at the tip of my tongue as I stepped out into the street.

And out of the rain.

I'd known rain to stop abruptly before, but this was different. Mostly, because I could still hear the rain behind me.

I think I knew what I was going to see before I completed my slow turn. Something at the back of my mind said not to look, but I had to. Heracles was standing there with his arms folded.

"Any ideas?" Damn him anyway, if he wasn't smirking when he said it.

I didn't find anything at all funny about the fact that the storm was centered over my house—and *only* my house. The clouds, with their soft flashes of lightning and gentle peals of low thunder, were directly overhead. The sky over the rest of the street was clear, faint stars sparkling overhead.

"Shit," I said with real passion. "Shit, *shit, SHIT!*" Stamping my bare foot repeatedly on the asphalt to punctuate the curses hurt like hell, but I didn't care at that point.

"Shall I hazard a guess that this has something to do with what you were up to with our winged friend?"

The anger and shock were fading, but they weren't gone. I began pacing.

"I don't know. I don't know what happened with Peter. But the storm came up just as we were..." I let the rest hang, but he'd gotten the message.

"Remember Pompeii," he said with a teasing note in his voice.

"Accident! It was just... an... *accident!*"

"An accident that conveniently happened as you were getting... acquainted... with a very unusual young man down on a nearby beach. An unusual young man who, it turned out—"

"Was the son of Poseidon and a mortal woman," I finished weakly as I sat down on the curb. Not a soul was stirring, not even a light as far down the street as I could see.

I leaned back a bit and jumped as I got splashed by the rain that was still falling resolutely on my yard. It felt better to lean forward and put my head in my hands anyway.

"I don't need this. I don't need something else. Tonight of all nights, I don't need this."

Heracles crossed the street and sat down next to me. "Cheer up. It could be worse. It could have been another Vesuvius. Or maybe some other horrendous disaster. At least we weren't buried like Pompeii."

"It's disaster enough, isn't it?" Still, I shivered a bit at what could have happened. We were nowhere near a volcano, but the New Madrid fault was close enough that it might have decided to give way during my little escapade. Just because the Earth moved for me, didn't mean it had to move for millions of other people. I decided to count my blessings.

"Mixed bloods, Medea. Mixed bloods can call up very unusual phenomena when they mate. Perhaps it's best we never were more than friends. Even when I was mortal, I was still half-god."

The rain was tapering off behind us. If there was any luck to be had, I hoped it would be enough to ensure that no one had bothered looking out their window to see a storm drenching only my house that night.

"I suppose we'd best figure out who and what Peter is, and whether he's any threat." Heracles rose, holding out a hand without prompting this time. I took it and let him pull me up.

"Just what I needed. Another mystery."

He trudged back through the grass. "Maybe this one will be easier to solve." He sounded nonchalant enough about it. I tried to let the mood infect me, but it kept its distance. I felt like one of the storm clouds hovering over my house had just floated down and taken up permanent residence over my head.

Chapter 39

By the time we got back inside I was so disheartened that I couldn't work up enough strength to get mad when I found Orphne and Peter in the study.

"He said he needed a drink," Orphne explained before I could ask. "You didn't say anything about keeping him in the basement, just keeping him in sight. Which I did."

I'd played the cheerful hostess with far worse than a winged lover, but the effort seemed truly monumental at that moment.

Heracles went over to the bar to pour himself a drink as well. He frowned when he picked up the decanter. It was seriously depleted.

"How much of that have you had?" I turned to Peter. He was slumped into the couch, a half-empty glass—no ice—in his hand.

"That's his third," Orphne answered for him. Peter didn't look like he was in good enough shape to form much of an answer himself.

"Well I certainly hope he is half-god. Or half-something," Heracles shook his head. "We weren't gone for more than a few minutes. I don't think the human body is made to take that much alcohol that quickly."

"The human body certainly isn't made with wings," I reminded him. "Keep an eye on him. And this time, don't let him go anywhere. We're going to get to the bottom of this."

It took longer than I anticipated to find what I needed in my sanctuary. I'd buried the box in a chest. The delay gave me time to do a little thinking, and by the time I got back to the study I had a rough game plan.

"Is that what I think it is?" asked Heracles when he saw what was dangling in my hand. Peter was still conscious, rocking softly back and forth. It wasn't easy for him. It looked like it was uncomfortable to lean back on the wings.

He barely looked up when I went over to the sofa, but he started struggling when I leaned down to slip my prize over his head.

"Don't touch me again," he slurred.

Heracles was there in a flash, his hands firmly on Peter's shoulders. That made it easy for me to drop the necklace around Peter's neck.

"A stone from the River Styx," I finally answered Heracles' question. He moved his grip a bit lower as Peter tried to raise his hands to it. Peter briefly strained against it but quickly gave up, his shoulders slumping.

The stone on the simple leather thong looked almost like obsidian, except for the dark red gleam underneath. If you looked at it for more than a couple of seconds you'd realize that gleam was moving and flowing on its own, like a dull liquid fire beneath the pitch-black surface of the stone.

"At least we'll be sure the answers are truthful," Orphne put in. She'd made herself comfortable in a chair next to the couch.

No one can tell a lie when touching a stone from the River Styx. The river is older than the gods, and so potent that they swear their most solemn oaths on its waters. The story goes that if any god breaks such an oath the waters of Styx will rise up and drown Olympus itself, not to mention our lovely little corner of the Universe. It sounds far-fetched, but there's usually a glimmer of truth in such stories. I hadn't heard of any god willing to test how much truth there was in this one.

Unfortunately the stones can only be used for a few minutes on humans. They have a nasty side effect: they secrete a corrosive liquid that can quickly burn into human flesh.

I leaned down, gripping Peter's chin lightly to force him to look me in the eyes. I let the masking glamour drop again. He might be immune to my natural gaze, but the golden eyes were eerie enough to intimidate most people. I needed every advantage I could muster.

"Who are you?" I demanded softly.

His eyes were glassy, and not just from the alcohol. He was in the semi-trance the necklace conjured to knock down any resistance to telling the truth.

"Peter Kirkpatrick," he said slowly, his tongue a little thick.

Heracles gave a reluctant grunt. "So it's really his name, is it? Or at least one of them."

A good point, and I seized on it. "Do you have any other names?"

Peter shifted a bit with a slight wince. The stone moved with him, revealing an irritated red patch where it had previously lain. It was already burning him.

"Chuckles."

"What?"

"My nickname is Chuckles." The words took some effort on his part.

"He's certainly not one of us, then." Heracles seemed a bit relieved. "Chuckles, indeed."

I wasn't amused in the least. "All right, Father Chuckles. What are you?"

There was a bit of fight creeping into Peter's eyes. Maybe the discomfort from having the stone on his bare chest was sobering him up.

"A priest."

Another drawback of the stone. You have to be precise with your questions. People touching the stone can't lie, but they can equivocate enough to avoid telling you what you really want to know.

"I mean, what kind of creature are you? You're not human, that's for sure."

"I *am* human. As human as—" he looked away, glanced at Orphne and then half-turned for a glimpse at Heracles. He exhaled and went a little more limp. "More human than any of you," he finished with resignation.

I looked at Orphne and Heracles. Both seemed at a loss.

"He can't lie," Orphne said finally.

"And there can be a difference between telling the truth and stating a fact," Heracles added. "Most of all, truth is a matter of viewpoint."

He was right. Peter was telling the truth as he knew it. A complication, to say the least.

"How long have you had wings?" I leaned a little closer. There was a slight acrid smell that told me I'd better hurry up. I reached out with a finger and shifted the stone slightly. It had been in one place long enough to give him a nasty first-degree burn. He winced as I pulled it off the tender spot and moved it to the other side of his chest.

"I never had them. Not before tonight. You did this, didn't you?"

I hardened my gaze. "You're not in a position to ask questions. But just so we're clear, I didn't do anything to you that would cause this.

"Now," I went on as I leaned forward. "Tell me about Hawk's Haven. Why did Paul give it to Shannon as a wedding present. Did she ask him for it?"

For a minute it looked like he might refuse to answer. But of course, that wasn't an option for anyone wearing the stone. The resistance was short-lived.

"She didn't. Not exactly, anyway. Her mother wanted it. Evelyn tried to buy it from us for months, but she finally gave up. We thought she'd forgotten about it, but then Shannon asked Paul for the vineyard as a wedding gift. She wasn't that kind of woman. We knew her mother put her up to it, but Paul couldn't refuse her anything."

I straightened abruptly at that. It was certainly not the response I'd expected, but it shed a new light on things.

I reached out a hand. Peter twisted and Heracles applied new pressure. I grasped the thong around Peter's neck and yanked it off. His chest was scarred with angry red welts the size and shape of the stone.

"Question time is over," I said resolutely. There was no need to put Peter through any more pain. One of the twelve Olypians might be able to lie while touching a stone from the River Styx, but no one else had the strength to resist it. Peter was telling the truth about everything, at least the truth as he saw it.

"So what do we do with him now?" Orphne asked. I wished she hadn't. I needed time to think.

"I'd say he's outlived his usefulness," Heracles volunteered.

It was a practical suggestion. Peter might be less trouble if he was dead. Getting rid of a body wasn't all that hard. I could almost do it in my sleep.

For some inexplicable reason, I knew I couldn't do it this time, awake or asleep. Not yet, anyway. Maybe after I'd had some rest myself I could work out a solution. One thing I'd learned over the years is that it never pays to make snap decisions, especially irrevocable ones. Once Peter was gone, he'd be gone. Even if I could bring him back the way I'd done with the men on Aiaia, it would only be for a few minutes. We might need a lot more than that from him.

Sleep wasn't such a bad idea. I quickly muttered the sleeping spell again, and Peter was briefly surrounded by a faint glow before he went entirely limp.

Heracles shot me a questioning glance. "A mercy killing? Put him out so he doesn't suffer?"

A thought came to me. "He knows the vineyard better than the rest of us. He might be able to help us figure out the best way to get in, and where the most likely spots for an ambush would be."

He considered that a moment. "I suppose, although I'd make sure he's wearing that stone. He could set us up for a trap as easily as help us unless he's compelled to tell the truth."

"Is that wise?" There was a note of concern in Orphne's voice. "He looks like he's been pretty badly damaged by it."

"Easily mended," I muttered. I didn't relish the idea of healing him just to put him through more pain, but Heracles was right. Peter "Chuckles" Kirkpatrick had no reason to help us willingly.

I put my hands over the burned areas and murmured the healing charm. I felt the power flow through me, sensed the changes beneath my hands that told me his flesh was healing. It should have ended there.

But it didn't. The power normally faded on its own when the healing was complete, but it didn't now. It was flowing stronger. I was too surprised to even try to curb it consciously, and after a moment I knew I might not be able to stop it anyway. I couldn't pull my hands away from Peter's chest.

The air around my hands was glowing bluish-white. That only happened with the most severe injuries. Peter's burns hardly fell into that category.

"Medea?" Heracles didn't bother hiding the note of worry.

"Can't... stop..." It was difficult to even get the words out.

"Look!" Orphne shot out of her chair and stood next to me. She pointed behind Peter.

I moved my head enough to glimpse what she'd seen. What I saw made my stomach flip.

Peter's wings were lifting up slightly, fluttering—and shrinking.

"By all the gods," Heracles whispered.

Within seconds they'd shrunk to a third of their size, and a moment later they vanished beneath his shoulders. Heracles pushed Peter forward. I was able to see well enough over his slumped form to see the wings wither to next to nothing, then slip into his back. Only small slits remained.

A second later the skin closed over them. The flow of power in my hands died, and I could finally break contact with Peter.

"A night of wonders, indeed," Heracles said slowly.

Chapter 40

"A night of problems," I countered Heracles' comment. "But also a night of answers. Orphne, can you run upstairs and get my purse?"

As she left I hurried over to my desk. I didn't have much on it and quickly found what I needed: the list of wedding guests I was supposed to help notify about Shannon's death.

A handwritten list, from Evelyn O'Neill herself.

Heracles laid Peter out on the couch and joined me. Orphne was back quickly. I dug through the purse, thanking Hecate that I'd remembered the note from the zoo which I'd crumpled up and stowed in there. The note which led me to the panda exhibit, leaving Paul alone and exposed to danger.

I found the paper and unfolded it. The handwriting was a match to that on the list.

"The old woman at all of the murders," I said with a sigh, remembering Lamia's warning. "Agave's spirit hasn't possessed Lyn. She's taken over her mother's body."

I'd been so busy searching for Lyn's connections to the murders that I'd overlooked the possibility that someone close to Lyn would have the same connections.

Heracles exhaled slowly. "Does it really fit, or is it just another twist?"

"It fits, all right." I ticked off the points on my fingers. "Evelyn would likely have known about the party Shannon's friends were throwing for her, and could have gone there. And she supposedly borrowed Lyn's car the day that girl was murdered in the sorority house. She might have been trying to set Lyn up by leaving it close to the house, hoping someone would see it."

If so, it hadn't worked.

"That might be how the grape vine you found got into the car," Orphne added. "It could have been accidentally dropped by Evelyn."

"Or maybe put there for me to find," I muttered. "Again, trying to shift attention to Lyn. Either way, I've been going down the wrong path." I was sure of that now.

"And it would have been no problem at all for her to get into the party at the zoo," Orphne continued. "If Dionysus didn't just transport her there along with Shannon, Evelyn could have just walked through the gate. It was open to anyone."

All of the circumstances that gave Lyn an opportunity to be at the murders worked just as well for Evelyn.

"So at least we know which woman to look out for," Heracles said thoughtfully. "Although it's Dionysus we have to be more concerned about."

"But there's something I don't understand," Orphne mused. "Peter just said Evelyn had been after them for some time to sell the vineyard. Only when that failed did Shannon ask for it as a gift."

I looked up at her, understanding. "If Agave possessed Evelyn months ago, the timelines don't match. The murders have just started. They haven't been going on for months."

"At least not that you know about," Heracles said quickly. "Maybe he's been able to keep it hidden until now."

I shook my head slowly. "I don't think so. I think you were right, and that someone has tricked Dionysus into drinking blood to reawaken his lust for it. Someone who put more time and planning into this than we first imagined. Agave came back months ago, got the vineyard, *then* Dionysus was brought into the plot."

"So you're willing to accept that—"

"*Someone*," I said with emphasis, deliberately avoiding naming Pasiphae directly, "is responsible. Someone who might have freed Agave's soul and enlisted her aid." I didn't want to admit that Pasiphae was the most likely suspect, with her deep hatred for Dionysus.

"But why would Agave agree to it? Surely she'd understand the danger," Orphne protested.

"She was crazed enough to kill her son Pentheus to help spread Dionysus' cult," I reminded her. "And if she's been drifting in some limbo for thousands of years, she could easily have come completely unglued. All she ever really had was love for Dionysus. If she was approached by someone who offered her a way to bring him back to power on Earth—"

"And possibly to surpass the power of the Olympians themselves, by usurping the Curse of Prometheus," Heracles put in.

"Except the Curse could drive him completely mad before he reaches that level of power," I cut him off. "Someone wants his downfall, wants it badly enough to take the most extreme steps to make it happen."

"Maybe you're overlooking the most important point," Heracles said with sudden sternness.

I looked at him, surprised at his tone. Hadn't he been the one who proposed Dionysus was set up?

"You're right," I said evenly. "Regardless of why he's doing it, we have to stop Dionysus from going further."

He seemed mollified at that, but his expression hardened again when I continued.

"Except that our reasons for doing it may have to change. We won't necessarily be running up to that vineyard tomorrow to get evidence to use *against* Dionysus."

"We may be going there to *save* him," Orphne concluded.

Chapter 41

"The *only* priority is to stop Dionysus," Heracles said firmly. "It's not up to us to work out his reasons for what he's doing. That will be taken care of at the proper time and place, and *not* by us."

That was enough to persuade me to shut up. I wasn't done with the conversation by a long shot, but clearly it wasn't the time to finish it. He'd made up his mind, and I knew him well enough to know there was no changing it. At least, not at the moment.

I drew myself up. If he wanted to play the dictator, I could certainly play the aloof priestess who wouldn't be cowed by a tantrum.

"Then perhaps we should get some rest. We'll have a long journey ahead of us." I kept my voice even. "We can take Peter back down to the basement couch. You can have this one."

It was a slight to be sure, offering a guest less than the best accommodations. I wasn't in any mood to mollify him. If he wanted comfort, he should have stayed on Olympus. I was certain his wife Hebe could entertain him. Since being relieved of her duties as cupbearer of the gods she had all the time needed to perfect her wifely duties.

"No need for that," Orphne piped up. "He can have my bed. I don't sleep, so I can just stay down here with Peter to make sure nothing happens."

"Sounds good to me," Heracles said. He turned without further ado and left.

Orphne waited a few seconds to make sure he was upstairs. "What was that about?"

I waved it off impatiently. "He's probably just under stress. We're going into an unknown situation against an opponent who could easily overcome him. Dionysus is far stronger than Heracles, and he knows it. He's used to having at least a slight chance of success at the outset and turning the odds in his favor. There's no wiggle room this time."

I wandered over to a window and peeked out. The rain was gone. A glance overhead told me the clouds floating over my house had dispersed. It was enough to bump my tension level down a notch.

"So how do we win?" Orphne persisted.

"We don't have to, necessarily. If Dionysus wants me, maybe I can distract him enough for Heracles to slip back to Olympus."

"There's another option," she offered. Hesitating, she finally continued. "Dionysus probably won't take too much notice of me. I can slip back to Hades—"

"And be tossed into chains immediately?" I spun around, as much fearful she'd do it as angry that she'd even suggest I accept such a choice.

"I could warn them—"

"The word of a fugitive won't carry much weight, especially if you're claiming one of the high gods has revived a blood cult." She looked a little hurt, but she had to face reality. Still, just because Heracles had snapped at me, I had no right to do the same with her.

I relented a little. She only wanted to be helpful. "You might be able to get away, though, and warn some of the other nymphs. Like we discussed earlier today. They could get word to someone who'd listen."

"I suppose that would work," she finally agreed. "But I wish we had a better plan. This seems chancy, at best."

My very thoughts, but a new one was clamoring for attention. I mulled it, weighed the risks, and decided anything that could give us even a slight advantage was better than nothing, no matter the downside.

I wandered back over to the couch and motioned her to join me. Peter was breathing deeply, fast asleep under the enchantment. I wondered if he was dreaming of me, as Endymion dreamed of Selene.

Wondered more where such a thought had come from, and why it would even matter to me.

"Help me get his pants down," I directed Orphne. She rolled her eyes.

"Haven't we had enough problems with that tonight?"

I smiled. "It's not what you think." She sighed and helped me work his pants down several inches. "That's enough," I said.

She looked puzzled. It was hardly enough to expose the most interesting parts fully, but it was enough for my purposes. Kneeling down, I tugged on his hip until he rolled over on his side.

My finger made a quick movement, remembering the pattern with years of practice as I recited the proper words.

By the time she realized what I was doing it was too late. Orphne's shocked outburst wouldn't alter anything.

"Are you *insane*?" she sputtered. "You can't—"

"Just did," I cut her off with a smile. "Help me work his pants back on."

She gave an exasperated grunt but did as I asked. "You've lost your mind," she muttered. "When she finds out what you've done…"

"As long as Dionysus doesn't know what I've done, we're OK. It may be enough to swing the battle in our favor."

It certainly couldn't make things worse for any of us, especially Peter, who'd just become the surprise behind door number two.

Door number one was far to the north, and in a different direction than Hawk's Haven.

Chapter 42

I knocked on the spare bedroom door just after three in the morning. We needed the cover of darkness for the entrance I planned. I hadn't gotten any sleep and from the looks of him, Heracles hadn't either.

"We'll get breakfast ready in a few minutes, if you want to take a shower first."

He grunted something that was probably an assent and shut the door again. I'd already showered to help clear my head, but coffee would be a welcome bolster.

Orphne helped me put together a passable meal. I hadn't had time over the past couple of days to do any proper shopping. Still, we had cheese, a couple of half-loaves of different breads, honey from Greece and homemade yogurt.

I made sure Heracles was downstairs before undoing the sleeping spell around Peter. Heracles was in the kitchen, within easy earshot. I kept several paces away from Peter, hoping it would make him feel a little less threatened. Things would be better for all of us if he was cooperative. After the charm was undone Peter sat up slowly, trying to get his bearings. When he saw me he backed away as far as the couch would allow.

"Why don't you just kill me and get it over with? I have nothing more for you." His gaze was steady, unafraid. I could change that last part if I wanted, but it seemed more expedient to try to reason with him.

I tossed him the shirt I retrieved from the basement. He made no move to put it on. "Your body-builder friend said I'd outlived my usefulness. Have I?"

I ignored the question. "I've no objection if you'd rather stay as you are. You have a very pleasing body. But you're going to find our journey cold without a little more clothing."

"I don't intend to go anywhere with you." He was keeping calm, stating it as a fact rather than a threat.

"You will if you want to bring your brother's killer to justice. We need your help to do it."

"I'm staring at her now, I think."

I moved closer to him. He tensed a little, but otherwise remained motionless. "You can think what you like, but at least use common sense. If I wanted you dead, you'd be dead. I have a hundred ways to do it, from brute force to poison to horrible things you can't even imagine."

I took another few steps towards him. "Twice now, you've woken up in my house after I put you to sleep. Doesn't it stand to reason that you wouldn't have awakened at all if that's what I intended to do with you?"

His eyes narrowed. "You already did something else with me, if I remember correctly." He reached behind him. "Was that just a dream, then?"

I sat down in the chair near the couch. "No. And I'm at a loss to explain it, because as I told you last night I didn't do anything that would cause wings to grow from your back."

He reached further back, rubbing his shoulder for a moment. "What happened to them?"

I picked up the stone from Styx, which I'd left on the coffee table. "Remember this?" He didn't answer, but I saw him flinch. "You remember the burns it caused. I healed them after putting you back to sleep. When I did, the wings disappeared."

Peter digested that. "I suppose if you had it in for me, you wouldn't have healed me. If that's what happened. I wasn't conscious so I have only your word. That doesn't count for much at the moment."

"Understandable. And unfortunately, all I have is my word to back up what happened to your brother."

He eyed me a moment longer before shrugging. He put his shirt on and sat up.

"All right. I'm listening."

I gestured in the general direction of the kitchen. "Why not join us for breakfast, then? You must be hungry."

I let him go first, noting his quick glance down the hall towards the front door.

"I wouldn't advise it," I cautioned as I pointed to the kitchen. After a moment's hesitation he made the wise choice.

"Still among the living, I see. For the moment, anyway." Heracles barely looked at Peter before biting into a large hunk of bread oozing with honey.

Peter eyed him warily and pulled up a chair at the far end of the table. I got us both coffee and sat down between them, across from Orphne.

"You've already met Orphne," I nodded in her direction.

"I'm sorry for the bad first impression. I would have preferred that you saw me this way from the outset," she said with a smile.

He managed a half-smile at that. "I've been taught not to judge by appearances. However..." He sipped his coffee but didn't bother to reach for any food. Maybe he was used to fasting, but I made a mental note to pack away some bread and cheese to take along in case he changed his mind later.

Again, I had a brief feeling of something not quite right. Why did I care if he ate or not, and why had I even wondered the night before if he was dreaming about me?

I shook my head to clear it. Stress did odd things to people.

"In my defense, the shape I chose was more practical for keeping you safe at the time," Orphne smiled over her coffee. Oh dear. I didn't want to have to play chaperone on top of things. Having a romp with me had disastrous consequences, and I was only half-nymph. There was no telling what would happen if Orphne got her hands on Peter.

He frowned as he reached for the yogurt, spooning some onto the plate in front of him. "What the hell were those women, anyway?"

"It's a long story, but you have a right to hear the short version," I said. "They were succubi, women who were tainted by a she-demon named Lamia, and became monsters. They survive by sucking the life force out of humans."

"So they're like vampires?"

"Living dead, to be sure. But they don't actually die before coming back. And the other woman you saw me talking to, the one floating in midair, was Lamia herself."

"I'm surprised they could come into hallowed ground like a church," he observed while reaching for some bread.

I had to smile at his naiveté. "Unfortunately, they can go anywhere that's not warded with stronger stuff than Catholic blessings."

He glanced up at that. "Should I be insulted?"

"Nothing personal, but you should know the truth. And they can't be killed by wooden stakes, in case you were planning to lay in a supply. Only special weapons can slay them, and no human can wield them without being killed themselves."

"But you did. So that makes you—"

I shrugged. "It makes me Medea." He didn't seem to get it. "You apparently know a little about Greek mythology, at least from what the folder we found in your office indicated. Surely you've heard of me."

That stopped him in mid-chew. He stared at me a moment, washed down his bread with some coffee, stared some more. "Medea. As in golden fleece Medea?"

I'd dropped the glamour over my eyes to reveal their golden hue. I raised my hand and called up a fireball. Just a tiny one, for emphasis.

"The one and only," I said with a smile. He drew back a bit, but that was the extent of his reaction.

"That would make you—"

"An older woman," I said emphatically to end the conversation as I snuffed out the fireball. I wanted to kick myself as soon as I said it. It had unsavory connotations considering what had happened the night before.

They weren't lost on him. He raised his coffee mug to me. "Here's to you, Mrs. Robinson."

I couldn't suppress the laugh. It felt good. I needed it.

Heracles cleared his throat a little too loudly. "I'm sorry," I said after getting control over myself. "I didn't mean to ignore you. Peter Kirkpatrick, meet Heracles. My bodybuilder friend, as you put it."

The slight humor that had crept into Peter's eyes vanished. He folded his arms on the table and laid his head down in them. "Medea. And Heracles. Energy vampires. Women who change into monsters, but only to protect me. I'm going insane. This can't be real. I died back in that church, didn't I? Died and went—somewhere. Somewhere that's not quite hell, but close enough."

I reached over and put a hand on his arm, strangely gratified when he didn't pull back.

"Although I wouldn't wish such a fate on you, I agree it might be easier to deal with than the truth. But this is real, Peter. And as crazy as it seems, we're the only ones who can stop what's happening. We're trying to prevent others dying the way Paul and Shannon died. And we need your help for that."

He stayed that way for a minute before taking a deep breath and raising his head.

"Then I need to know the truth. How *did* they die?"

Chapter 43

I gathered my thoughts for a moment, wondering how much to tell him. For starters, I wanted to see how much Peter already knew.

"In the church, you asked me about the maenads. You were on the right track. What made you come up with it?"

"Mostly the circumstances of Shannon's death. I remembered hearing about them in a college class on classical mythology. I did a little research and found a lot of similarities. Shannon's friends were in some kind of daze, and they'd...."

He looked a little green, so I decided to help him out. No need for him to discuss the gruesome details over breakfast. "You're right. That's exactly what the maenads used to do. What they're doing again."

He rubbed his temple and took a few sips of coffee.

"You're telling me Shannon's friends got mixed up in some kind of cult?" He kept his eyes on me while I poured him more coffee. "Someone has actually brought back this crazy practice?"

"Not just someone. Dionysus himself."

He held up a hand. "Wait a minute. You're telling me Dionysus is *real*?" He looked extremely skeptical.

"You've just met Medea and Heracles, and you have a problem with Dionysus?"

He left his coffee untouched. "It's different. You're both... well, maybe not ordinary people, but people nonetheless. I can accept that the stories about both of you were based on reality, although it's a little hard to fathom that I'm sharing coffee with someone who walked the world before Christ. But you're telling me that Dionysus—an actual god— exists? That would mean my religion is based on lies. And I can't accept that."

I hadn't expected that turn in the conversation. "No one is saying your god doesn't exist, just that there are others. Dionysus and the rest of the Olympians don't need your belief to exist. But you'd be foolish beyond saying to think non-belief would protect you if you got on their bad side."

"Why would he do something like this if he's a god? It doesn't sound very god-like to me, killing people like that."

I started to answer but caught a warning glance from Heracles. This was bad enough business without humans learning the full extent of the evil. The less they knew about the Curse of Prometheus, and their role in it, the better.

"All I can say is that he's likely been tricked into it," I finally said. "It's something that, under normal circumstance, none of the gods we worship would do, not even the darker ones."

He let out a deep breath. "And now you're asking my help to banish some pagan god? If Catholic blessings aren't enough to keep that Lamia person and her minions of a church, how do you expect me to help you beat someone who has to be a lot stronger than her?"

"You're stronger than you think," Orphne said with a meaningful glance in my direction as she rose. "Excuse me a moment."

"We need your help navigating the vineyard at Hawk's Haven," Heracles added.

Peter seemed surprised. "You think he's at Hawk's Haven?"

"We think it all ties together with Evelyn putting Shannon up to asking for the place as a wedding present," I said.

His brow furrowed. "I might have known that dragon would be involved somehow." Wow. So much for love thy neighbor.

"It's fair to say we don't think she's quite herself these days," Heracles added casually.

Peter looked to me for an explanation.

"We think she's been possessed by the spirit of a woman named Agave. She was one of Dionysus' most devoted followers when his cult first developed."

He took that in. "So she helped him get the vineyard. You think he's using it as some kind of headquarters."

Heracles nodded. "We were ambushed there by maenads last night. That was after Medea found several dead men lying there."

I tensed a bit, but he seemed to understand that it wasn't the time to tell Peter his brother had been in that pile of bodies. "We'd just as soon have someone along who knows the lay of the land, who can tell us where they might be hiding so we can avoid another encounter," Heracles continued. "Someone who could also take care of getting us into the vineyard by stealth, through a hidden path."

"We don't need to worry about that," I interrupted.

Heracles raised an eyebrow.

"Oh?"

"He'll expect a sneak attack. Maybe he'll let his guard down a little more easily if he thinks I've decided to accept his invitation."

"Invitation?" asked Peter.

I smiled, but there was nothing nice or inviting about it. "Let's just say he's made some overtures. He's undoubtedly looking for allies. If he thinks he's won me over…" I shrugged and let the rest go unspoken.

"He might slip up somewhere," Peter finished for me. "I guess if we're dealing with a real-life god ordinary force won't be much use."

"Precisely," I said.

He shook his head thoughtfully. "There are a lot of places someone—or some*thing*—could hide up there. But there are a few hills that will give us a good view of the vineyard."

My smile deepened. "We'll have a much better view than that before we actually head in."

Understanding dawned on Heracles' face. "Medea, you aren't thinking about using—"

"I am," I said emphatically.

"What?" Peter looked a little alarmed.

"Nothing to worry about."

"Don't believe it," Heracles said quickly to Peter. "When this one starts scheming, you can bet there will be trouble."

"Thanks for the warning," Peter replied easily. "But I already gathered I'm in trouble. I've been kidnapped, after all. And you've evaded my question." He turned to me, completely serious now. "How did Paul die? Did Dionysus kill him and just throw him into the leopard's cage?"

I couldn't demur any longer. "I think he lured Paul in there. It's possible Dionysus took control of the leopards and made them maul him."

"But there's another possibility." Orphne's comment was followed by a soft *thud* as Shannon's severed hand landed on the table in front of Peter.

He recoiled a bit, got his wits back and peered at the thing more closely. "My God... is that a *hand*?"

I couldn't believe what Orphne had just done. I looked up at her, my eyes flashing, but she wasn't cowed. "Tell him, Medea. He has a right to know everything we're up against."

She was right. I'd been trying to couch things too nicely.

"Yes, Peter. It's a hand. Shannon's hand."

He looked at me in total disbelief. "She was among the maenads who attacked us last night," I went on. "Dionysus brought her back from the dead. Her hands were like that when we found her. I assume they were normal when she was buried."

He nodded slowly. "They were. I gave her Extreme Unction. It was rough." His voice cracked a little, but no blame to him there.

I took a deep breath. This wasn't going to be any more pleasant. "I told you Dionysus may have lured Paul into the leopard exhibit. It's possible Shannon was the bait. He and I were trying to meet up. When I checked in at the gate they gave me a note that said to head to the panda exhibit. Now I know Evelyn wrote that note, a ruse to get me away from where I was supposed to meet Paul.

"We were on our cell phones while we tried to connect. He was just passing the leopard exhibit when he noticed the cats were outside. The last thing I heard him say was, 'It's her!'"

Peter put his head down again. "And then the leopards killed him."

It was no use avoiding the worst possibility. "Look closely at the hand, Peter. It's been transformed into a cross between human and animal. The claws would be deadly weapons. She would have been completely under the control of Dionysus or Agave. Do you understand?"

He didn't raise his head. He'd already seen enough. After a moment I realized he was crying.

When he finally looked up there were still tears on his cheeks, but his expression was resolute.

"All right. I have a hard time believing this, but what you've told me makes more sense than my brother just ending up in some wild animal exhibit on his own. If you think you can bring some sort of justice, then I'm in. What do you need me to do?"

I got up from the table and headed towards my sanctuary.

"For starters," I tossed over my shoulder, "you can take your clothes off."

 *Chapter 44*

"How is he holding up?"

Heracles strained to make his voice heard over the rush of the wind and the beating of the dragons' wings. He was riding one of them, and from the look on his face he was having the time of his life.

Orphne had changed herself into a stone again and was safely lodged in my pocket. There was only room for two in the chariot.

I glanced behind me to where Peter was half-crouched, clinging desperately to the side of the vehicle. His eyes were squeezed shut, and over the din I heard him practically screaming.

"Holy Mary, Mother of God, pray for us now and... and... now is just fine. Now is when I need it. Please, pray for me now."

I turned back to Heracles. The dragons, magical beings at their finest, only needed the merest thought from me to take the fiery chariot wherever I wished. They didn't need GPS to locate it, either, so the reins were really not needed. But holding them made me feel a little more in control.

"As well as can be expected," I yelled the answer. Heracles nodded, whooped a bit, and slapped the side of his dragon. It hissed and roared, turning its head back slightly and breathing out a cloud of sulfurous fumes.

"Be nice to them!" I admonished. "It's the first exercise they've gotten in a long time."

It had still been pitch dark when we arrived at the Etowah mounds where my chariot was hidden, the dragons in slumber. Peter nearly fainted when I spoke the spell that caused the mound to crack open, and the chariot and dragons to rise up to the surface. He screamed a bit and stumbled back when one of them croaked a reptilian protest at being awakened. Even at rest the chariot glowed brightly enough to light the entire area. Fortunately I'd already located the rangers on duty and used my eyes to ensure they wouldn't remember anything about the disturbance.

Now we were streaking high over the land, flames trailing the chariot in a meteor-like tail. We were so high that anyone seeing us in the still-darkened sky would probably assume we were indeed a meteor. Still, I kept a close eye out. I was nervous that we'd show up on radar, and I had no doubt any jets sent to intercept us would determine we were a hostile aircraft.

We were, but there would be no way to communicate to the fighter pilots that our hostility was directed towards Dionysus at the moment.

It would certainly be a grand entrance when we touched down in the vineyard. I just hoped we wouldn't have to jump out and start fighting right away. I'd have to give Peter a few moments to compose himself.

To his credit, he hadn't balked back at the house when I told him why I needed him completely naked.

"This ointment will protect you from harm until the sun goes down," I said as I showed him the jar.

"I'm sure I can manage full coverage," he said, slightly wrinkling his nose as he took a whiff.

"It won't make you smell like lilacs, but no weapon can harm you for the rest of the day. Unfortunately I have to apply it. There's a certain spell I have to recite as I'm doing it to make it work."

"You're sure it *will* work?"

I gave him a look that told him to get on with it. He hesitantly pulled off his shirt. "I gave it to Jason. My father forced him to yolk a fire-breathing dragon and plow an entire field in order to win the fleece. Aeetes expected Jason to die within seconds, but thanks to this he survived without a scratch."

Peter turned. I started applying the ointment to his neck, working slowly down as I murmured the spell.

"So it worked, and Jason got the fleece, and you."

I stopped for a moment. "My father was never one for keeping his word," I said, not bothering to hide the coldness in my voice. "We had to resort to other means."

I went back to work, quickly covering his back. "Pants," I said in between verses of the spell. After a moment's hesitation he dropped them and the boxers as well.

He jerked a bit when I reached his side. "Sorry," I said. "I know it's cold."

"It's not that. I'm just ticklish."

"I'll try to be careful." But I couldn't resist a playful touch when I reached the other side. He snorted a bit and flinched again.

"Cut it out! It's bad enough I've allowed myself to have recourse to witchcraft. That's another sin I'll have to confess."

He didn't say anything more, and I decided it was best to avoid mentioning the far bigger sin he'd be confessing thanks to my actions the previous night. "Is this why they call you Chuckles?" I asked to lighten the mood. The first round of the chant was done; time to start again at the beginning.

"Mmm," he confirmed. "Paul gave me the nickname. He used to get great delight tackling me and tickling me until I couldn't breathe for laughing."

It was a sweet image, and I couldn't help smiling. "Sounds like a nice childhood." I worked quickly over his rear, then smoothed some of the ointment onto his right thigh and started reciting the spell again.

"Who said it stopped there? He did it to me at the church's Labor Day picnic. Damn near broke my arm when he tackled me from behind." I glanced up and saw his shoulders slouch more. It was hard for him, realizing there would be no more sneak tickle attacks.

After that, and on the long drive north to the Etowah area, we didn't say more than a few words. There didn't seem to be a need.

Now all his attention was directed to reciting some sort of hybrid version of the rosary. I assumed he was ad libbing freely, unless they'd added "Holy crap, I'm going to puke!" as a prayer between Hail Marys.

Thanks to the ointment he was surviving the chariot ride unscathed. An unprotected human would have been incinerated in moments. I'd brought along one of the unbreakable chains that we'd bound him with while he was dozing in my basement. I hoped strapping him into the chariot with it would make him feel a little better. It didn't appear to be working.

At least the ointment I'd used was. I'd had to put it everywhere, even coating his hair with it to make sure his scalp was protected. He looked good with a slicked-back style. He had a bit of a cowlick that responded quite well to the unguent. Maybe I could make him a more cosmetic version for everyday use when this was over.

The chariot started descending. We were getting close. I began planning the aerial pattern we'd trace over the vineyard to scope out hidden groups of maenads. The fiery chariot would cast more than enough light over the place.

As I willed the dragons to level off I briefly wondered why on Earth I'd even thought about making hair cream for Peter. If we got through this, he'd have no reason to want anything from me, much less continued contact with me.

No reason at all.

Chapter 45

It didn't take long for me to conclude aerial surveillance was out. We only made a few passes over the vineyard before Heracles turned back to me.

"He's made the foliage impossible to see through!"

I'd already discerned that much. The vines, which had been lush beyond belief a day earlier, were now almost obscenely full. The light from my chariot revealed that they'd joined together in a tight-knit canopy over the fields. We couldn't see through it, but I didn't need to. I knew there was an army of maenads down there waiting for us.

I steered the dragons close to the front of the property. The parking lot would be big enough to accommodate them, and far enough off the road that they wouldn't be spotted.

We touched down lightly. Heracles leaped off the dragon and began reconnoitering the vicinity.

I turned to dismount and nearly fell over Peter, who was still clutching the sides of the chariot, eyes squeezed shut. "It's all right," I said, putting a hand on his shoulder. He looked up tentatively. "We've landed. Firm ground."

He raised himself up enough to see over the side of the chariot. A second later he was out, walking in an unsteady gait to the nearest tree.

As I turned to tend to the dragons I heard the sounds of retching. I was grateful he hadn't let loose while we were airborne.

I murmured soothing words to the dragons, stroking their heads lightly. The low growl in their throats was one of contentment. They lay down and curled their tails up over their snouts, their glowing green eyes half-closed.

A slight shift in my pocket reminded me of someone else who needed tending. I gently withdrew the stone and set it on the ground. A moment later Orphne was in front of me. She'd kept her human guise but added a Xena-like costume that made her look a lot more daunting.

"Weapons?" she asked. I reached into the chariot, where several large slots along the front provided perfect containers for swords and knives. I handed her an old bronze sword that had once belonged to Hippolyta, queen of the Amazons.

I took a similar sword, though it was much newer. The poisoned knife I'd kept in my purse was sheathed and hooked to my belt now.

Heracles jogged over. "No sign of anyone," he muttered. "I don't like it."

"They're here, no doubt of that," I said. "But they'll be hiding in that jungle we just flew over."

Peter staggered over. "Was that really necessary? Couldn't we have just taken the car?"

"I want as many weapons as I can get. Those dragons can kill a score of humans in a matter of seconds. Their hides are impenetrable, and I can summon them mentally. If we're overrun by maenads, they'll give us a huge advantage."

"And what about Dionysus?"

A warm breeze moved past us, much warmer than it should have been for pre-dawn hours at that time of year. It felt like the vineyard had just responded to the name of its new master. The glow of the chariot revealed the trees around us were still in their autumn finery. Apparently Dionysus' beneficence only extended to his precious grape vines.

"We can't kill him. We have to use our wits," I said coldly.

He sat down on the ground. "Mine were scared out of me a ways back. Just before you made that sharp turn and my spleen flew out of my mouth." He was breathing more normally now. I figured he'd be fine in another minute or two.

A few moments later he seemed distracted by something. He was looking around the parking lot. "That car—I recognize it. It belongs to Deidre, the manager." He looked towards the office building and saw the same thing I did.

"The lights are on." Those few words said enough; something was wrong. He got up, steady now, and started walking towards the building.

I grabbed his arm. "Wait a minute! It's probably a trap!"

"The whole place is a trap, isn't it? I heard what you and Heracles were saying. There was no way to see anything from the air, which means there's something he wants hidden."

I reluctantly let his arm go, motioning for Orphne and Heracles to join us.

We moved carefully up the stairs, but I quickly realized it didn't matter. They creaked enough to give us away, as if the clamor of the chariot and dragons landing a few yards away wasn't enough to announce us.

Peter was at the top and just about to open the door when Heracles bounded ahead of me. "I'll go first," he said in a tone that brooked no argument. After a second's hesitation, Peter wisely decided it was the best plan.

Heracles slowly pushed the door open and stepped inside. He'd grabbed a large spear out of the chariot and held it at the ready. Aside from my knife it was the only magical weapon I'd brought. Its blade was also impregnated with the venom of the Hydra. There was no point carrying too many weapons like that. We could easily be hurt by a careless move from a comrade if we ended up fighting in close quarters.

He turned, giving a slight movement of his head indicating it was safe for the rest of us to come in.

The smell hit me almost as soon as I walked through the door. We were in some sort of lobby area. The entire rear wall was nothing but windows. Undoubtedly during the day it would be a marvelous view, though perhaps not on this day. A large fireplace surrounded by leather couches stood cold and dark to our left.

To the right was a doorway, through which light gleamed brightly.

"Is there anyplace else for someone to hide?" I whispered to Peter, indicating the room beyond.

"The basement, but the staircase to this level is very narrow. It wouldn't be very convenient for a group trying to attack. That's our showroom. It's big enough for maybe two dozen people. If it's empty, we're probably OK."

Heracles was already heading there. The rest of us crept a few paces behind. The smell got noticeably stronger.

Heracles stepped inside, looked around. His gaze lingered a bit on one spot, but I couldn't see enough beyond his massive frame to tell what caught his attention.

"It's all right," he said in a normal tone of voice, though there was a bit of resignation to it. He moved further into the room, giving the rest of us enough space to squeeze in.

"Gods of hell," I said softly when I saw what he'd been looking at. Or rather, who.

A woman, I could tell that much. There was still enough of her face and hair left, though both were caked with gore.

"My God," Peter said hoarsely. "What did they do to her?"

Pretty much what they'd done to their other victims, it seemed. She was naked, but scraps of clothes were scattered about, a few thrown carelessly up onto the decorative wrought iron racks. There were some bottles in the racks, but there were a lot of empty spaces. It didn't look like the type of place to let its shelves go empty.

Dionysus evidently wanted to slake his thirst with more than blood.

Peter walked slowly over to the body. I wondered if he'd be sick again, but he seemed steady enough. I followed, getting a closer look at the damage.

A lot of flesh was missing. There was blood on the floor, but much of that seemed missing too. Most of it would have flooded onto the floor with so many wounds, unless it was caught in libation bowls.

She was much more damaged than Shannon had been. I considered whether that meant more maenads had been here, or whether they were merely growing more savage in their frenzy. I felt a tinge of regret that I hadn't bothered looking at the office the day before, but she'd likely been dead before we arrived. It wouldn't have mattered.

"Is it the woman you mentioned? The manager?" Orphne asked.

"I can't tell," Peter said after a pause. I put my hand on his shoulder again, wondering briefly if I was really being solicitous or whether I was just looking for excuses to touch him.

Because, after all, the "spell" I'd been murmuring as I covered him in the protection ointment had just been a child's lullaby, chanted in my native Colchian tongue. He really could have taken care of covering most of his body, with just a little help from me for those hard-to-reach places. The ointment needed no additional magic.

But that would be my little secret for the moment.

"There's nothing you can do for her," I said, pushing those other annoying thoughts out of my mind. I forced myself to break contact with him.

"I know," he said miserably. "I wonder if I'll be able to do anything to keep this from happening to more people. If any of us can stop it."

"Not if we stay here in this charnel house," Heracles said stridently. "We should get moving into the fields. Medea, we'll need you to call up some of your fireballs to light the way."

He turned purposefully and headed back out of the room, Orphne on his heels. I gently pulled Peter's arm in that direction. He stood his ground for a moment, then made the sign of the cross over the body.

"Go with God," he said softly before answering my grasp.

For her, the battle was over.

Chapter 46

The trek up the path to the small rise was quick. We mounted the rise and Peter stopped cold when he saw the fields before him. It was his first glimpse of what I'd already seen from the air. I'd cast several fireballs over the field, partly to light things up and partly to see if there'd be a response. Nothing.

"My God," he whispered as Heracles came to his side. I moved to the other side.

No, I thought. *Not your god. A very different one.*

The air emanating from the fields was balmy and humid from the exhalations of the dense foliage. It was like standing in a field after a summer storm as the sun dried the rain, making the air thick with moisture. The temperature had to be at least in the mid-80s down there.

Peter wavered a bit beside me, but regained his composure just as I set a reassuring hand on his back. I kept the touch brief.

"You were right, Medea," he said with a mixture of horror and wonder in his voice. "I can't believe what I'm seeing."

"Believe it, Peter," I responded. "And understand, there's no shame in ending your role here. You can go back and wait for us at chariot. I think you finally have a good inkling of what we're dealing with."

He stiffened at the suggestion. "No. I'm in this with you until the end."

"All right then," Heracles said with determination. "We take a direct approach." He pointed to the left. "We go two-by-two down the rows." He turned to Orphne. "That was quite a punch you used on me yesterday. I assume there's more where that came from?"

"I know how to take care of myself," she said solemnly.

"Good enough. You and Peter will be together. Take care of him as well."

"No," Peter said forcefully. "I'm going with Medea."

I was too surprised to say anything. After what happened the previous night, I expected him to take any option available to stay away from me.

"This is no time to argue," Heracles snapped with equal passion. "He'll be less likely to pay attention to the two of you anyway. Medea and I are the bigger threats to him. You'll still have a chance to get away if he's occupied with us."

"He's right, Peter," I said soothingly. "Dionysus won't care about either of you. If Heracles and I are together, he'll focus his energies on us and leave the two of you alone. Orphne can still get away and get help. She has contacts."

"And can change her shape, too." Peter said sardonically. "Is this your real shape?"

"No," she said simply.

"Was it what you became in the church?"

"No."

"Do I get to see the real you?"

She regarded him for a few moments before shaking her head. "I think not. If we get through this, ask me again in a few years. The memories you'll have of today might be fading, and you'll need some new fodder for your nightmares."

Peter closed his eyes and shook his head. "All right. You and I go together. I can't wait to see what you'll become if we get into trouble."

"Are there any large open areas in the fields?" I asked. "It might be a place where Dionysus would set up court."

"There's a good-sized garden close to the back of the property. It's surrounded by a boxwood maze. We have weddings and summer parties there occasionally."

"How far do the fields stretch?"

He thought a moment. "I don't know the exact acreage. Paul handled most of the vineyard business after my father died. We should make it to the back of the property by late morning."

"Any odd landscape that would provide extra coverage for an ambush party?"

He shook his head. "The rows are fairly even and straight all the way back to the maze. At least, they were."

Message received. Of course he couldn't guess what Dionysus had done to the place. None of us could.

There didn't seem to be anything else to cover, so I silently started down to the fields.

I called up fireballs for each of us, using an additional spell to keep them floating a few paces ahead of us. We started down the rows in silence.

Heracles and I moved quickly and quietly. After a few rows it became clear there wouldn't be an all-out assault right up front. Too bad. That would have broken the suspense.

There was an edgy feeling in the air. Not knowing when the peace would end made it difficult to truly enjoy the silence.

Heracles finally broke it. "Your young man seems highly protective of you, Medea. Is that part of the magic you used last night?" Heracles asked the question lightly enough, but I heard the intimations behind it.

"No," I said rather too quickly.

"Ah," he replied simply. We walked in silence again. A few more minutes were enough to convince me that talking was preferable, even if it was a distraction.

"I suppose we won't see anything like this again on Earth if we're successful," I ventured. "I assume Dionysus will be banished to Tartarus for his acts. Do you think all the vineyards will just wither up and die without him?"

"For sure, Dionysus will be expelled if we get enough evidence against him," Heracles said carefully, but left it at that.

I waited a moment. Something wasn't being spoken.

"And?"

He shrugged. "Once a seat among the high gods is created, it can't be undone. Dionysus himself doesn't have to be the god of wine anymore, but *someone* has to fill the slot."

Now there was an interesting twist I hadn't really considered. I'd just assumed that his throne would remain vacant if Dionysus was ousted.

"You're saying if Dionysus falls, someone will benefit. In a very large way," I said.

Becoming one of the Twelve meant gaining essentially limitless powers. We'd broached the possibility that someone had slipped Dionysus human blood to awaken his old thirst for it and undo him. But Heracles had been focused on revenge as the motive, hence his suggestion that my aunt Pasiphae did it.

Now I saw a new motive. "Advancing through the ranks sounds like a good reason for seducing Dionysus with a drink of human blood. Anyone would know what that would do to him."

I was becoming excited about that avenue, mostly because it gave me a reason for turning the spotlight away from Pasiphae.

But Heracles seemed surprised by my thoughts. "I didn't intend to imply that," he muttered. He suddenly seemed uncomfortable.

"Well, who would benefit from it? Who would most likely be raised to fill the throne of Dionysus?" I asked excitedly as we reached the end of the row—

—and stared a dozen armed maenads right in their cold, dead eyes.

Chapter 47

Heracles made a quick move to shove me behind him, just as he'd tried to shield me the night before. This time I was already twenty feet above him, fireballs in hand. I'd just had time to jam my sword through my belt before levitating.

Heracles glanced up and growled in annoyance. He'd lost another chance to defend poor helpless Medea. Of course *that* Medea never existed. He spun angrily and began laying into the maenads to work out his frustration. Like the ones who'd come after us the night before, all of them were naked.

"They're here!" I screamed as I twisted towards the row where Orphne and Peter were. They stared up at me a second before running towards the sounds of the fray.

Looking down towards Heracles I saw three maenads on the ground already. More were piling on him but he was swinging around, oblivious to their weight, his right fist crashing wildly into others nearby. He'd dropped his spear, but when humans were concerned his fists were just as deadly.

With a shriek I hurled both my fireballs into a group of advancing maenads. I called up more fireballs and lobbed them too. After a few rounds I counted five maenads dead or dying in agony. Several more were being held at bay by the furiously burning bodies blocking the path.

I made a hasty decent before any of the maenads got the bright idea of throwing her thyrsus at me like a spear. Only about half the women were carrying those damnable staffs. The rest had an assortment of nasty weapons, including maces and spiked clubs. So much for tradition.

Three maenads had snuck up from behind. Orphne had already dispatched one and was fighting with another. The third was circling Peter with a sword.

I gasped involuntarily as she made a sudden lunge and swung the blade down at him. He held up his arm defensively. The blade slammed into it in a blow that would have normally severed the arm clean through.

But his arm was anointed with my magic salve. The blade glanced off him as harmlessly as if it had hit pure iron.

Peter seemed amazed at first, but he didn't have much time to ponder it. The maenad wasn't about to back down. She swung down twice more, the second time catching him neatly on the shoulder with equal ineffectiveness, though it sliced through his shirt.

On the next blow Peter had the presence of mind to take a side-step and give her a shove. The maenad lurched off-balance and he quickly grabbed the sword from her flailing hand. But instead of pressing his advantage he backed away.

What was that line about being a lover, not a fighter?

Orphne took care of the maenad for him. In the next moment she had half-taken the woman's head off with a single blow of her sword. The body swayed a bit, blood spurting up from the huge gash in the neck, before it sank slowly to the ground.

The maenad's mouth was still moving in a wordless scream.

Peter heaved dryly and turned away. Orphne went over and roughly grabbed his arm, spinning him around and forcing him to look at the body.

"*That* is what you have to do!" she said urgently, pointing at the dead woman with her sword. "You can't hesitate. You can't show weakness. You must kill them, Peter. That's the only way."

He looked at her in horror.

"They can't be saved," she hissed. "They belong to Dionysus now. If you care so much about souls, this is the only way to free theirs from his control."

And with that she let go of his arm and stalked over to me. I'd been watching the pile of bodies growing around Heracles. It wasn't that I didn't want to help him, but I knew it would be stupid to get too close to him when he was in battle frenzy.

Orphne glanced at the plume of smoke fueled by the seared bodies of the maenads I'd taken out.

"Looks like there's no disguising our intentions now," she said coolly.

"You looked like you were enjoying yourself back there," I commented.

"The busier it gets in Hades, the less chance they'll know I'm gone. So I'll send as many shades down there as possible today."

The reasoning seemed a little sketchy, but I didn't have time to debate. I heard a clamor coming from one of the rows of vines behind us. Apparently the maenads I'd held off with fire had decided to try again. And from the sound of things, they had reinforcements.

Time for another surprise. "Distract them a moment, will you?" Orphne grinned and ran towards them.

As she moved out of the way I saw Peter. He was staring in my direction without seeing me, his jaw slack, arms at his sides. I recognized the beginnings of shock. It was all coming to a head for him now, the terrible things he'd already endured suddenly combined with what I assumed was his first up-close look at bloodshed. Certainly his first encounter with battle.

I paused a moment, hoping he'd look at me so I could try to project courage and comfort to him. But he didn't, and I didn't have more time to waste.

Within a second I was hovering high enough to see the maenads approaching. Orphne was doing a taunting dance, waving her sword in the air one moment, the next turning around and waggling her rump at them.

The women weren't taking the bait by running towards her. Too bad for them. She would have killed them a lot more quickly.

I screamed a charm, causing them to look up. Their eyes were back on the ground a second later as a rustling sound grew louder and louder. The vine leaves around them were shivering, shrinking…

And changing.

Another second, and the maenads were screaming in pain as dozens of hand-sized scorpions clambered up their bodies, tails stinging again and again.

One of the maenads who'd been straggling escaped the furious arachnids and quickly turned to run. She got only a few steps before my fireball turned her into a running torch.

She dropped after another half-dozen steps. Her shrieks mingled with those of her sisters, who were now bloated with venom. Some had been stung so many times their skin was bursting in places. The sounds of their death-cries soared over the vineyard like an unearthly hymn.

From my aerial vantage point I glanced around. For the moment it looked like we were clear. I didn't think we'd have long to wait or far to go before running into more trouble. I floated back down to the ground.

"Well, we couldn't have announced our arrival much more loudly," I muttered as the rest gathered around me. Peter turned his eyes away from the dead maenads. The scorpions, their purpose outlived, crumbled away into dust.

"So now what? In a few minutes this place will be teeming with maenads, or worse," he said. He seemed to be a bit out of breath. I figured he was trying not to get sick again.

Heracles was looking impatiently down the main path that divided the fields. "Hmph," he said when he saw the still burning bodies. "Maybe we should just go down one of these rows and start ripping through the vines. Taking a short-cut through the—"

His thought was cut off as a bellow of pain erupted from him. Heracles crumpled to one knee and let loose another cry.

The spear he'd dropped earlier was embedded in his thigh. A maenad who'd been wounded, but clearly not seriously enough, was grinding her teeth as she gripped it with both hands and tried to force it further into the muscle.

With a furious shriek I ripped my sword from my belt and ran forward, plunging it into her throat. I turned to Heracles. He'd already grasped the spear. Biting his lip to steel himself he abruptly yanked it free, choking down another cry of pain.

He dropped the weapon and collapsed to the ground, his hand clamped as tightly to the wound as he could manage. Silvery ichor flowed through his fingers and down his leg. As a god, blood no longer flowed through his veins.

But there were streaks of purplish black in the fluid. It was Hydra venom released when the spear pierced his flesh. It would cause him crippling agony.

I knelt beside him, putting my hand over his. I chanted the strongest healing spell I knew, trying to keep the desperation out of my voice as I focused on reducing the damage.

Panic was already welling in the back of my mind. I knew none of my magic was strong enough to completely remove the poison from the long-dead Hydra. It hadn't lost any of its potency over the centuries and worse yet, it was one of the few toxins for which even I had no antidote. The only known cure lay in Apollo's palace. On Olympus.

I repeated the healing spell again, forcing my voice to reflect a calmness I didn't come close to feeling. It was stupid to maintain the façade in front of Heracles of all people.

He knew better than any how corrosive the Hydra's venom could be. He'd slain the beast himself, but was later poisoned by some of the venom through treachery. It had burned the last vestiges of his mortality away, leaving him a full god. But it nearly destroyed him in the process.

He was remembering it himself. "Hurts just as bad all these years later," he said through clenched teeth. A ragged exhalation burst through his lips, and he quickly sucked in fresh air.

The sound of tearing cloth distracted me momentarily. I turned my head and saw Peter ripping up his shirt. He ran over, strips of the cloth dangling from his hand.

"How far up is it spreading?" He directed the question to Heracles, who hesitated only a moment before indicating a spot a few inches above the wound. I hadn't told Peter exactly what the spear was, only that he had to stay clear of it and the knife I had, especially if we were still caught in the field after sunset when he'd no longer be protected by my salve. He must have guessed they were imbued with poison.

I bit back a protest. I knew full well the venom would have gone far higher than Heracles was indicating, and that it was so virulent even a proper tourniquet wouldn't stem it for long. The flimsy strip of cloth Peter was quickly tying around Heracles' leg would be useless.

Heracles knew it was pointless as well, but he let Peter do it. It was just like him to accept a caring gesture honestly offered, no matter how useless, even in the face of blinding pain. They don't call them heroes for nothing.

Peter quickly tore another strip from the mangled shirt and tied it just above Heracles' knee.

"This should stop the..." He started to say bleeding before taking a look at what was flowing out of Heracles' wound. Normally the skin would have sealed itself by then, but the Hydra's poison was strong enough to slow the normal healing process even for a god. He bit back the comment and finished tying the knots.

He had two more strips ready. He wadded up the rest of the shirt over the wound and bound it on.

"I wish I'd thought to grab the first aid kit from the wine shop," he muttered. "This shirt isn't exactly sterile."

Heracles managed a half-smile. "No worries. The poison on that spear is a lot worse than any random dirt that might be on the cloth. My thanks to you Peter, both for the shirt and your ministrations. You bind a wound quite neatly."

"I'm a Boy Scout," Peter said casually as he rose.

Heracles frowned a bit and nodded. "We had plenty of men like that back in my day, mostly in Athens. But I thought it had fallen out of favor."

If the situation hadn't been so grave I would have laughed a good ten minutes at Heracles' interpretation of the term Boy Scout. But after laughing I'd have to tell Peter that Heracles now assumed he was a pederast. That wouldn't be so amusing.

"We should try to get you back to the chariot," Orphne said softly.

Heracles waved an impatient hand, but it took him a few breaths before he could speak. "I'm still the strongest among you," he said in a strained voice. "I can't defeat Dionysus, but if he chooses to make an appearance I can delay him long enough to let you get away. We have to stay together."

"And how will *you* get away?" Peter asked as he looked down at Heracles struggle to ignore the pain. Heracles held his hand out to Orphne, and she started pulling him to his feet. Peter quickly moved to drape Heracles' other arm over his shoulder to help prop him up. Heracles pointed at the spear, and Orphne retrieved it.

"Can't leave it lying around for another maenad to find," Heracles said tightly. "Not a few minutes into battle, and I've already endangered us with my carelessness."

I was about to protest his self-criticism when my ears perked up. For a few moments there was nothing but the slight whisper of the breeze through the vine leaves.

Then I heard it again. A low growl, answered by at least two more.

No mistaking it. We had more company.

Chapter 48

"Cluster together, back to back!" Heracles shouted. The low growls were getting closer, along with the distinct sounds of footfalls. Several sets of them, rustling the grass just slightly.

I broke away from our cluster. From the location and intensity of the faint sounds, I estimated I had less than a minute to act.

"What are you doing now?" Heracles said in a distracted whisper. "No levitation! Cats can jump!"

True, but they'd be less inclined to jump through a barrier like fire. I quickly used my sword to dig a rough circle in the grass around us, then conjured up more fireballs. Carefully laying them on the ground I whispered a charm. The fire liquefied and flowed easily into the shallow makeshift trench. I jumped back with the others just before the circle was completely alight. The flames surged higher with another short spell.

Just in time. Three leopards appeared from the vines, two from ahead of us, one from behind.

"Holy shit," Peter whispered. "Can you use magic to control them?" he asked with a half-turn of his head in my direction.

"I don't have much luck with larger animals. Except wolves and dogs," I said.

I felt Peter tense as one of the leopards gave a fierce snarl. They were circling the fire, eyes wide and ears lowered, ready to make a leap. The fire was burning up to shoulder-height, but that didn't make a difference. It would only have held off leopards that were acting under their own instincts, not those controlled by a god.

"Too bad there aren't any dogs around," Peter muttered. He tensed again as the leopard closest to us gave a quick snarl and an exploratory bat of a paw at the wall of flames.

I digested Peter's unintentional suggestion. It was dangerous with a mortal in the group, but it just might work…

"Peter," I said quietly. "I need you to close your eyes."

"I'm not afraid of the leopards, Medea."

"They're going to be joined by that dog you mentioned. And you can't look at him, or you'll die, invulnerability ointment or not. Now close them! And don't open them again until I tell you, no matter what you hear. Or feel."

"Feel?" He whirled to face me completely at that.

"Do it NOW!" I yelled, spinning away from him to end the conversation. I lifted my arms and began the incantation, one of several I'd had to master during my apprenticeship in Hades.

"*Ancient guardian, implacable and incorruptible, you of clashing teeth and brazen claws, whose foaming mouths are as the pits of*

197

Tartarus, whose fury is as the roiling fires in the Earth's belly, Cerberus, spawn of Echidna and Typhon, attend me now..."

With the first few words dark clouds appeared out of nowhere, quickly extinguishing the faint glow that indicated dawn was near. As the chant progressed the black clouds thickened and boiled in fury, low rumbles of thunder echoing through the hills.

I finished the chant and clapped my hands three times. An enormous bolt of lightning shrieked through the sky and seared the ground in front of me, just outside the circle of flames.

The leopards were screaming in fury, clearly terrified at the uproar but unable to disobey their master's commands to attack us. But they were going to have a lot more to face than the four of us.

The sizzling plot of ground targeted by the lightning bolt split open, a crevice at least eight yards long forming and deepening. The cracked ground began to split and draw apart, and noxious fumes rose in thick clouds.

"Keep your eyes closed, Peter!" I had to yell at the top of my voice to be heard over the din coming from the fissure. "Don't open them for *anything*!"

The groans from the wounded, shifting Earth were suddenly augmented by deeper, more menacing rumbles. Abruptly a mournful howl emerged from the cleft, followed in quick succession by two more. All coming from the same source.

With an enormous bay from one head, snarls and barks from the other two, Cerberus leapt from the fuming ground.

His eyes glowed orange with darker red pupils. His black fur was shot through with streaks of blood red. It bristled stiffly, especially around his neck. Each of those hairs was needle-sharp. This was not a lap-dog, even for the dread Lord Hades.

The unholy beast's chest would have topped Heracles' head even if Heracles wasn't slightly hunched from his wound. He knew well and good what was behind him, but he wasn't about to turn his back on the leopards in front of him.

The leopards shrieked again, their high pitched protests barely audible over the sounds emanating from the opened ground. I couldn't leave that portal open long.

"Cerberus, guardian of Hades' dark realm, obey me!" I looked him directly in the eyes, which was no small feat considering there were six of them. "As Hecate's priestess I command you, hunt down these creatures which now threaten us. Destroy!"

With that final word all three heads of the beast rose and howled in unison. The leopards were growling and screaming at the top of their lungs. They'd backed away several yards, crouched low so they could leap at a moment's notice.

It was a moment they didn't have.

With a single growl Cerberus leaped high over us and landed on the other side of the circle, untouched by the flaming barrier. Two of his heads made quick work of the leopards there. There wasn't much left of either.

The hellhound spun around, blood still dripping from one set of lips, and soared over us again. All three heads took a turn with the final target.

With two heads lowered and snuffling for the scent of more prey Cerberus circled back in front of me. The center head was sniffing the air. After a few moments all three heads turned to me. The left one gave a slightly disinterested half-bark. I took that to be a message that there were no more beasts prowling around.

I couldn't keep Cerberus detained any longer for my needs. From the smoking cleft in the Earth something else was emerging. A hand, greenish and furry, with more than the normal complement of fingers, was tentatively exploring the earth.

"Cerberus," I said urgently. "You must go now. Your duties await. My thanks, faithful companion of Hades."

Two of the heads spotted the thing trying to crawl from the portal to Hades. With a raging bark and a couple of howls Cerberus leaped back into the opening, knocking the would-be escapee back into the pit with him. The ground shook beneath us. A rumble of grinding rocks echoed across the fields and the cleft closed seamlessly, a final wisp of brimstone escaping and dissipating.

I heaved a deep breath. It was taxing having to use so much magic in so short a period of time.

Peter must have noticed the sudden calm. "Can I open my eyes now?" I turned to find him with his eyes scrunched more tightly than they'd been in the chariot.

"All clear," I said. My voice was a bit ragged. I was really craving some ice cream. Peter opened his eyes cautiously. I muttered a quick spell and the circle of fire died out. He sat down heavily, his eyes gazing back towards the rise that divided us from the front of the property.

A grunt behind me drew my attention. I spun just in time to see Orphne catch Heracles as he collapsed.

"Medea!" she cried. "It's getting worse. Isn't there anything you can do?"

I knew my healing spells were useless. Perhaps I could try one to ease the pain—

"Medea..."

Peter's voice had an odd tone to it, but I was too impatient to pay attention to the subtleties.

"Not now—" I began. But Heracles was looking past me too, his eyes growing wider.

"RUN!" he yelled.

I turned instead, and wished for once I'd just listened to Heracles. A shadow was swooping towards us, and it wasn't another leopard.

Dawn was breaking, and in the light I could see a wall of green surging higher and higher. I realized too late what was happening. The land itself was rising up in a wave, like an emerald tsunami. I saw rows of vines being swept up as it roared towards us, each contributing to its height.

I spun around and started to run as if the Devil himself was after me. Orphne had already grabbed Heracles around the waist. Peter scrambled over to help out, but she shoved him away.

"Go!" she screamed over the increasing roar of the living wave behind us. "I can get him!"

"Let me help—" Peter's comment was cut off as Orphne swung her other arm under Heracles' legs and picked him up in both arms as if he was a child. She started running. Orphne's human guise made her look about a third of Heracles' size and about a sixth of his weight, but as they say, looks can be deceiving.

The incongruity made Peter freeze momentarily, but as he turned and got another look at what was coming for us he got over it. He started running too and quickly caught up with me.

Suddenly the looming shadow swept over us. A sound like a thousand trees in a windstorm was quickly growing louder just behind us.

"Faster!" I yelled back to Peter.

I felt the ground rising beneath our feet. Within seconds we were both off balance, tumbling into each other. We fell, but we were still moving. I felt rather than saw Peter sliding over me. He grabbed me around the waist as we moved forward. We were surrounded by vines that were twisting around us and over us, binding my limbs so tightly I couldn't move.

Peter's voice came to me over the roaring around us. He must have been shouting, but oddly, it sounded as if he was whispering directly in my ear.

"I'm with you! I'm here, Medea!"

It was the last thing I heard before the darkness closed in and the din abruptly ended.

Chapter 49

The darkness felt so nice. Cool. Soothing. Like my mother's hand on my cheek the winter I had that terrible fever, when I was still a girl years away from making the decision to become a priestess.

But the comfort of the darkness, like that memory, was fading. As consciousness pressed in on me so too did a thousand aches.

Crap. Where was I?

I opened my eyes but didn't gain any insight. It was nearly pitch black. There seemed to be a muted light several yards to my right.

I sat up slowly, giving myself a once-over. My ankle was throbbing. I knelt, raised that leg and put a little pressure on it as if to stand, gasping as the pain sharpened.

It was broken, but that was a minor inconvenience. I sat back for a few more minutes, breathing in to clear my head. Then I put my hand over my ankle and spoke a healing spell. The pain resolved into a throb, then an ache. Within seconds there was nothing.

I gingerly got up. No other major damage that I could discern. I felt a little stronger so I called up a fireball to light the scene.

The first thing I saw was a heavy barred gate in front of me. I panicked for a moment, thinking I must have been transported to some desolate spot. But when I turned, I saw rows of bottles behind me. I could see the Hawk's Haven logo on them.

A little good news, at least. I was still at the scene, and maybe the rest were too.

I walked over to the door, tried it. Locked, of course. When I tried the normal spell to open doors the lock glowed a bit, but didn't pop. I tried a stronger one. Nothing.

Of course Dionysus could easily make the lock impervious to magic. He wasn't about to let me get away.

And after what had happened, I doubted he'd buy the ruse that I'd decided to accept his invitation. Good allies don't usually slaughter your minions.

I looked as far through the bars as I could. A hallway of some sort. The wall at the close end had windows up high. I figured it must be some kind of wine cellar under the main shop. The rest of the hall stretched into darkness. I couldn't tell how far it went.

But maybe there were more chambers like this.

"Hello?" I called, trying project confidence. There was a slight echo, but no response.

"Heracles? Orphne?" Again, nothing. "Peter?"

Only the faint echo of my voice, coming off from the dark end of the hall.

I turned back to explore my prison cell. It was large enough to walk around comfortably. A small crate in one corner looked like it would serve as a passable seat. Certainly, there was no shortage of wine.

Well, why not? It could be a long wait.

I walked along the walls, willing the fireball to float with me so I could check out the selection. I finally chose a merlot. A simple charm, and the cork eased up and popped out.

Even if Dionysus had made my prison door impervious to magic, he wasn't blocking me from using sorcery otherwise.

I took the bottle over to the crate and sat down. A quick taste told me the wine was respectable enough. I couldn't drink too much, but I needed something to quench the thirst that was growing more insistent.

Whether the wine was relaxing me more, or whether I was just more comfortable sitting, it seemed easier to think after a few swallows. I weighed my options.

The walls were stone, so using fire to burn my way out wouldn't work. Maybe I could conjure a hot enough fire to melt the grated door?

I decided that would be a last resort. I needed to conserve energy. If he'd made the door impervious to magic, Dionysus had probably made it invulnerable to other forces as well.

The thought came to me that if I could call up a portal again, as I had the night before, I might be able to slip away. Maybe with a little more concentration I actually could get to Aiaia, or Hades if necessary. Even if I didn't end up where I wanted, I'd still be better off.

I took another couple of swallows of wine, trying to decide whether I could work up the nerve to attempt it. More importantly, whether I could figure out *how* to attempt it. I still had no clue how I'd done it the first time.

"That wine won't help you if you're serious about getting out of here, Medea."

I didn't have a yardstick, but it was probably one of the higher jumps I've made after being startled.

The young woman at the door was eying me curiously. She didn't have vine leaves in her hair or a thyrsus in her hand. She wasn't naked, either. She was wearing something that looked like a patent leather body suit.

I've always loved subtle.

I tipped the bottle towards her. "I'd offer you some, but the bars look a little narrow. I don't think the bottle would fit through."

"Easily solved," she said as she held up something glittery. She slipped it down to the lock. A second later the door swung open.

I had no intention of approaching her. Let her come to me, if she had honest intentions.

"I guess he didn't think about blocking the obvious way to open a lock," she observed casually. She made no move to come into the space. Smart girl.

I looked at her a little more closely. Her hair was dark, probably black, but it was hard to tell from the diffuse light in the hall. My fireball cast a little glow over there, but not much.

"Are you just going to sit there all day?" she asked, a little hint of impatience in her voice.

"I might. You can just leave the door open and be on your way. Unless you'd like to come in and introduce yourself."

She smiled a bit. "I'd rather stay here, if it's all the same. You're free to come over and walk out with me."

Well, it wouldn't hurt to try. Or maybe it would. But I could probably give a little hurt in return, at the very least.

"You still haven't given me a name," I said as I eased up. I didn't intend to make any sudden movements.

"You can call me Nyx."

The godddess of night, except I'd met the real one. They didn't look remotely similar.

Black hair, black outfit, suitably Goth name. Cute.

"And before I just walk out the door and into what's probably another trap, do you mind telling me why you're here?"

The smile didn't change. "I'm not working for Dionysus, if that's what you think. I've been keeping my eye on the old woman while you've been chasing down other leads, trying to play catch-up. If only you'd done the same, you would have gotten to the vineyard in enough time to save those field hands, and the woman in the shop."

I walked slowly towards her, the fireball floating with me. "Why didn't you save them?"

She shrugged. "Couldn't give myself away. But he's known *you've* been after him all along."

"And how do I know you weren't the one to tell him, since it seems you know so much about what I've been doing?"

She shrugged again. "You don't. But at the moment, I'm the only one who can get you out of this building undetected. He thinks you're trapped in here. He won't be expecting you. And you might still have time to save the others."

I had no idea who she was, but I had a very good idea what my tolerance threshold for bullshit was. She'd just surpassed it.

I quickened my pace. She didn't flinch. I'd reflexively called up the glamour that masked my eyes when I was waking up, but now I dropped it.

"All right. I don't know who you really are, but—"

I stopped dead in my tracks. We were close enough to see eye to eye. I don't know what she made of mine, but I knew what to make of hers, especially the serpent-slit pupils.

Dammit. She was one of Lamia's bitches.

Chapter 50

I jumped back and called fireballs into my hand.

In a shot Nyx sidled out of the way and did the same.

What the *hell*? Lamia's brats had higher than normal strength and could climb the sheerest surfaces, backwards if necessary. But none of them had ever done *that*. Had Lamia found a way to give them new powers?

"We can have a duel if it suits you, Medea," she said stridently. "But it would give us both away to Dionysus. Don't you think it would be nice to try discretion for once?"

I narrowed my eyes. "Sorry if I'm skeptical. Lamia and her family haven't exactly been close friends."

"Take care, Medea," she hissed. "Lamia could teach you a thing or two about how to treat family."

The witty repartee came to a standstill. We stood there sizing each other up for what seemed an eternity. Finally, Nyx dropped her hands, allowing her fireballs to go out.

"I don't have time for this," she spat as she spun around.

"Wait."

She half-turned to me. I hesitated, then lowered my arms slowly and let the fireballs go out. "I suppose if you were going to attack me, you'd have done it. And since Dionysus already had me, I suppose he wouldn't have sent you to play games with me."

She faced me fully. "Now you're showing some sense. Who, by the way, do you think gave Lamia the information about the old woman?"

I took a tentative step towards Nyx. "Is there any other information you can give me that will help me?"

She turned again, motioning for me to follow. "Even if I had a book's worth of information, it wouldn't do you any good. What it comes down to is power, Medea. And you don't have enough to defeat Dionysus, even with Heracles. Especially now that Dionysus has killed scores of people and consumed their blood."

The implications chilled me. "All here in Atlanta?"

"Many, but not all. And his maenads have come here from far afield as well. It's been hard to count, but I estimate more than a hundred here, not counting the ones you've killed. I've heard them talking. He's started setting up bases elsewhere."

We were moving into the darkened portion of the hall. I tensed a bit. It was the perfect place to be waylaid, if Dionysus had sense enough to post guards in case I escaped.

Sense, however, might not be a trait Dionysus had in abundance now. If he'd drunk as much blood as Nyx implied, he'd be well on his way to insanity through the Curse of Prometheus.

"How have you managed to avoid being detected?"

I sensed rather than saw her look over her shoulder, just as I sensed a cynical smile. "For starters, I didn't storm in here with a flaming chariot drawn by dragons. And when I came across dead bodies in the fields—and there are far more out there than the handful you found—I left them alone, rather than spiriting them off somewhere for some kind of arcane ritual."

"It proved most enlightening," I offered.

"So has discreet observation," she countered. The light was getting a bit brighter. "And I haven't gotten attacked. Just a little further," she said.

We'd been moving fairly carefully. It was obviously a courtesy to me. Lamia's daughters can see like cats in the darkness. She could have covered the distance in a third of the time without me in tow.

Just as her outline became firmly defined in the half-light she turned sharply to the left.

"Up here."

I followed carefully, stubbing my toe on the first step. I muted a curse. It was my own carelessness, after all. The stairs wound in a tight circle, the walls narrow enough that I could touch them without fully extending my arms.

A burst of light dazzled my eyes. Nyx had opened a door and was looking to each side.

"Clear," she said as she moved up.

I quickened my pace but checked both ways as well before coming through the door. We were back in the shop. I hadn't noticed the door the first time around. The smell from the dead body hadn't improved any.

Nyx stepped over the body and headed into the lobby.

"This way," she motioned me impatiently. She was already at the front door.

"Your dragons and chariot are safe. You should be able to get away if you act quickly."

"And do what?"

She smiled wickedly. "Do what you should have done to begin with. Go straight to Hell." She opened the door. "By now, you should have enough information to get Hecate herself to listen. If you can't, then you're more incompetent than I expected."

I bit back a snappy reply and headed to the door. She was right, damn her. I'd botched it royally. There was no way to know where Heracles and the rest were, and no way for me to save them if Dionysus was keeping an eye on them. Maybe Peter, being human, would be left unguarded, but he wouldn't do the others much good.

A noise stopped me in my tracks.

"What was that?"

"Nothing to concern you," Nyx said, another hint of impatience in her voice.

The sound came again, clearer now. It was muffled, but it was definitely human. It was coming from near the fireplace. I strode over there, stopping briefly when Nyx gave a disgusted snort. I turned to face her.

"Is there something you don't want me to see?" I demanded.

"If you want to waste time, that's your business. I'm not waiting any longer. Getting away is your problem now."

What happened next was so quick it took me several seconds to digest it. Nyx faded—not vanished, but faded—from view. Then the door slammed.

No wonder she'd been able to evade detection. She had the power of invisibility—another trait Lamia's daughters had never exhibited before. It was she, not an errant wind, who slammed the door.

What the hell was Nyx, then? A sorceress, perhaps, who'd run afoul of Lamia and been changed. If so, I could see why Lamia had sent her to spy on Dionysus.

The muffled noise came again. I decided it was worth the few extra minutes to investigate. Nyx didn't think it was worth it, but then she wasn't exactly keeping the best company. She didn't indicate it was any kind of threat, so what was the harm?

I found a closet next to the back of the fireplace. It must be some kind of small storage space. I ripped the door open, ready to fight if necessary.

It wasn't. There was a white bundle on the floor. It jerked when I tore the door open. I could see enough to determine it was human.

I stepped inside. Whoever she was, she looked like she was wrapped in some kind of sheet. There was a strip of cloth over the lower half of her face, a small protrusion where the mouth would be indicating it held some kind of gag in place.

I moved over and began loosening the gag. I could see her hands bound behind her back, but decided to let those bonds stay until I could figure out who the hell it was.

It didn't take long. The gag came loose and I pulled it away.

Lyn O'Neill stared up and me and began sobbing in relief.

Chapter 51

"Ms. Keres!" she said between sobs. I was busy with the cords that tied her hands. Her feet were unbound. It took me only a moment to get her hands free and pull her up. We staggered out of the closet.

"Thank God," she whimpered. "I didn't think anyone would ever find me. I thought it was him…" She trailed off weakly, but she didn't need to elaborate. I had no doubt who she was talking about.

I'd thought she was wound in a sheet, but as she moved the folds fell into place. She was in a chiton, a Greek garment held together along the top edges with small broaches and belted at the waist to form a simple gown.

"Why are you dressed like that?" I asked gently.

She looked up to answer, but the words caught in her throat. She looked petrified. "Your *eyes*—"

I hadn't bothered replacing the masking glamour. "Never mind that, Lyn. I'll explain later. I'll help you get out of here if I can. Are you injured? We'll have to walk several miles to find help."

She backed away a bit, shook her head. "I can walk, but it's no good. We can't leave. He said there was a barrier around the vineyard. No one can get out."

"Who said that?" I prompted gently, staying where I was. She was cowed by my golden eyes. I didn't need to frighten her further my moving closer or appearing too intense.

If the information was accurate, I was in trouble. I wouldn't be able to use the chariot to get out. I certainly couldn't try to take Lyn in it. She'd be incinerated before she even stepped foot inside. I'd used up my reserve of invulnerability ointment on Peter. Of course she probably wouldn't have the backbone to get within twenty paces of the thing, invulnerable or not.

I moved towards one of the couches and motioned to another one. "You can sit down, if you like. Tell me what's going on so I can help you."

She balked a bit before picking her way over to the couch. We both sat down.

"You said someone told you about the barrier," I reminded her. "A man, was it? Who is it?"

"I don't know his name!" she blurted out in frustration. "But he says things to me. Horrible things. He says my place is here with him, and that I'm never going to leave him!"

She started snuffling again, wiping the back of her hand against her nose before brushing impatiently at her eyes.

"He's—I don't know. There's something not right about him. He's tall, very tall, almost like he's a giant or something. And his head...." She stopped for another sniffle, but I didn't need to press her again. She pointed to her forehead. "He's got *leaves* growing out of his head, circling around like some kind of crown."

"Does he have a beard?" I asked, though I already knew the answer.

"It's black, just like his hair. It almost doesn't look real, the way it curls so perfectly."

"He does things," she went on, her voice pitching higher with fear. "He makes things appear out of nowhere. Food," she looked down at herself. "These clothes. He said he's the one who made all the grape vines start growing again. Have you seen them?"

"I have," I said. "It's frightening, what he's done." I wondered if she knew just how frightening. There was no point in giving her the "You're In Danger" speech. She'd figured that much out herself. Time to move beyond that. "Lyn, I need to know if your mother is here."

She nodded, squeezing her eyes shut. She put her hand over her mouth and tried to choke back the sobs. After a few moments she calmed down enough to answer me.

"She's the one who brought me here. She said now that Shannon is dead, the vineyard is mine. That I had to take over for Shannon." She gave a sound halfway between a laugh and a sob. "I thought she was just bringing me up here to sign papers or something. I didn't know..." She stopped, took a couple of breaths. "Didn't know she was one of them. That she's with *him*. How could she be involved in this?"

"One of them?"

She sighed. "There are a lot of other women up here. But there's something wrong with them. They don't act right. It's like they're on some kind of drug. And they—"

"Run around naked," I finished for her. I almost had enough, but something made me push just a little further. "She's changed, hasn't she? Your mother is different. Has been for some time now."

Her breathing was becoming steadier now. I figured having someone there to talk with was the best medicine for her. "It's been a few months. I thought she was just getting edgier because of the wedding and all. And then when Shannon died... I understood why she was so distant. But it's like she's become a totally different person."

Couldn't have said it better myself.

"Have you seen your mother and the man together?" I prodded gently. I hoped she knew that I didn't just mean in the same place at the same time. Dionysus' appetites in the sexual arena were legendary.

From the grimace that marred her face I figured she understood clearly enough. She pressed her hands to her face. Small choked sounds came from her throat.

She stopped after a moment. "Are you here with Father Kirkpatrick?" she asked in a meek voice.

I leaned forward. "Yes! You've seen him? Were there others with him? A large man and a woman?"

She nodded. "They were all in the maze with Mother and that man. But..." She closed her eyes and began to cry again.

"What, Lyn? You have to tell me."

"I think they killed Father Kirkpatrick."

"How?" I asked, trying not to let my feelings show.

"I didn't see it. I turned away. But I heard him screaming. It went on for a long time. Finally Mother told that man she didn't want me there, because I was such a coward. She had some of those other women bring me here and tie me up. She said she'd lock me up until I learned to accept reality."

She broke down again. I let her whine to herself. I needed the time to think. Just as her sobs ebbed I made my decision.

I went over to her and took her by the arm. "Take me to the maze."

"No!" She pulled away, but not hard enough to break my grip. "You don't know what you're saying!"

"I know exactly what I'm saying!" I said firmly. "We're going to get out of here. But I need the help of my friends to do it. Will you help me find them?"

She looked away. "I'm scared..."

"You're always scared!" I yelled as my grip tightened into a vise. "And what has that gotten you? Being timid, being meek, being a good girl... look where it's landed you! You're in far worse trouble than you know, Lyn. If you don't learn to fight you're always going to be someone's pawn. Right now it's your mother, but even if you get out of this, you'll end up dancing to someone else's tune unless you change!"

She cringed deeper into the couch as I vented my frustration.

"I'm going," I said, dropping her arm and stalking away. "You can stay here if you like," I tossed over my shoulder. "I can find the maze without you. Peter gave me a good idea of the layout of the place. But I can't promise I'll be able to come back for you. My first duty is to find my friends."

She remained silent.

"Wait!" she yelled as she dashed to catch up with me. I didn't break my stride.

"I know I'm no good to anyone in a fight," she said as we stepped up the pace. "But I won't get in the way. I want to get away from here. From everything. Especially her. Mother is sick, but that doesn't mean I have to suffer too."

I slowed a bit and turned towards her. "That's a sensible approach, Lyn." I yanked open the door, half expecting to see a crowd of maenads there. There wasn't.

Lyn yelped when we walked out of the building and she saw the chariot. Evelyn must have dragged her into the building through a back door.

"Don't worry about them," I said. "They're with me. And don't even ask."

As we passed by one of the dragons lifted its head in my direction. "Not yet," I said firmly. "But soon. Be ready." A low reptilian hiss told me the message was understood.

"Is there a way to reach the maze undetected?" I asked as we moved towards the rise. Lyn nodded.

"Just a bit over the hill there's a stretch of trees to the right of the fields. It goes all the way back to the maze and garden. If it's just the two of us it should be enough to provide some cover. There are a couple of small breaks, but if we hurry past them there shouldn't be a problem."

I climbed the rise slowly, crouching just before the crest to edge my head up. The coast was clear. I nodded to Lyn and went over the top.

She followed, more quickly than I would have expected in the chiton. They're elegant but not the easiest outfits to maneuver in when you're in a hurry.

The trees were the perfect cover. I'd only glimpsed them in bits and pieces during my previous forays and hadn't realized they stretched almost unbroken for such a distance.

We moved silently as I kept an eye out for any foot patrols. I kept peering through the trees to make sure we didn't overshoot the mark.

We kept on until I spied a clearing on the other side of the trees. It went on for several yards before a large stand of boxwood appeared.

I moved closer and carefully peeped through the trees. Sure enough, four maenads armed with swords were standing along the front of the maze, two flanking each side of the entrance. At least now I knew what we'd be up against if we had to get out of the maze that way.

I turned back to Lyn. "Stay here," I whispered. She looked confused but didn't argue. When I judge I was a safe distance from the front of the maze I moved through the trees, staying on my hands and knees.

I called a fireball and quickly moved it along the boxwood wall, tracing a decent-sized half circle. The branches caught fire, green though they were. I mentally guided the flames to burn quickly through to the other side, forming an arc-shaped tunnel.

I didn't hear any commotion from that side of the boxwood so I chanced a quick crawl through, carefully peeping to either side. The coast was clear.

"What are you doing?" asked a voice from behind me.

"Getting into the maze," I told Lyn. I wasn't surprised that she'd followed me. "Come on." I shimmied through the hole, and Lyn followed through a second later.

She stood up, brushing stray leaves off herself. "What now?"

I hardened my expression. "You know exactly what we're going to do now. You're taking me to Dionysus. The game is up, Agave."

Chapter 52

A disdainful look crossed Lyn's face before she started changing. Her hair grew longer and curlier, dark brown with streaks of grey. The face looking back at me still had a lot of Evelyn in it, but there was no doubt someone else was there too.

"So my disguise did not fool you," she said cooly.

"But it fooled Paul Kirkpatrick when you stood outside Lyn's sorority house after helping Dionysus commit another murder, didn't it? He really thought Lyn was involved. Were you trying to frame her to make it easier to get personal control of the vineyard? Hoping he would call the police instead of me?"

She merely smiled. "I have heard so much about you, Medea," she said, not bothering to hide the contempt in her voice. "And now I meet you, the greatest sorceress of the ancient world, and find you spend your days chasing petty demons, as if you were a menial. You had ample opportunities to rule, Medea, yet you shrank from taking power. How pathetic."

"There is more to ruling than the power to command men's deaths, Agave. How pathetic that *you* never saw those truths." It was my turn to be disdainful, and I've had plenty of practice putting the note in my voice. "You will learn this day that I shrink from *nothing*."

I gestured in the general direction of the fields. "Your minions fared badly out there, Agave. We slaughtered all you sent against us. You are a poor leader. Since you will never command loyalty, perhaps you should try your hand at learning competence before sending your underlings to face their betters. Their betters, and yours."

Her nostrils flared as her false smile disappeared, replaced by a glare.

"You insolent witch—" Her invective was cut short as I called a fireball into my hand and shot forward. She drew back instinctively.

"Insolent, perhaps, but no coward," I sneered. "I am of blood as royal as yours, Agave. And in my father's kingdom we were taught to stand our ground, not to quaver in the face of attack."

I allowed the fire to go out and stared down at her. "Were you about to run to Dionysus for protection, Agave? That is another difference between us. I fight my own battles rather than cowering behind dark Hecate's skirts. She would never have chosen me as her priestess otherwise."

I smiled slowly, taking yet another step towards her. She didn't move back, but I was rewarded by seeing a twitch in her legs that told me she'd thought about it.

"Tell me, great Agave" I drawled slightly. "Since we speak of skirts, does your god still wear them? As he did when he hid among the nymphs, gathering them about to protect himself?" It felt good to remind her that Dionysus had once been an outcast, hunted by Hera who was jealous of Zeus' affair with his mother.

Her eyes narrowed to slits. "See for yourself what he wears!" she hissed as she spun away from me. She thrust her hand sharply towards the inner side of the maze.

The greenery split open in front of her, bending to either side in great ripples that flattened the shrubs to the ground. A second later the next row of shrubs parted, and the next, until the final barrier to the center of the maze was down.

Having witnessed many terrible things in my life, several of them in the past day, I was able to keep an impassive face at what I saw there. Or rather, who.

He was at least nine feet tall for the moment. Like the other Olympians he could grow in an instant to any height he desired, towering over mountains if he wished it. But apparently Dionysus was content to keep a low profile in his new stomping ground.

That didn't mean he'd held back displays of his power in any other area.

His clothing was sumptuous, far more elaborate than the simple covering he was normally depicted with in art. A silk chiton in richest scarlet, heavy with brocade at the neck and hem, hung in luxurious folds around him. A leopard skin was draped from one shoulder.

Every finger had multiple rings of silver, gold and precious gems. Heavy necklaces of amethyst and pearls circled his neck. His ears were pierced, hung with large crescents of carnelian wrapped with gold wire. On any other male the outfit would have been ridiculously effeminate, but on him it merely looked decadent, speaking of someone who liked his pleasures and equally enjoyed showing himself off in splendor.

The hair that flowed past his shoulders was so dark and luxuriant it almost looked like a wig. The surreal effect was heightened by the living grape vines that sprouted from his brow and circled his head. They were intertwined with thick gold wire that trailed loosely down, separating his hair into large hanks without really confining it.

There was no gold twined through the beard. It was just as I remembered it from my visions in the Sybil's mirror and on Aiaia: thick, curled precisely and heavily oiled, gleaming richly. Almost everything was exactly as I'd seen in the visions.

Except for his eyes. Just as mine glowed golden, his glowed too. They were red.

The realization sent a little chill over me. When I'd seen his eyes in the vision on Aiaia they were verdant, appropriate for a god whose powers were related to cultivation. But now they burned like angry coals. It could only mean one thing.

The madness from the Curse of Prometheus was taking firm hold of him. This was the worst scenario possible. I'd only held scant hope that I might be able to reason with him, but at least it had been something. Now that little wisp of hope was gone too.

Agave might have seen the flicker in my eyes. She smiled slightly and gestured for me to proceed forward.

I got a broader view of the scene around the mad god as I drew closer to the heart of the maze. There was a low table of marble flanked by flaming torches. Behind it was an enormous seat on a dais. It was impossible to tell what material it was made from, because it was entirely draped in animal skins. I spotted hides from leopards, bears, wolves. A couple of over-stuffed pillows in gaudy violet silk provided a place to lean in ease against the low back.

The maenads were there, too. As I drew closer to the inner perimeter of the maze, I saw them spaced in neat formation around the circle. All of them were armed. None of them were smiling.

Dionysus' eyes fell on me, and I quickly turned my gaze away. I'd have no way to defend myself against his power if I made eye contact. It would be hard enough to resist him in any event.

As I looked past Dionysus my heart leaped in my chest. Heracles!

But just as suddenly my heart slowed and grew a little heavier. He was hanging from his wrists, which were bound over his head, in what looked like an enormous geode. His feet were several inches from the bottom. The huge cleft rock glowed softly in amethyst light, which sparkled off the crystal facets embedded in the inner wall. He was unconscious, but as near as I could tell he was otherwise unharmed.

I turned my head impassively back towards Dionysus' general direction and looked up, careful not to meet his gaze.

"So, you join us at last, Medea," he said casually, as if greeting an old friend who was just a trifle late for a soiree.

I risked a slight lift of my head. "I am here, but make no mistake. I will *join* you in nothing," I said evenly.

People had been obliterated for speaking like that to a god, but he merely chuckled. The sound was colder than the waters of Styx. He made an idle gesture towards Heracles. "I wanted to have your hero awake for your arrival, but he does love to fight. It was quite entertaining for awhile, but I'm afraid he hadn't the stamina to keep it up. He needed a nap."

He slowly walked towards the glowing geode and regarded it. "Have no worries, though. Heracles won't be leaving anytime soon. No, I think I'll keep him here to play with awhile longer. After all, we're half-brothers. Brothers should sport together now and again, don't you agree?"

He knew I wouldn't bother responding. Dionysus resumed his slow amble towards his throne. He took his time ascending the dais and sitting down.

I could see enough of the wine god's face to tell he was smiling. "You must be wondering about that little prison, Medea. Pretty, isn't it? A portal to a world of my own creation. And very effective. Heracles can't set so much as the tip of a toe on this Earth. Nor will the other gods be able to find him, including that troublemaker who sent him after me."

He made another slight move of his hand in Heracles' direction. "You seem dubious, Medea. Go on, try it for yourself. See that he is perfectly sealed."

When I didn't move a slight hint of steel entered his voice. "I insist," he said, the precise enunciation making it clear I had no choice.

Well, no need to start the fighting just yet.

I went over to the geode. Aside from the fact that the interior was suffused with shifting purple light that had no discernible source, there seemed to be nothing unusual.

I tentatively lifted my hand and carefully moved the palm towards the opening. A tingling started almost instantly, growing more intense as my palm got closer to the edge. I suspected full contact with the open space through which I could see Heracles would be quite painful. But perhaps not as painful as disobeying Dionysus so soon.

I took a deep breath and thrust my hand the final inch.

No pain, only a slight numbness. I tried to press my hand further in to touch Heracles but found I couldn't. I was pushing against something invisible but with definite give, almost like gelatin. I couldn't get my hand past the outer edge of the prison.

I turned towards the dais. "Where are the others?" I asked coldly. Might as well get the bad news over with.

"It doesn't matter," Agave spoke from directly behind me. I hadn't heard her coming up, but I was proud that I didn't jump even a little at the unexpectedness of her voice.

I turned my head slightly in her direction, a half-acknowledgement that one used when a servant spoke, implying they weren't worth your full attention. The slight wasn't lost upon her.

She circled around me, her aggravation apparent. "You won't see your friends again, including that pretty little boy you've been sporting with," she said with pure spite. She pointed to the geode. "Heracles was your only hope of getting word to the high gods. And now that hope is gone. He is trapped between worlds, in a place none can find him."

She allowed a slight smile to quirk the edges of her mouth. "And soon my lord Dionysus will be strong enough, our followers plentiful enough, that it will matter little whether the Olympians know what we're doing."

She was moving towards the dais now. As I watched her form shifted yet again, the plain white chiton becoming cloth-of-gold. It trailed beneath her feet, but she gracefully held the front hem up just enough to keep from stepping on it.

Heavy jewels appeared at her wrists and neck from nowhere and an ornate tiara seemed to grow from her brow as she turned around to face me again and sat at the feet of her god.

My eyes were focused on her jewels. They flashed brilliantly. They were encrusted with precious stones, some of them amethysts or sapphires, others new and exotic gems which I'd never seen before, and which I doubted had ever been seen by any human. Perhaps they were created from nothing, perhaps they were dragged from areas of the Earth so deeply inaccessible that men would never reach them in a thousand lifetimes.

But none of them looked like the jewels the mysterious woman in the Sybil's mirror had worn.

Evelyn—*Agave*, I reminded myself—noticed me staring at her adornments. She smiled, her eyelids lowering a bit. "You see how generous my lord can be, Medea," she said with a slightly cajoling tone.

Of course. The insinuations would start first, then the open invitation to join their ranks. Dionysus now knew from my escape the previous night that I had powers no one—not even me—had known about. There were only two options for him.

Win me over, or get rid of me for good.

Chapter 53

"But I forget myself," Dionysus said languidly as he leaned back against one of the cushions. "I wouldn't want to be accused of violating the laws of hospitality. Forgive me, Medea. Have some refreshments."

He turned a hand palm-up and slightly lifted the first three fingers. My arm rose with it. A nice display of power, proving he didn't need to look me in the eyes directly to make me his puppet. He wasn't causing me harm, so he technically didn't violate the laws against laying a hand on a priestess in violence. Nice way to skirt the rules.

Instantly I felt something solid materialize in my hand, and I looked to find a golden goblet. Ruby cabochons were spaced around it, but they were not nearly as red as the contents.

The smell of copper wafted up to me.

"Drink, Medea, dear guest," Agave purred. "It's a vintage that will soon become quite popular." I glanced up to see she had her own goblet from which she sipped delicately. The slight smear of red on her lips told me the contents of our cups were the same.

But not the contents of our hearts.

Mastering all my strength, I twisted my wrist. It felt as if I were trying to move in a skin-tight iron vise. It was excruciating, but I finally managed to turn my hand enough to spill the blood on the ground. With a final surge of willpower I relaxed my fingers enough to allow the cup to slip from my grasp. It made a dull thud as it hit the neatly manicured grass of the maze.

Dionysus feigned a disappointed exhalation. "Such a waste. He was so nice looking, young and strong. Do you think he'd appreciate your refusal?"

I knew he was implying Peter was dead, but I wasn't biting. I'd known Agave was lying when she said the same thing back at the office.

"I suppose he'd be insulted, at least as much as an animal can be," I said through clenched teeth. "Was it one of your precious leopards who died to fill my cup?"

A harsh laugh burst from Dionysus as he sat upright and clapped his hands in glee. "Well done, Medea, well done! How did you know?" The pressure on my arm disappeared as he gave another laugh.

I allowed myself the smallest smile of satisfaction. "It takes little wit to realize you won't be wasting human blood on anyone else yet. Not when you have to build your own power to challenge the high gods."

"Mmmm," he sighed as he leaned back once more. "Your reputation for cleverness is well earned. It was a bull, by the by. I don't kill my leopards. They are cunning and loyal. As you yourself appear to be. Such traits should be rewarded."

"Loyalty, yes," Agave said, leaning against the back of the throne and coming within inches of Dionysus' leg. "But those who are cunning must be carefully watched. Deception is second nature to them."

"As you would know best," I shot back. Her mouth compressed enough to let me know my barbs were getting to her.

"And yet it is so useful," Dionysus said as he reached down to stroke Agave's hair lovingly. She craned her neck, closing her eyes in ecstasy and reaching up into the touch as a cat leans into a caress. To see a human behave that way was sickening.

"Did you know, Medea, that it was my dear aunt Agave who came up with the plan for spreading my cult over the Earth again?"

"No," I said with as much disinterest as I could fake. "Based on the crudeness of the killings, I had no idea there *was* a plan. In fact," I tried adding a note of flattery, "I had a hard time convincing myself that *you* were involved at all, Dionysus. But if the plan was Agave's, well, I can see why it looked so haphazard."

Her eyes shot open and her legs tensed, but Dionysus put a hand on her shoulder to prevent her from leaping up in outrage. His head shook with silent mirth. "I can see Heracles isn't the only one who likes to play. Oh, you will be good company, Medea. Perhaps I should have *two* high priestesses?"

Agave's sharp inhalation might have been from fury, or the slight increase in pressure I noticed as Dionysus' fingers made deeper indentations into her golden robe.

"Tell her, dear aunt, what your plan is." His voice was mild enough, but it still took several seconds for Agave's shoulders to relax. When they did Dionysus resumed his gentle strokes on her head.

"The plan is simple, Medea. Even you should have figured it out by now."

I shrugged. "You want to corrupt as many women as possible to revive the long-dead cult of Dionysus. That hardly takes much guesswork."

"Exactly," she said. "As you know, the maenad's ecstasy is transferred from woman to woman by close contact."

"Like an illness," I said with coldness.

She waved away the insult. "Happiness is also infectious, I'm told. In the old days, of course, it was simple. Women naturally congregated, since they were by and large segregated from the men. And they often welcomed visiting kin, or even strangers from nearby villages, into their gatherings. So it was easy to spread the touch of our god across the countryside.

"But there was a difference. Back then, women held no power. Even I, mother of a king, could not wield enough influence to allow my lovely lord Dionysus to formally establish his worship in our city of Thebes."

"An obstacle which you found a way to overcome," I noted tartly.

The reference to her brutal murder of Pentheus, her own son, didn't faze her in the least. "Just so. But it mattered little even then. Our influence could only spread so far. But now, the story is different.

"Now, women have a far greater role in the world. They are scientists, healers, politicians, even military officials. Teachers, industrialists, police. Some lead countries, or are in line to lead them, and in these days they need no husband to establish their claim to power. They have it on their own merit."

She was sitting up, leaning forward just enough to show her warming enthusiasm for the subject without breaking away from Dionysus' caress.

"It is a network, Medea. Not a network of mere village gossips and midwives as it used to be. It is a vast system of power and influence whose members know how to cooperate because they have all had to fight harder and longer to gain their positions. And with such shared experiences, naturally they meet with each other quite frequently. Giving ample opportunity for a god's touch—*my* god's—to spread among them to bless their lives."

I saw it in my mind as she spoke. Women of power networking and meeting. Small groups within cities, multi-city conventions, international conferences... women from every possible walk of life and profession coming together, drawn by common interests and pursuits but equally bonded by simply being women.

Agave had found the perfect tool for infiltrating multiple layers of society to the deepest levels. Once he had control of enough women, Dionysus could bring the world itself to a standstill.

Police, militaries, intelligence agencies... all of them would be thrown into chaos if the women among them turned against them. Women in financial institutions could engage in mass stock and commodity selloffs, plunging word markets into panic and triggering economic collapse in every major country. Women who were doctors and nurses could use their knowledge of medicine to hurt as well as heal. It was the perfect scenario for terrorist infiltration.

How quickly could Dionysus gather enough followers to sabotage an entire planet? Considering the amount of personal and professional travel women did these days, it might just be a matter of weeks.

And no one would see it coming until it was too late.

"Our guest seems distracted," Dionysus pouted. "Perhaps we should bring something to lighten her mood." He lifted his hand from Agave's neck and gave two staccato claps.

A loud rustling began behind him. A large mass of dark brown emerged into view from behind the throne. As it shuffled mindlessly forward I realized it was roughly human in form. It was made out of dark, dried vinestalks. Some kind of automaton, I guessed.

But what came out next made my breath race through my throat. An arm, then a shoulder. Then—

I couldn't control the outburst.

"Peter!"

Chapter 54

The vine-man had Peter under the arms and was dragging him slowly into view. The movement was jerky, but the pauses were long enough that I could tell Peter was still breathing. I quickly scanned him for marks. None were visible. My ointment was still protecting him.

The scarecrow jerked Peter upright, holding him roughly by both arms. Peter's eyes fluttered open as his head bobbed up.

"Medea," he said weakly. "They said they killed you."

"But it failed to break your spirit. Still, the day is not yet over," Agave said icily. "But it will be soon." She glanced to the sky. Only then did I realize how far the sun had sunk. It must be late afternoon already. There was only an hour, perhaps a little more, until the sun set.

Until Peter was vulnerable.

Agave knew it. "This witch's magic will dissipate with the sun's light, and *you* will die, Peter Kirkpatrick." She turned to me with a satisfied gleam in her eyes. "That shall be your entertainment, Medea. You shall watch your young lover bleed out. But do not be sad. His death will bring more power to Dionysus."

I masked my emotions well, but inside my heart was pounding. "What did you do with Orphne?" I demanded. Agave's leer was fixed, but Dionysus raised his eyebrows in mock surprise.

"You mean you haven't seen her? Why Medea, she's been here the whole time. Come closer. Look at the altar."

I knew if I resisted he'd force me to come anyway, the way he'd forced my hand up to accept his goblet of blood. I used all my willpower to keep myself steady as I approached the table.

As the surface came into clearer view I could see it was streaked with blood. Not perfectly fresh, but the stains were recent. That was no matter. Like Heracles, Orphne's veins flowed with silvery ichor. I gave it a quick perusal then looked up, tilting my head to elicit an explanation.

"In the corner," Dionysus said with patience. I bent a little lower. There was a small blob of gold in the corner closest to me.

I didn't bother keeping the confusion out of my face as I straightened up. I pointed at the blob. "Are you telling me that's her?"

His smile was full of mirth. If his eyes hadn't been glowing like coals in the fading light the expression would have been almost benevolent.

"Indeed, indeed," he said with a laugh. "That little bit of gold you see around her is actually a chain. A very special chain. A chain made by Hephaestus himself."

He got up abruptly and hurried off the dais.

"That chain ends in two cuffs, also of gold. No one who's bound by it can escape," he said with excitement.

I nodded. It seemed a good idea to encourage him. "I know. I've got several of them myself, though mine don't have cuffs. I don't tend to keep the things I bind up around for amusement."

His lips pursed in commiseration. "Of course not. You've had a hard time of it, chasing all those demons."

He waved it away, back on his own tangent. "Now of course, I had no idea your friend had a Tear of Nereus. Imagine my surprise when suddenly she shifted into a cat!"

His hands balled into fists, which he shook with the delight of a child presented with a marvelous new toy. "But the chain shifted size with her, binding her front paws! She tried again, becoming a bird, but the chain and cuffs bound her wings!"

He started to scurry back and forth in front of the dais. I realized then that his borderline mania was another symptom of madness from the Curse of Prometheus.

"I thought she might try to become something big. An elephant, perhaps, or maybe something from the old days. A Cyclops would have been good," he mused as he stroked his beard. "But she seemed to have trouble shifting. And then it hit me. The chain was so well-made it changed size with her, of course. I realized all it could do was shrink! It couldn't expand, and neither could she become something larger than her last transformation while she was still bound!"

He smiled as if he'd devised the cuffs himself. "Isn't that wonderfully clever? Anyway," he hurried on as he rounded the altar, stopping mere feet from me and stooping a bit so I wouldn't have to crane my neck to see his face. "I think I must be right, because she changed twice more after that, once into a lizard and then again into a beetle. And now that's the form in which she's trapped!" I maneuvered my head slightly to keep from looking directly in his eyes.

What the hell was he talking about? There was no beetle on the altar. Just a tiny blob of gold.

Hope flared a bit within me. Was the chain empty? Had Orphne figured out a way to escape after all? If so she might still be nearby, waiting to help. I had to keep Dionysus from looking at the altar and realizing Orphne was gone.

"A pity I don't have the Tear of Nereus," I said quietly. "I'm sure I could have found a form that would have stumped your efforts to contain me. Perhaps..." I let my voice trail off deliberately. "But no. It wouldn't have been much fun at all."

"Fun?" he demanded. "And why would you find trying to escape the inevitable to be a source of amusement?"

I waved my left hand as if to dismiss the thought entirely and smiled wistfully. "I had merely thought that you might join me in a game of transformation. To see who could come up with the best guise."

I turned away a little bit, pretending to be demur. "But I have seen so much, living on Earth for hundreds and hundreds of years. And you have been on Olympus, where things never change. I suppose your repertoire must be somewhat... stale."

"Stale!" he drew himself up, growing another three or four feet in the process. "Witch, you forget your place!" His voice thundered across the maze.

I backed away, bowing my head slightly. "I apologize. Of course you would find many amazing forms to don. I have no doubt of it." I put just enough doubt in my voice to goad him.

Suddenly he was gone. I was facing a man in leather and metal battle gear, holding a rough-hewn spear. There were a few patches of bronze highlights in the thick red hair and rough beard. A puckered scar trailed from the corner of his right eye down his cheek, pallid against the otherwise ruddy complexion.

He was well in his forties, developing a paunch but still sporting the arms and shoulders of a man ten years younger. As he smiled the gaping hole from a missing eye tooth seemed to mock me.

It was a perfect image of my father Aeetes as I last saw him, the day he thought he'd lead Jason to his death.

I smiled as sweetly as I could. "Father, how lovely to see your kind face again. And how fortunate I know glorious Dionysus is behind it. I wouldn't wish to bring the charge of sacrilege against myself by spitting in your eye, as you deserve."

He brought a hand tenderly to my cheek.

"How good to see you again, Medea," he said. His breath even stank of beer and rotting teeth, just as my father's had. Wow, Dionysus went all out when he played this game.

"And so good to touch you again," he cooed. "Just as we did so long ago..."

"Until Mother found out you were sneaking into my chambers at night, and why, and told Aunt Circe, who used her magic to wither your manhood to nothing before sending me to my apprenticeship with Hecate. Then Mother left you and your blighted member to yourself, and returned to the sea."

I boldly reached down. "Have you added that little detail to this guise of yours, Dionysus?" I asked softly, putting emphasis on *little*.

I stopped before making contact with him, but I heard a sharp intake of breath from the dais and knew Agave must have shot to her feet, outraged that I'd gone as far as I did.

But the man in front of me held up a restraining hand. A hand that, like the rest of him, was changing.

He was becoming far younger. Barely twenty now. The face so familiar, tanned from months on the unforgiving waters of the Black Sea as he sailed with his comrades to my birthplace in Colchis.

I kept myself from looking into eyes that should have been a soft amber-brown. I knew they would be red, and that I would be lost if I glimpsed them. Instead I focused on the hair. A rich chestnut, curling slightly where it met his shoulders. It matched the short beard, streaked through with gold from the relentless sun.

The beard framed a mouth that still had the fullness and softness of youth, not a trace of chapping despite his exposure to the cruel elements. It was a mouth that begged to be kissed and promised to be marvelous at returning it.

I avoided that temptation, though it was hard. Instead I allowed my hand to trace the arm. So well-muscled from his turns at the oars, which he insisted on taking even though he was leader of the band.

He leaned into me, the feeling of his body so familiar against mine. I smelled honey and salt, and a slightly heavier musk wafted to my nostrils now and again. The scent of hardship and deprivation willingly embraced, the sadness of friends lost along the way, and an underlying fear that he would never again see his home.

If the situation had been any different I could have almost forgiven Dionysus for taking Jason's form. Almost, because no matter how much it hurt to see my first love's likeness again, there was something else too.

This was how he had looked when we first met alone, after he landed in Colchis on the quest for the Golden Fleece. It was enough to remind me the breathless excitement of infatuation which I'd mistaken for love. I'd never felt quite the same way with any other man.

"Sweetly done," I murmured, allowing my lips to just caress the edge of his ear. "But we have a saying these days. I'm over you." I pulled back and turned away.

The movement was so subtle I almost mistook it for an errant shadow. Orphne?

I glanced back to my right. The movement came again. It wasn't Orphne. Nyx had just appeared, quickly. She saw that I was looking, put a finger to her lips to silence any possible giveaway I might make, and just as quickly vanished.

Was she going to help me somehow? She had some tricks up her sleeve, but I doubted they'd be enough to get us very far. Still, she had the one thing I desperately needed now: the element of surprise.

"I was right," I sighed as I took a few thoughtful paces. "You've been stuck on your holy mountain too long. You think these images from my past will hurt me. But you're wrong, Dionysus. I long ago came to terms with my father and Jason, and their memories. They wronged me, but in revenging myself I committed my own wrongs. I forgave them. I had to, so I could forgive myself."

There was a slight sound of footsteps behind me. But they were softer than they should have been for a man of Jason's size.

"And have you really forgiven yourself?"

My veins ran cold at the sound of the child's voice. My breathing quickened, but my heart slowed so much it might have been pumping lead. My eyes squeezed shut involuntarily at the pain that voice sent surging through me.

A small, cool hand slipped into mine.

"Have you forgiven yourself," the voice repeated. "Mother?"

Chapter 55

I drew a shuddering breath. Then another. Each one felt like my lungs were filled with red-hot nails.

I slowly turned and looked down at one of the forms that haunted my worst nightmares.

"Pheres." The name jerked from my throat, as it had on so many nights when I woke from the tear-flooded dreams. Pheres, youngest of my two boys, the one who looked most like his father. True, he had my blond hair. But his father's features gazed up at me. The stubborn set of the chin, the curve of the cheekbones, even the eyes…

No! Don't look at the eyes!

The strangeness of the warning was enough to jerk me to semi-awareness so I could turn my gaze away. Out of the corner of my eye I caught the gleam of red, not the cool amber-brown the child's eyes should have been.

I thought quickly enough to maintain the burgeoning look of grief on my face, but part of me was in another frame of mind. Had I just heard a voice?

A faint buzzing sound peaked and dimmed in my ear as a fly moved away.

A fly. A fly on the wall.

It was Orphne I'd just heard! Faint, as if the warning came from the smallest of throats. She was free, and waiting for me to act. And she'd warned me in the only way she knew, flying by me and speaking in my ear somehow!

But the boy before me….

"Pheres," I sobbed as I fell down to my knees, flinging my arms around him. "Oh, my boy, my precious, precious darling!" I couldn't get any more words out. The sobs were coming too hard. It wasn't all an act, either.

I felt the tentative squeeze from the four-year-old's arms. "Mother, why did you leave us? I was so scared. And then she came… she hurt us. Why did you let her hurt us?"

The sobs came harder now. I could barely force the words out.

"I… had to leave… you," I was wracked so hard, taking in huge gulps of air in between words. I had lapsed unthinkingly back into ancient Greek. "You would have died in my chariot! I didn't have time to make any of the protection ointment. I left you in the temple so your father could get you to safety…" I couldn't go on.

"But he didn't. He abandoned us too. I was there alone with Mermeros. And she came. She was beautiful. I thought she was going to

227

help us. Maybe even be our new mother, since you'd left us. But she didn't."

He pulled away from me, and I collapsed to the ground, face to my knees, my fingers digging into the sod as I wept.

"My babies," I sobbed. "I want my babies. I want them back! I want them baaaaack...." The futile prayer ended in more shuddering sobs.

"But they *can* come back, Medea," the soft silky voice said from above me. The voice of Dionysus. "I can bring them back to you," he murmured. "All you have to do is follow me."

I looked up to where the god stood, staring down at me with what seemed to be infinite compassion. "Did I not bring Agave back? I can find their spirits for you, restore them to you just as they were when you left them. All you have to do is worship me."

I looked up at him, nothing but contempt in my eyes. It was now or never, and I hoped Orphne knew it.

"You have brought nothing back but death and corruption. And Agave's the worst of it. I won't worship you, won't ever call your name in honor again."

I rose, pointing an accusing finger at him. "In Hecate's name, and in the name of all the gods, I declare you anathema!"

I took a step closer, raised my head, and spit in his face.

"Unclean!" I screamed. "Unclean!"

The shock on his face was rewarding. To be so cursed by a priestess was no light burden, even for a god.

With perfect timing, Orphne made her move. As Dionysus stood there, his fingers touching my spittle on his cheek, something loomed behind him. Something very large and menacing.

I allowed myself a smile of triumph even though I knew the triumph might well be temporary. "It looks like you're going to get your wish, Dionysus."

He took a step towards me but froze instantly at the low reptilian growl that erupted behind him.

"Orphne decided to turn into something large after all," I said with satisfaction. That satisfaction grew as the mad god turned around and came face to face with a thirty foot tall, reddish-orange dragon.

I jumped out of the way just in time. With a wild cry and a swipe of her taloned paw, Orphne sent Dionysus flying a good forty feet. He sailed over the throne where Agave cowered and landed rather unceremoniously behind it.

The maenads around us finally found their wits and began rushing forward, screaming. But there was another surprise in store, one even I hadn't anticipated.

Another round of cries filled the air, coming from outside the inner wall of the maze. The maenads stopped in confusion. The boxwood shook and trembled as if we were in an earthquake.

Without warning, they flooded over the hedge.

There was no mistaking what they were. No humans could have scrabbled so easily over the hedges and down the other side. Others came bursting through weak points in the foliage, while still more poured in through the entrance to the inner circle.

If I'd had any doubts, they were banished once I saw the eyes of those closest to me. Serpent-slitted, every last one. We were surrounded by scores of Lamia's daughters.

Nyx appeared abruptly, halfway between me and the maenads. She thrust aloft a glittering sword.

"Attack!" she screamed. "Kill every one of them!"

At that the she-demons surged forward in a wave, some running, others scuttling quickly on all fours. The look was truly gruesome. But if they were scared, the maenads didn't show it. They quickly rushed forward to meet the challenge.

And their deaths.

Lamia's brood work quickly even when the hunt is casual. The demonesses quickly grabbed random maenads. Though Dionysus' followers were in ecstatic madness, their opponents had unnatural strength and quickly turned the tide.

One of them overpowered a maenad just feet away from me, turning her so the back of her head was exposed. With a shout of triumph the demon thrust forward to the woman's neck. There was a squishing sound, a grunt from the maenad, and then the sound of feeding.

Like Lamia, her daughters have a retractable spiny protrusion on their tongues which they use to pierce the soft hollow where the skull meets the neck, straight into the spinal cord. They use the connection to draw every bit of life force from their victims through the nervous system.

One by one the maenads were falling, nothing more than shriveled husks.

"Still think Lamia's set a trap instead of helping us?" hissed Orphne.

"I'll suspend judgment for the moment," I promised as I raced towards Peter.

The vine-thing was still holding him tight. Its head was a good six feet above Peter. Its rudimentary intelligence would be centered there if it was like the other automatons I'd encountered.

Jumping up I engaged my power of levitation, floating over Peter to come eye-to-stalk with the thing holding him prisoner.

"How about a little fire, scarecrow?" I screamed as I threw a fireball with all my might to the center of its head.

Flames shot up through the dry vine stalks. A hideous rasping sound that was probably some sort of scream came from the general direction of what would have been its mouth, if the thing had one at all. I quickly dropped to the ground. The thing released Peter to bring its crude hands up to its head, which was now fully engulfed.

Of course that was the worst possible move because the hands simply caught fire as well. But the creature was designed to be a guard, not a neurosurgeon. High intelligence wasn't a prerequisite.

Peter's eyes shot from the blazing automaton to the slaughter Lamia's daughters were carrying out with efficiency, if not grace.

"God in heaven, Medea, are you trying to kill us all?" he yelled. I didn't care.

As stupid as it was I flung my arms around him and kissed him. A second later he returned it.

A snapping sound put me back into action. I yanked Peter away from the swiftly collapsing vine-thing. We ran a few paces before I slowed and turned to speak to him again. But the words caught in my throat at what I saw.

Chapter 56

An enormous monstrosity suddenly sprang from behind the throne. It was serpentine, as thick around as one of the fabled cedars of Lebanon, covered in greenish-black scales. A hideous face that still bore traces of Dionysus's features dangled from one end, the jaws unhinging to reveal multiple rows of serrated teeth. It looked far more dangerous than a shark's mouth.

A small tremor shook the ground as the thing reared up even higher. The mouth opened wider, giving an eerily hollow cry. A clawed foot suddenly shot up from behind the throne, the next second coming down and smashing the dais to pieces as the thing advanced.

I realized what else was wrong with the scene. Agave, who'd been cowering on the dais during the battle, was nowhere in sight.

It looked like my real problem was much, much bigger, but the thing that used to be a god paid me no heed as it lumbered by us. Its eyes were on Orphne's dragon form, which had been casually watching the maenads' slaughter.

The grotesque serpentine thing half-slithered and half-crawled to where Orphne was rearing up again. She unfurled great bat-like wings and hissed menacingly.

"So what now?" Peter asked with a trace of hysteria growing in his voice. I couldn't blame him there.

"We have to find a way to free Heracles," I yelled over the din of the monsters. Orphne and Dionysus were tentatively circling each other, making exploratory feints with their claws and snapping their teeth in warning.

There were dozens of corpses on the ground, and I was willing to bet none of them were—

Wait. Where were they?

I scanned as much of the area as I could around the hulking menaces. Sure enough, Nyx and her cohorts were gone.

Well, I hadn't expected them to stay around all night. Hadn't expected such help at all, for that matter. I wondered what Lamia would demand in return.

Ear-shattering roars buffeted us as Dionysus launched his attack against Orphne. He flew at her, his face snapping down towards the vulnerable area where the dragon's neck joined the torso. She twisted out of the way just in time.

In a lightning-fast thrust her head shot forward and her vicious teeth sank in just behind the head of the snake-beast. It gave a bellow of pain and rage that left my ears ringing.

Peter was watching with a mixture of horror and fascination.

"Heracles," I said emphatically. Peter looked like he wanted to say something in return, but in the end he gave up and ran with me to the geode. He reached up to unfasten Heracles' bonds and quickly encountered the same energy barrier that had stumped me. After a few seconds of futile pushing and probing he looked at me.

"What now? I can't get to him."

I had no answers. Dionysus said the geode was a portal to a world of his own making. And that meant only he had the means to open the portal.

The ground shuddered beneath me. Peter and I spun around in time to see Orphne land hard on her back, her dragon form crushing huge portions of the maze's rings.

The snake-creature whipped around fully to face me.

"You have failed, witch!" the thing said in a horribly hollow voice. The words sounded as if they were coming from the bottom of a dry well, but there was a flatness to them that made me think inexplicably of insect carapaces, or dead leaves whirring along a gravel path.

Orphne wasn't moving. Her dragon form heaved a groan and went limp.

The mouth of the walking snake stretched into what might have been a smile. It dripped with vile brown ooze. "I have sunk enough venom into her to make her wish she could die. But she will not. Your friend will live and suffer, and keep suffering, until I choose to remove the venom from her. And I promise you, it will be a long, long time before I do."

The snake's words came slowly as it lumbered towards me. There were many open wounds on its legs and body, but they were healing themselves as I watched. The thought of Orphne going through such agony infuriated me.

"Now I shall take this boy-child of yours and drain him dry as you watch," the thing said with relish. "And you will watch me drain others. Hundreds, thousands. I will make you watch day after day as I drink their lives to the last drop. You can see the price of your failure over and over again. You will do NOTHING to stop me."

The rage within me was building, fueled by the images the words conjured up. The monstrosity wormed a step closer.

"You are useless," it said slowly, punctuating each word. I hung my head, feeling a warmth in me that was oddly familiar. As if a star was breaking from an iron shell....

"You are weak," it said in the same cadence as it took another step. Then another.

"You..."

Another step. "Are..."

Another step. "Nothing!"

It was so close I could feel its cold stinking breath on me. Close enough.

My head snapped up as the star's light inside me broke free. I could feel it pouring out of my eyes as energy surged through my hands, the way it had on Aiaia when I raised the dead men.

I took one step towards the abomination that had once been a god. "No," I said, feeling the power start to crackle in the air around me. "I... am... MEDEA!"

My arms shot over my head as a cascade of sparkling light burst forth. Within an instant it formed a glowing cloud around Peter, Heracles and me. Another second and the cloud soared above the maze.

The snake-beast lurched back, giving a sharp cry of surprise. But I wanted more than its surprise.

I wanted its pain. The desire to see him suffer as he'd made so many suffer, as Orphne was now suffering, overwhelmed me. I felt all traces of civilized emotion crumble as something far older and more primeval reared up within me.

I focused that thought and the cloud expanded again, this time outward, until it crashed against the monster. Bolts of energy crackled like enormous lightning strokes, sizzling as they hit the thing's hide. The high-pitched screams it emitted were immensely gratifying.

But I wanted more.

I wanted to destroy Dionysus, to *taste* his death. I wanted to feel him being rent to pieces under my hands, to see him beg for mercy so I could tear his throat out with the pleas still half-spoken.

I bared my teeth in a mixture of triumph and anticipation. I took another step, trying to keep up with Dionysus as his beast form scuttled unsteadily back. It was hard to move forward, as if I had to drag an immense weight with me. I realized the energy was weighing me down as much as it was protecting me. But if I could call up even more power...

You are the granddaughter of Titans! Circe's words rang in my head, urging me forward.

The hideous creature had regained its balance. I felt new anger welling within me as I remembered its threats to kill and kill again. Another burst of lightning bolts surged from the cloud around me and struck Dionysus along the length of his body. The shrill scream of pain whetted my appetite for more.

I knew the key to raising this energy was rage. A dangerous key, to be sure, because it can slice your hand open as easily as a real key opens doors.

Doors. As in portals.

Dionysus clambered back behind Orphne. The bastard was trying to use her as a shield. Little did he know I had a new target.

The geode.

"NO!" The cry of protest came too late from the snake-thing as I turned back and fastened my hands to the side of the rock. Like I would have listened anyway. The cloud around Peter and me shrank as I concentrated all my energy on Heracles' prison.

The crackles of energy around me didn't do much to mute the sound of crystal shattering. Shards of something that looked like glass flew from the geode's opening. Peter was thrown off his feet by the outward blast. But that was a good thing, because he was out of the way. A moment later hairline fractures started rippling across the geode's surface, radiating out from the points where my hands were making direct contact.

The rage within me was dying. With a final cry of desperation I willed all of my energy into the geode. A sound like dozens of trees falling filled the air as the smaller fissures split open simultaneously.

I knew what was coming but I was still taken off guard when the thing exploded. I felt myself flying back. A moment later I was on the ground, trying to stand up. I felt like every muscle was on fire.

As I staggered up I saw Heracles' limp form on the ground.

Peter was staggering to his feet as well. The remnants of the shattered geode were scattered on the ground between us, some of them still steaming from the explosion.

A rasping squawk drew my attention. Something was trying to climb over Orphne's prone form. It was dark and looked like it might be wounded.

"What the hell is that?" Peter asked as he pointed to the wriggling thing. It looked small compared to Orphne's size, but it was probably about eight feet long.

"I have no idea." My voice betrayed my sudden fatigue. It was no surprise, considering how much energy I'd just expended. More than I ever thought I'd have. To break through a prison created by an Olympian was no small feat. Well, there might be time later to celebrate it. We had more immediate issues.

I pointed to Heracles. "Try to wake him," I said as I moved towards the wriggling thing. "I'll deal with this."

"Stay where you are!"

Agave was there, restraining the real Lyn O'Neill in a chokehold. Lyn was in a plain white chiton, the same type of garb Agave had affected when she impersonated Lyn. The sketchy light of the fading day glinted dully off the knife Agave held to Lyn's throat.

"One move from either of you and she dies," Agave said through clenched teeth. "You've not triumphed yet, Medea. But I will give credit where it's due, witch. You've slain many of our followers. Many, but by no means all.

"Even now others are out in the world, spreading the touch of Dionysus. Even if you escaped this place, which you will not, you could not possibly find and kill them all!"

Ancient as she was, Agave clearly hadn't learned an important lesson: don't stand their gloating until your enemy is completely vanquished. She'd been too busy giving her wicked-little-villainess speech to notice my lips moving silently.

The knife flew from her hand and into mine. I smiled her stunned expression. "You keep calling me 'witch' as if it's merely an insult. You seem to forget what it really means, Agave."

Lyn abruptly twisted free and ran. Not towards Peter and me, but at that point it was no surprise that she didn't trust us any more than the woman who used to be her mother.

Agave flung out her hand, releasing a shimmering orb that struck Lyn sharply on the back. She flew forward and hit the ground with a loud thud, lying motionless after that.

"Witch or no, you have not outwitted *me* yet," Dionysus said from behind me. I snapped around in time to see him complete the transformation from the black wormy thing into his true form. But he didn't look as imposing as he had before. He looked injured.

Had I done that?

Dionysus looked down at the remains of the geode. "Impressive," he conceded. "It was wrong of me to forget that while you have chosen to live as a mere sorceress, you have the blood of Titans in you. It would seem you have inherited abilities from that side of your family. But you lack control. It's almost as if you're just discovering who you are, Medea."

He smiled laconically as he took measured steps towards me. "I think we can work together. With someone like you on my side, any battle with the high gods would be shortened. I can teach you how to use your powers, Medea. You don't have to be a servant of Hecate any longer."

He took another step towards me, holding out a hand.

"I can make you a goddess in your own right. You will outstrip even your aunts. You are wrong if you think I want to have this world to myself. I am willing to share. All you have to do is give me your hand, Medea, and you will have your portion."

I looked impassively at his outstretched hand. "I would rather serve Hecate in honor than rule with you in shame. And at your side, there could be no option *but* shame."

The inviting smile didn't change, but the hand withdrew.

"Have it your way, Medea. I cannot kill you, but I can keep you as one of my pets. But first, there is something else to attend to," the god said as he narrowed his eyes slightly and turned towards Peter.

An imprecation rose in my throat, but it stayed there. I couldn't speak, nor could I move. Apparently Dionysus had gotten over any shock from my assault. Mad though he was, he wouldn't be lax enough to give me another opportunity to use those powers.

I felt his hand on mine as he gently pried the knife from my fingers.

I didn't know whether Peter was frozen as well, or simply very, very brave. He didn't quaver at all as Dionysus raised the point of the dagger to his heart. The god waved his hand, and a shower of sparks flared around Peter as the magic from my ointment was neutralized.

The god smiled slowly. "Did you really think mere sorcery would stop me? I don't have to wait for sunset." He shook his head, chuckling softly.

"Time to eat."

Chapter 57

Just as Dionysus touched the tip of the blade to Peter's chest, lightning shot up the knife and into the god's arm. It danced around him for several seconds as he screamed in agony. With a burst of light he flew back, the lightning shimmering around him, holding him in a net.

I could move again, and so could Peter. We both jumped back, then jumped again when another agonized shriek pierced the air from behind us.

Agave was limp on the ground, holding her head, feeling her god's suffering. Couldn't happen to a nicer priestess.

"What the hell—" Peter began, but I held up a hand. The sounds of thunder were already gathering in the distance.

I put my arms around Peter, and after a moment he returned the embrace. Let him think I just needed some comfort. On some level, I did. I was relieved that my plan had worked, but horribly saddened that I'd had to drag Peter into it. Worse yet, that I'd endangered him by what I'd done to him. Still, he proved to be the secret weapon that led to victory, even if he didn't know it.

"I think the cavalry is about to ride in," I whispered. Just as I finished the ground started shaking. The mild tremors quickly grew until we had trouble keeping on our feet.

The echoing yawn of the ground cleaving open was joined by the growing sounds of thunder overhead. Clouds were rushing in, converging directly over our heads. Lightning started streaking from them.

Light also sprang from the rent in the ground, flickering as if a thousand torches were down there. There weren't a thousand, though. Just two really, really big ones.

She emerged quickly. The torches she held in each hand glowed like miniature suns in the real sun's fading light. They gleamed off the golden oak leaves that, along with a twining wreath of snakes, formed a crown in her flowing black hair.

Her equally black eyes reflected the torchlight perfectly. It looked as if she had flames flickering in her pupils.

The sounds of dogs baying filled the air.

The ground stopped shaking so abruptly that Peter fell backward and landed hard. He didn't seem to notice. His eyes were fully on the scene before us.

Hecate is always quick to respond if she feels she's been slighted.

"Who dares to raise a weapon against one under my sanctuary?" Her voice echoed loudly through the sky, punctuated by another round of baying from the dogs. She loomed over us, at least five stories high.

The baying almost drowned another sound that was quickly growing louder. It first seemed to be the sharp call of some kind of bird of prey, but soon resolved into comprehensible words.

"Sacrilege! Sacrilege!"

It quickly became clear that there was more than one voice. Three, to be exact, coming closer and closer as the whir of wings cleaving the air grew louder as well.

They looked so much alike from a distance that there was no way to be sure which of them broke through the clouds with the first barrage of lightning. But I knew all their names: Alecto, Megaera, Tisiphone. The Erinyes, goddesses of vengeance, swooped down on wings of brass that sounded like swords slicing through the air. They stopped about a hundred feet overhead, which was plenty close because they'd chosen to make themselves almost as large as Hecate.

She looked above her. "Bear witness, you who are the avenging hand of Zeus, god of oaths and king of Olympus!" She pointed a torch towards Peter. I was close enough to him to feel him flinch, but he didn't move beyond that.

"This mortal was placed under sanctuary in my name, by my chosen priestess. And that sanctuary has been violated by one of the shining gods! I demand a penalty for this crime. I demand justice at the hands of Zeus himself!"

Hecate's statement drew another round of shrieks from the hovering Erinyes. Their silvery-black robes merged well with the roiling clouds, but the flaming whips they carried and the glow of Hecate's torches reflecting off their brass wings provided enough light to make them stand out.

"Who dares violate the laws of the gods so grievously?" Tisiphone shrieked. There was an answering peal of lightning and thunder from the clouds.

Megaera swooped down until she hovered barely twenty feet over us. The heat from her whip was searing. "Name the one who has done this Medea, priestess of Hecate!"

Despite the terrifying sight of her and the scorching heat from her whip, I stood erect and pointed in the general direction of the problem at hand.

"It was none other than Dionysus, son of Zeus, who violated the rules of sanctuary." I was proud that my voice rang strong and clear even though I was shaking inside. A huge volley of lightning shot from the clouds.

"There is more, Megaera. Dionysus has committed worse crimes still! He raised a weapon to this man," I gestured towards Peter, "not merely to kill him." I took a deep breath. This was the moment I'd been waiting for, though I hadn't had any clue it would come in quite so spectacular a confrontation.

"Dionysus planned to drink this man's blood, to increase his own power through the Curse of Prometheus. His followers have already killed many humans so he could drink the blood! I myself witnessed visions of him drinking the blood of slain mortals, visions I called up from the very bodies of the victims! And I was not alone, for Circe and Pasiphae, daughters of Helios, and Heracles, son of Zeus, witnessed these same visions!"

I pointed again to where Dionysus was still struggling and screaming in the web of lightning. "As priestess of Hecate, I accuse him of the worst of all sacrileges, and call on you Megaera," I paused and looked up. "And you, Alecto and Tisiphone, to bring him to Olympus for justice at the hands of the high gods."

Megaera gave an ear-splitting shriek as she shot higher to meet her sisters. Peter put his hands over his ears. I had the same urge myself, because her cry of rage was like the scream of a falcon magnified a hundred times. Not the most pleasant sound on the ears.

Alecto wheeled and dropped lower, pointing at Dionysus with her whip. "Crime upon crime!" Her piercing voice cut through me, but I stood my ground.

Megaera shot down to her. "Then there must be a trial," she said forcefully.

"A trial!" Tisiphone agreed as she plummeted to join them.

The three of them cackled, delighted at the prospect of what promised to be a swift and violent vengeance against a wrongdoer. Their favorite pastime.

But something didn't feel right. Something was...

NO! I turned to where Dionysus was imprisoned by the glowing net.

He wasn't there. The cackling of the Erinyes had drowned out the hoarse laughter of the huge flock of ravens that now filled it...

Ravens that were wiggling through the spaces in the net.

"He's getting away!" I screamed. But it was too late.

The birds burst through the net in an instant, shattering the light like so much ice. Screaming in fury the Erinyes dove towards the cloud of scavengers, whips crackling as they knocked bird after bird onto the ground.

"Find them! Find them all!" Megaera screamed.

Hecate wheeled as well, power surging out from her in a circle of fire. "I'll burn the hell-spawned bastards myself!" she screamed, and dozens of the ravens erupted in fire at the touch of her rage.

I dove towards Peter, knocking him to the ground.

"Get down!" I screamed. A battleground of gods was no place for a mortal.

If I hadn't been in that position, I never would have seen the lone raven cackling from the ruins of the throne. Why was there just one there?

Decoys. The rest were just decoys!

I raised myself to warn Hecate, but just as I opened my mouth the raven did to, a rasping laugh mocking me. Its eyes gleamed red.

Hecate turned, saw what I was looking at and raised her torches high to bring them crashing down.

On emptiness. With a flash, the bird was gone.

"He's escaped!" Hecate screamed in rage.

"Impossible!" Alecto screeched back.

"It cannot be done! No one escapes our justice!" Tisiphone protested.

"He has, sisters," Megaera said, defeat in her voice. "He has gained too much power through his cursed sacrifices. We must hunt, and hunt, never stopping, until he is found."

Alecto swooped down to me, pointing her whip. "And you, Medea, must go to Olympus to tell the high gods what he has done. You must bring your charges before them."

"But what proof is there?" Tisiphone demanded. "Only the visions she has called up. The gods will not be swayed by a sorceress' visions!"

"There is proof."

The voice was so ragged that I scarcely recognized it.

"Heracles!" I rushed over to where he was propping himself up weakly on the ground.

"I saw him drinking blood," he looked past me to the Erinyes. "I witnessed it with my own eyes. He killed a man, drank the blood, and tossed the body to his maenads, who consumed the rest of him until only bones were left. Upon great Zeus' thunderbolts, I swear it."

Gods be praised! Dionysus had been reckless enough to reveal himself before Heracles! But the speech, short as it was, was too much for him. He collapsed again.

"He needs help!" I turned desperate eyes to Hecate. "He's been poisoned by Hydra's venom."

"Help he shall have, if the Gracious Ones will take him back to Olympus," she said firmly, using the polite title for the Erinyes. "I would have a word with you, Medea."

"So be it," Alecto agreed. "We have heard his testimony, and shall report it to Zeus. Come sisters. Let us return." With a slight gesture from her hand, Heracles' unconscious body rose from the ground into her arms. Without another word they turned and soared silently into the clouds.

Chapter 58

The thunder and lightning died but the dark clouds remained, roiling less but not dispersing. The field was still lit by Hecate's torches.

I quickly took a few steps in her direction and cast myself on my knees, head tilted low.

"Rise, Medea," she said. The voice was suddenly faint, and the area seemed to be much darker. I lifted my head and saw that she had reduced her size to that of an ordinary human.

She drew closer. "You still please me, Medea. You have taken great risks to expose this crime. And it would seem you have learned a few new tricks. I saw the signs of battle on Dionysus. He is an Olympian. It takes a great deal to leave them marked."

I bowed my head.

"He said he fought with Heracles," I offered.

"You have many good qualities, Medea. But I think it is time you dropped humility from that list. I have no cult on Earth for the moment, so you may live your life as you wish. But I would advise you to relearn how to carry yourself as a priestess. You may need it sooner than you think."

I bowed in slight acknowledgement. "Yes, lady," I said. It had been many years since I'd seen her face to face, more than a thousand since I'd seen her on Earth. It was nice to meet on my home ground rather than in Hades for a change.

Hecate released the torches from her hands. They remained in place, hovering above the ground. She came over to me then gestured to Peter to join us. He looked slightly confused, as if she must have mistaken him for someone else. I gave a short, urgent nod to ensure he didn't delay.

She regarded him appraisingly. "I think Medea was wise to give you protection," she said. "And yet, I do not see the sign of my sanctuary on your brow." She looked to me. If she was truly puzzled, she gave no hint in her expression.

"It is a story best left for the ears of the gods," I replied with a bow of my head. I hoped she'd accept that, because I didn't want Peter to know I'd set him up as a human booby-trap.

"If that is the case, then we should make haste to tell them," she said. "You will find appropriate attire in your chariot. Ready yourself, and start on the journey at once."

She held out an open palm. There was a flash of light and a small silver medallion appeared. It bore an etched triskele. She held it out to me and I took it, noticing the arms of the triskele rotating slowly. It was almost hypnotic.

"Place this charm about your neck, and you will be granted admittance to Olympus."

She looked like she was about to go. I didn't want to lose the chance that presented itself. "A moment, my lady, if you please."

She raised an eyebrow.

"I would ask you to keep your blessing on this man. He has been involved in a dangerous business this day. Dionysus may seek vengeance against him if he is left unprotected. Please, keep him under your sanctuary, at least until the threat from Dionysus is over."

The corner of her mouth raised slightly in what was the closest approximation of a smile that she ever gave.

"I see he means something to you, Medea. Very well. I have not yet heard why you placed him under my protection, but your judgment has been sound over the years. I give my oath that I shall not revoke my sanctuary so long as Dionysus remains a threat."

I bowed deeply, elbowing Peter. He looked over at me, confused, but then picked up on my cue and bowed slightly.

"My thanks, great Hecate," I said.

Her expression hardened as I straightened up. "But there is one who cannot have my blessings, at least in this matter."

She turned to where Orphne's dragon form still lay. All of my happiness vanished.

"We would have lost without her..." I began weakly, but she stopped me with a look.

"She left her appointed duties without permission," Hecate replied crisply, her voice tinged with ice. "Stealing the Tear of Nereus from me, no less. She will have to answer for it. If her reasons were compelling, perhaps Lord Hades will show her mercy. Since she undoubtedly aided you in this, I will speak on her behalf. But I cannot guarantee anything."

There was nothing else to say, and I knew it. Unfortunately Peter didn't.

"She's injured," he said hastily, as if it would make a difference. "Dionysus said he pumped her full of venom."

I felt myself pale at his tone but Hecate merely raised an eyebrow.

"I'll forgive the implication that I'm colossally stupid, since I know you're not used to speaking with gods face to face. Consider this you're only warning: don't point out the obvious to us. She will be healed before we decide whether she merits punishment. We will certainly not let her suffer needlessly. The gods of Greece are civilized."

She gestured towards Orphne, who faded from sight, still in her dragon form. Hecate glanced to the horizon that was now visible through the shattered maze. It was tinged with red under the clouds.

"You cannot delay your journey to Olympus, Medea," she said in a softer tone. She turned to Peter. "Are you willing to wait for Medea in her home, or is there some other place you would like to go?"

He looked dumbfounded for a moment, as if he couldn't believe she was speaking to him again.

"I guess that'll do," he said uncertainly. "I'm not sure I can go back to my own home. Not yet, anyway."

She nodded, and with a slight flare of light he was gone. She backed away, growing taller with each step until she reached her former height. The torches flew to her upraised hands and grew as well.

"Make haste, Medea. Already the remaining Olympians are gathering in council."

"Yes, my lady," I replied. As I raised my head she slowly faded from view.

I had to get ready, but first—

I spun to where I'd last seen Agave writhing on the ground. What I saw stopped me cold. But not as cold as Agave.

She was solid rock. I walked over slowly, ready for some kind of trick. She did have the power to change her shape, after all.

I gave the statue a tentative poke. No doubt about it. This wasn't just some sort of external glamour. The statue was laying on its back. The face looked as if she'd been frozen in mid-scream. I'd heard that the mere sight of the Erinyes could do that to humans guilty of the worst offenses against the gods.

A muffled whimper caught my attention. I looked a few feet beyond and saw Lyn hunched over in the grass. She'd apparently recovered from the blow Agave gave her, but I was certain she'd be in shock after everything that just went on around her.

"Lyn," I said hesitantly, not wanting to frighten her.

I walked carefully over to her and put a hand on her shoulder. "Lyn," I repeated in the same gentle tone of voice.

Her face snapped around, a snarl of rage fixed on it.

"You haven't won yet!" she spit. Her eyes were an animal's eyes. I jumped back as hair began springing from every one of her pores. The light was dim but I didn't need to see details. I knew it would be yellowish hair, with black spots all over it. The face shrank and grew rounder as the teeth grew longer. Within seconds a growling leopard was staring back at me.

I called a fireball but she was too quick. With a scream of frustration I hurled it at the darting cat.

By the time it hit the ground Agave was already gone.

Chapter 59

The wind felt glorious as it rushed past. We were sailing higher and higher, heading for the clouds. It had been a long time since I'd flown in this garb, a white silk chiton with a cloak streaming behind me. My hair was done up simply but elegantly with the pins Hecate had thoughtfully left in my chariot along with the robes and sandals.

I'd never flown to Olympus before, but the dragons seemed to instinctively know how to get there. We entered the clouds, and for a moment the cool mist chilled me.

The shift was subtle. One moment I was flying through dampness, the next, the clouds had parted. Light was streaming from far on the horizon, a light so pure that I knew it had no earthly source.

True to Hecate's word, the medallion had led me to another dimension without any effort on my part. We quickly approached the light, or perhaps it was rushing to meet us. Maybe a little of both. One can never tell in the dimensions of the gods.

Banks of clouds were swirling around the light, glowing with their own auras in brilliant shades. One bank was light green, another darker green and gold, a third flaming red and orange, and another cool blue with splashes of mauve.

The cloud banks shifted as we drew closer still, taking on very human features. The faces of women with long trailing hair formed in each bank. They were the Horae, goddesses of the seasons, who guarded the entrance to Olympus.

As we approached I felt the medallion growing warm. I looked down and saw it glowing. A beam of light shot out from it, straight towards the dazzling whiteness I now knew to be Olympus itself.

Recognizing the beacon, the goddess-clouds drew back gracefully, revealing the full glory of the home of the gods.

It seemed to stretch on forever. In a sense it did, because Olympus is the very embodiment of "forever". There were beautiful halls and spires on verdant hillsides, as well as the more traditional columned buildings that reflected Greek architecture's apex. I knew these were the palaces of the high gods as well as their lesser vassals like Heracles.

We flew directly in, then mounted a little more. There was one building standing on the highest hill in that fair land, a building of gleaming alabaster and gold. The throne-hall of Olympus, where the Twelve—now Eleven, I reminded myself—held their councils.

The dragons landed easily on a broad patch of the lushest grass I'd ever seen, just outside the hall. Immediately a group of nymphs came over. I dismounted, handing the reigns to one nymph while taking the chalice offered by another. It was carved of a single giant ruby.

I drank deeply, immediately refreshed as the nectar slid down my throat. All of the aches and pains of battle, emotional as well as physical, vanished the instant the drink of the gods touched my tongue.

"We were told you might want this as well," another nymph said as she offered up a golden dish.

I laughed. It was chocolate ice cream. A thoughtful gesture, although it slightly disturbed me that the gods knew so much about my habits. If they were so all-knowing, couldn't they have stopped Dionysus sooner?

I didn't allow my discomfort to show on my face.

"Thank you, but I don't wish to delay any further. You may have it, and share it with your sisters."

She frowned slightly. "What is it?"

Suddenly I remembered Orphne. I couldn't repress a sigh.

"Fluff and sugar," I said as I turned to the entrance.

Inside another nymph welcomed me and led me quickly to the main hall.

Twelve thrones lined the far end in a huge semi-circle, but they were empty. All were lit by an unseen light, except one. It was in pitch darkness, silent testimony to a grave and unthinkable change in a realm where nothing was supposed to change.

Hushed voices came from in front of the thrones, where several tables were laden with foods and drinks humans could only dream of. There were figures milling about.

If I hadn't known who they were, the scene would have looked like a costume party. They were tall, though still within the bounds of human normalcy. But there was no mistaking the high gods, huddled in small clusters. It took no guesswork to know what they were discussing.

Demeter and Apollo were closest, he in a golden tunic with equally golden hair and sandals. Her hair was much paler, the color of wheat, and crowned with woven stalks of that grain interspersed with scarlet poppies. Her diaphanous green gown swirled easily around her.

Artemis, in a knee-length silvery tunic, her bow and quiver strapped to her back, was talking animatedly with Poseidon and Hermes. A sudden laugh burst from Hermes, drawing the attention of the rest.

From the other side of the semi-circle Athena cast a disapproving glance with her grey eyes. Ares and Hephaestus were with her, neither one looking very pleased.

Nowhere did I see Hestia. Since her power was stolen she no longer claimed a place among the Twelve proper, though the Greeks and Romans had still honored her highly. Legend said that after the withdrawal she removed herself to live alone in a far cave on Olympus, where she tended a perpetual fire, the physical remnant of her stolen power. The story went that so long as the fire burned, there was hope she would reclaim her power in full, but until that time she would remain a recluse.

Still, she was Zeus's own sister. I had thought he might seek her counsel in so grave a matter, particularly since it involved the consequences of her stolen power.

The nymph who led me into the room approached the group. "The Lady Medea, high priestess of Hecate," she announced in a clear voice that echoed through the hall. She bowed and vanished.

All eyes were on me. It was a distinctly uncomfortable feeling. I'd met most of the gods individually over the years, but always on Earth. This was a lot more daunting.

"You may approach, Medea," Athena said. "My father and his wife were conferring with Hecate in private. They will wish to know of your arrival."

She strode up the steps of the dais and disappeared behind the two central thrones, which were the most elaborate. The seats of Zeus and Hera, king and queen of heaven.

I took a few tentative steps towards the group. I didn't sense any outward animosity, but that didn't mean anything. They were experts in hiding their true feelings, and they had no reason to have any high regard for me. I was a mere witch in their eyes, and now I had come to their sacred precinct to speak unthinkable things about one of their own.

A flash distracted me. I raised my hand instinctively to shield my eyes as I turned to it.

A vision of loveliness, with golden hair flowing down to her feet and a transparent rose gown that left little to the imagination, had appeared. She was walking; the flash had come not from her materialization, but from the ornate bracelets and necklaces adorning her. All were set with emeralds, her favorite stone.

Aphrodite, goddess of love and beauty, had decided to make an entrance. Fashionably late, of course. But then, what were such trivial matters as human sacrifice and betrayal on the part of an Olympian god to her? She had other affairs to attend to. Emphasis on *affairs.*

I wondered which of the gods was her paramour this week, then banished the thought. It was unseemly for me to have such rude musings on holy Olympus, especially with the severity of my mission.

Athena swept back into the room. A second later a low gong began ringing.

Everyone in attendance faced the thrones and bowed deeply. I went one better and got down on my knees. It seemed appropriate, given my low status.

A wind rushed through the hall, and the sound of thunder echoed against the walls. I sensed, rather than saw, the newest arrivals.

"Arise, and let us convene this council!" The strong voice rang clear through the hall, a voice used to commanding.

The voice of Zeus himself.

I lifted my head while staying on my knees, beholding the fairest of the gods. Why artists insist on representing Zeus as an old man is beyond me. Far from it. His form was young and strong, a larger version of Heracles, with reddish-gold hair and a beard with no trace of grey in it.

His wife Hera was equally fair, with dark streaming hair and green eyes that rivaled Aphrodite's emeralds. Together they made a royal couple who could inspire love and loyalty in anyone.

Almost anyone, that is. We were here because someone had violated that loyalty.

Hecate had entered with them, and was standing a little to the side. She spied me.

"Rise, Medea, and come here. We will now hear what you have to say."

I rose and moved forward. The gods gathered together in a half-circle. Zeus and Hera were in the center, with Hecate at Zeus' right hand. An honored guest, which, I hoped, foreshadowed an objective, if not welcome, reception of her priestess.

I halted a respectable distance away, but Zeus made a brief gesture.

"Closer, Medea. There is no need to be afraid."

I obeyed, stopping just a few feet away from him. He waved his hand, and a small pedestal appeared in front of me.

I recognized what was on it instantly. It was a larger version of the stone from Styx that I had used to compel Peter to tell the truth. Well, I couldn't blame the gods for this one. They had to make sure.

I placed my hand on the stone.

"Begin your story, Medea," Hera commanded.

I did. The telling of it took less time than I anticipated, but it was still uncomfortably long. I was chilled by the shocked looks on the faces of the gods, even, at one point, Zeus, when I told them how Shannon's dead body had been resurrected and transformed, her hands made into leopard's paws to kill Paul. Despoiling the dead is one of the most hateful crimes to the gods.

Finally, I was finished. The silence was palpable. I just wanted to be out of there. Wanted to be away from Olympus, away from everything. And yet, where would I go but back to Earth? Earth, where Dionysus was now a fugitive at best, an implacable new enemy at worst.

"If things were as you say, Medea," Demeter asked slowly, "then when you placed this Peter Kirkpatrick under Hecate's sanctuary, you were—what do they say now? Setting him up. You were using him as bait in a trap."

I nodded. "He was the only human among us. I knew Dionysus had regained his bloodlust, and it seemed logical that he would try to sate himself with any expendable human. Or if he didn't, that he might amuse himself in...other ways... with Peter. Ways that would also violate the laws of sanctuary."

There was another silence. It had been an evil thing to do, I knew. But the stakes were too high. What was the life of one man risked, if it meant that I could stop a mad god who would kill a hundred thousand men without any thought at all?

"And you still have no idea why Lamia's minions helped you?" Poseidon asked with a frown. "She has no reason to love you, nor you her."

"I have only a guess," I said.

Artemis nodded. "Tell us, then. We must know as much as possible, and solid conjecture could be as valuable as hard facts."

I took a deep breath. "The plan was for the maenads to infiltrate all levels of society. Dionysus was using them to gain entry to key sectors such as finance, law enforcement, politics, medicine. I believe he was a threat to Lamia because she plans to use her daughters to do the same thing."

There was a murmur among them.

"It would be a dark day indeed for her to gain such a foothold," Zeus said gravely. "But her daughters are monsters. One has only to look at them—"

"Not necessarily a problem," Athena offered. "Medea, you shield your own eyes from human sight with a minor charm, yes?" I nodded. "Then Lamia, using her knowledge of the black arts, could give her daughters the same disguise. They could pass, if they had enough control to keep their unholy hunger hidden."

We all knew it was true.

"Then perhaps we should let them battle each other," Ares suggested. "Let Lamia's daughters destroy the maenads, and—"

"NO!"

No one was more surprised than me, that I'd interrupted a god in mid-sentence. They didn't say anything, although Ares looked like he'd like to have my head on a platter for my insolence.

"You can't let that happen," I went on, pressing my advantage. "How many innocent people will die? And both Lamia and Dionysus will just step up their efforts to enslave women. It will be Armageddon even if neither succeeds in getting enough of their followers into places of influence to carry out their plots."

There was silence after that. Finally Athena broke it.

"Medea is right. This is not our way. We may have removed ourselves from the affairs of men, but we cannot sit by and allow them to be slaughtered wholesale by the treachery of a rogue god."

"We have not yet formally passed that judgment on him," Zeus cautioned. "But I agree it would be in bad form to sit by idly." He turned to me. "Medea, there is one question I still have. You placed Peter

Kirkpatrick under sanctuary, but Hecate says when she arrived, she did not see the seal of her power upon his brow."

"Yet I felt it, certainly enough. I knew him for one of my own," Hecate said. "So, while your hand is still on the stone of truth, tell us Medea. How did you accomplish this marvel?"

I'd dreaded this moment, but there was no avoiding it, especially since I was compelled to answer. So I did.

If they'd looked shocked when I tallied up my summary of Dionysus' crimes, the gods were positively aghast now. Several darted hasty glances in Hecate's direction. Hermes, who was closest to her, edged away until he was practically standing on top of Hephaestus. For his part, the smith god was cringing and looking like he wanted to be anywhere Hecate wasn't.

I couldn't blame then for wanting to put distance between themselves and the pending eruption.

Hecate took several deep breaths. Her eyes glittered strangely. "My holy sigil," she said slowly. "The symbol of all that I am, of all my powers. You drew my holy sigil on his *ass*?"

Chapter 60

"It seemed expedient to keep it hidden, and I could think of no place that Dionysus would be less likely to look for a symbol of protection," I said hastily.

I'd expected her to lash out, to threaten me. Perhaps to beat me right then and there, which certainly would be her right. But I was totally unprepared for her reaction.

After a moment of silence, she threw her head back and laughed. It was a harsh sound, no doubt because she had so little practice with it. But laugh she did, the rasping bursts echoing through the halls.

Hermes relaxed and gave Hephaestus a little more personal space. I noticed Demeter and Apollo hiding half-smiles behind their hands. Even Athena's mouth twitched a bit.

Zeus seemed to be the only one who wasn't amused. "Entrapment," he muttered. "You tricked him into violating the laws of sanctuary."

"And did believing the mortal was unprotected give your son a right to lay a hand on him in violence?" Hera demanded coolly. She had to accept many of the byproducts of Zeus' affairs with humans, including Dionysus and Heracles, but she didn't have to pretend to love them.

"The symbol of a god is supposed to be placed on the brow of the protected, for all to see," he objected.

She lifted her chin. "That may be traditional, but there is no law that says it must be so. Medea was not constrained to announce her intention to Dionysus."

Zeus knew he was beaten. He pressed his lips together discontentedly but said nothing more.

"There was another reason I used the gift of sanctuary," I offered. Everyone looked at me with curiosity, although Hecate was still shivering a bit with unaccustomed mirth.

"I had no proof until I saw Dionysus in person that all of it, the murders included, was not some trick of Lamia's. And I knew that if she harmed Peter—"

I left the thought unfinished, since they could pick it up. If she violated the laws of sanctuary, her own protection from Zeus would be null and void, and she would be fair game. I wouldn't have to kill all of her daughters before destroying her.

Wouldn't have to kill her first daughter, the one I dreaded confronting. The one I'd lost to her. Lamia said in the church that Clymene was still alive. But I'd have to see it to believe it, considering the source.

"You have a well-deserved reputation for cleverness, Medea," Hermes said as he strolled over to a table and helped himself to a chalice of nectar. "But even the clever are not allowed to attend the private councils of the high gods. We must consider what you have told us, and decide how to respond."

I bowed in acknowledgement. "Then with your leave…"

Hecate nodded. "Go, Medea. There are many pleasures on Olympus. You have my leave to enjoy yourself. We will let you know if we need you further. "

I bowed to her, and kept myself in that position as I backed out as gracefully as possible. Only when I was close to the door again did I turn my back. They were already deep in conversation, not paying me any attention at all.

I hurried out of the hall.

It turned out to be interesting, wandering across the hills and fields that surrounded the palaces and feasting halls of the blessed. But eventually my thoughts overcame me. I just wanted to sit and mull them over, but I where to do it? There was too much frolicking and merriment among the lesser denizens of Olympus.

As if conjured by my thoughts—which it likely was, things being that way on Olympus—I saw a path out of the corner of my eye. It hadn't been there a moment earlier, and as I glanced down it I noticed it led to a place in the trees that was shaded.

Curious, I followed the path deeper and deeper into the copse until I realized that the eternal light of Olympus had dimmed. The place was filled with opalescent mist and deeper shadows. It seemed quite peaceful. Even the gods might tire of perpetual daylight. Sometimes they, too, might need the comfort of a darker place to brood over some thought or other.

I found myself in a small, out-of-the-way garden. The great palaces of the gods gleamed through the mists on the hillsides above me. How far away they were I couldn't say, since distance as humans know it is but a dream on Olympus. I supposed they were as far from me, or I from them, as I desired.

At least the garden offered the soothing murmur of a fountain and the whisper of scent from exotic flowers waving lazily in a slight breeze. I closed my eyes, tried to still my mind with the meditation techniques I had learned during apprenticeship. I followed the pattern of my breath, but only focused on the exhalation, not the inhalation.

I was sinking easily into that state of awareness in which thoughts become perfectly still. I hardly noticed the sounds at first. But the excitement and exhaustion of the day had honed my nerves too much; they sprang to life quickly, bringing with them my senses.

Voices.

CURSE OF PROMETHEUS: A TALE OF MEDEA

I was not alone, but I was apparently unnoticed. I opened my eyes, turning slightly towards the sounds of hushed conversation.

It was coming from an alcove a short distance away. The alcove was in a wall I would have sworn hadn't been there before.

Two voices, male and female. I heard muted words filled with excitement and, if I wasn't mistaken, affection. Well then, at least someone was unperturbed enough about the events of the day to hold a tryst in an out-of-the-way place. Bully for them.

I couldn't hear well enough to make out what was being said, and the mists were for some reason growing thicker in the garden. Probably summoned to give the couple an extra screen of privacy. The mist was just dense enough, and the angle of my view just skewed enough, that I couldn't see who was there.

I started to move behind a border hedge, intending to make my way back to the more populated areas. No matter that it was obviously an amorous encounter of some sort rather than an ambush. Being out there with no backup, in the presence of two unknown shadowy figures made me nervous. A slight movement from the alcove, and the sight of one of the people moving to leave it, only reinforced my desire to get out of there.

But I paused when the mist cleared a little and revealed one of the figures. Heracles! My heart gave an excited flutter. He'd been healed of the Hydra's poison, and was well enough to take a stroll.

I thought about calling to him, then decided to give him privacy instead. He was there for a tryst of some kind, and who was I to interrupt? Undoubtedly this misty grove was a popular place for assignations. Perhaps I could see him later.

I was about to withdraw discretely from the garden, but another movement stopped me. The other person was coming into view. And with her came a sudden shock that chilled me to the core.

The arm was heavily laden with jewels. Rings and bracelets, all encrusted with emeralds. So Heracles was having a liaison with Aphrodite herself.

Bad enough, but worse still when a cloud of mist drifted past, dimming the view of her gems. Changing the color so that they didn't appear at first glance to be emeralds, but some other precious stones that were more blue than green.

Stones that were the exact same shade as the jewels worn on the unidentified hand I'd seen dabbling its fingers in the bloody ruins of a human torso in the Sybil's mirror.

I'd like to think I would have had enough self-control to keep from gasping out loud, but I'll never really know for sure. The hand that came over my mouth would have muffled it.

The hidden assailant's other arm circled my waist and dragged me back so quickly I didn't even have time to think about screaming.

Chapter 61

Circe was in front of me.

"Say nothing, make no sound!" she whispered urgently. I was released and turned to find Pasiphae had been the one holding me. She motioned for me to follow them.

We raced through a field to a small outbuilding. We slipped inside, and I was slightly surprised to see a few lamps had been lit. Had the aunts planned to waylay me?

"What the hell is going on?" I demanded as Pasiphae and Circe sat on a bench. Both were in golden robes that complemented their hair and eyes. Circe's hair was loose and flowing, but Pasiphae had bound hers up, crowning her brow with the royal diadem of Minoa. To remind everyone who she'd been, undoubtedly.

"You've already guessed much of it, I suspect," Circe said as she patted the cushion next to her. I considered whether I really wanted to play some game with them. But I was safer with them, especially now that I'd learned something potentially devastating.

I sat down next to Circe. "I know Aphrodite is having an affair with Heracles," I began cautiously, not sure how much I should reveal to her. After all, much of it was just supposition, and I was still struggling to accept facts that were swiftly falling into very uncomfortable places, where they were fitting all too nicely.

"What else?" she demanded, not unkindly, but with an urgency that wouldn't be denied. Her golden eyes bored into my own.

"I believe she's the one who killed the man I saw in the Sybil's mirror. When I saw her, just now, the mists were thick enough to change the color of the emeralds on her jewelry. They were the same color as the gems on the hand that I saw caressing the dead body in the mirror."

I paused, took a deep breath, then took the plunge.

"I think she somehow tricked Dionysus. She killed a man, here on Olympus of all places, and gathered his blood. She probably kept it, waiting for an opportunity to slip some to Dionysus unnoticed. It wouldn't be hard, with all the feasts and parties up here on Olympus. Once he drank even a trace of blood, it would be too late."

Pasiphae smiled. "And of course, Aphrodite would have ways of finding out where Agave's spirit was being kept, and releasing her so that she could come back to Earth," she added.

"But why would she do it?" I queried with a helpless gesture. "As near as I know, she's never had a quarrel with Dionysus."

"Do you know what's going to happen now?" Circe asked.

"Most likely Dionysus will be consigned to Tartarus for what he's done."

"And?" she pressed.

I hadn't thought beyond that point. The betrayal wrought by Dionysus was monumental enough. It didn't seem to need an epilogue.

"Who will fill his place? Who will ensure the vineyards still produce fruit, and that the magic which transforms that fruit into wine still occurs? Who will be elevated to sit on his throne?" she prodded me, like a schoolteacher trying to get a pupil to see the answer for herself.

I thought a moment. Heracles had said something about that... once a throne for a high god is created, it must be filled. Someone would have to take over the duties of Dionysus.

"Possibly Ganymede," I said, not really comfortable with speculating about such matters. It was a decision for Zeus ultimately, though he would undoubtedly take counsel from the other gods.

"A strong candidate," Pasiphae replied matter-of-factly, as if she was just discussing a common horse race rather than the filling of one of the thrones of Olympus. "He is cupbearer of the gods, so it would be appropriate. But there is another possibility."

I tried to think of who would be in the running.

"Consider this, Medea," Circe said. "Ganymede was mortal-born. He was not always the cupbearer. There was one who held those duties before him, who has a higher claim to a vacant throne because of her own birth."

And it all became clear.

"Hebe," I breathed. Hebe, the goddess of youth, daughter of Zeus and Hera. A princess of Olympus. She had been the honored cupbearer of the gods before Zeus fell in love with Ganymede's beauty and spirited him away to Olympus to make the boy immortal and eternally young.

Elevating Hebe to one of the high thrones would not be unusual.

And if Hebe was chosen to replace Dionysus her duties would be many. She would have little time to pay attention to her husband. That would free Heracles to dally with Aphrodite as much as he desired.

I should have been enraged, but the first thought that came to my mind was that Pasiphae was in the clear.

The anger wouldn't be denied though. Anger on behalf of Dionysus, tricked into becoming mad. Anger for the innocent lives that had been lost or destroyed.

I had another target for my rage as well. Though there was no doubt in my mind that Aphrodite was author of this mayhem, it was all too clear to me that Heracles was fully involved in helping her achieve it. I would never be able to respect, much less trust him again. He had tried to poison my mind against Pasiphae, my own kin, to divert attention from the plot.

"We have to stop it," I said with determination. "We have to tell the truth. We can't let Dionysus suffer for their crimes."

"No," Pasiphae replied simply. And waited.

My jaw eventually re-hinged itself so I could talk. "Dionysus is innocent!" I exploded. "I know you hate him because of what he did to you, but—"

"He is not innocent!" Circe interrupted forcefully. "In the end, Medea, even if he was tricked into reawakening his old lust by drinking human blood, there was a point at which he could have said no. There was a point at which he knew what was happening, a point when he could have sought help. He above all others knows that, because he was helped before.

"But he chose to let it take him. He chose to follow the old bloodlust, chose to reinvent his deadly cult and use it to kill innocent humans. He may not have intentionally reawakened his thirst for blood, but believe me, Medea, he is not free of guilt. He gave in to it, accepted it. And that is his crime, and it must be punished."

I digested what she said. "Then Aphrodite and Heracles must be punished as well. They instigated this nightmare. If they are not called to account, can you be sure it will end here? What else might they dare if they succeed in this?"

"And how would you bring them to justice, Medea?" Circe asked with what appeared to be real curiosity. I couldn't believe she had even asked the question. Wasn't it clear?

"I would tell the truth," I said with more heat than I intended. I took a breath to steady myself and return to the cool logic which was my only hope of winning the argument.

"And what proof would you offer? You know the gods will not accept mere accusations." Pasiphae sounded as if she was reasoning with a child.

"I saw them," I protested. "I saw Aphrodite and Heracles together!"

"You saw two figures in the mist."

"I saw *them*," I protested.

"In the mist," she repeated. "A mist which was thick enough to distort your perception of the jewels she wore. That means it was thick enough to obscure true sight. That will be enough to discount what you witnessed as proof of anything."

I was stunned by what I was hearing and its implications. The aunts were actually going to pretend it hadn't happened, that they hadn't seen what I had seen even though I knew they couldn't possibly have missed it. They were going to remain silent.

"And if it was accepted that you saw Aphrodite and Heracles together, what of it?" Circe continued. "The gods are known for their dalliances. What connection would you be able to prove to this situation with Dionysus? Only that you saw jewels that appeared to be the same color as the ones you saw in the Sybil's mirror."

I looked away, even though I knew she wasn't mocking me or trying to attack me. I hated it, but I had to admit that she was making sense.

"There are two more things to consider, Medea," Pasiphae chimed in. "Zeus has already lost one son today. You must understand what would happen if he suddenly lost another son as well as his most beloved daughter, if he was forced to punish Aphrodite and Heracles. You must consider whether you really want to be the instrument of that outcome."

The thought was sobering. I had basically been asking for Heracles and Aphrodite to suffer the same fate as Dionysus. Expulsion from Olympus, exile to Tartarus.

I might also be opening the door for my own set of torments. If I was responsible for forcing the gods to punish not just one, but three of their own, I could rest assured of a feud based on pure vengeance. The vengeance of the king of the gods.

It was bitter as bile. I had revealed the truth about a series of murders, brought at least some justice for the victims. But it was incomplete, because the real culprits would get away with it. Only their pawn would be punished.

And if justice is incomplete is it really justice, or a palliative?

"You said there were *two* things to consider," I finally said. I couldn't imagine what else they could hit me with.

Circe gathered her thoughts for a moment before speaking.

"You are not here by chance, Medea," she said. "Apparently you do not realize how orchestrated this situation was. Do you really think it was coincidence that the sacrifices to Dionysus took place right where you live, out of the whole wide world? And that you were drawn in because some of the victims were either people you knew, or connected to people you knew? That the woman who became possessed by Agave was someone you knew? Did you think the vision in the mirror happened by chance?

"If the only purpose of this whole sordid business was to get Dionysus out of the way, then he would simply be poisoned with the blood and allowed to ravage where he willed. Most likely he would have chosen territory more familiar to him, in Greece or Asia Minor. But even that aspect of his downfall was controlled."

I drew in a long, shuddering breath as Pasiphae picked up the thread.

"Agave did not choose a vineyard close to you by mere chance. She was instructed to use that one, and not by Dionysus. By the one who freed her, the same one who gave Heracles leave to go to Earth. One who knew you are dogged in your determination once you set your mind to accomplish a thing, even if that thing is solving a mystery that others would flee from out of fear. The same one who sent you the vision in the mirror, concealing her identity, though not, it seems, well enough."

She paused then, but I was ready to finish it.

"Aphrodite. It was all a setup. I was lured into it so that I would find the truth, bring it into the light and take it to the high gods," I murmured.

"In a way that could leave you implicated if you are not careful," Circe said.

"Because it could be argued that I was helping my old friend Heracles," I replied softly, suddenly very interested in the floor. Focusing my gaze there ensured I didn't have to rein in the emotions on my face as much. "That I was working with him and Aphrodite. That I was involved with the murders, with the whole plot to unseat Dionysus, from the start. That my connection to the victims really was too convenient, and that I didn't solve any mysteries because I had the answers all along,"

"Just so," Pasiphae nodded.

It was flawless. Aphrodite had known I wouldn't run away from solving murders that touched me personally, but she left nothing to chance. It was done in a way that would ensure my silence if I followed the puzzle to the end and figured out she and Heracles were responsible.

As it was, I had only the flimsiest evidence to link them to the crime. If I ever got firmer evidence, I wouldn't be able to use it without cutting my own throat, metaphorically speaking. I had no doubts that if Aphrodite went down she would drag me with her. She would argue that I got involved to avenge the wrongs Dionysus had done to my kin, Pasiphae and her children.

But the realizations coming to me went deeper still. My eyes were blazing as I faced my aunts.

"You knew all along. You knew what they were doing."

Chapter 62

"We suspected," Pasiphae put in quickly, keeping her voice low.

"And you said nothing. Innocent people died."

"Innocents die every day on Earth," she pointed out.

"There was a time when you would have spoken up."

"A time when I ruled my own domain as a living goddess," she retorted. "Do not presume to preach to me, Medea. We may have said nothing to stop this thing from happening, but believe me by the time we had enough knowledge to make the words worth hearing the damage had already been done. The outcome would have been exactly the same as it is now."

I remembered now how she greeted Heracles when we arrived on Aiaia: *back so soon?*

"They tried to get you to help them, didn't they?"

Circe shrugged. "Heracles contacted us. He didn't reveal exactly what was planned, of course. He merely said there was a problem that needed to be dealt with among the high gods."

"And you said no."

"Of course we said no! We have no need to get involved in the quarrels of the Olympians. Harming Dionysus would not have restored Pasiphae's children or her queendom to her, and it would have exposed both of us to danger."

"But when you figured out what was going on, you didn't try to stop it. More, you didn't warn me when I came to Aiaia. The gods might need proof of what Heracles and Aphrodite were doing, but I wouldn't have. I would have believed whatever evidence you gave me."

"And done what with it?" she countered. "Tried to confront Aphrodite directly, or more likely Heracles. You would have been in far greater danger then, because you would have been a threat to them."

I got up and began pacing.

"Don't you see?" Pasiphae asked with exasperation. "As long you were performing your amateur sleuthing and gathering the evidence they needed to fulfill their plot, you were safe. They *wanted* you to succeed, and would have done anything to ensure you fulfilled that purpose, including protecting your from Dionysus.

"If you knew the truth you might have betrayed yourself. You would have become a liability, and even if Heracles had qualms, Aphrodite wouldn't have hesitated to attack you or have Dionysus do it for her."

The hollow feeling inside me seemed to throb gently. It took a few moments for me to realize the throb was actually coming from outside me. Almost imperceptible vibrations were filling the air.

It was a summons, probably one tailored especially for me.

I wanted nothing more than to be done with the whole day, to just have everything over with. The deception, the treachery, the withholding of evidence by my own kin, all of it.

I headed to the door without a word.

"Medea…"

I knew I shouldn't let anything delay me even an instant from responding to the summons. But something in Pasiphae's voice made me turn back anyway. When I faced her, I saw golden tears brimming in her eyes. Circe was in control, but still regarding me intently. She let her sister do the talking.

"You must know we would never have let anything happen to you, even if we had to deal with Dionysus in his madness and Aphrodite in her anger. I lost Ariadne and Megalitheros. I won't lose you. You must believe it."

Whether her tears were artifice or sincere didn't matter. They had the intended effect. I calmed down.

No matter how angry I was that they'd kept me in the dark, I knew they were right. If I'd known the truth, I would probably have lost my temper and confronted Heracles. Pasiphae and Circe had done the only thing they could think of. They let me continue digging so that I could complete Aphrodite's dirty work for her, because it was the one way to guarantee my safety.

"I love you too," I whispered.

But I didn't go to embrace them as I would have when I was younger, and the compelling throb vibrating through the air was only part of the reason I turned again and left.

I stepped outside, momentarily dazzled by the brightness. More dazzled still that on Olympus, a kingdom of pure light, there were shadows darker and more treacherous than any in Hades itself.

Chapter 63

The eleven remaining high gods were waiting for me, arrayed again in a semi-circle. The refreshments had been cleared away. I chanced a glance at Aphrodite, but if she'd seen me in the secret garden she gave no sign.

This time I approached without being bidden, bowing when I judged I was close enough. They all seemed taller now. The gods often shift in form slightly without intending to, simply because they're distracted. They certainly had enough to distract them now.

"Medea," Zeus began, "you have done well. While I cannot say I approve of all of your methods, the fact that you were willing to take such risks to expose horrendous crimes is most impressive."

I bowed my head in acknowledgment.

"Unfortunately, you did not go far enough." I kept my head bowed a moment longer, ensuring that my face bore no trace of the shock that coursed through me at Athena's statement. When I judged myself to be in control I looked up.

"What you have given us is not enough proof, though certainly Dionysus' presence on Earth, surrounded by women who appeared to be maenads, raises unwholesome suspicions," Apollo said smoothly. "But nevertheless, we do not have proof of the gravest crime, the crime for which we would surely expel him to Tartarus forever. We do not have proof that he is conducting human sacrifices."

Easy, Medea, I thought. *Don't explode.*

"Heracles said he witnessed it," I reminded them, in a respectful tone. "He took an oath before the Erinyes."

Hera looked pointedly at Zeus. "However, my husband believes that, too, is not enough."

Zeus was clearly uncomfortable, as well he might be. Her temper was worse than his, and that was saying something. "It is just that Heracles was under the influence of the Hydra's venom," he said a little petulantly. "If it wasn't for that, there would be no issue. But what if he was delusional? We cannot rule it out, and we cannot take so severe a path as unseating one of the Twelve if there's any possibility it could be a mistake."

"So, Medea, we must ask your help again," Artemis said, tactfully trying to turn the attention back to me.

I looked to Hecate, who was standing at the right hand of Zeus. "Yes, Medea. I am in agreement. You know the modern world better than any of us, and you will be able to detect signs of Dionysus' activity that we might miss. We will, of course, be watching, both the gods of Olympus and we of the Underworld. You will not be alone this time."

"It is especially good that Dionysus has seen you use powers he didn't know about," Hermes added. "You were able to open a portal on your own to escape him, and you were able to shatter the prison in which he trapped Heracles. You were even able to injure him in battle."

"It is a surprise," Hecate interrupted. "But perhaps, being kin to the Titans, you have abilities we were unaware of until now. If Dionysus doesn't understand those abilities, it is a sure bet he will want to prevent you from using them against him. He may still try to win you to his side, but one way or another he will seek you out."

Oh no. I didn't like the sound of that at all.

"You're going to use me as *bait*?" Only when I replayed the scene in my head much later did I realize how impudent that must have sounded. But they didn't take offense.

"You did not hesitate to use Peter Kirkpatrick the same way," Ares said evenly. "And at least you have the advantage of being immortal, and a cunning sorceress as well."

"It's the only way, Medea," Zeus said, softening his eyes a bit. "He is on the run now, but if he has indeed rekindled his taste for blood he will need to feed. Soon he will have to seek new victims. He may get careless and betray himself that way, but if not, you will be our lure. He will try to capture you. And when that happens, we will be waiting for him."

Fine. If they were going to put my ass on the line, let them give me something in return.

"I'll need help," I said, making sure to keep my tone respectful.

"We can certainly provide guards, if that's what you want," Hera said.

I pretended to consider it, even though I'd already decided what I really wanted.

"They might be more of an encumbrance. They'd draw too much attention. Let Orphne help me."

Hecate stiffened at that, opened her mouth to protest. I didn't give her any space to object. "She knows how to use the Tear of Nereus to assume any shape, including human. She knows how to fight, too."

"Orphne is a fugitive!" Hecate exploded. "She left Hades without permission, and if you remember, she stole that Tear of Nereus from my very palace!"

"If Orphne committed a wrong in leaving Hades," Demeter said thoughtfully, "She more than made up for it by risking herself to pursue Dionysus. She stayed with Medea, rather than running and turning truly fugitive even though she had a means to blend in with humans."

"If she needed any punishment," Poseidon added, "then surely the agony she went through after Dionysus injected her with his venom during their battle was enough. As my sister has said, she stood by Medea in honor."

"I think a small clemency can be shown," Aphrodite smiled at Hecate, who definitely was not inclined to return the expression. "It would look ill for us to punish one who tried to stop the abominations Dionysus was carrying out. Especially since he is still on the loose, committing who knows what outrages. It might appear we were trying to take our frustrations out on her. This is not the way of Olympus."

"It is not unreasonable to have her help Medea," Athena put in.

"And rather convenient," Apollo added. "Since she already knows what she's up against, and can take care of herself. And apparently she has made a place for herself with Medea easily enough. I add my voice to those of the others. Let Orphne go free and return to Earth with Medea."

The set of Hecate's mouth indicated displeasure, but she knew when she was bested.

"Very well," she said. "I will take the message to my lord Hades myself. She has been healed of her wounds, and may return to Earth immediately." She turned her eyes to me, and I couldn't help cowering a bit at what I saw there. "But I warn you all, you may find she is not quite what you expect."

And with that, she was gone.

"We know the risk we are asking you to take," Zeus said to me kindly. "Dionysus is, at best, unpredictable now."

"There is one other thing," Hera added. Of course. Isn't there always? "Lamia seemed inclined to help you, although I must agree it was likely for her own purposes. Nonetheless, perhaps it would be prudent to seek a partnership with her. Temporary, of course."

I couldn't stop my eyes from widening at that, but at least I kept my mouth closed.

"We know this will not be easy," Athena said. "We know only too well what she took from you. But consider this, Medea; her daughters are many, and live in all corners of the globe. Her ability to gather information is formidable. Wasn't it she who provided the information that helped you determine Agave was on the loose as well as Dionysus?"

She had me there. Even with Orphne, I could only do so much, only go so far. Lamia had resources I couldn't command. And she would use them ruthlessly, even if it meant losing a few of them, to keep her plans secure.

"Consider it, Medea," Zeus said. "We must work for the greatest good in this matter. And we all know that if Dionysus is really intent on reestablishing his blood cult, he is by far the greatest evil humans have faced in a long time."

We stood in silence awhile. Finally, I decided there was nothing else to do. The gods might present something as a suggestion, but there is never any doubt it is anything but a free choice.

"As you command," I said, bowing. "And now, with your permission, I will return to my home."

"Will you not stay on Olympus awhile to rest? You have earned at least that much respite," Hephaestus offered.

I forced a smile, inclining my head in a gesture of gratitude. "Your offer is kind, but as long as Dionysus remains a threat it would be unwise for me to indulge in relaxation."

Hera nodded. "So be it. But keep that medallion, Medea," she indicated the charm I'd all but forgotten around my neck. "You may use it to return to Olympus whenever you have need, especially if there is danger."

I bowed again in thanks. "By your leave," I said. No one objected, so I turned and left.

What I had left unspoken was my desire to be away from all of them. The gods themselves, who were supposed to represent the highest seats of authority and morality, had equivocated when meting out justice came too close to home. Worse still, one of the Twelve had committed an unthinkable act of treachery just to make the road smoother for her to entertain a paramour.

Even the dragons sensed my somber mood and remained unusually cooperative and quiet during our flight back to Earth. As my chariot descended from the clouds into a cool October night high over Georgia, I reminded myself coming home was a far better choice than staying on Olympus.

On Earth, at least I'd have the security of rushing into a known danger. Olympus had once been pristine, but it had changed. Beautiful still on the outside, corruption had somehow tainted the innermost workings of the realm. Now it was a place where plots and deception were blithely disguised by thin veneers of light.

If I'd found out as much in such a short time there, it meant those veneers were starting to wear. I didn't want to be around when the cracks became too large to ignore.

Chapter 64

By the time I got back home it was after two in the morning. I felt an aching tiredness and remembered I hadn't had sleep in nearly 48 hours, except for my blackout at the vineyard.

Whatever's waiting for me will have to wait a few more days, I thought as I shut the garage door. I planned on sleeping that long, waking up just long enough to order a pizza or two.

But some of the things waiting for me didn't want to be put on the back burner. When I walked through the door Peter was there. He'd found an old sweatshirt of mine in the hall closet and put it on, though it was a tad short for him and he couldn't zip it up all the way.

He glanced at me, still clad in my Greek attire. I'd left my regular clothes in a Dumpster at the vineyard. They were torn and covered with blood, beyond repair. I knew I looked exotic, and it probably helped that the nectar I'd drunk on Olympus had the side-effect of enhancing beauty. The effect would eventually fade, but that would take a few days. Now, I bet I looked pretty damn good, tired as I was.

Finally he found his tongue.

"Is it over?"

What should I tell him? That the gods who were supposed to be the embodiment of justice had hesitated, had decided against immediately condemning his brother's killer?

I regarded him coolly, trying to wrap myself the aura of a priestess long enough to formulate an answer. I wouldn't lie to cover up what the high gods had done—or rather, hadn't done. There'd been enough lies. But there'd been enough disappointment too. I could finesse the truth.

"You saw him escape," I said evenly. "There will be a hunt. I've been instructed to help them."

"But not alone."

My heart jumped at the new voice. Orphne came into the room, smiling broadly. We embraced. At least one person had come out ahead in all of this. She'd gotten what she wanted. She'd be on Earth with permission now.

Something seemed off. It took me a moment to realize the Tear of Nereus was gone.

"The Tear—" I began.

Her smile deepened. "Don't need it any more. Hecate said it was too great a risk that I might lose it somehow and that it would fall into the wrong hands. So she just gave me the power of transformation outright."

CURSE OF PROMETHEUS: A TALE OF MEDEA

Suddenly Arnold Schwarzenegger, in his role of Conan the Barbarian, was holding me in his arms. "Will this work for a battle-guise? I saw him on TV the other night. He seemed to be a very good fighter."

I cleared my throat diplomatically. "Yes, I'm sure he was. But this will be a little... unsubtle. We're supposed to keep a low profile."

She was back in her human form in a flash. "Well, I'll keep practicing."

We were walking to the kitchen, Peter behind us. "Spill it, Orphne," I demanded. "How did you get out of those manacles Dionysus threw you in?"

She'd already laid out a dish of ice cream for me. I dug in, realizing I hadn't eaten since morning. It was lousy nutrition, but who cared?

"I realized that the cuffs were changing size with me, and that I could only go to smaller and smaller shapes. But then I remembered that I came to the vineyard in your pocket as a stone, so—"

The spoon was halfway to my mouth and not going any further. I put it down and laughed. "Brilliant!"

"And of course, a stone doesn't have arms, so the cuffs slipped away," she finished triumphantly. She gave Peter a casual glance. "Well, I think I'll head upstairs. They've been rerunning a show called "Lost" and I love it. I don't want to miss it."

Of course it was just an excuse, but I welcomed it.

I couldn't finish the ice cream. "Do you want anything? I think there's some cold chicken..."

Peter shook his head. "Orphne offered too, but I just don't have an appetite."

Another uncomfortable silence. "Join me for a drink in the study?" I was grasping for some way to keep up the conversation.

He hesitated, then, "Sure."

I poured a couple of double scotches and we headed to the couch. "So I guess you'll get back to the church now," I started. "I hypnotized your secretary to believe you'd been kidnapped by a group of men—"

"I'm not going back," he cut me off, keeping his eyes on his glass for several seconds. He took a deep sip.

"How can I? Today I lost everything I've been taught is real. I saw gods and goddesses I'd been told were nothing but myths, walking, talking, fighting. But my God wasn't among them.

"When I was threatened, he didn't send down an angel to save me. It was your goddess who came up to defend me, because you'd placed me under her protection. Even if I made up some fantastic story about escaping my kidnappers and they bought it, what would I tell my parishioners? To keep praying, keep believing in the God of Abraham? How can I do that? *I* don't believe any more. When it came down to it, the gods who appeared to my eyes weren't that God. If he exists at all, he abandoned me."

It was understandable, but it still saddened me. I remembered the statue of Mary in his Church, and how it had brought back memories of a real flesh-and-blood woman whose simple faith and kindness had taught me to be a little kinder myself.

That brought another issue up, one I'd shamelessly forgotten about from the moment I kidnapped Peter.

"What about your mother? She must be frantic with worry, and after losing Paul..." I really felt like a heel now. No doubt the police had told her Peter was kidnapped. How could I, who knew what it was like to lose my sons, have shoved that issue out of my mind for so long?

He finished his drink, went back to the bar and poured another. I couldn't blame him.

He was quiet for a few minutes, and I wasn't inclined to prod him. He'd been through hell and back, and needed time to process things.

"We lost mother awhile ago," he said quietly.

Was he in some kind of trauma? "But I saw her," I gently reminded him.

"You saw who she used to be," he said slowly. "She's been... declining. It's gotten worse this past year. When I told her Paul had died..." His voice broke. He struggled to regain control.

"She said she was sorry to hear it, and asked if he'd been a close friend of mine," he finished quietly. I was a little heartened when he put the drink down. Many others would drown their sorrows in it, and tonight I wouldn't have blamed him. But he was showing more restraint than the previous evening.

He bent forward, clasping his hands tightly. "The last few times I saw her, she called me James. That's her brother." He smiled a bit. "It was probably the collar. He was the one who inspired me to be a priest."

He sighed. "Uncle James has been dead for five years. Massive coronary."

Before I knew it I was beside him, my arm around him. It was clearly hard for him to talk about it. I wondered if he'd talked to anyone about it before. Maybe Paul? At least I hoped so. A man who spent much of his life helping others with their troubles should be first in line when it came to getting a shoulder to cry on.

"She'll be OK," he said after awhile, his voice stronger. "There was plenty of money, and we'd already made arrangements. Her sister was flying in this week to start taking care of her, since Paul is gone and I... well, I could have been reassigned to another parish any time. We all knew that."

We stayed that way for awhile.

"You're free to stay here, Peter. As long as you like. It might be safer to be around me. We're going to be watched closely in case something happens."

"You mean in case he comes back," he said flatly as he turned to me. He was haggard, unshaven, but still very handsome. His blue eyes had seen so much that day, but they shone clear.

He was looking deeply into my eyes as well, and I realized that I hadn't bothered to call up the masking glamour. He was looking at their true golden hue.

"Is that the only reason you're asking me to stay?"

It surprised me to hear a priest ask a question like that, but what surprised me more was the answer that I found.

"No. Not the only reason."

His hand traced my cheek lightly, and then... well, things just got a little fuzzy. It wasn't the scotch. What I remember clearly was the sight of the wings filling my vision again as I looked over his shoulder when we both got what we were seeking.

Afterwards, he didn't comment on them. We leaned back into the couch for awhile, but a sudden thought sent me hurrying to the window. I couldn't repress an exclamation of delight.

Instead of dark storm clouds hovering over my house, the entire sky was filled with lights that danced and shifted, changing colors every second. Greens, purples, reds—the aurora. We rarely got the lights this far south, and never so intensely.

Peter came behind me, peering over my shoulder.

"Beautiful," he murmured. I took his hand.

"Let's enjoy them outside."

He slipped his pants back on, and I slid into my London Fog. We stood in the backyard in silence, just taking in the show.

"Quite a display, isn't it?"

Not as good a display as the sight of my heart nearly flying out of my throat when the voice blasted over the back fence. Fortunately I managed to swallow it back down.

"Mr. McCaffrey," I stammered. "What are you doing up so late?"

"Oh, the dogs got excited and woke me. Thought they just needed to go out, but they probably saw this going on through the windows. Who's your friend?"

Oh hell, *hell, HELL*! He'd seen Peter. Peter with wings, no less. Time to get close enough to snare him with my eyes.

"I'm James," Peter said quickly. "Nice to meet you, sir." Wow. A good lover who could keep his cool and ad lib.

"Nice costume you have there. Getting ready for Halloween?" McCaffrey asked amiably.

I heaved a sigh of relief. "Yes, I was just helping him get it together when we saw the lights and came outside."

"Ah," he said with an understanding tone. "Well, I'll let you enjoy it. I'm a bit tired now. Have a good night."

He ambled away from the fence.

"Well, that could have been worse," Peter observed. He reached back to touch the wings. "Since we can only pull that Halloween stuff for another week or so, do you think you can do something about these?"

I drew his head down and answered him with a kiss. He could interpret it any way he chose.

Chapter 65

The heavy fog rolls by me. I hear the slow churning of a bus moving a couple of blocks away. In the fog, it sounds even more distant than that. Almost as if it's a ghost bus ferrying the dead to Hades.

There's not much traffic down the street where I'm walking slowly. The skyscraper ahead of me is closed until morning. Only the first floor is visible through the fog. I know I'm vulnerable out here, but it has to be this way.

The past few days went by quickly, tinged with the constant feeling that something was about to happen. It didn't. Wherever Dionysus has fled to, he seems content to keep a low profile.

One thing bothers me: there hasn't been any mention on the news of a mass murder up at Hawk's Haven. Surely someone would have noticed the manager missing, if not the field hands, and police would have investigated and found the dead maenads.

Perhaps the Olympians took care of cleaning up the mess. With so many women missing, there had to be some intervention to keep it out of the news. Had the gods erased all memory of them to avoid a massive investigation?

The fact that Dionysus is still among the missing is more disturbing, since he's likely plotting some new atrocity. I have no doubt Agave, now in Lyn's body, has managed to find him again. It's become clear now that they don't intend an imminent strike.

So I'm walking the misty streets right in the heart of Atlanta, hoping to tempt them to action. I keep my ears open for anything strange, especially the mocking caw of a raven or the sound of something winging through the night.

If only humans realized their world is just like a city in the fog. There's so much they can't see, stretching beyond their limited vision. But it's their fortune that they don't see so far. If they knew what lay beyond the mists that separate this world from the others—

There is it. The sound I've been waiting for. I knew he'd find me, sooner or later. The beating of wings comes closer, closer...

With easy grace Peter lands in front of me, touching down so gently it seems as if an invisible god is setting him down, a priceless, fragile prize displayed on a shelf. Except the shelf is a step leading to the side entrance of a skyscraper.

My pace quickens, and I reach him in seconds.

"What are you doing here? How—"

"I figured out how to get them to come out on my own. Without us... you know. I thought it might be a handy skill to have, if I'm going to help you fight him."

269

I kiss him. Kiss him again, deeply.

"There's just one thing. I haven't figured out how to get them back in. So I'll need your help."

"Now?"

He shakes his head.

"It's incredible," he says between kisses. "Flying up there, looking into windows, feeling the wind blowing across me."

"Looking into windows?" I try not to sound too alarmed, but it's hard.

He laughs. "Relax. Only the darkened ones in the office buildings."

Sanity scores a point. It's been a little on the thin side in my life lately, but I'm happy to say it's not totally gone.

I smile in the middle of a kiss.

"What?" he asks softly.

"I was just thinking how peaceful it must be to fly with wings."

"You've flown," he breathes into me.

I laugh a little. "In a chariot pulled by dragons. They're a little feisty."

We kiss again. He's the one who pulls back just a bit this time, and I feel the shape of his mouth forming the words I want to hear most this night.

"Fly with me."

We keep kissing as I call the power of levitation. He feels me drifting up and circles my waist tightly, his mouth seeking me deeper and deeper. Like this, I weigh nothing.

His wings beat slowly and we rise. Up and up until the mist closes around us. It enfolds us like a cloak, and for an endless moment I am suspended between the cares of world below and the promise of heaven just above.

The sound of his wings keeps time with my heart.

Author's note:

While I wanted to give the reader a sense of places in and around Atlanta in this book, many of the places described in these pages are fictional.

There are several wineries in north Georgia, but to the best of my knowledge Dionysus is not hanging out at any of them. Hawk's Haven is a fictional place I created after visiting some of the wineries, and should not be construed as representing a specific place in Georgia or anywhere else. If the reader has an opportunity to taste some of the wines produced in Georgia, I hope you will do so. Many of them are quite good.

Like Hawk's Haven, St. Helen's Catholic church and Elliswood are fictional places.

While Atlanta has several colleges and universities, Elliswood is not based on any of them. Nor should any inference be made about any specific sororities, since Delta Kappa Iota is a fictional sorority.

The statue of Mary that I placed at the fictional St. Helen's church is based on a real statue, which is found at Gethsemani monastery in Kentucky.

Zoo Atlanta does not have a leopard display as described in this book. The zoo did have a single male clouded leopard named Moby for many years. Sadly, Moby had to be euthanized in 2013 due to declining health.

www.ingramcontent.com/pod-product-compliance
Lightning Source LLC
Chambersburg PA
CBHW072206170626
46813CB00003B/810